CHRISTMAS MITTENS MURDER

Books by Lee Hollis

Hayley Powell Mysteries
DEATH OF A KITCHEN DIVA
DEATH OF A COUNTRY FRIED REDNECK
DEATH OF A COUPON CLIPPER
DEATH OF A CHOCOHOLIC
DEATH OF A CHRISTMAS CATERER
DEATH OF A CUPCAKE QUEEN
DEATH OF A BACON HEIRESS
DEATH OF A PUMPKIN CARVER
DEATH OF A LOBSTER LOVER
DEATH OF A COOKBOOK AUTHOR
DEATH OF A WEDDING CAKE BAKER
DEATH OF A BLUEBERRY TART
DEATH OF A WICKED WITCH
DEATH OF AN ITALIAN CHEF
DEATH OF AN ICE CREAM SCOOPER
DEATH OF A CLAM DIGGER

Collections
EGGNOG MURDER
(with Leslie Meier and Barbara Ross)
YULE LOG MURDER
(with Leslie Meier and Barbara Ross)
HAUNTED HOUSE MURDER
(with Leslie Meier and Barbara Ross)
CHRISTMAS CARD MURDER
(with Leslie Meier and Peggy Ehrhart)
HALLOWEEN PARTY MURDER
(with Leslie Meier and Barbara Ross)
IRISH COFFEE MURDER
(with Leslie Meier and Barbara Ross)

Poppy Harmon Mysteries
POPPY HARMON INVESTIGATES
POPPY HARMON AND THE HUNG JURY
POPPY HARMON AND THE PILLOW TALK KILLER
POPPY HARMON AND THE BACKSTABBING BACHELOR
POPPY HARMON AND THE SHOOTING STAR

Maya & Sandra Mysteries
MURDER AT THE PTA
MURDER AT THE BAKE SALE
MURDER ON THE CLASS TRIP

Books by Lynn Cahoon

The Tourist Trap Mystery Series
GUIDEBOOK TO MURDER
MISSION TO MURDER
IF THE SHOE KILLS
DRESSED TO KILL
KILLER RUN
MURDER ON WHEELS
TEA CUPS AND CARNAGE
HOSPITALITY AND HOMICIDE
KILLER PARTY
MEMORIES AND MURDER
MURDER IN WAITING
PICTURE PERFECT FRAME
WEDDING BELL BLUES
A VACATION TO DIE FOR
Novellas
ROCKETS' DEAD GLARE
A DEADLY BREW
SANTA PUPPY
CORNED BEEF AND CASUALTIES
MOTHER'S DAY MAYHEM
A VERY MUMMY HOLIDAY
TWO CHRISTMAS MITTENS

The Kitchen Witch Mystery Series
ONE POISON PIE
TWO WICKED DESSERTS
THREE TAINTED TEAS
FOUR CHARMING SPELLS
Novellas
CHILI CAULDRON CURSE
MURDER 101
HAVE A HOLLY, HAUNTED CHRISTMAS

The Cat Latimer Mystery Series
A STORY TO KILL
FATALITY BY FIRELIGHT
OF MURDER AND MEN
SLAY IN CHARACTER
SCONED TO DEATH
A FIELD GUIDE TO MURDER

The Farm to Fork Mystery Series
WHO MOVED MY GOAT CHEESE?
KILLER GREEN TOMATOES
ONE POTATO, TWO POTATO, DEAD . . .
DEEP FRIED REVENGE
KILLER COMFORT FOOD
A FATAL FAMILY FEAST
Novellas
HAVE A DEADLY NEW YEAR
PENNED IN
A PUMPKIN SPICE KILLING

The Survivors' Club Mystery Series
TUESDAY NIGHT SURVIVORS' CLUB
SECRETS IN THE STACKS
DEATH IN THE ROMANCE AISLE

Books by Maddie Day

Country Store Mysteries
FLIPPED FOR MURDER
GRILLED FOR MURDER
WHEN THE GRITS HIT THE FAN

BISCUITS AND SLASHED BROWNS
DEATH OVER EASY
STRANGLED EGGS AND HAM
NACHO AVERAGE MURDER
CANDY SLAIN MURDER
NO GRATER CRIME
BATTER OFF DEAD
FOUR LEAF CLEAVER
CHRISTMAS COCOA MURDER
(with Carlene O'Connor and Alex Erickson)
CHRISTMAS SCARF MURDER
(with Carlene O'Connor and Peggy Ehrhart)

Cozy Capers Book Group Mysteries
MURDER ON CAPE COD
MURDER AT THE TAFFY SHOP
MURDER AT THE LOBSTAH SHACK
MURDER IN A CAPE COTTAGE
MURDER AT A CAPE BOOKSTORE

Local Foods Mysteries
A TINE TO LIVE, A TINE TO DIE
'TIL DIRT DO US PART
FARMED AND DANGEROUS
MURDER MOST FOWL
MULCH ADO ABOUT MURDER

Cece Barton Mysteries
MURDER UNCORKED

Published by Kensington Publishing Corp.

CHRISTMAS MITTENS MURDER

Lee Hollis
Lynn Cahoon
Maddie Day

Kensington Publishing Corp.
www.kensingtonbooks.com

This book is a work of fiction. Names, characters, businesses, organizations, places, events, and incidents either are the product of the author's imagination or are used fictitiously. Any resemblance to actual persons, living or dead, events, or locales is entirely coincidental.

To the extent that the image or images on the cover of this book depict a person or persons, such person or persons are merely models, and are not intended to portray any character or characters featured in the book.

KENSINGTON BOOKS are published by

Kensington Publishing Corp.
119 West 40th Street
New York, NY 10018

Copyright © 2023 by Kensington Publishing Corp.
"Death of a Christmas Mitten Knitter" copyright © 2023 by Rick Copp and Holly Simason
"Two Christmas Mittens" copyright © 2023 by Lynn Cahoon
"Murderous Mittens" copyright © 2023 by Edith Maxwell

All rights reserved. No part of this book may be reproduced in any form or by any means without the prior written consent of the Publisher, excepting brief quotes used in reviews.

All Kensington titles, imprints and distributed lines are available at special quantity discounts for bulk purchases for sales promotion, premiums, fund-raising, educational or institutional use.

Special book excerpts or customized printings can also be created to fit specific needs. For details, write or phone the office of the Kensington Special Sales Manager: Kensington Publishing Corp., 119 West 40th Street, New York, NY, 10018. Attn. Special Sales Department. Phone: 1-800-221-2647.

K and the Teapot logo is a trademark of Kensington Publishing Corp.

Library of Congress Control Number: 2023938827

ISBN: 978-1-4967-4424-1
First Kensington Hardcover Edition: October 2023

ISBN: 978-1-4967-4426-5 (ebook)

10 9 8 7 6 5 4 3 2 1

Printed in the United States of America

Contents

Death of a Christmas Mitten Knitter
Lee Hollis
1

Two Christmas Mittens
Lynn Cahoon
119

Murderous Mittens
Maddie Day
223

DEATH OF A CHRISTMAS MITTEN KNITTER

Lee Hollis

Chapter One

Hayley was just reaching for the door handle to make her escape from her still buzzing restaurant, Hayley's Kitchen, when her manager, Betty, suddenly swooped in to intercept her.

"Hold on. Reverend Ted would like to have a word with you before you go."

"I was so close to getting out of here! Can you tell him you just missed me?"

Betty's eyes flicked across the restaurant to a table near the fireplace. "I could, but then he'd know I was lying because he is literally staring at us this very moment."

"What is it this time? Is his steak not pink enough *again*?"

"No, he's finished with his steak and moved on to dessert and coffee," Betty said. "The Yule log cake, his favorite."

"Okay," Hayley sighed, steeling herself as she forced a smile and nodded while she weaved her way around the tables of patrons to head to where Reverend Ted was dining alone. There were bits of chocolate on both corners of his mouth as he devoured Hayley's special holiday Yule log cake.

"Good evening, Reverend. Did Kelton get the temperature of your rib eye right?" Hayley asked brightly.

Reverend Ted snorted. "Eventually."

"I'm sorry about that. Dessert's on me tonight."

"Thank you," Reverend Ted said, beaming. Hayley felt as if she had just saved herself from a snippy Yelp review.

She knew giving him a discount would solve the problem of his earlier complaint. Although beloved by his congregation at the church and known throughout Bar Harbor as kind and warmhearted, if Reverend Ted did have one flaw, it was that he was rather cheap, a proud and often irritating tightwad. So a free dessert was very much appreciated.

"This cake really is quite delicious, Hayley. I just wanted you to know that."

"Ahhh, yes, the Yule log cake here is quite popular this time of year. Well, enjoy, I'm just heading out."

She did a quick turn to leave when he reached out and grabbed her by the wrist. "Wait, there is something else I need to discuss with you."

Hayley braced herself.

"As you know, the church's Christmas bazaar is coming up in a week, and I was hoping you might make a contribution."

Oh, good.

All she had to do was write a simple check.

Easy peasy.

"Of course, Ted. No problem. I can drop off a check to you at the church tomorrow, or if you have Venmo, I can just transfer the amount right into the church's account and we can save a tree."

"That's very kind of you, but I was hoping to enlist your exceptional baking skills instead of relying on a donation of cold hard cash this year. We are raffling off gift baskets at the bazaar, and I believe that if you prepared a Hayley's Kitchen dessert basket, maybe include one of your locally famous Yule logs, those delicious Christmas Crinkle Cookies that practically taste like a rich fudgy brownie and perhaps even a gift certificate for a dinner for two from Hayley's Kitchen, then we'd make a killing."

"You have certainly thought a lot about this," Hayley remarked, full of dread.

"Honestly, who wouldn't want to put a raffle ticket in the jar to win a prize like that. I would bet it would be the most popular gift basket of the whole bazaar."

Hayley took a deep breath. "Reverend, I would really love to help out, but as you can see, I have been so busy here at the restaurant it's hard to find a free moment, especially this time of year. But again, I would be more than happy to make a financial donation . . ."

"I understand, Hayley. I can see you have a very successful business to run. And I am sure the needy families who benefit from the money we raise from the bazaar will understand as well."

And there it was.

The carefully timed guilt trip.

Still, Hayley was slightly annoyed that Reverend Ted was not interested in a direct cash donation, which would essentially achieve the same goal. Lift the spirits of local families during the holidays with money to buy food and toys.

Hayley opened her mouth to try one more time to offer a generous donation, but Reverend Ted spoke before she had the chance. "Your brother Randy's business is also doing remarkably well, even during the off-season."

"Yes, he's got a fully stocked bar that comes in mighty handy during the cold winter months here in Bar Harbor when almost everything else is closed for the season."

"And yet he was more than happy to offer his own Drinks Like A Fish holiday gift basket loaded up with some of his top-shelf booze, various cocktail mixes and shot glasses and all sorts of goodies and special trinkets. Wasn't that thoughtful of him? Your brother has always been so public-spirited."

Checkmate.

Hayley nodded, accepting defeat. "When do you need my basket?"

"Friday would be just fine," Reverend Ted said without missing a beat. "Now, if you would be so kind as to have Betty bring me my check, I need to get back to the church. There is so much still to do before the big bazaar." He finished the last forkful of Yule log cake, and then grabbed his napkin and wiped his mouth clean. "Can I give you a lift home?"

"Oh no, I'm not going home. I'm meeting friends at Drinks Like A Fish," Hayley blabbed without realizing.

Reverend Ted nodded knowingly.

It finally dawned on her.

Too busy to make a gift basket for the Christmas bazaar but not too busy to drink with friends even while her restaurant was still open.

Not good optics at all.

"We're celebrating. Liddy sold that mansion down on West Street that's been on the market all year," Hayley offered weakly.

"Well, please, don't let me keep you," Reverend Ted chirped, working hard not to show any judgment on his face but failing miserably. "I will see you Friday when you deliver your basket."

Yes.

Friday.

When she would have the time to pull it all together was

still an open question. But right now, her focus was on getting out of here before there was another crisis in the restaurant she would have to deal with, such as a dissatisfied customer, a lost reservation, a fire in the kitchen. She had seen it all this holiday season.

After waving good night to Betty and the waitstaff and extricating herself out from under the watchful eye of Reverend Ted, Hayley jumped in her car and sped over to her brother Randy's bar, which was mostly empty at this late hour except for a couple of regular bleary-eyed fishermen at the end of the bar downing shots of whiskey and Liddy and Mona chattering on top of stools at the opposite end. Mona was guzzling her usual Budweiser from a can, and Liddy was sipping her typical cosmo.

Hayley hopped up on a stool next to Mona. "Sorry I'm late. I got hung up at the restaurant. Reverend Ted cornered me and talked me into—"

Mona interrupted her. "Donating a gift basket for the church Christmas bazaar. Yeah, we already know. He stopped by my lobster shop earlier today and asked me to do the same. I told him I was already going to hell, so why bother kissing up to the church? But that didn't seem to stop him from pestering me! He just wouldn't let up with the arm twisting until I finally yelled, 'Uncle!' So I think I got an old picnic basket in the attic I can use and I'll throw in some gift certificates for lobsters and scallops and maybe a few touristy trinkets I sell in the shop like those cute lobster trap magnets for the refrigerator."

"I think that's adorable, Mona. You do you. But my basket is going to be the big grand prize of the raffle," Liddy insisted.

Hayley cocked an eyebrow. "He got to you, too?"

"Oh yes. He showed up at my office yesterday and told me how much I smelled good, and I told him it was this very expensive new body lotion I got on my last trip to New York, Laura Mercier Ambre Vanille Soufflé Body Crème. Well, the next thing I knew, I was volunteering a gift basket full of beauty products and spa creams. So I win."

"It's not a contest, Liddy," Mona growled.

"People who say that know they can never win," Liddy snorted.

"She's right," Randy concurred as he delivered Hayley her usual Jack and Coke. "Besides, if anyone is going to win a contest on who can make the best holiday gift basket, it's going to be me hands down."

Hayley nodded. "He's right. No one can compete with a basket full of booze."

"I can!" Liddy cried. "I guarantee you my basket will get the most raffle tickets!"

The annual Christmas bazaar tradition was to set out a goldfish bowl next to each holiday basket and all the attendees would deposit one or more of their raffle tickets in the bowls for the drawing. Often people would buy twenty tickets at once and stuff them all in the bowl for the basket they really wanted, so the most popular basket was always obvious, given how the goldfish bowl next to it was overflowing with tickets. Hayley had reasonable confidence in her baking skills and felt that she would garner a healthy pile of tickets and be able to at least compete with Mona's seafood and Liddy's spa package, but Randy remained the wild card. She could see him walking away with it.

But with her healthy competitive streak, she was now willing to give it a try. And the unofficial contest for the most popular Christmas bazaar gift basket between the four of them was underway.

Chapter Two

The great Congregational church Christmas Bazaar Gift Basket competition turned out to be not much of a contest after all. Just as Hayley feared, Randy's impressive holiday basket boasting a wide variety of very pricey spirits won in a walk. No one was particularly surprised to see a large crowd hovering around Randy's prize, eagerly stuffing their raffle tickets into the bowl next to it until it was overflowing and tickets were falling onto the floor.

Reverend Ted dashed off to find another bowl for people to use to vie for the Holiday Cheer package. Luckily Hayley, Mona and Liddy were all doing brisk business as well, just not nearly as much as Randy. Still, the dozens of attendees did spread enough tickets around on the other baskets to not make it completely embarrassing.

That is, with the exception of the deserted table in the far corner of the church basement that featured the donations of Helen Woodworth's knitting circle. All five members—Helen, Abby Weston, Esther Willey, Betty Dyer and Doris Crimmons—had put together their own gift baskets with personally knitted items they had all made over the past year such as mittens, scarves, and hats. Doris was even offering an afghan blanket that had taken her eight months to complete. Unfortunately, despite their best efforts, nobody seemed particularly interested in wasting their valuable raffle tickets on any of them, and Hayley could see Helen and her group fuming in silence as most people passed them by.

Then Reverend Ted made the faux pas of asking Helen if she and Abby could use the same bowl to collect tickets and they would just draw from it twice, once for each of their baskets.

A miffed Helen barked, "Why do you need *my* bowl?"

Reverend Ted nervously glanced at the less than a dozen tickets lying on the bottom of Helen's bowl. He cleared his throat. "It's just that Randy's bowl is completely full and people are starting to get antsy waiting to add their raffle tickets, so I thought I would just borrow yours until I can dig up something that will hold all those tickets for the drawing!"

"I'm surprised, as a Man of God, you would even allow him to offer a basket stuffed with bottles of alcohol!" Helen sniffed.

"Come on, Helen, even Jesus drank wine!" Mona yelled from across the room.

"Mona, that's probably not helping," Hayley admonished.

Helen chose to ignore Mona's snide remark and kept her blazing eyes squarely focused on poor Reverend Ted, who had not yet dared pour the tickets into Helen's bowl out of fear that she might pop him one in the nose.

Reverend Ted set Helen's fishbowl gently back down on the card table next to her basket of knitted goodies. "I'm sorry, Helen, you're right. I will find another solution. You hang on to your bowl. No sense in anyone getting upset. This is supposed to be a joyous day of giving."

"I just don't understand why those flashier baskets are more popular than the old-fashioned ones like ours that our families have been donating to the church Christmas bazaar for generations. Don't these people have a sense of history and tradition? Frankly, if you ask me, the booze, the lobster, the facial scrubs, they're all just trying too hard!"

"Actually no one asked you, Helen!" Mona couldn't resist cracking before Hayley nudged her in the rib.

Helen's face flushed with anger and she turned her head away from Mona to complain to her knitting circle as Reverend Ted dashed away to the kitchen to find a giant serving bowl that was big enough for all the raffle tickets Randy was currently raking in.

"Reverend Ted looks a little frazzled. Maybe I'll go see if he needs help. Can you two keep an eye on things here?" Hayley asked Liddy and Mona.

"Sure," Liddy said. "But hurry back. I have been on my feet all day, and if I don't get a cocktail soon, I'm going to have to conduct a secret raid on Randy's basket when he's not looking."

Hayley smiled and headed off toward Reverend Ted, who had been stopped on his way to the kitchen in the church basement by Scooter Beauchemin, bald with a graying goatee, a wealthy New York hedge-fund manager who had recently moved from Manhattan to Maine with his gorgeous wife Tawny for a simpler, quieter life.

Hayley stopped short of interrupting them but was close enough to overhear their conversation. Reverend Ted was staring at a piece of paper Scooter had just handed him. His eyes were nearly bulging out of their sockets.

"Are you sure you didn't accidentally write too many zeroes on this check?" Reverend Ted gasped.

Scooter threw him a self-satisfied grin. "No, that's the correct amount. What can I say, I had a good year."

"I'm not sure we have enough raffle tickets to sell you."

Scooter chuckled. "I'm not interested in taking home any gift baskets. Tawny and I have everything we need. I want that money to go directly to the church programs."

"This is beyond generous, Mr. Beauchemin. You can't imagine the good this will do," Reverend Ted gushed, his eyes still glued to the massive amount scribbled on the check.

"Well, I know there are a lot of disadvantaged kids on the island, and I simply want to make sure they all have a very merry Christmas."

Tawny suddenly appeared at his side, handing him a glass of white wine. He gave her a sweet kiss on the cheek, which caused her to blush. "We both do."

"I can't thank you enough. And the kids thank you," Reverend Ted said, beaming.

Scooter nodded, and Tawny offered a wan smile as they wandered off to mingle with a few locals. Reverend Ted folded the check and stuffed it into the breast pocket of his LL Bean flannel shirt, and then continued on toward the kitchen before Hayley managed to stop him. "Reverend Ted, you seem to be out straight, so I was just wondering if I could offer you a helping hand?"

A big happy grin spread across his face as he patted his breast pocket with the palm of his hand. "Not anymore. But thanks anyway, Hayley."

And off he went.

Hayley shrugged and then spun around to return to Liddy and Mona when she noticed in the hallway off the main room Helen Woodworth and her fellow knitting circle member Esther Willey having a serious, intense, heated conversation. Esther was wagging a finger in Helen's face, spewing out angry words, her face as red as a beetroot, as Helen tried standing her ground but seemed overwhelmed by Esther's tirade. She shrank away the more Esther forcefully confronted her. Then, unable to take any more, tears streaming down both cheeks, Helen bolted away from Esther and out a side door. Esther watched her go, fuming.

Hayley made a beeline back to Mona and Liddy.

Liddy sighed. "Oh, good. You're back. Now it's your turn to hold down the fort while I get something to drink. I was told there were only sodas and iced tea here, but I just spotted Tawny Beauchemin sail by with a glass of white wine."

"Hold on a sec, Liddy, give me five more minutes," Hayley said.

"You already had your break, and I cannot stand another minute of listening to Bah Humbug Mona drone on and on about how much she hates Christmas."

"Cut me a break! I got all seven kids coming home this year, and I'm already stressed out about feeding them Christmas dinner. Most of them are full grown now, but they still eat like a pack of hungry wolves!"

"Seven? I thought you had eight kids," Liddy remarked.

"Wait, don't you have nine?" Hayley added.

"What? You expect me to remember?" Mona barked. "I was bedridden for most of them, so I have managed to block all the pregnancies out of my mind!"

"Listen, I just need to go check on Helen Woodworth. She ran out of here looking pretty upset."

"Come on, she can't take a little joke?" Mona scoffed.

"It has nothing to do with you. I saw her arguing with Esther Willey."

"All those women in that knitting circle are always bickering and complaining about something! They're so petty, and they're constantly judging other people, like hens on a fence. I'm sure it's nothing too serious," Liddy said.

Hayley debated with herself.

Maybe Liddy was right.

She should probably just let the two of them work it out on their own.

But Helen left the church crying.

Whatever conflict was boiling over was definitely not some silly inconsequential disagreement. It appeared far more grievous.

Hayley touched Liddy's arm. "Please, just five minutes."

Liddy threw her hands up in the air. "Fine. But I expect you to bring me back a Sauvignon Blanc and make sure it's chilled."

Hayley turned to go when a man started shouting from across the room. All eyes turned to Ed Willoughby, the owner of the local jewelry store, Willoughby's Rock Shop, who was standing at a card table with an empty display case situated in the middle and a clipboard of silent auction bid sheets and a ballpoint pen next to it.

"It's gone!" Ed Willoughby cried.

Reverend Ted came running from the kitchen, alerted to the commotion. "What's gone, Ed?"

Ed Willoughby took a deep breath and exhaled, trying to collect himself before announcing with great distress, "The ring I donated for the silent auction. Someone just stole it! It was right there in the case. I turned away for just a few seconds, and when I turned back, it was suddenly missing! Someone stole it! That ring is worth two thousand dollars!"

There were surprised gasps from the crowd.

Hayley grabbed her phone from the back pocket of her slacks. "I'll call the police!"

Chapter Three

Randy's husband and Hayley's brother-in-law, Bar Harbor police chief Sergio Alvares, who had arrived just moments earlier, was busy questioning a discombobulated Ed Willoughby. Poor Ed was still in a state of shock from the brazen theft of his expensive diamond ring. Meanwhile, Hayley watched an agitated Reverend Ted, nervously chewing on his left thumb fingernail, race around the room taking inventory of all the donations to make sure nothing else was missing.

It was total pandemonium in the church basement as people wanted to leave the bazaar to go finish their Christmas shopping or decorate their tree or visit relatives, only to be corralled by Lieutenant Donnie and Officer Earl as if they were flustered chickens clucking around in a coop. No one was allowed to leave until Chief Sergio had the opportunity to question each and every one of them and search their bags and purses. It appeared to Hayley to be a fruitless task since in the ten minutes it took for the police to arrive after she called them there were about two dozen people who had slipped out. And it was entirely possible that one of those people had left with the stolen ring.

Liddy and Mona stood by their baskets, protectively guarding them so no sticky-fingered thief could attempt to make off with them, although Hayley highly doubted there was any cause for concern. Pilfering a small ring in the palm of your hand was much easier than trying to snatch an oversized cellophane-wrapped gift basket.

Hayley approached them. "I heard Reverend Ted is considering postponing the raffle until tomorrow since Sergio still needs to question everybody and that could take hours."

Liddy sighed loudly. "Great. Just great. I had two holiday parties I was going to go drop in on tonight, and one of them was at the home of Ethan Brandt, that studly single lawyer who just moved to town, and now I'm going to miss out! Why do these things always happen to *me*?"

"Technically this did not happen to you, Liddy. Ed Willoughby is actually the victim here," Hayley reminded her.

"Oh, please. I'm sure that rock was insured!" Liddy snapped. "But I still don't have a date for the New Year's Eve extravaganza at the Atlantic Oakes Hotel, and I was hoping Ethan might ask me to accompany him at his party tonight. But now that's never going to happen, is it? Because I'm stuck here. So yes, Hayley, I am a victim, too!"

Hayley decided it was probably wise not to argue with her further at this point.

Mona just shook her head and turned to Hayley. "Sometimes I think she knows how ridiculous she sounds but she keeps on running her mouth just to screw with us."

"FYI, Mona, I can hear you. I am standing right here!" Liddy snapped.

"Good! You need to know how silly you act sometimes!" Mona yelled.

Hayley stepped between them. "Come on, you two, relax, will you? I know this is a huge imposition, but staying put and allowing Sergio to do his job is the right thing to do. Besides, it's Christmas. 'Tis the season to be jolly."

"Jolly? People with big bellies are jolly, Hayley. I lost seventeen pounds on Nutrisystem this year. If anyone is jolly here—"

Mona held a finger up to Liddy's lips. "I would advise you to stop right there, Liddy. I wouldn't want you to be cancelled for fat-shaming me!"

Liddy finally took Mona's words to heart and wisely kept her mouth shut.

Hayley glanced around the room. Liddy and Mona were not the only ones on edge. Everyone appeared restless and unnerved, especially Rosana Moretti, the wife of Hayley's old boss Sal Moretti, editor-in-chief at the local paper, the *Island Times*. Rosana stood off in a corner flanked by three women, all of whom Hayley recognized as members of Rosana's own knitting circle, the Happy Hookers. Rosana, who normally was very sweet and unobtrusive, some might even describe her as mousy, was in a state of distress as her friends buzzed around her trying to comfort her. Hayley wondered what was bothering her so much, but she did not have to wait long to find out, because just as Chief Sergio finished speaking with Ed Willoughby and turned to confer with Reverend Ted, who was hovering directly behind him, Rosana let loose her bottled up rage, spewing, "Hey, Chief Alvares, if you want to know who swiped that ring, just ask Helen Woodworth!"

Helen, who had returned to the basement and was huddling with some of her own knitting circle, the Crochet Mafia, including Betty Dyer, Doris Crimmons and Abby Weston, balked. "I have no clue what you are talking about, Rosana!"

Rosana pointed an accusing finger at the ladies across the room. "Helen, Betty, Esther, Abby, Doris, they're all liars and cheats and thieves! The whole lot of them!"

Rosana's group nodded in full agreement.

The rest of the crowd in the church basement watched with rapt attention.

"If you have proof we have done something wrong, then why don't you just present your evidence to the chief?" Helen challenged her.

Sergio hustled over to insert himself between the two warring factions before a rumble broke out like the Jets and the Sharks in a geriatric all-female version of *West Side Story*. "Ladies, please, why don't we just bring down the temperature here a little bit and stop hurling wild accusations without any evidence to back it up?"

"I've got plenty of evidence! *And* a witness!" Rosana cried.

Sergio was suddenly interested. "Go on, Rosana. I'm listening."

"Our knitting circle way back in June decided that all our members would knit fifty pairs of Christmas mittens for the church bazaar raffle this year. I told everyone to keep it under wraps, but Binki Welles, one of our members, was in St. Petersburg, Florida, when we had our meeting, so I brought her up to speed when we were having our hair done next to each other at Roberto's salon after she got back. Well, Shirley, the shampoo girl, told me she noticed Helen two dryers down eavesdropping on our conversation."

"Shirley the shampoo girl? That's your witness?" Sergio asked with a withering look.

"Yes!" Rosana huffed. "Well, I didn't think much of it at the time because I am not a suspicious person by nature, and I usually choose to see the good in people. So imagine my surprise when I got wind of the fact that Helen's group was suddenly on course to knit seventy-five pairs of Christmas mittens for the bazaar! It was painfully obvious that she had stolen my idea! We had to change course at the last minute and make scarves instead!"

"You can never have too many Christmas mittens," Hayley interjected, suspecting the comment would land with a thud and have little effect. Which it did.

"You're deluded if you think I could hear anything you said under that dryer at the salon, Rosana!" Helen roared.

"Who knows? Maybe you can lip-read!" Rosana replied.

Helen bristled. "Shirley doesn't know what she's talking about! And to think I always tip her so generously. I will tell you one thing, she's never getting another hard-earned penny out of me!"

"Stop blaming Shirley! You know what you did!" Rosana cried.

Helen took a long, deep, slow breath, as if trying to collect herself, and then, eyes narrowing, growled to Rosana, "You listen to me, Rosana Moretti, I came up with the mitten idea completely on my own. Maybe you were the one who tried stealing it from *me*!"

"That's absurd!" Rosana scoffed.

"Oh no!" Betty Dyer screamed at the top of her lungs, stunning the whole room into silence.

Helen whipped her head around toward Betty, who stood at the table staring at her specially made gift basket. "What's wrong now, Betty?"

Betty plucked a lone mitten out of the basket. "One of the mittens I made is missing! It was right here just a few minutes ago." She fixed her angry gaze on Rosana and her Happy Hookers. "Did one of you take it?"

Rosana laughed. "You've got to be kidding me! Why would any of us want to steal one of your lousy, poorly made mittens?"

Betty waved at Chief Sergio, who stood watching the

whole embarrassing scene with frustration. "If you want to arrest the guilty party and recover the ring and my mitten, you might want to consider a body search of Rosana Moretti's evil coven of witches!"

Sergio's shoulders sank.

It was going to be a long night.

Chapter Four

Hayley had not really meant to eavesdrop on Sergio questioning the attendees at the Christmas bazaar in the church basement, but as she wandered down the hall upstairs near the reverend's office she could clearly hear the chief talking with a woman, whom Hayley quickly recognized as Abby Weston. She was a nondescript pleasant woman who once dated a local seafood company owner, who had sadly passed last summer. After the sudden passing of her boyfriend, Abby was grateful to be a long-standing member of Helen Woodworth's knitting circle because it gave her something to focus on, allowing her to keep her mind off her grief. Hayley had heard through the grapevine that it was Abby, as one of the founding members, who had thought up the name for the group, the Crochet Mafia.

Hayley had to strain to hear what Abby was saying, since Abby was usually so demure and soft-spoken, so she quietly tiptoed down the hall until she was literally loitering right outside the door, which luckily was open just a crack.

Hayley craned her neck around and peered through the door, spotting Abby sitting in a hardback chair, her pert nose twitchy as she anxiously fidgeted with her sweater.

"You seem nervous, Abby," Sergio observed.

That was quite an understatement.

"I suppose I am," Abby whispered. "I am not used to being so closely associated with a crime."

That was not entirely true.

Abby's boyfriend, the seafood king, had been the victim of foul play, although it turned out she had nothing to do with his untimely demise.

"What do you mean by *closely associated*?" Sergio gently asked.

Hayley could see Abby's body stiffen. "What I meant to say was, I am not in the habit of being around a crime scene. The thought of that makes me very uncomfortable. When I was ten, I went to the five-and-dime with my older brother and he stole a package of licorice and I got so scared I hyperventilated to the point where the cashier had to call for an ambulance, which of course led to one of the paramedics spotting the licorice sticking out of my brother's coat pocket. They didn't dare charge him, because they were so afraid I would suffer a seizure on the spot, so they let him off with a warning."

There was a long pause as Sergio took in all of this information. Then he said, "I am no doctor, Abby, but it looks like you might hyperventilate right now. Does that mean you saw something?"

"No!" Abby shot back much too quickly.

Hayley could practically hear Abby's heart thumping in her chest from the hallway.

Sergio leaned closer toward her. "Are you sure?"

"Please, Chief Alvares. You are putting me in a very awkward position," Abby cried.

"By asking you a few questions?"

"But I told you, I don't know *anything*," Abby said.

She was a terrible liar.

"Abby, in my experience, it's always best to tell what you know as soon as possible. Because the truth will come out eventually. And if it turns out you lied or withheld information, then you could find yourself in trouble as well," Sergio warned her.

Abby reared back, horrified. "Are you going to arrest me?"

"No," Sergio said before pausing and ominously adding, "not if you come clean with any information you know."

Abby sighed. "I just don't want to get anyone into trouble."

"If you know the identity of the thief who stole that ring, then that person is already in a heap of trouble, so you might as well fess up now."

Visions of being booked and fingerprinted by Officer Earl for obstruction of justice were undoubtedly swirling through Abby's head, because Sergio did not have to press her any further into spilling the beans.

"I think it may have been Esther!" She let that hang in the air for a moment before dropping her head, defeated, consumed with guilt over ratting out her dear friend.

Sergio cocked an eyebrow. "Esther Willey?"

Abby nodded slightly before opening her purse and pulling out a tissue to dab at the tears pooling in her eyes and then blowing her nose.

Sergio waited for her to collect herself before he continued. "Did you actually see her take the ring?"

"Not exactly," Abby sniffed. "But I did see her milling around the table with the display case, and she was clearly coveting it. At one point when Mr. Willoughby wasn't looking, she took it out to try it on. But no, I did not see her physically put the ring in her pocket. Still, just moments later, I looked back and Esther was gone and Ed

Willoughby was shouting to the rooftops that someone had stolen his ring! The whole thing just looked highly suspicious."

"Do you believe that Esther is capable of theft?"

"I honestly don't know. But I will say, of all of us in the knitting circle, she's the one who is always borrowing things and never returning them, or buying a dress to wear to a party and taking it back to the shop the next day claiming it's too small or too big, or pretending to find a bug in her salad in order to get away with a free meal."

Hayley could corroborate that last point.

Esther had been with Doris Crimmons in her restaurant just a few weeks ago and complained that she had found a strand of hair in her fried calamari. Hayley had comped their entire meal.

"So she has a history of lying and cheating," Sergio said matter-of-factly.

"No, I would not go that far. Esther is a good person. There is just, shall we say, a dark side to her personality."

That was all Hayley needed to hear.

She made a beeline back downstairs to Liddy and Mona, who were impatiently waiting to be interviewed by Sergio next. "Have either of you seen Esther Willey?"

Liddy shook her head. "No, not for a while. Maybe she made her escape right before the cops got here."

"No, I think I saw her huddling with Betty Dyer when Donnie and Earl were trying to get everybody to stay put," Mona said.

Hayley glanced around the room.

There was no sign of Esther, but she did spot Helen Woodworth, now recovered from her dustup with Esther earlier, sitting in a corner furiously knitting a winter cap to keep herself measured and calm.

Hayley turned to Liddy and Mona. "Okay, we need to

find her. It's important. You two search the building. I'm going to go talk to Helen."

Without waiting for them to respond, Hayley dashed over to Helen and hovered over her. "Helen?"

Helen willfully ignored Hayley, her knitting needles clicking and clicking against each other as she worked feverishly on her hat.

"Helen, have you seen Esther?"

"No," Helen muttered, eyes intently fixed on her project.

"Is everything okay between the two of you?"

"Of course," Helen growled. "Why would you ask me something like that?"

"Because I saw you arguing with her earlier, and I was just worried because you two have been close friends for so long."

Helen finally raised her eyes to meet Hayley's. "I don't know what you think you saw, but Esther and I are fine. More than fine. We're closer than ever. Now I would appreciate you leaving me in peace."

Helen went back to staring at her incessantly clicking needles.

Hayley knew she was not going to get anything more out of Helen Woodworth, so she made the rounds chatting with the room full of locals who had been present at the time when Ed Willoughby's ring had been pinched. Most claimed they had not even noticed Esther Willey at the Christmas bazaar; not surprising, since there was very little traffic around their gift basket table. But finally Betty Dyer's grandson, who had been whining to his grandmother that he wanted to leave because he was hungry and wanted a pepperoni pizza, told Hayley that he thought he had seen Esther Willey leave the church out a side door that led to the exit upstairs shortly before the police had arrived. Hayley thanked him and scooted down the hall, out the side door and up the steps to the exit, which led to the church cemetery.

It was eerily quiet as Hayley walked past the rows and rows of white headstones, many of them faded, with the family names from the earlier settlers, dating back to when the town was first founded in 1796. Bar Harbor was initially incorporated as the Town of Eden, after Sir Richard Eden, an English statesman, in a document signed by Samuel Adams.

The winter chill in the air was almost debilitating. Hayley, who had hurried outside without putting on a coat, was about to turn around and retreat inside when she spotted what looked like a shoe.

A woman's shoe.

A tan dress pump with a low heel.

Was it a discarded shoe, or was someone still wearing it? She could not tell because a gravestone was blocking her view.

Hayley cautiously approached, crunching through the snow, until she was able to see over the gravestone and what was behind it.

Hayley gasped and stumbled back, almost losing her balance.

The shoe, which had somehow fallen off, was just a few feet from the dead body of Esther Willey, laid out flat on her back with a sharp chrome steel knitting needle stuck in the middle of her Santa's reindeer sweater and Betty Dyer's missing Christmas mitten stuffed in her mouth.

Island Food & Spirits
by
Hayley Powell

When I was in high school, Home Economics was a required class, and I did everything I could to avoid it. Which worked until the start of my senior year, when I could not put it off any longer.

My mother, knowing how important this class was, and that if I failed I might not graduate with my class, informed me that if I did not pass this class, then I would not be joining my best friends, Liddy and Mona, for our upcoming Christmas break ski trip to Squaw Mountain that Liddy's mother had so graciously agreed to take us on.

This, I must say, was indeed a motivating factor for me as I marched into the Home Economics class on its first day.

I sat down with my freshly sharpened pencil, a new notebook, and most important, a positive attitude, which my mother told me I would need to have or else.

Our teacher, Mrs. Blake, who started off by telling us to call her Mrs. B, stood in front of the class and explained that she would be showing us how to enjoy running a household smoothly and efficiently and that she would also teach us the basics of sewing, knitting and cooking.

I just sat back in my seat and groaned. This was the 1990s, not the 1950s. Who in the world wants to knit nowadays? In hindsight, however, that might not have been a bad thing for me to learn considering what's been going on recently this holiday season in Bar Harbor.

First up was sewing. We all chose a pattern from a well-worn smelly old box that looked like it was also a relic from the 1950s.

Most of the students chose to make skirts and dresses, but both of those projects looked extremely complicated to me, so luckily I came upon a pattern for a simple pair of sweatpants. I mean, sweatpants, come on, how hard could that be to make? I quickly snatched it out of the pile and thought, "Jeez. Easy A."

For the next few weeks in class, everyone worked like busy little bees. I made a show of focusing on my sewing project whenever Mrs. B passed by with her arched eyebrow checking on everyone's progress, but in reality I spent most of the time just fooling around, chattering away to everyone about basically everything but sewing.

When my mother asked me how the class was going, I would give her a thumbs-up and say things like "Great!" or "It's not as bad as I thought it would be!"

But eventually the hens came home to roost. Mrs. B held me after class and told me that she had noticed that I had not been working on my sewing project and wanted to remind me that I had only two days left before it was due.

I was shocked.

It had been two weeks already?

I quickly dashed back to my table and pulled out my material, staring glumly at it, realizing I had frittered away all this time and still had no clue how to follow a pattern or sew the sweats. All I could see was my mother's irate face. In a panic, I just grabbed a pair of scissors and started cutting.

I wish I could say I surprised myself and that

my sewing project was the work of art that I imagined it to be. But alas, no, an easy A was not in the cards. I could tell from the look on Mrs. B's face when she inspected my project that she was not impressed. And the D Minus she gave me for a grade pretty much confirmed it. She told me in a very haughty tone that the only reason I did not fail completely was because I had at least made some kind of effort to complete the task.

I could suddenly see my Christmas ski trip in serious jeopardy and knew I had to try much harder on the next project, which was knitting a scarf or a pair of mittens. Of course I picked a scarf because it seemed to be the easier of the two to get done.

Well, it didn't take long, just one class to be exact, to learn I was hopeless with a pair of knitting needles. I felt overwhelmed and soon lost focus, and before I knew it, another two weeks had passed by, and I found myself handing in a half-finished scarf. I gulped when I saw Mrs. B's face. She looked even less impressed with my scarf than she did with my sweatpants.

Needless to say, I got an F.

It would take a miracle for me to even have a snowball's chance in hell of going on that fun-filled weeklong ski trip.

But as luck would have it, I received my miracle! Mrs. B announced that, for our last project before Christmas break, we would be learning the basics of cooking and preparing a couple of simple dishes.

Finally!

A subject I knew something about!

All I had to do was perform well enough to get a passing grade and my ski trip might be back within my reach. I went home after school, happily skipping through the front door, but came to a screeching halt when I came upon my mother standing in the middle of the kitchen, angrily waving a piece of paper.

Apparently the teachers had mailed out school progress reports, a minor detail that had slipped my mind. My mother was none too pleased to discover that I was on the verge of failing Home Economics. She warned me that if I did not pass with a C or better, I would be spending my Christmas vacation cleaning out the garage. No ifs, ands or buts.

Thankfully I was acing the cooking portion of the class, and after a few successful dishes, I stopped by Mrs. B's desk when the bell rang to dismiss us for recess and asked about my grade. She gave me a foreboding grim look and explained that unfortunately, although I was definitely improving, it was unlikely that I would be able to make a C with my two awful previous grades.

I was devastated.

No ski trip.

But then Mrs. B offered me a lifeline. She told me that if I could make an extra credit dessert that wowed her, there was a slight chance I would get my C. Maybe even a C plus.

I eagerly accepted the challenge and raced off to start perusing recipes.

After a long night of searching for the perfect dessert, I finally decided on a Christmas Rum Cake. But I was not going to take any chances of screwing it up. I practiced making the rum cake at home first, testing three different cakes out on my brother, mother and friends, all of whom pronounced each one grade A delicious!

I knew I was ready.

The night before I was to present my cake to Mrs. B, I had a eureka moment! If my rum cake was delicious with rum extract, then I bet the flavor would be over the top with *real* rum! Mrs. B had challenged me to wow her, so maybe this was the key to a major win! I looked into my mother's liquor cabinet, and lo and behold, found a bottle of Captain Morgan Dark Rum.

Then I set about making my final cake.

Not knowing how much rum to use, I erred on the side of more is better and kept pouring more and more rum into the batter. I also decided to use it in my glaze since it was a rum cake and sure to be a yummy one at that.

The next day I proudly carried my cake into class and set it down in front of Mrs. B. Her eyes lit up with delight. She declared it a lovely cake, and then she proceeded to cut a slice for everyone in class, setting the pieces on paper plates with plastic forks. I proudly passed them out to everyone, basking in my glory, and then I held my breath while Mrs. B picked up her fork, scooped up a big hunk of the cake, and shoveled it into her mouth.

As she began to chew, I could plainly see the puzzled look on her face. She scooped up another piece with her fork and ate that one, too. Suddenly she threw her fork down, jumped up from her chair and began screaming for everyone to stop eating as she frantically ran around the classroom grabbing everyone's cake from them and telling all the students that they were excused for early recess. Everyone except me!

I just stared in shock, my cheeks flushed, tears in my eyes. Did it really taste that bad?

Before I could even ask, Mrs. B ran out of

the room and soon returned with the principal right behind her.

They both grabbed a plastic fork and tasted more of the cake. They warily glanced at me as they whispered to each other, their mouths full of cake. All I could make out were a few words like "damage control," "reeks of alcohol," and "call her mother."

I still had no real sense of what was going on other than a bad feeling I would be spending Christmas break hauling junk out of our garage. I couldn't hold back the tears any longer and just broke down sobbing.

The next thing I knew I looked up and my mother was storming through the classroom door. I knew at this moment that my young life, as I knew it, was over.

There were more harried hushed tones. My mother was handed a fork, and then all three women were munching on my Christmas Rum Cake and nervously eyeballing me.

Finally, the principal asked me about the rum, and I explained that since it was a rum cake, I thought real rum would taste better than the extract. I saw them all nodding in agreement, and I began to feel better.

Mrs. B explained that the use of alcohol was not permitted on school grounds, but since I had made the cake at home and was unaware of the rule, then the school would not hold it against me. She also added that I had made one of the most scrumptious rum cakes that any of them had ever tasted, and therefore I would be passing the class (barely) with my extra credit project. She did warn me, however, not to bring one of my special cakes to school anymore. They should be enjoyed at home, reminding me that I was always welcome to drop one at her house after school hours.

That rum cake became a Christmas tradition in our home that continues to this day. I also made one for Mrs. B every year until she retired from the school and moved to Boca Raton.

I'm going to share my easy recipe with you, and it just might become a staple of your own holiday gatherings. But first, why not have some refreshing Christmas punch?

Christmas Punch

Ingredients
4 cups cranberry juice, chilled
2 cups lemon lime soda, chilled
2 cups ginger ale, chilled
2 cups sparkling apple juice, chilled
2 cups vodka or light rum
1½ cups frozen cranberries
1 lemon, sliced
1 lime, sliced

Combine the first six ingredients in a large punch bowl and mix well.
Add your lemon and lime slices to the punch.
Serve and enjoy.

Hayley's Home Ec Christmas Rum Cake

Ingredients

Cake
1 cup chopped walnuts (pecans if you prefer)
1 package (15.25 ounces) yellow cake mix
1 box (3.4 ounces) vanilla instant pudding & pie filling
4 large eggs
½ cup cold water
½ cup vegetable oil
½ cup dark rum

Glaze
8 tablespoons butter
¼ cup water
1 cup sugar
½ cup dark rum

Preheat your oven to 325 degrees. Grease and flour a 12-cup Bundt pan. Sprinkle the chopped walnuts over the bottom of the pan.

Mix together the rest of the cake ingredients, and pour this mixture over the nuts in the Bundt pan. Bake 1 hour or until an inserted butter knife comes out clean.

Cool the cake, and then invert onto a serving plate.

Make the glaze by melting the butter in a saucepan. Stir in the water and sugar. Boil for 5 minutes, stirring constantly. Remove from heat, and stir in the rum.

Prick holes all over the top of the cooled cake with a fork, and then pour the glaze evenly onto the cake, letting it drip down the sides and absorb into the top of the cake. Use all of the glaze.

Let the cake sit for about 30 minutes to absorb the glaze.

Slice and enjoy!

Chapter Five

Word spread fast through the crowd that had been herded like cattle into the basement of the Congregational church that poor Esther Willey had been discovered dead in the cemetery outside. There was a constant chatter as the people began to realize that not only was there a thief among them, now there was a cold-blooded murderer who had wielded a knitting needle to stab his or her victim to death.

Sergio tried to get the chaos under control by announcing that more officers and county detectives would be arriving shortly to help him interview everyone again, but that did little to assuage their already frayed nerves. After all, there was no guarantee the killer would not strike again at any opportune moment.

"Excuse me, Chief Alvares!" Ed Willoughby shouted above the din of the crowd. "I have a question!"

"Yes, Ed, what is it?"

"I am sorry about what happened to poor Esther. Really I am. But does this mean you will be shifting focus away from my stolen ring and concentrate all your efforts on finding who speared her with that knitting needle?"

Sergio stared at him, dumbfounded. "Uh, yes, Ed, that's

correct. I'm sorry, but right now I'm afraid murder trumps theft."

"I don't mean to sound insensitive to what happened to Esther, but that ring was worth a lot of money and it would be a shame for the culprit to just get away with it because the police department dropped the ball."

"To be honest, Ed, whether you mean to or not, you are coming off as completely insensitive," Hayley scolded as she huddled with Liddy and Mona at their gift basket table.

"That's easy for you to say, Hayley. No one wanted to steal your measly basket of baked goods," Ed huffed.

"Shut up, Ed!" Mona roared. "Stop making a damn fool of yourself."

"Nobody asked for your opinion, Mona Barnes!" Ed clapped back.

Sergio raised a hand for order. "Okay, everybody, let's just freeze out for a minute!"

The crowd exchanged baffled looks.

Randy stepped forward. "What he meant to say is, let's all chill out for a minute."

English was Brazilian native Sergio's second language.

"That's what I said!" Sergio barked defensively.

"No, not really, but why quibble?" Randy whispered.

Sergio spun back around to face off with Ed. "We will do our best to recover your ring, Ed. Trust me, my department can multitask, but right now my top priority is finding out what happened to Esther, which unfortunately means that we need to go through the interview process all over again with everybody here."

There were a lot of discontented moans and groans.

Woody, Helen Woodworth's bald, plump and scruffy-faced husband, shot a hand up. "Do you think we'll be out by six? There's a Patriots game on TV that I think we *all* want to be home to watch!"

Sergio sighed. "I will try to work as fast as possible, Woody, but let me reiterate, a woman has been *murdered*!"

"A woman nobody really liked," Mona muttered.

Hayley elbowed her in the rib cage.

Rosana Moretti piped up. "You should start by interrogating Betty Dyer! I heard her missing mitten was found stuffed in Esther Willey's mouth!"

There were surprised gasps from the crowd.

Betty's eyes widened in despair. "How could you be so cruel and say something like that, Rosana?"

"Because it's no secret there was a lot of internal strife inside your quaint little knitting circle, and maybe you had reached a boiling point with Esther and thought it would be easier just to take her out!" Rosana cried, pointing an accusing finger at the entire Crochet Mafia, who were huddled together, hugging one another, sobbing.

"Esther was my friend! We were all her friends! We would never do her any harm!" Betty wailed.

"Then how did your mitten wind up between her teeth?" Rosana shouted.

"I have no idea!" Betty sobbed, falling into Helen's arms as Helen gently patted her on the back, trying to comfort her.

Liddy whispered into Hayley's ear. "And the Oscar goes to . . ."

Hayley glanced at her, surprised. "You really think Betty Dyer is capable of murder?"

"If you ask me, I think any one of them in that knitting circle could have done it," Liddy said.

"Lightning may strike when I say this, but for once I actually agree with Liddy," Mona declared.

Sergio had heard enough. "Okay, enough speculation from the cashew gallery . . ."

More puzzled looks.

Randy stepped forward again. "Peanut gallery."

Sergio shot him another annoyed look.

Randy cleared his throat. "Just trying to keep everybody up to speed."

Sergio mumbled something under his breath in Portuguese as Hayley quietly approached him to offer a suggestion. "Why don't you search everyone's knitting bags to see if anyone is missing a needle that could have been used as the murder weapon?"

"I already thought about that. But after searching Esther's belongings, we found a matching needle, which means the murder weapon belonged to Esther," Sergio whispered. "Her killer must have grabbed it out of Esther's bag and impaled her with her own knitting needle. But that stays between you and me. I don't want that specific detail made public yet, so you better warn Bruce that he will be in a world of hurt if that little fact suddenly pops up in one of his crime columns."

"Of course," Hayley assured him.

Sergio then pointed at Rosana. "Mrs. Moretti, come with me upstairs to the reverend's office, would you please?"

Rosana gasped. "What? Me? Are you saying I'm a suspect?"

"No one is a suspect yet. I'm going to get to everyone eventually, but I have decided to start with you, and so I would appreciate your cooperation."

Rosana tentatively walked across the room with her head held high and followed Sergio up the stairs as the highly emotional Crochet Mafia members stayed in their cluster, eyeing the crowd surrounding them, sensing their suspicion, and frantically whispering to one another.

Hayley noticed Reverend Ted standing off in a corner by himself with a shell-shocked look on his face. She could tell he was spiraling emotionally. She walked over to him and put a comforting arm around his shoulder. She could feel him shivering. "I'm sorry the Christmas bazaar didn't work out the way you had hoped, Ted."

"This is a disaster. Why did these things have to happen, today of all days? This was supposed to be a celebration, a chance to give back to the community, and now we're dealing with a theft and a murder on church grounds. I know I'm supposed to be a voice of reason and comfort in difficult times, but I'm in shock, Hayley. I don't know what to do or say."

"It's a shock to everyone. You cannot be expected to be a rock at all times. But you will find your voice. And I am sure you will deliver the perfect sermon to honor Esther on Sunday."

"I just don't see how things could get any worse!"

"Excuse me," a man's voice said from behind them.

Hayley and Reverend Ted turned around to discover Scooter Beauchemin and his wife, Tawny, both gloomy and exhausted from all the drama.

Reverend Ted did his best to collect himself. "Yes, Scooter, how can I be of service?"

"You can give me back that check," Scooter said flatly.

Reverend Ted's mouth dropped open. He was speechless. He took a beat, processing the request, swallowing hard. "I-I beg your pardon?"

"To be completely honest, Reverend, I have to be fiercely protective of my public image. My entire business has been built on my reputation. I cannot afford a whiff of scandal, no matter how good the cause. So the last thing I need is for my money to be associated with a theft *and* a murder." He thrust out his hand. "So I would appreciate it if you just returned my donation."

Reverend Ted shakily reached into his pocket and extracted the check. Scooter snatched it out of his grasp before he even had the chance to hand it over. "Thank you, Reverend. I'm sure you understand. I wish you all the best." He took his wife by the arm. "Come on, Tawny, let's see if the chief can take us next so we can get out of here."

They walked away, leaving Hayley behind to console the now-devastated Reverend Ted.

Chapter Six

Hayley usually had her Christmas tree up and decorated in the living room by the first week of December, but this year in particular had been unusually busy at the restaurant. Between her business, Christmas shopping and attempting to wow everyone with her gift basket, there had just been no time.

Bruce had bought a fine-looking eight-foot-tall balsam fir tree at the local tree farm, and she had dragged all the boxed decorations out of the garage that morning so they could whip up some spiked eggnog and decorate the tree together when she returned home from the church's Christmas bazaar.

Unfortunately, given the unexpected events and the endless questioning by the police, Hayley did not make it through her front door until almost seven that evening. She found Bruce, bleary-eyed, sitting in the middle of the living room floor trying to untangle the colored Christmas tree lights like a frustrated child. Judging from the empty glass mug next to him, not to mention his watery eyes and beet-red face, she guessed he had already gotten a head start on the bourbon-laced eggnog.

"There you are!" Bruce cried, dropping the lights and climbing to his feet but stumbling into the couch. He grabbed the armrest to steady himself and then enveloped her in a big bear hug. "Merry Christmas, my love!"

"You started without me!" Hayley scolded him.

"I had no idea how long you'd be stuck at the church answering questions, so I just set up the tree and was going to start stringing the lights. I would never put on the ornaments without you. I know that's your favorite part."

"No, my favorite part is drinking your world-famous one-hundred-proof eggnog while sorting through all the old decorations!"

"Coming right up!" Bruce promised as he scurried off to the kitchen.

"And don't forget I like a dollop of whipped cream on mine!"

Hayley shed her jacket and boots and began to open the boxes of decorations and empty all the ornaments onto the coffee table. She took great care with the ones she had inherited from her grandmother after she passed, some dating back to the late nineteenth century. They were mixed in with midcentury pop art collectibles, including a porcelain Andy Warhol and a Rolling Stones album cover, a portrait of her beloved dog Leroy inside a tiny frame, as well as some homemade ornaments her kids had made in grade school that she had held on to for their sentimental value.

Bruce returned with her eggnog, and after just one sip she felt as if she were wrapped up in a warm blanket. She and Bruce spent the next hour covering the branches of the tree with all the decorations. Bruce went to retrieve the stepladder from the garage so he could affix the Northstar light on top, then set about ripping open the packages of tinsel. Before Hayley could stop him, he was flinging the silver tinsel haphazardly everywhere just like her kids were prone to do growing up.

"Bruce, no! You do this every year! You can't just hurl it! It'll look like some tinsel monster threw up all over the tree. There is an art to it. One strand at a time."

"That will take *all* night!"

"Nobody ever said art was easy. Here, let me do it." She snatched the half-empty box out of his hand and began carefully applying one tinsel piece at a time over the branches.

"What am I supposed to do?"

"You can make more eggnog."

"I love that idea!"

He eagerly bounded back into the kitchen, leaving her in peace. She had maybe put on five or six pieces of tinsel when the doorbell rang. She glanced at the clock above the fireplace. It was almost nine o'clock. She walked over and opened the door and was greeted by Reverend Ted and his church choir, all bundled up in winter coats and scarves and muffs and mittens, all of them holding lit candles as they began singing the lyrics to "The First Noel."

"*The First Noel the Angels did say*
Was to certain poor shepherds in fields as they lay . . ."

Hayley plastered on a bright smile, trying her best to act surprised and full of joy at finding Christmas carolers on her doorstep.

"*In fields where they lay keeping their sheep*
On a cold winter's night that was so deep . . ."

"Oh, how wonderful!" Hayley cooed, although she was tired and a little buzzed from the spiked eggnog and knew this song could go on endlessly. She assumed Bruce was hearing all of this and currently hiding out in the kitchen in order to avoid getting dragged in as part of the audience.

"*Noel, Noel, Noel, Noel*
Born is the King of Israel!"

Hayley applauded. "That was beautiful, thank you so much!" She went to shut the door but they kept going.

"They looked up and saw a star
Shining in the East beyond them far..."

Finally, Reverend Ted turned around and waved his arms at everybody. "You know what, why doesn't everyone take a little break so I can have a private chat with Hayley?"

Doris Crimmons from the Crochet Mafia, who also sang in the church choir, stepped forward, annoyed. "But this is only our second house! We don't need a break already!"

"I noticed you were a little off-key, Doris. Why don't you hum a few bars with the rest of the choir and get yourself back in tune before we continue! I will be right back!"

Before Hayley could protest, Reverend Ted slipped through the front door and slammed the door shut on his choir just as a man in the back groaned, "But it's twenty degrees outside!"

He sheepishly turned to Hayley. "I'm sorry, this will only take a moment."

"What is it?" she asked curiously.

"I would like to enlist your services."

"Trust me, Reverend, I have no intention of joining the choir. I have a *terrible* singing voice."

"Oh, don't worry! I know! I've heard you sing a few hymns at church. As Simon Cowell once said, if you lived two thousand years ago and tried to sing, I fear they might have stoned you."

Hayley grimaced.

He could have stopped at "I know."

"Then what is it you want?"

Reverend Ted took a deep breath and sighed. "I want you to investigate Esther Willey's murder."

Hayley shook her head. "I understand I have a reputation for being an eager amateur sleuth, but I think it's probably wise to leave this case to the police."

Bruce strolled in with two mugs of eggnog, grinning at Hayley. "Who are you, and what have you done with my wife?"

He had a point.

It was the rarest of occasions when Hayley actually turned down the opportunity to do some snooping.

Before she had the chance to take a mug of eggnog from Bruce, Reverend Ted reached out and snagged her hand. "Please, you must! I'm begging you! I need you to find out what happened!"

"Why is it so important to you?" Hayley asked.

"Because my fear is the police will act too slow, drag out the investigation, and time is of the essence because if you can prove that whoever killed Esther was not a part of the church, then maybe I can convince Scooter Beauchemin that he should rethink withdrawing his donation. Think of all the kids, all the families, who will go without this Christmas season if the church can't provide food and presents because this year's bazaar was a scandal-plagued bust!"

"But why me? I just don't see—"

"You know, I know, the whole town suspects Esther's death had something to do with those knitting circles. Some of those women are downright vicious!"

"Actually we honestly don't know that for sure—"

He cut her off again. "Besides, I heard you briefly belonged to Helen Woodworth's group. You know them all well, they probably trust you. I'm sure you will have an easier time investigating them from inside the circle than the police will," he reasoned.

The little voice inside her was screaming at her to politely but forcibly turn down Reverend Ted's request. But the desperation she could see in his eyes was almost too much to bear.

And he was right.

The faster Esther's killer was brought to justice and the church was cleared of any involvement or connection, the better the chance that Scooter Beauchemin might give back his check so the neediest families in town could have a merry Christmas.

Hayley went from shaking her head to slowly nodding, resigned. "Okay, fine. I will do it."

"And there it is." Bruce laughed, not the least bit surprised, as he slurped on his eggnog and got whipped cream all over his upper lip.

Chapter Seven

Even though Hayley had attended only one meeting of Helen Woodworth's knitting circle in the past, and that was a blatant attempt to extract information from the members on another investigation she had so zealously embarked on, Helen appeared not the least bit nonplussed by Hayley's sudden appearance on her doorstep on this snowy, cold Tuesday afternoon when the Crochet Mafia held their weekly meeting. In fact, Helen ushered her inside her home as if she had been expecting her.

"We're having champagne in the living room, sort of a celebration of life for poor Esther. Why don't you join us?"

"Thank you, Helen, that's very kind of you," Hayley said, following Helen down the hall to join the other surviving members of the group—Doris, Abby and Betty—who were all seated on the floor, their knitting needles clicking away on a joint project, different corners of what looked like the beginning of a large blanket.

Hayley marveled at the progress they were making. "What are you working on?"

"It's a memorial quilt to commemorate Esther's life. We're going to include a bunch of different types of clothing and fabric and some of her favorite designs she knitted during her time in the Crochet Mafia," Helen explained.

"When we're finished, we're hoping the YWCA will hang it on the wall in the gym for a time this spring since Esther did a lot of fundraising for them."

"What a lovely gesture," Hayley said as Helen poured her a glass of champagne and handed it to her. Hayley raised her glass. "To Esther."

Helen raised her own glass as Doris, Abby and Betty set down their knitting needles and picked up their flutes of champagne to clink for the toast.

There was a beat of silence before Abby finally spoke. "I still can't believe she's gone."

Hayley glanced at two empty champagne bottles on the coffee table in addition to the one Helen held in her hand. The ladies of the Crochet Mafia were definitely drinking away their sorrows on this somber day, which might prove useful. The more their guard came down, the more loose-lipped they might become. After all, Hayley was here to ask questions. She wanted to try to find out whether any of them knew anyone who might have had it out for Esther besides Rosana Moretti and her Happy Hooker crew, none of whom, Hayley staunchly believed, had anything to do with Esther's murder. She had known Rosana for far too long as the devoted wife of her old boss Sal Moretti, and she knew Rosana's heart. She might talk a good game, but deep down Rosana was a shy, docile little pussycat incapable of stepping on a spider.

"Did you bring your knitting needles, Hayley?" Doris asked.

Before she had a chance to answer, Helen jumped in. "Of course she didn't bring her own knitting needles, Doris! She's not here to knit or drink champagne with us!"

Hayley took another sip. "Actually, the champagne is quite lovely."

"Then what is she doing here?" Doris asked.

Helen sighed. "Oh Lord, Doris. Where have you been, living in a cave? Haven't you seen Hayley running around town all these years investigating local crimes? What do you *think* she's doing here? She's here to pump us for information about Esther."

So much for subtlety steering the conversation to Esther Willey's murder. Helen had already done that for her.

Doris shot Hayley a disapproving look. "Don't you think it's a bit too soon to be doing that? At least give us a day or two to properly mourn the loss of our friend."

"Well, I for one am happy she's here," Abby insisted. "I want to know who took our dear friend away from us."

Betty Dyer remained suspiciously silent, her eyes glued to her end of the quilt, which piqued Hayley's curiosity. She was not the only one who noticed.

Helen plopped down on her couch after gulping down her champagne. "Cat got your tongue, Betty?"

Betty snapped out of her thoughts. "What?"

"You're being awfully quiet," Helen said, eyes narrowing.

"It's hard to get a word in edgewise with all of you chatterboxes!" Betty snapped.

"Oh, you usually manage just fine," Doris scoffed.

"I didn't do it, all right? I know what you're all thinking, but I never touched a hair on Esther's head, so stop acting like I'm some kind of suspect!"

There was a stunned silence.

"Relax, Betty, nobody here believes you killed Esther." Helen laughed.

Hayley, however, could not resist following up on what was just put out there. "Why would anyone have reason to think that, Betty?"

"Because it's no secret Esther and I had our issues. I wanted to open my own Christmas shop, which I was going to call Frosty's Treasures, and I found the perfect space to lease. But I didn't have enough money for the down payment, so Esther and her husband, Bub—this was before he died—they agreed to co-sign the loan, which I would pay back with interest as the business got going," Betty explained breathlessly. "But they got cold feet at the last minute and pulled out after I had already signed the lease and put down my half of the down payment using my entire life savings. Esther swore it was Bud who made the decision, but she just let it happen and didn't fight him on it. I get it, he was her husband, I was just a friend, but I felt so betrayed. We were never the same after that."

"Oh, for goodness sake, Betty, that was years ago. And Esther was telling you the truth. It was cheapskate Bud who squashed the deal, not Esther. I was there when he came home from the bank and told her they weren't going to help you. Esther did stand up for you and tried very hard to convince him otherwise, but the bastard just didn't want to hear it. His mind was already made up."

Doris cackled. "I do remember you being so mad that when Bud keeled over from that stroke, I said to myself, 'Maybe Betty slipped something into his Mountain Dew,' which he was always drinking."

Betty's eyes bulged out. "I did not kill Bud! Why is everyone suddenly ganging up on me?"

Helen sighed. "Betty, stop being so paranoid."

"Helen's right," Abby said. "Bud had a stroke because he weighed over three hundred pounds and could never diet. He would always chase the diet pills he was taking with a Twinkie."

There was a palpable tension in the air, mostly coming from Betty, who always despised being the center of attention.

"I'm sorry, I fear my presence here is keeping everyone

on edge. Maybe I should come by another time," Hayley said.

"Nonsense, Hayley, you are welcome to stay as long as you want. I even have an extra pair of knitting needles you can use if you want to help with the quilt," Helen said.

"No, Doris is right," Hayley said. "You should all have some time to grieve. I will swing by in a couple of weeks. It would be an honor to contribute a section of the quilt. It's going to be beautiful."

She eased out of the living room and headed to the door. Behind her, she heard Abby say, "I left some yarn I need out in my car. I'll be right back."

Hayley had just stepped onto the front porch of Helen Woodworth's house when Abby followed her out and shut the door behind her so they had some privacy.

"Hayley, wait," Abby whispered. "I have something to tell you."

"Of course, Abby, what is it?"

"I don't think it was Betty."

"Good. Neither do I."

"It wasn't Betty because . . ." She paused, looked back at the door to make sure no one had cracked it open to eavesdrop. "Because someone else in the group had a much stronger motive for wanting to see Esther dead."

Hayley snapped to attention. "Who?"

Abby lowered her voice again to a barely audible whisper. "Helen."

"*Helen?*" Hayley found herself almost yelling.

Abby put a finger to her lips. "Shhhh. Helen would kill me if she knew I was telling you this. Of course, I mean that figuratively." Abby thought about it. "But then again, if Helen did knock off poor Esther, I guess I could mean it literally."

"Abby, tell me, why Helen?"

She leaned in closer to Hayley. "Esther once admitted to me that she was having an affair with a married man. Well, Esther was always joking and telling stories, so I didn't put much stock in it. But then, one of my students at Emerson Conners, who lives next door to Esther, claimed he saw Woody Woodworth sneaking into Esther's house late one night when he was using his telescope to look up at the constellations. Of course, the kid's a regular Peeping Tom, always spying on people, so I don't buy the whole looking at the stars story, but honestly, why would the boy make up something like that?"

It was a doozy of a rumor.

If it was indeed true.

"Did Helen know?" Hayley asked.

"No. She was totally in the dark until recently. But then I heard she found lipstick on Woody's collar. It was raspberry glaze. Esther's favorite color. You know she had such thin lips so she was very particular about her lipstick."

Hayley swallowed hard.

If Abby had her facts straight, then Helen Woodworth was Hayley's first major suspect.

And it would explain why Helen fled the church basement in tears after exchanging terse words with Esther Willey at the Christmas bazaar.

Chapter Eight

"Helen! So nice to see you!" Hayley chirped as she strolled into the Christmas Vacation Shop, which sold a wide variety of holiday decorations nearly year-round, to find Helen Woodworth perusing a shelf full of tree ornaments. Hayley glanced over at the clerk behind the register. "Hi, Debbie, happy holidays!"

The gray-haired woman, although in a festive red and white sweater, lacked even a hint of Christmas cheer and simply grunted a reply, not taking her eyes off the Louise Penny mystery novel she clutched in her hand.

Hayley shrugged and swiveled back in Helen's direction. "I hope you can forgive me for crashing your knitting circle meeting yesterday. It was so rude of me to just show up unannounced."

Helen did not seem at all perturbed about it. "No worries, dear. I'm just sorry you didn't get any useful information and it was a complete waste of your time."

She was wrong about that.

Hayley did walk away with a doozy of a rumor.

One she desperately needed to confirm.

Which was why she came flying into the Christmas Vacation Shop after spotting Helen inside shopping for decorations. She had just happened to be passing by after picking up a gingerbread latte at the coffeehouse next door. It was a fortuitous coincidence.

"Looks like we're both behind the ball with decorating our Christmas trees," Hayley commented as she began browsing the ornaments next to Helen.

Helen gave her a curious look. "I thought you said that you and Bruce put up your tree the other night. At least that's what you told us at the meeting yesterday."

Did she?

Hayley could not remember.

She had been so focused on digging up information on who might have had a reason to kill Esther Willey.

But it was entirely possible she had mentioned that inconvenient fact, so she had to think fast.

"You're right. We did. But as luck would have it, Bruce went to plug in the Christmas tree lights and accidentally bumped into my favorite ornament, an adorable glittered glass hummingbird, and he knocked it right off the tree and it fell to the floor and smashed to pieces. Now it looks bare in that spot, so I'm here for a replacement."

Hayley eyed Helen, who did not flinch or shoot her a skeptical look. She actually seemed to buy Hayley's off-the-cuff excuse for being in the shop.

Or she just did not really care all that much.

Hayley picked up an ornament from the shelf. "This Santa on Skis ornament is cute."

"I was going to buy that," Helen barked.

Hayley quickly handed it to her. "Here. It's all yours."

Helen walked over and set it down on the counter in front of Debbie the cashier. "Put this with my other purchases, would you, please, Debbie?"

Debbie grunted again, her face still buried in her paperback.

Helen returned to continue shopping for more decorations.

"Bruce and I always drink spiked eggnog when we decorate the tree. It's so yummy. Do you and Woody have any traditions you do every year?"

Helen gave her a withering look. "The only tradition Woody and I have is to stay out of each other's way, and that one's not reserved for just the holidays. We try keeping it up year-round."

Hayley was taken aback by her forthright honesty.

She had not expected that.

"I'm so sorry, Helen, I had no idea that you and Woody—"

Helen cut her off. "Of course you did, Hayley. You don't have to pussyfoot around me, trying to find a natural way to get me to open up about my crumbling marriage. I saw you walk by the window, then come back and peer inside to make sure it was me, and then waltz in here pretending you were just shopping to replace a broken ornament. Although I give you credit for the whole glittered glass hummingbird. It was so specific I almost believed you. *Almost!*"

Wow, Helen was good.

And she had rightfully called Hayley out.

"Someone told you about my marriage troubles. Who was it? Betty? Doris? Abby? They all know about it. Abby! I bet it was Abby!"

Hayley hesitated answering because she certainly did not want to reveal her source and possibly cause even more friction within the already fractured knitting circle.

"Did she also happen to mention that Woody was having an affair with Esther behind my back? They thought they were being so clever sneaking around and hiding it from me, but when I saw Esther's signature lipstick on

Woody's collar, I just had to laugh. I mean, really. What a stupid rookie mistake."

"So you weren't mad?"

Helen stared at her blankly. "Mad? Why would I be mad? I don't care one whit about what those two were up to behind my back!"

The loud conversation in the tiny shop finally garnered Debbie's attention. She casually set her paperback down, stood up, walked around the counter and began rearranging the nativity scene in the display window nearby so she was close enough to eavesdrop.

"Look, Hayley, this is none of your business, but if you must know, my marriage died decades ago."

"Then why stay together? Your kids are all grown up now and gone. Why punish yourselves?"

"Because frankly neither of us is willing to move out of that grand house we built together when we were newlyweds. We both love that house. If we got divorced, then one of us would be forced to leave it behind and neither of us is willing to do that, so now we're basically just roommates. Woody is a lout, a slob, and a pain in my backside, but he can do whatever he wants as long as he doesn't interfere with my personal pursuits like my knitting circle and my time share in Boca Raton."

"I don't understand. But if you've known all along, and don't care, then why were you and Esther fighting at the Christmas bazaar? You ran out crying!"

"Oh, that!" Helen exclaimed. "Of course I was upset. You would not believe what that woman did."

Hayley leaned in. "Try me."

Even Debbie stopped fumbling with the ceramic Baby Jesus to get the full story.

Helen's eyes welled up with tears at the mere mention of the painful memory. "That woman . . . she . . . she told me that the reindeer sweater I was wearing at the bazaar looked tacky."

Hayley had to bite her tongue.

What reindeer sweater does *not* look tacky?

Hayley could hear Debbie suppressing a chuckle just a few feet away from them.

"What Esther didn't know was that my long-dead grandmother Flossie knitted that sweater in her own circle way back in the 1950s and saved it for the granddaughter she hoped to have one day."

Hayley remembered the sweater Helen was wearing at the bazaar. The 1950s? No wonder it had the distinct aroma of mothballs.

"Grandma Flossie gave that sweater to me as a Christmas present on my eighteenth birthday, a few months before she died." Helen choked up. "I have worn it every Christmas since and cherished it my entire adult life. It has enormous sentimental value. So you can imagine what a slap in the face it was for Esther to so cruelly laugh at it. That's why I ran out. I was terribly upset."

So Helen Woodworth held a knitted wool reindeer sweater in much higher regard than her own flesh-and-blood husband of nearly forty years.

"And so we are crystal clear, Hayley, before your mind starts going to any dark places, just because Esther hurt my feelings, that is *not* enough for me to chase her down in the church cemetery and stab her with her knitting needle, so don't start jumping to conclusions!"

Hayley held her hands up in surrender.

She actually believed Helen was telling the truth.

Which meant that Helen did not have any real motive to murder Esther.

Leaving the burning question.

Then who did?

Chapter Nine

Hayley had never held much affection for Helen Woodworth's husband, Woody, but she had to admit that he was a master craftsman when it came to boat building. Woody had been working at Collier Yachts for decades, ever since he was in his late teens, and quickly earned the respect of the owners, brothers Tom and Brett Collier. Their family had started the business over forty years ago. The Collier family from Philadelphia had discovered the natural beauty of Mount Desert Island in the late 1800s and immediately embraced the down-east traditions of sailing and the area's rich history of boat building. The family-run company had since produced a long line of stunning yachts that never failed to turn heads. Their clientele had included presidents, kings, athletes, Wall Street titans, and Hollywood stars among a long line of deep-pocketed sailing enthusiasts. They had always relied on the support of a highly skilled team of professional boat builders to keep their creations flawless, the height of perfection. Boats made for boat lovers. And no one was more valuable to the company than Woody Woodworth. What he lacked in couth and kindness, he made up for in raw talent.

When Hayley pulled up to the large warehouse that housed the boats in production just across the bridge from

Mount Desert Island in Trenton, she found Woody loitering outside taking a smoke break. If he was surprised to see her arriving at his workplace, he did not immediately show it.

Hayley jumped out of her car and sauntered over to him. "How's it going, Woody?"

He gave her a flirty wink. "Better now that you're here."

Oh God.

This was par for the course with Woody, who had the mistaken impression that he was God's gift to women.

"Maybe you and me can take one of the boats out and have ourselves a cozy little picnic in the bay, just the two of us."

"I'm married."

"So am I," he cackled, tossing her another suggestive wink.

Gross, Hayley thought.

Woody gave her a lascivious smile. "Still waiting for an answer."

"Hmmm. Let me think about it. No."

"By the way, you can tell that brother-in-law of yours that I still got a beef with him. He kept us at that church so long firing questions at us, I didn't get home to see Saturday's Patriots game until almost halftime."

"What's the big deal? They lost. Badly."

"Don't matter. Win or lose. I never miss a game. So now he's in the doghouse as far as I'm concerned."

"You can tell him yourself. I'm sure he'll be coming around to see you real soon."

Woody took a long drag on his cigarette and eyed her curiously. "Why do you say that?"

"Because I'm guessing sooner rather than later he's going to find out that you were fooling around with Esther Willey before she ended up dead in the church cemetery. And I'm also guessing you probably did not share that juicy little tidbit with the chief when he was keeping you from your football game."

Woody dropped his cigarette into the gravel and snuffed it out with the heel of his boot. "Now wait a minute, Hayley, how did you hear—? Who told you that?"

"It doesn't matter. But word is spreading fast. So you might want to buckle up."

Woody no longer appeared so smarmy and self-assured. He was downright scared.

Hayley sniffed the air. "Is that fear I smell?"

She could tell he was spiraling into a state of panic. "Hayley, please tell me you didn't spill the beans to Helen, because I can't afford that kind of drama right now . . ."

"I didn't have to tell Helen anything. She already knows *all* about it."

The blood drained from his face as he croaked out a barely audible "What?"

"You can relax, Woody. Your wife could not care less. According to her, you're free to do as you please."

Woody's mouth dropped open. "She actually *said* that?"

Hayley nodded.

"I don't know if I should feel relieved or insulted."

"Maybe a smidgen of shame might be appropriate in this particular situation."

Woody leaned back against the wall of the warehouse and exhaled, popping out another cigarette from his pack. "I was afraid if she knew, she might file for divorce and I could lose the beautiful house I broke my back building for the two of us when we got married. A cheating spouse isn't exactly a good look in any kind of tough divorce negotiations. I was so worried Esther might slip at some point and give Helen the opportunity to take me to the cleaners."

He lit the cigarette and took a long, thoughtful puff.

"That habit will kill you."

Woody laughed derisively. "Which is probably why Helen never pestered me to quit."

Hayley could not help but laugh, then her face got serious. "You know, you just admitted to a motive."

Woody continued to suck on his cigarette. "What are you talking about? A motive for what?"

"Murdering Esther."

"Hayley, are you crazy? Why would I want to murder Esther? We were dating. Sort of."

"You just said you were living in fear that Esther might leak the affair to Helen and you couldn't risk losing your precious Cape-style home."

"No! I adored Esther! She made me laugh. We had a good thing going. I didn't want it to end. You can't imagine what went through my head when I saw her lying there in the cold—"

"Wait, when did you see the body?"

Woody nervously pursed his lips. "Huh?"

"The police kept everyone inside the church once I discovered the body. Forensics was all over the place. You never had an opportunity to see Esther's corpse unless you saw it before I did!"

"I didn't kill her, Hayley, I swear! I went outside for a smoke during the bazaar and nearly tripped over poor Esther. I was in shock. I saw that knitting needle sticking out of her chest, and my first thought was Helen. I figured she must have somehow found out about us and the two of them got into some kind of scuffle and Helen stabbed her."

"Why didn't you call the police?"

"I don't know. I was terrified. What would happen to Helen? I mean, we may live our own lives now, but she's still my wife. I couldn't bear her going to prison. I wasn't thinking clearly. I wanted to do something to throw the cops off her scent."

The truth suddenly dawned on Hayley. "So you went back inside the church, pilfered one of Betty Dyer's Christmas mittens, and stuffed it in Esther's mouth so the police would direct their attention toward Betty instead of Helen!"

"I'm not proud of it, but I've always despised that mouthy busybody Betty Dyer. I don't care about what happens to her," he growled. "After you discovered Esther's body, I went to see Helen, and I saw how shaken and upset she was, which surprised me. She was truly broken up over losing Esther, so I just assumed it was all for naught, that she was still in the dark about the affair and my secret died with Esther. I had nothing to worry about."

He blew smoke in Hayley's direction. Annoyed, she waved it away with her hand.

He shrugged. "Sorry, smoking calms my nerves."

"Well then, perhaps you better swing by the Big Apple and stock up on a few more cartons."

"Why do you say that?"

"Because you may be off the hook for Esther's murder, but you intentionally interfered with a crime scene, which means you're about to be in a whole world of trouble."

She almost enjoyed saying it.

Especially when he began coughing and choking on the smoke from his own cigarette.

Hayley spun around and marched back toward the car, determined more than ever to dig up whatever other secrets the people around Esther Willey were desperately trying to bury alongside her.

Chapter Ten

When Hayley blew through the door to the *Island Times* office, her previous place of employment before leaving to open Hayley's Kitchen, her old boss, editor-in-chief Sal Moretti, was standing at the coffee station, slurping down a mug of coffee before spitting it out and bellowing to no one in particular, "If I wanted it cold, I would've added some ice cubes! How hard is it to make a pot of *hot* coffee?"

Hayley shut the door behind her, startling Sal and causing him to spill a few drops of coffee on the front of his shirt. She winced as he gave her the once-over.

"Well, well, well, look who has decided to come grace us with her shining presence! The highfalutin restaurateur!"

"It wouldn't be Christmas without you playing the part of Scrooge," Hayley countered.

"Bah humbug!" Sal bellowed. He grabbed a napkin and began dabbing at his stained shirt. "I hear your joint is doing pretty good, so I assume you're not here to beg for your old job back. Your replacement has been a complete disaster!"

"You can stop calling her my replacement. She's been here for two years now, and you also need to give her a break, because she is doing the best job she can working for someone who is nearly impossible to please!"

"When did you get so sassy?"

"When you stopped signing my checks."

Sal grumbled and Hayley smiled. He made a habit of pretending to be annoyed with her all the time, but deep down she knew he loved their unusual rapport.

"So what are you doing here?" Sal asked.

"I came to pick up Bruce."

"He already left. You can probably find him at home."

"What? But we agreed I would pick him up here at the office. I texted him earlier and told him I would drop by after Lydia Partridge made her ice-cream delivery at the restaurant. Why didn't he text me back and tell me he was going to leave?"

"How the hell should I know? I don't have time to monitor all your texts and communications. I'm not the FBI!"

"He always gets so distracted when he's working on a big news story," Hayley said.

"News flash! I don't care!" Sal hollered as he poured what was left in the coffeepot into his ceramic mug and put it in the microwave. "But speaking of Esther Willey, when I saw you come in, I figured you were here to question me."

"*You?* About what?"

He punched in forty-five seconds on the microwave key pad and pressed start before turning back to face Hayley. "Come on, it's all over town. My wife's a murder suspect! She despised Esther and that whole knitting crew. I haven't seen her so wrapped up in knots since Harry and Meghan ditched the royal family for a life as Oprah's neighbors."

"Oh, come on, Sal. Rosana is so sweet and demure. I hardly think she is capable of murder."

"Have you talked to her lately? It's like her whole personality has changed ever since she went to war over those stupid Christmas mittens. She used to defer to me, and now she barely listens to a word I say."

"Rosana may be a little on edge lately, but really, Sal, a murderer?"

"Why not? She's been slowly killing my spirit every day for the last thirty-two years." Sal laughed at his own joke.

What he did not know was that Rosana had suddenly appeared with a small box in her hand from the office's back bullpen and was standing directly behind him, face flushed, seething.

Hayley cleared her throat and shook her head, trying to warn him. "Sal, you don't mean that."

"Are you kidding? Sometimes I like to watch my wedding video running backward so I can see myself walk out of the church a free man!"

Now he was howling.

Hayley remained stone-faced.

"You gotta admit, Hayley, that was a pretty good one."

Hayley averted her eyes to a fuming Rosana. "What do you think, Rosana?"

Sal's face froze.

"Typical Sal humor. Lazy and lame."

Sal spun around, instantly softening. "Baby doll, when did you get here? I didn't see you come in."

"I made Christmas cookies for the staff and was just dropping them off. You weren't in your office, so I figured you were in the bathroom sitting on the toilet playing Wordle on your phone."

Hayley chortled.

She knew that was exactly where he had been.

Sal went in for a kiss, but Rosana pushed past him and marched up to Hayley. "Despite my husband's inexplicable suspicions about me, I can assure you, Hayley, I am far from capable of anything so dastardly as driving a knitting needle through poor Esther Willey's heart. We may have had our differences, but I would never wish her any physical harm."

Just psychological.

"Honestly, Rosana, I just came by the office to pick up Bruce. I wasn't snooping around for clues. I believe you. One hundred percent."

Rosana glared at Sal. "I wish my husband had as much confidence in my innocence as you do."

"I was just playing around, sweetie pie," Sal protested. "Of course I don't think it was you who impaled Esther."

She ignored him, turning back to Hayley. "Luckily I can prove it. Right before you discovered Esther's body outside the church, I posted a TikTok video."

Sal scratched his head. "TikTok? I thought only kids used that app."

Rosana sighed with a withering look and kept her focus on Hayley, not her husband. "Can you believe the editor-in-chief of a newspaper is so out of touch with what's going on in the world?" She shot Sal a brief look over her shoulder. "Everyone uses it."

"What kind of video did you record?" Hayley asked.

"A rap song," Rosana declared.

"A *what*?" Sal cried.

"A rap song. For our knitting circle to perform at the bazaar. I wrote it myself."

Sal, mouth agape, just stared disbelievingly at his wife. "How is it possible that you, who has every song Barbra Streisand ever recorded on her playlist, wrote a *rap* song?"

"There is something called eclectic taste, Sal. Look it up." She excitedly turned to Hayley. "I adore Snoop Dogg. Did you know he's friends with Martha Stewart?"

"I heard," Hayley said, smiling.

Rosana's eyes sparkled. "So do you want to see it?"

"Of course!" Hayley exclaimed.

She wasn't lying.

This was something she *had* to see.

Hayley and Sal gathered around Rosana, who punched her passcode into the phone and tapped the TikTok app. In a few swipes, she was playing the video.

Rosana and her Happy Hooker knitting circle were decked out in all the Christmas sweaters and hats and mittens that they had made and were lined up in a row as rap music played through a portable speaker on the floor in the background. They danced and sang as a small crowd surrounded them, watching the performance.

"I'm a happy, happy hooker,
Got dinner in the slow cooker,
'Cause my needles are ready to knit,
Making a holiday sweater that fits,
With a Christmas tree on front,
It's gonna be rad I'll be blunt,
Frosty the Snowman on back,
Don't be talkin' smack,
The Crochet Mafia can take a rest,
'Cause the Happy Hookers are simply the best,
Sorry your sad mittens are a major flop,
C'mon girls it's time for the hookers to do a mic drop!"

Hayley was mightily impressed. Rosana and her knitting circle were joyful to watch. They were truly putting their hearts and souls into it.

Sal stared at the screen, dumbfounded. This was a side of his wife he had clearly never seen. He put an arm around Rosana's shoulders. "Honey, you're brilliant. I love it."

Hayley suddenly noticed something on the video as the crowd applauded and the Happy Hookers took a bow. "Wait, Rosana, go back!"

Rosana scrolled the video back a few seconds and played it again. Behind the women as they were finishing their performance with a flourish, they could plainly see Esther Willey leaving up the stairs toward the exit of the church.

And she was not alone.

Doris Crimmons, a key member of the Crochet Mafia, was accompanying her.

Island Food & Spirits
by
Hayley Powell

Every Christmas, my favorite thing to make is peanut butter fudge. And believe me, I always have to limit myself to making it only once a year because I absolutely cannot get enough of this rich and delicious treat! If I allowed myself to make those pans of peanut goodness year-round, by the time December rolled around, I'd have a belly so big I could deliver all those Christmas presents in a reindeer-led sleigh myself!

Unfortunately, as much as I love peanut butter fudge, my BFF Liddy loathes it. It's not because of some peanut allergy, or that she simply doesn't like the taste of it; she claims it's because my peanut butter fudge ruined her life!

You can probably see a story coming.

And you'd be right.

It was our senior year in high school, and yes, it was the same year as my rum cake debacle in Home Economics! Liddy, Mona and I were walking together to the lunchroom, making plans to go shopping over the weekend for our winter Snow Ball dresses while discussing which boy in school would be our fantasy date for the dance. Mona, who was not a fan of dating, swore she'd prefer to draw a face on a soccer ball and call it a day, like Tom Hanks did when he was stranded on a desert island in that movie that came out a few years later.

Suddenly Liddy stopped in her tracks, staring straight ahead. Mona and I strolled past her and then spun around and exchanged puzzled looks.

What was wrong with her?

Liddy, her bottom lip quivering, muttered under her breath, "Who is that?"

Before either of us could turn back around to check out what had caused her to suddenly freeze in place, we heard a familiar voice behind us. "Hello, girls. That's Jon Black."

Mona and I visibly shuddered. We knew that voice. It was my high school archnemesis Sabrina Merryweather (you could say we are friends now, let bygones be bygones).

Just ahead of us, we all stared at a handsome dark-haired boy wearing an MDI letter jacket and standing at his locker.

Liddy was mesmerized.

Sabrina, speaking with an air of superiority, explained, "Jon's a new transfer student. His father recently retired from the U.S. Air Force, his mother is a doctor of genetics at the Jackson Laboratory, and they recently moved from Los Angeles, California, into the old Myer house on Holland Avenue." Sabrina took a dramatic pause before icily adding, "And he is going to be *my* date for the Snow Ball!"

It was that last sentence that seemed to snap Liddy out of her googly eyed trance.

She glared at Sabrina, eyes narrowing. "What do you mean he's going to be *your* date? Did he ask you?"

Sabrina shrugged. "Not yet, because I haven't actually met him, but I'm about to!" She winked at Liddy and then whipped around and bounced off in the new boy Jon's direction with Liddy chasing after her, hot on her heels.

Mona snickered. "Sounds like it's going to get a little exciting around here!"

We watched as Sabrina and Liddy, elbowing each other, made a beeline for the poor unsuspecting Jon Black, who did not have the faintest clue that he was about to be trapped in a love triangle from hell.

That first introduction, however brief because the class bell rang just as both girls managed to get their names out, set off a stiff competition that lasted a whole week, with Liddy and Sabrina vying for Jon's attention. They would both sit with him at lunch and laugh uproariously at everything that came out of his mouth, even when he wasn't trying to be funny. They both somehow got their hands on his class schedule and managed to situate themselves in the perfect position to casually run into him so they could walk with him to his next class. He had no privacy, as they were both in the immediate vicinity of his locker whenever he arrived at school in the morning or was leaving in the afternoon.

As heated as the competition was, it only got more frustrating for Liddy and Sabrina because Jon seemed to be immensely enjoying the slavish devotion both girls were piling on him and he just didn't seem to feel any urgency to choose between them. However, his two self-proclaimed love interests were reaching their breaking point. The Snow Ball was fast approaching. Time was running out. He was going to have to make a choice.

The two girls went into hyperoverdrive. They turned up the flirting, brought little gifts, handed out endless compliments about his physique, his test scores, his feeble attempt to grow a mustache that looked more like a baby caterpillar clinging to his upper lip. And both girls were relentless with their not-so-subtle hints about the Snow Ball. However, neither one still seemed to be making any headway.

I could see that Liddy was going absolutely bananas, so I finally had to step in. I pulled her aside and told her in no uncertain terms that she needed to give up this ridiculous quest. It was just getting to be too much and embarrassing to watch. But Liddy was intractable. In her mind, this was a battle between good (her) and evil (Sabrina), and it was a war she had to win.

I sighed and said, "Okay, fine. But let me offer up a little advice. My mother always says, 'The best way to a man's heart is through his stomach.'"

Liddy's eyes lit up. She hugged me and told me I was a genius, and then she ran off without another word.

The next morning before classes, Mona and I were sitting at the lunchroom table watching Sabrina fawn all over Jon, both of us wondering where in the world was Liddy. As if on cue, Liddy came sailing into the lunchroom with a beautifully wrapped box and presented it to Jon. "A little birdie told me you love peanut butter fudge!"

She had borrowed the recipe from me.

Well, Jon's face lit up with pleasure as he handed the fudge to Sabrina to hold for him while he stood up and pulled Liddy in for a long grateful hug. Liddy smiled sweetly over his shoulder at a seething Sabrina, who had to restrain herself from hurling the box of fudge across the room.

Liddy snatched the box of fudge back from Sabrina and handed it to Jon and told him to open it right away so he could enjoy some. He happily complied and began chomping it down, in between bites raving to Liddy that it was the most delicious fudge he had ever tasted. Liddy euphorically soaked up the accolades while Sabrina silently sulked.

After a few minutes, Sabrina finally decided she had endured enough humiliation. She jumped to her feet and told Liddy that she was undeserving of a boy like Jon, that she should set her sights much lower. Liddy was not about to take that kind of a slam and began screaming at Sabrina, calling her a sore loser and telling her that she should just suck it up and admit defeat.

As the two girls shouted at each other, neither noticed that Jon had begun coughing and choking and holding a hand to his throat while frantically waving for help with his other. His face was starting to turn blue. He was trying to signal Liddy and Sabrina for help, but they were both ignoring him.

Before any of us had time to react, as if from Heaven itself, a curly haired girl with glasses appeared, grabbing Jon from behind and expertly performing the Heimlich maneuver. Another girl near Jon got the attention of Liddy and Sabrina, who finally stopped screaming at each other, now realizing the seriousness of the situation.

The girl gave a final thrust with her hands, and Jon let out a gasp as a peanut went sailing through the air, landing on the floor. Everyone watched in stunned silence before bursting out in applause for the heroics of the girl who saved

Jon's life after he nearly choked on the peanut that had lodged in his throat.

Sabrina opened her mouth to blame Liddy for nearly killing poor Jon with her deadly fudge, but before she could say a word, Jon held up his hand to silence her. Then he turned to his rescuer, whose name was Anne, a pretty senior, a girl most students barely noticed because she was always so quiet and shy around other people.

Jon grabbed Anne in a hug, thanked her profusely and then said that if she ever needed anything, anything at all, she only had to ask.

Anne broke out into a wide smile, glanced playfully at Liddy and Sabrina, then looked at Jon, batted her eyes a few times and whispered coquettishly, "Well, if you don't already have a date, I would love for you to take me to the Snow Ball this weekend."

"Of course! It would be my honor!" Jon replied with a big grin. Then he took her hand and they began to stroll away together, but not before Jon stopped, came running back for his box of fudge and then dashed off to join Anne again.

Liddy swears to this day that between Sabrina and that cursed peanut butter fudge, her life was ruined. I don't argue with her for my own peace of mind, but just for fun, every holiday season I make her a batch of my own peanut butter fudge to stir things up.

I know it's the Christmas season, but any time of the year is a good time for a margarita! Here is my favorite Christmas Margarita, which I love serving at my holiday gatherings. Disfrutar!

Christmas Margarita

Ingredients:
3 ounces cranberry juice
1 ounce triple sec
2 ounces tequila
Garnish, optional: orange slice and cranberries

Rim a cocktail glass with your favorite salt or sugar.
Add all of your ingredients into a cocktail shaker filled with ice, and shake well.
Strain into your ice-filled cocktail glass. Garnish. Salut!

Hayley's Chocolate Peanut Butter Fudge

Ingredients:
1½ cups semisweet chocolate chips
1 can sweetened condensed milk
1 cup mini marshmallows
¾ cup peanut butter
2 teaspoons vanilla

In a medium saucepan over medium heat, add your condensed milk, chocolate chips and marshmallows, stirring to combine. Add your peanut butter and vanilla, and then stir again until well combined.

Remove from heat, pour the mixture into a greased 9 × 9 pan and spread with a spatula to smooth the top.

Place in the fridge to chill until firm.

Slice into 1-inch pieces, and store in an airtight container.

A happy holiday treat!

Chapter Eleven

Dick Crimmons's Christmas Tree Lot—located just outside of town at his small farm across from the Hulls Cove schoolhouse, which served as a community center for wedding receptions, birthday parties and high school reunions—boasted an impressive array of Christmas trees and wreath products for sale during the holiday season. Because there was stiff competition from other sellers around the island, Dick went that extra mile to make his own lot special. Every Saturday and Sunday in December leading up to Christmas Day, Dick and his wife, Doris, would dress up as Santa and Mrs. Claus to greet their customers. He even enlisted the help of a small band of local teenagers to serve as elves, serving hot cider and helping people load and secure the trees on their car roofs or in the back of their flatbeds.

Dick was a natural performer and relished playing the role of St. Nick. He would strap a giant pillow around his gut and glue on the fluffy white beard. And whenever a car would pull into the lot, he would bellow at the top of his lungs, "Ho Ho Ho!" Doris was less of a method actor than her husband, refusing to obscure her slim figure with any kind of padding. She opted for just a bulky sweater instead. She didn't want to mess up her hair wearing a gray wig with a bun, but she did relent to putting on a pair of granny glasses and resting them at the bridge of her nose to complete her look. She did love her rouge, so some rosy red cheeks were okay as long as it didn't make her look too much like a clown. Less was always more, in Doris's opinion.

Dick worshipped Doris and always claimed he was put on this earth to keep his wife happy, joking, "In my marriage, I always make sure to get in the last two words. 'Yes, dear!'" They had been together forty years, raised five children, all grown up now, and happily doted on their nine grandchildren, some of whom were dressed as elves today raking in a cool twelve dollars an hour.

When Hayley arrived at the Crimmonses' Christmas Tree Lot, she spotted Dick as Santa Claus showing off an eight-foot-tall Fraser fir tree to a young couple with an infant in a baby sling that was strapped to the father's chest.

Hayley scanned the area for Doris, finally catching sight of her sitting on one of two high-backed hand-crafted hardwood Canterbury celebrant chairs that served as Santa and Mrs. Claus's thrones, where they would greet any children who wanted pictures or to present their Christmas lists. At the moment, no one was waiting. Doris was knitting a Christmas stocking, and a mug of hot cider was on top of her armrest.

Sensing someone approaching, Doris raised her eyes from her knitting needles and grimaced slightly before forcing a smile. "Hayley, are you just getting around to buying a tree? You're usually the first one in town to have one up and decorated."

"That's the second time someone's told me that. I had no idea I had such a reputation for being so eager to start celebrating Christmas. But no, Bruce and I are officially done. We just have to hang the stockings."

Doris showed off the stocking she was knitting. It was a beautifully woven green one with the name Jason emblazoned around the top. "This is for my youngest grandson. I've already knitted seven, so after this I only have one more to go for little Selena."

"You're a very talented knitter, Doris," Hayley said.

"Why, thank you," Doris cooed, blushing.

At least Hayley thought she was blushing.

It could have just been the liberally applied rouge for her Mrs. Claus look.

Hayley figured it could not hurt to butter up Doris a bit because she was about to steer the conversation into a very uncomfortable turn.

"If you don't need a tree, can I interest you in one of our Christmas wreaths? Dick makes them himself. Fresh noble fir with incense cedar, and then he adorns them with juniper, canella berries, dogwood and pine cones. They're ready to hang and only $49.95."

"Thank you, Doris, but we're good on wreaths. Bruce brought one home for the front door the other day."

"I hope it wasn't one of those cheap ones from the Shop 'n Save! I think they're the tackiest things I have ever seen," she sniffed. Doris read Hayley's expression and saw that it was indeed one of the cheap, tacky wreaths from the Shop 'n Save for half the price, so she quickly followed up with "But I'm not one to judge."

"Actually, Doris, I just happened to be driving by . . ."

So not true.

She had made a point of coming here today.

"And I thought I would stop and ask you if you saw the cute TikTok video that Rosana and her knitting circle posted."

Doris snapped her head back so fast Hayley thought the granny glasses on her nose might fly right off. "Why on earth would I ever do that? I long ago made the decision not to expend any of my energy thinking about that contentious group of awful women."

"I totally get it. But I watched it recently, and there is something I noticed that piqued my interest, and it has to do with you."

Doris raised an eyebrow. "Oh? What was that?"

Hayley pulled out her phone. "Why don't you see for yourself?"

She opened the TikTok app, scrolled down for the video and pressed play, handing the phone to Doris.

"I'm a happy, happy hooker,
Got dinner in the slow cooker,
'Cause my needles are ready to knit,
Making a holiday sweater that fits . . ."

Doris shook her head, unimpressed. "I stand corrected. Forget the Shop 'n Save Christmas wreaths. *This* has to be the tackiest thing I have ever seen in my life!"

"You didn't see them perform this number at the bazaar?"

"Of course not! I may have heard some noise in the background, but I was busy with the raffle, and I certainly would not have wasted my valuable time watching this monstrosity! My word, imagine women that age acting so silly and immature!"

She tried to hand Hayley her phone back, but she refused to take it. "Please, Doris, keep watching."

"Do you get some kind of perverse pleasure torturing me like this, Hayley? Rosana is so off-key, my ears hurt!"

Doris turned her nose up as she continued watching the video until the key moment when she was clearly seen heading up the stairs toward the exit with Esther Willey.

Hayley tapped the screen with her finger. "There. That's you . . . walking toward the exit with Esther."

Doris practically hurled the phone back at Hayley. "So what?"

"*So what?*" Hayley repeated incredulously. "Doris, consider the time line. You are clearly seen on the video leaving the church with Esther just minutes before I discovered her murdered in the cemetery!"

"Are you accusing *me*? How dare you! Esther was a dear, dear friend!"

Hayley scrolled the video back and paused it, zooming in on Doris's face as she was leaving. "Look, you're scowling. Obviously you were upset about something."

Doris's armor was slowly starting to crack. "I-I don't remember . . ."

"Come on, Doris, you expect me to believe that? It will be a lot better for you if you just tell me the truth."

Doris sighed, cornered. "It was nothing, Hayley, really. I had just heard some rumor that Esther was spreading malicious gossip around town about me, that I was hated in the knitting circle, that they called me 'stitchin' bitch' behind my back and that they were going to vote to kick me out of the Crochet Mafia. I was furious. I co-founded that circle with Helen. It was just as much mine as it was hers or anyone else's. I asked Esther if we could talk in private so I could confront her about it, and so we went outside."

"Did Esther confess to bad-mouthing you?"

"No! She furiously denied spreading any rumors about me or anyone. And I believed her because she appeared to be as genuinely angry as I was. She guessed that the rumor probably got started by someone in Rosana Moretti's circle, one of the Happy Hookers! Every single woman in that hateful group was singularly focused on driving a wedge between us and blowing up the Crochet Mafia. It's downright shameful!"

That struck Hayley as entirely possible.

Except Hayley was having a tough time picturing Rosana Moretti acting so malevolently. She just was not a spiteful, wicked person.

Still, there were others in the Happy Hookers who might be prone to poison the well without a second thought. Or, the fact remained, Esther could have been doing a masterful job of covering up her own misdeeds in front of Doris.

Doris could read the troubled look on Hayley's face as she considered all the angles. "Esther and I had known each other since high school. I could tell when she was fibbing and when she was telling the truth, and believe me, Hayley, when it came to those vicious lies about me, I knew in my heart that Esther was being sincere. That's why I had to confront her, just to be sure, for my own peace of mind."

"So after you confronted her, you two made up?"

"Yes, we hugged it out. Like friends do. Esther even cried a little because she was so upset at the thought of me believing her capable of such nasty behavior."

Doris spotted her husband, Dick, dressed as Santa Claus, approaching.

"Please, don't mention any of this to Dick, he'll just worry. But I promise you, Hayley, when I went back inside the church, Esther was still very much alive!"

"Ho ho ho, Hayley, you want to sit on Santa's lap and tell me what you want Santa to bring you for Christmas?" Dick cackled.

"Don't be creepy, Dick, she's a grown woman," Doris sighed.

"Yes, Mrs. Claus!" Dick said, before turning to Hayley with a wink. "I guess we know who wears the red suspenders in this family! Ho ho ho!"

Hayley had to give him credit for never breaking character, and thought he should consider auditioning for the local community theatre.

"Now, Mrs. Claus, it's awfully chilly here at the North Pole Christmas Tree Farm, and I'm starting to get cold. Do you have one of those festive holiday scarves in your knitting bag I can wear before frostbite sets in?"

"Of course, dear," Doris said, opening her knitting bag and pulling out a red scarf dotted with tiny green Christmas trees.

"Ho ho ho, you're a treasure for the ages, Mrs. Claus!" Dick announced loudly as he wrapped the scarf tightly around his neck and bounded off to greet some more customers who were just arriving.

Doris left her knitting bag open to reach for her mug of hot cider and take a sip when Hayley glanced down and noticed something glistening inside. She casually took a step closer, peering into the bag. She suddenly choked back a gasp as she realized what she had just seen.

The sparkly diamond ring stolen from Mr. Willoughby at the church Christmas bazaar was sitting on top of a ball of red yarn in Doris Crimmons's knitting bag.

Chapter Twelve

Hayley stood there, stunned. She was not sure what to do. Doris closed her knitting bag just as Dick returned accompanied by a family of four—father, mother and two redheaded, freckled twin girls around five years old in matching LL Bean color-block down jackets and white boots.

"Ho ho ho! Mrs. Claus, these two beautiful bright little girls would like to have their pictures taken with us!"

"Heavens, yes, of course," Doris cooed, playing her part perfectly. "Do you girls live here in town?"

"No, Millinocket," one of the girls answered.

"How nice!" Doris said, clapping her hands. She reached over and picked up a paper plate sitting on a side table. "Would you girls like a sugar cookie?"

One twin grabbed two cookies.

The mother smiled. "Just one, girls."

The second twin grabbed three.

They obviously were not in the habit of listening to their mother.

Dick plopped down in his chair next to Doris. "Come sit with me and tell Santa Claus what you sweet cherubs would like to find under your Christmas tree, and we'll see if the elves can make it in Santa's workshop."

The girls stomped over, both jumping up in Dick's lap so fast he had trouble balancing them at the same time.

"Careful, girls, Santa just had knee surgery," Dick said through gritted teeth, wincing in pain.

The father excitedly whipped out his phone to take pictures.

"I want the new iPhone, a horse, and I mean a real one, not a plastic one, I want a Barbie Club Chelsea Doll and Carnival Playset, a Bluey Mega Bundle Home, a Dressy Dotty Baby Doll, Magic Mixies Magical Misting Cauldron—"

"Whoa! Are you going to remember all this, Mrs. Claus?" Dick asked, turning to Doris.

Doris shrugged. "Sure."

The girl pouted and snapped, "I'm *not* done!"

The parents laughed, under the mistaken impression that their daughter's greediness and rudeness was adorable.

The second twin chimed in. "I want a Lego Pet Day Care Center Kit!"

"I'm *not* done!" her sister growled.

The father ignored their selfish behavior. "Okay, girls, smile. You too, Santa!"

Doris plastered a fake smile on her face and leaned in closer to get in the picture.

"Just Santa in this one," the father insisted. "You can be in the next one."

Stung, Doris flushed with anger and sat back down in her chair, fuming. Hayley seized the opportunity to send a quick text to Sergio. She had debated how to deal with this prickly development. It might have been better to try to talk to Doris first, but she also did not want Doris getting rid of the ring in the time it would take for Sergio to arrive. So she decided it would be best to fill him in on what she had just seen and allow him to handle the situation as he saw fit.

Five minutes later, after the twins had cleaned Santa and Mrs. Claus out of all their sugar cookies and candy canes and peanut butter fudge and were both now flying around the lot on an intense sugar high as their parents half-heartedly chased after them, a police squad car pulled into the lot. Sergio got out and made his way over to Dick, Doris and Hayley. Hayley was still loitering, pretending to look at Doris's homemade Christmas stockings that were displayed on a nearby cardboard table.

"Ho ho ho, Chief. Merry Christmas!" Dick bellowed.

"Merry Christmas to you," Sergio said quietly, staring at Doris somberly.

She instantly appeared nervous, suspecting something was up.

"We're out of sweets, but we can offer you a hot cider," Doris said.

"I'm fine. Thank you."

Hayley picked up one of Doris's knitted stockings, looking it over, but she was obviously eavesdropping.

"What can we do for you today, Chief? Do you and Randy still need to find a tree? I got a real nice balsam fir, big too, nearly nine feet, perfect for your living room with the high ceiling."

"No, thank you, Dick, I mean Santa, we're good. My husband the environmentalist prefers an arthritis tree."

Hayley bit her lip, determined not to correct him and give herself away for snooping.

Dick guffawed. "I've never heard of a tree with arthritis! Must have some pretty stiff branches!"

"Do you mean an *artificial* tree?" Doris asked, suppressing a giggle.

"Sure, yes, a fake tree!" Sergio said, losing patience. "I

am not here looking for a tree. I have recently received some information about the diamond ring theft at the church Christmas bazaar, and I was wondering if you would mind me taking a quick look inside your knitting bag, Doris?"

Doris sat up straight in her chair, stupefied. "What? Why? Who gave you this so-called information? And what does it have to do with my knitting?"

"Please, Doris, just help me out here," Sergio said, rubbing his eyes with his thumb and forefinger.

"Do you have a warrant?" Dick asked.

Sergio sighed. "No, Dick, do I need one?"

"Of course you don't," Doris said. "I have nothing to hide. Here, knock yourself out."

She scooped the bag off the floor and handed it to him. Sergio opened it up, glanced down, and then reached inside and plucked out the stolen ring.

Doris gasped and threw a hand to her mouth.

Dick's jaw nearly hit the floor.

Sergio kept his calm and held up the sparkling ring. "Do you have any idea how this ended up in your knitting bag, Doris?"

"No!" Doris cried. "Of course not! I didn't steal it! I've never stolen anything in my entire life!"

"What about that roll of Mentos breath mints you didn't pay for at the Big Apple last month when we stopped to gas up the truck?" her husband reminded her.

"That was a mistake, Dick! It just slipped my mind! I had every intention of buying it! I didn't even realize I walked out without paying until we got home."

"Yeah, but did you ever go back and make good on what you owed?"

Doris's nostrils flared at her husband. "You're not helping, Dick!" She then focused on Hayley, who was desperately trying to stay invisible, her back to them, having just moved on to Doris's hand-painted Christmas ornaments that were for sale. Hayley could feel her pointing an accusing finger at her. "Is *she* your undercover informant?"

Sergio scratched his head. "Informant? Who said anything about an informant?"

Doris folded her arms, miffed. "I'm hardly surprised it was you, Hayley! You always seem to be everywhere accusing everyone of something!"

Hayley turned to face her head-on. "I'm sorry, Doris, but when I saw the ring in your bag, I didn't know what else to do. It's stolen property!"

"Someone is trying to frame me!" Doris wailed.

"Look, Doris, I have known you for years. You have never struck me as the sticky-fingered type," Sergio reassured her softly. "I believe if you knew the ring was in your bag, you would not have been so amenable to me looking inside. So I have to ask. Did you give the bag to anyone at any point at the bazaar?"

"No! Definitely not! It was in my sight the entire time!" Doris insisted. "And I would never . . ." Her voice trailed off.

Sergio took a step closer. "What, Doris? Anything you can remember could be helpful."

Her eyes flicked back and forth as her mind raced. "No, it couldn't have been her."

"Who?" Sergio, Dick and Hayley said in unison.

"Tawny Beauchemin."

"Scooter Beauchemin's wife?" Sergio asked.

Doris nodded. "Yes. She asked for a mint, and I told her I had some in my bag and she should help herself. I remember her rummaging through it for a few seconds. But why would she need to steal a diamond ring? She's one of the richest women in town. She and Scooter have millions. It makes absolutely no sense. No, it had to be someone else. It had to be one of the Happy Hookers! You should be dragging the whole lot of them down to the station for a thorough interrogation!"

Doris Crimmons was right.

Why would a millionaire have any reason to steal a diamond ring from Willoughby's shop when she could fly to New York and buy one twenty times more expensive at Tiffany's? And despite Doris's eagerness to indict the Happy Hookers, the ring was inarguably found in Doris's possession. She and Dick appeared, at least on the surface, to be financially sound. Unless they were hiding a mountain of debts that had yet to come to light. But Hayley agreed with Sergio's initial assessment that Doris was not a calculating thief, at least on the basis of the information they had so far.

But if Tawny Beauchemin was the only other person to come in contact with Doris's knitting bag, was there something they were still not seeing?

Hayley accompanied Sergio back to his office at the Bar Harbor Police Station, where he sat down at his computer and started a background check on Tawny while Hayley went down to the bakery on the corner for some muffins and coffee. By the time she returned and handed Sergio his coffee, he had already come up with the answer they were looking for.

"She's got a rap sheet."

Hayley nearly dropped the bag of muffins on the floor. "*Tawny*? It must have been from years ago, before she married Scooter."

"No, she has been arrested for shoplifting in four separate incidents since she's been married. The last time was just last year. She tried to walk out of Bergdorf Goodman in New York with some Prada platform sandals worth about a grand."

"But I don't understand. She could afford a hundred pair of those shoes. Why would she resort to stealing them?"

"Maybe her husband keeps the purse strings tied really tight and doesn't allow her access to the credit cards," Sergio surmised.

"Or she has kleptomania. A lot of rich people suffer from it. They don't steal out of need, it's more of a psychological problem. Years ago they caught Winona Ryder walking out of Saks Fifth Avenue with about five thousand dollars' worth of merchandise, and she was an Oscar nominee!" Hayley exclaimed.

It was a plausible theory.

And Hayley was determined to find out if it was true.

And in any way connected to the murder of Esther Willey.

Chapter Thirteen

Hayley and Bruce had an annual tradition during the holidays of spending an evening the week before Christmas driving around the island and marveling at all the Christmas light displays. People usually went all out decorating their homes. But the one house everyone saved for last and agreed was peerless in its pageantry was the Scooter Beauchemin estate. Usually the five-acre gilded-age property with its sprawling waterfront mansion, ten-car garage, caretaker cottage and two guest houses was closed to the public thanks to an imposing locked iron gate. But during the holiday season, the Beauchemins kindly opened their home to everyone who wanted to enjoy their opulent, Disneyesque Christmas light display. An endless parade of cars would be parked along the road, and families would file in to take in the magnificent, over-the-top, most elaborate presentation in Maine, maybe even in all of New England, featuring thousands of dazzling white lights, a candy cane lane lined with edible sweets like gumdrops and gingerbread cookies for the kids, festive displays of the nativity scene, Santa's workshop, a brightly lit sleigh and reindeer suspended in the air over the main house, a giant snowman that also served as a bouncy house for kids to play inside. The estate was more like a carnival than a private home during the month of December.

By the time Hayley and Bruce arrived and parked their car outside the gate just before ten o'clock, their last stop on the tour, the nightly party at the Beauchemins' was just winding down, and a few stragglers were strolling out past the gate and heading to their cars. A guard stood watch outside to make sure everyone left in an orderly fashion.

"Hey, Pete," Bruce said, waving at the guard.

Pete was a twenty-five-year-old local paramedic who did double duty as part-time security for Scooter Beauchemin.

"Evening, Bruce, Hayley. Sorry but we're getting ready to close things up for the night."

"We just want to take a quick look around. Won't take more than five minutes," Bruce promised.

"Okay, but I gotta clear out the last people and then get to the hospital. I'm on duty at eleven. Could you close the gate behind you when you leave?"

"Sure, no problem," Bruce said.

Pete trusted them enough not to fear they might make off with some of the more expensive decorations. He then bounded over to the snowman bouncy house where, not surprisingly, the young couple with the twins whom Hayley had met at the Crimmonses' Christmas Tree Lot were having a devil of the time coaxing the two rambunctious girls out. The little devils were screaming and laughing as they jumped around inside the snowman's belly. The parents refused to yell at them to get out, that it was time to go home, so Pete had to play bad guy.

Hayley gaped at the wondrous display as they made their way down Candy Cane Lane. "They really do go all out, don't they?"

"I would too if I had their money," Bruce cracked,

plucking a gumdrop off a squishy white fence made of marshmallow and popping it in his mouth. "Their electric bill alone could probably pay down the national debt."

Hayley watched as Pete climbed into the snowman bouncy house and started chasing the two girls around, stumbling and falling and bouncing around as the twins' far too lenient, pampering parents laughed hysterically.

"I wonder how much one of those bouncy houses cost?" Hayley asked.

"Doesn't matter. Tawny probably stole it," Bruce snorted, chewing on his gumdrop.

"Bruce, don't make light of it. Kleptomania is a serious affliction. I feel sorry for her. She must have some real emotional issues."

"Yeah, I guess what they say is true. Being rich doesn't necessarily make you happy. But I sure would like to test that theory for myself."

All the lights were on inside the main house, and Hayley and Bruce could see Tawny standing in the living room near a massive-sized white Christmas tree. She sipped from a mug as she rearranged a few ornaments from branch to branch, never seeming satisfied. There was no sign of Scooter.

"I'd say she has more than a few emotional issues if she stabbed Esther Willey to death," Bruce remarked.

"She may have stolen Ed Willoughby's ring, but that does not necessarily mean she killed Esther. The two crimes may not even be connected."

Pete had finally managed to corral the twins, and he handed them over to their parents. Dad picked the girls up, one in each arm, and the family finally made their way off the property and to their car. Pete turned and waved goodbye to Bruce and Hayley as he hustled off to get to his night shift as a paramedic.

Bruce stared inside the house at Tawny, who was now pacing back and forth in front of the Christmas tree, appearing to talk to herself. "Do you think Sergio has already been here to question her?"

Hayley shook her head. "I don't think so. There was a town budget meeting tonight, and Randy mentioned that Sergio had to be there to argue for an increase in the police funding, and given the Beauchemins' status in the community, I'm reasonably sure he was not going to hand over the reins of the investigation to Lieutenant Donnie. He would most likely want to handle this himself with a little discretion."

"Makes sense," Bruce said. "Well, we're definitely not discreet. Should we go talk to her?"

"Bruce, it's late. We can't just drop in unannounced."

"Why not? I'm a crime reporter. That's what I do. You always want to catch a subject off guard, that way they're far more likely to reveal a piece of info they were not planning on sharing."

Hayley could not argue with him.

It was a reliable tactic that she had used multiple times in her own amateur investigations.

"Okay, we'll just ring the bell and compliment them on the Christmas display, and if they invite us in, then great, but if not, we go home and let Sergio handle it," Hayley insisted.

Bruce was already halfway to the front door.

Hayley had to scurry in order to catch up. By the time she reached him, he was ringing the bell, which had been reprogrammed for the holidays with chimes that played a Christmas carol medley.

They stood there a few minutes before the door finally opened a crack and Tawny peered out, mug in hand.

"Bruce, Hayley, good evening. I'm sorry, were we expecting you?"

"No, we were just admiring your Christmas lights display. It truly gets more impressive and resplendent every year," Hayley said.

"Thank you, I am so pleased you like it," Tawny said, still confused as to what they were doing at her front door. But ever the hostess, she could not stop herself from adding, "Would you like to come in for some hot cocoa?"

Hayley put a hand up. "Oh no, it's late and—"

"We'd love to!" Bruce declared, pushing past her into the foyer, noticing Tawny's off-kilter reaction, as if the last thing she had expected was for them to actually accept her kind invitation.

"We won't stay long," Hayley promised.

Tawny led them inside the large home through the foyer decked out with potted poinsettias, mistletoe, a life-size Rudolph reindeer with a lit-up red nose and even an eight-foot candy cane made of metal. She guided them into the living room with a fireplace mantel adorned with stockings, garland, lanterns and ribbon. Hayley stopped in her tracks, in awe of the enormous towering Christmas tree. "That's got to be one of the most beautifully decorated trees I have ever seen."

"That's lovely of you to say. Both Scooter and I are absolutely nuts when it comes to Christmas. We just can't get enough of the holiday spirit," Tawny said. She walked over to a silver serving tray and poured two mugs of hot chocolate, adding a dollop of whipped cream with a serving spoon, and then handing them to Bruce and Hayley.

"Thank you," Hayley said, taking a sip. "Delicious."

Bruce looked around. "Where's Scooter?"

"He's not here. He had to fly to New York late last

night to take care of some business. He should be back sometime tonight if our plane doesn't run into bad weather."

Private jet.

Of course Scooter Beauchemin had his own airplane.

"I heard there's a nor'easter coming up from DC. Let's hope it blows out to sea before it reaches us," Bruce said.

Tawny eyed them curiously. "Did you have something you wanted to discuss with Scooter?"

"Yes," Hayley answered, improvising. "As a close friend of Reverend Ted's, I know how much he wants to help the disadvantaged here on the island, and when Scooter withdrew his donation, I know that utterly devastated him. So we were hoping we might be able to persuade Scooter to reconsider."

"I don't know about that," Tawny said. "Once Scooter makes up his mind, he hardly ever changes it."

"I understand," Hayley sighed. "It's just that it's for such a good cause."

"With all that went down at the bazaar, you must sympathize with Scooter's point of view. His reputation means everything to him. He can't risk being tainted by theft and murder all around him."

Tawny Beauchemin had just offered up a very clear and concise motive, one any prosecutor would probably love to get her hands on.

"Yes, scandal is never good for business," Hayley remarked. "Especially when it's so close to home."

Tawny's polite smile slowly faded. "I'm not sure what you mean."

Bruce and Hayley exchanged quick glances. Bruce signaled Hayley that since she had started the ball rolling, she might as well continue with it.

Hayley cleared her throat and proceeded cautiously. "I'm simply saying that if it were to get out that, say, someone near and dear to his heart, take you, for instance, hypothetically, if you had snatched Ed Willoughby's diamond ring when no one was watching, and the news became public, well, that would be a huge blow to Scooter's sterling reputation."

Tawny's face tightened. "But I didn't steal it, so as you pointed out, it's all just hypothetical."

"Yes, but it's easy to draw that conclusion given your past history," Bruce said quietly.

Tawny's eyes widened. "Past history? What do you mean?"

"Your issues with kleptomania."

She gasped, horrified. "How did you find out about that? Scooter got that buried."

"Maybe he got the press to bury it, but it's still very much a part of your record, which the local police here have access to."

Tawny, her hands now shaking, set her mug of hot cocoa down and lowered herself onto her obscenely expensive white leather couch. "Chief Alvares knows?"

Hayley nodded solemnly. "I'm afraid so. It's only a matter of time before he shows up here to question you."

"But I heard a rumor earlier tonight that the police believe Doris Crimmons stole the ring. They found it in her knitting bag, at least that's the story going around! That lets me off the hook!"

"Except for the inconvenient fact that Doris claimed that you had asked for a breath mint and she allowed you to rummage through her bag, where you could have easily planted the ring, fearing the police might find it on your person if they searched you. It was never about keeping the ring, it was about the feeling you got by stealing it, that emotional high you craved by not getting caught, what that did for you."

Tawny's mind was clearly working overtime trying to figure a way out of this colossal mess. "I never touched her bag. So there you have it. It's her word against mine. Who do you think people are going to believe? My husband and I are pillars in this community."

"Given your spotty track record obeying the law, the fact that you're terrified of embarrassing your husband and that we can probably scrounge up a few eyewitnesses who saw you going through Doris's knitting bag, I'd place my bet on Doris," Bruce said, downing the rest of his hot cocoa and wiping some whipped cream off the sides of his mouth.

Tawny, suddenly struck with a crushing fear, slowly began to crumble. "Please, Scooter cannot find out about this. You can't tell him! You have to promise me!"

"We can't make that kind of promise, Tawny, we're sorry," Hayley muttered.

"But there is a clause in our prenup which explicitly states that if I ever steal again, Scooter will divorce me and I will get nothing, not a penny! He put that in the agreement to discourage me from shoplifting again! But I can't help myself! It's an illness! He just doesn't understand!"

Hayley took a deep breath, glancing at Bruce. "Esther Willey saw you steal the ring, didn't she?"

Tawny shot to her feet defiantly. "*What*? No! Yes, I was weak! I took the ring! But I did not kill Esther! I could never take the life of another human being! Besides, didn't they find Betty Dyer's mitten stuffed in Esther's mouth? You should be talking to her!"

"Yes. The mitten belonged to Betty, but she didn't put it there. Woody Woodworth did. He stupidly believed Helen had killed Esther and he was just trying to throw the police off Helen's scent."

"Then maybe *he* killed her! Or Helen did it!"

Bruce shook his head. "No, Tawny. You were the only one with a clear motive and opportunity."

Hayley frowned. All the pieces were now coming together. "You were desperate, terrified your husband was going to find out that you had slipped up again. You couldn't resist grabbing that ring when you thought no one was looking. But Esther saw you take it. She confronted you about it and there was no denying it. Esther was going to ruin everything. Your whole future was now in doubt. You had to do something."

Tawny, wild-eyed, took another step back. "No! No! You're making this all up! It's a fantasy!"

Hayley plowed on. "You saw Esther go outside with Doris. You were panic-stricken, afraid Esther was going to expose you, so when you saw Doris come back inside the church, that was when you went outside to find Esther and . . ."

"No! I did no such thing! I would never, not in a million years, stab poor Esther with her own knitting needle!"

Checkmate.

Hayley and Bruce fell silent.

Tawny shifted her insolent gaze between the two of them. "What? What is it?"

"It was public knowledge that Esther was stabbed with a knitting needle. But the police never said the needle belonged to Esther. Only the killer would know that specific detail."

Tawny shrank back, flailing, in a state of disbelief that all of this was happening, that the walls were closing in around her. "I just assumed it was hers. Who else walks around wielding their knitting needle as a weapon?"

"A lot of people. There are four knitting circles right here in town that I can think of just off the top of my head," Hayley reminded her.

Tawny was losing patience. "My point is, that's hardly enough to convict me. Have the police dusted the needle for fingerprints? When they do, I'm certain they won't find mine!"

"Because it was twenty-four degrees outside that day, so I'm certain when you went out to find her you were wearing gloves," Bruce said.

"You've already admitted to us you stole the ring and why, Tawny, so you might as well admit to killing Esther, the one witness who could finger you, to keep her quiet about it."

Tawny slowly backed away.

They had her dead to rights.

"Fine, yes, so what if I did it?" she spat out. "You've got nothing. Where's your hard evidence?"

"We just heard you confess," Hayley said.

"And I will deny it. I will say you were so desperate to prove yourself as some remarkable amateur sleuth, you were willing to do anything to pin the blame on someone just so you could claim another victory!"

Bruce turned to Hayley. "She's right, honey. The cops are going to need more than just our word for it in order to make an arrest." He smiled. "Oh, wait." He reached into his coat pocket and pulled out his phone. "I totally forgot, Tawny. We've also got *your* words." He pointed his phone at her. His recording app was on, taping their entire conversation. "A full confession."

Tawny's face went ashen.

Then her eyes welled up with tears.

Hayley felt a twinge of sympathy for her.

But then she thought of poor Esther Willey, who had paid an enormous price for being in the wrong place at the wrong time.

Bruce pocketed his phone and turned to Hayley. "I'm going to go outside and call Sergio."

As he started out, Tawny, feeling desperate and cornered, picked up the large metal candy cane by the door and, before Hayley could react, raised it above her head and swung it down hard on top of Bruce's skull. He collapsed to the floor in a heap, unconscious.

And then Tawny, with a murderous look in her eye, turned her attention toward Hayley.

Chapter Fourteen

"Bruce!" Hayley cried, running to her husband, who was crumpled up on the floor. She bent down to shake him by the shoulder, desperately trying to revive him, when suddenly Tawny, waving the heavy metal candy cane around, charged forward to whack Hayley with it. Hayley popped back up to her feet and ducked just as Tawny viciously swung it, missing the top of Hayley's head by a few inches. The tip of the giant candy cane smashed into the wall, leaving a dent.

Hayley sprang out the front door, stumbling around in the snow, blinded by the awesome, overwhelming display of lights. She ran as fast as she could, diving into the Frosty the Snowman bouncy house, rolling around, landing on her tummy, and peering out at the property. She saw Tawny, still armed with the large candy cane, searching the massive front yard for any sign of Hayley.

Hayley went completely limp, trying not to move inside the bouncy house, fearing Tawny might spot Frosty jiggling and then know Hayley was hiding inside.

Tawny started hunting around the manger scene, knocking a stuffed donkey aside, making certain Hayley wasn't hiding behind any wise men or animals or the Baby Jesus's stained wood crib. Swiveling her head about, Tawny was growing more and more agitated and frustrated.

"Come on out, Hayley! I promise I won't hurt you. Let's talk about this," Tawny said sweetly. She paused, waited a few seconds for any kind of response and, when she received none, flared up with anger and slammed the candy cane down in the snow-covered frozen dirt. Then she stormed back inside the house.

Hayley waited, and then quietly rolled out of the bouncy house and carefully made her way toward the front gate when suddenly everything plunged into darkness.

Tawny must have cut the power by turning off all the circuit breakers. Hayley was totally blind, reaching out with her hands into the darkness, trying to make her way out.

She heard Tawny behind her calling out to her in a singsongy voice. "Come out, come out, wherever you are! I'm going to find you, Hayley! I know every inch of this property. I know all the good hiding places! You can't get away from me!"

Hayley shivered in the cold, pressing forward, confident she was not that far from the front gate, where she could slip out and then head into the woods, where it would be much easier to hide. She tripped over a bush and pitched forward, getting tangled up in some string of Christmas lights that had been draped over the bush. Her breathing got heavier as panic began to set in. The lights were wrapped around her arms and legs. She fought to free herself and feared she was making too much noise when she heard a sharp crack, and a bullet whizzed past her right ear, nearly nicking it. Tawny had gone inside to get a gun and was now hunting her down like a deer.

Hayley crawled to her feet and finally managed to shed

the string of lights. She figured Tawny would instinctively follow her to the front gate, the obvious escape route, and so instead she darted around behind the manger scene and back toward the main house. She bumped into several displays before craning her neck back to try to locate Tawny. It was pitch black. She couldn't see anything, but she could hear some labored breathing as Tawny doggedly tried tracking her down.

Hayley dropped to her knees and crawled up onto the front porch and through the front door, where she bumped into something in the dark. She heard a muffled groan and realized she had just slammed into Bruce, who was still lying on the floor.

"Bruce, are you all right?" Hayley whispered.

He moaned softly.

At least he was alive.

"Hayley! I'm starting to lose patience with you!" Tawny roared from outside. Hayley stood up and made her way down the hall to a utility closet, hoping she might find the circuit breakers so she could switch them on again.

No such luck.

Then she made her way upstairs, tripping over a few steps in the dark. On the second floor, she found herself in the main bedroom, where just outside the large bay window attached to a small balcony was the sleigh and reindeer suspended in air. She unlocked the window, slid it open and noticed a small toolkit on the floor of the balcony that someone had used to secure the display. She unzipped the kit, grabbed a screwdriver and began to loosen the screws. She paused several times, peering down over the side of the balcony, trying to zero in on Tawny's whereabouts. At first, she heard nothing, but then there was the distinct sound of crunching. Like someone walking through the hardened snow. It was getting closer and closer. Then she saw a stream of light and could make out Tawny, hunting rifle in one hand, a flashlight in the other, marching back toward the house, presumably to flick the lights back on to make it easier to locate Hayley and shoot her.

Hayley waited and waited until Tawny was directly down below, and then she shot her hands out with a forceful shove, pushing the sleigh and reindeer forward. The screws popped out and the display sailed through the air like Santa arriving at his next stop from the night sky and slammed into Tawny, knocking her to the ground and pinning her in the snow.

Hayley jumped to her feet and stared down at the scene. The flashlight illuminated Tawny as she wildly kicked and screamed, very much alive, trapped under the weight of Santa's sleigh.

Hayley then ran back inside, down the stairs and out the front door to retrieve the rifle, which luckily Tawny had dropped upon impact, safely out of her reach.

She grabbed the rifle, ran back inside to check on Bruce and immediately called 911.

Chapter Fifteen

Bruce winced as he gingerly touched the lump on his head with his left index finger as he and Hayley stood on the front porch of the Beauchemin house.

"Does it hurt?" Hayley asked as she held his arm to steady him so he didn't get dizzy and lose his balance and fall to the ground.

"Only when I touch it."

"Then you probably should stop touching it," Hayley said with a wry smile.

"Thank you, Doctor Obvious," he joked as they watched Chief Sergio escort Tawny, her wrists handcuffed behind her back, to his squad car.

Just as Sergio was about to place the palm of his hand on top of Tawny's head to slowly lower her into the back seat, a gray Mercedes came barreling down the driveway toward the main house. Scooter Beauchemin jumped out of the car, the flashing blue lights from the police vehicle washing over his face as his eyes widened at the sight of his wife under arrest and in handcuffs.

"What the hell is going on here?" Scooter demanded to know.

Tawny did not answer her husband. She just defiantly

pursed her lips and blew her long bangs out of her face with a gust of air.

"Tawny, what's happening? What did you do?" Beauchemin yelled, racing toward his wife.

Sergio had to stick an arm out to stop him from getting too close. "I'm booking her for murder."

Scooter stumbled back, like he had just been gut-punched. "What?" he croaked, deflating like a flat tire. "Murder? W-Who did she kill?"

Tawny averted her eyes, ashamed, as she climbed into the back seat of the squad car and Sergio slammed the door shut. "Esther Willey."

Scooter's face was a blank. "Who on earth is Esther Willey? The lady who got stabbed at the church bazaar?"

"Yes. She was a nice lady who simply saw something she shouldn't have," Hayley offered.

Scooter still looked puzzled.

Sergio filled him in on the rest.

His wife stealing Willoughby's diamond ring.

Esther witnessing the crime.

Tawny's abject fear that her husband might find out and the drastic lengths she went to make sure that would never happen.

It took a few moments for Scooter to digest everything he was hearing, and then his face flushed with anger. He lunged toward the back seat of the squad car, banging on the window with his fist. "How dare you, Tawny! What kind of maniac are you? Do you have any idea how this will damage my reputation?" he wailed.

"Please step away from the squad car before you break my window, Mr. Beauchemin. Otherwise you might find yourself in handcuffs sitting in the back seat with your wife."

Scooter wisely stopped pounding on the window and took a step back, giving Sergio a wide berth.

"You can follow us down to the station, if you'd like," Sergio said.

He did not respond to the chief.

Hayley wondered if he even cared what would happen to Tawny. As Sergio got behind the wheel of the squad car and drove away, Scooter stood in the middle of the large circular driveway in front of the main house, staring after the car, shell-shocked, his cheeks red from the cold. It started to snow, and little white flakes began landing on his bald head and graying goatee.

"How could she do it? She knows this could ruin me," Scooter muttered.

"Maybe you should be less concerned with your reputation and more interested in getting your wife the help she needs. She's obviously suffering from a mental illness, one she's probably had to deal with for years without any help from you," Hayley spat out.

Scooter chose to ignore her and stalked into the house, slamming the door shut behind him.

She turned to Bruce, who was still measuring the size of his lump with his finger. "Come on, let's get you to the hospital."

"I don't need to go to the hospital," Bruce insisted.

"You're going to the hospital. We need to make sure you don't have a concussion."

"Really, Hayley, I'm fine. I just want to go home and snuggle up on the couch and watch *A Christmas Story* on TV."

"We can stand out here in the cold arguing about this for as long as you want, Bruce, but we both know how this will eventually end."

He sighed.

Of course he did.
They headed straight to the hospital.
Because Hayley always won.
And deep down, he knew she was right.
Better safe than sorry.

Two hours later, after some quick tests, Bruce was given a clean bill of health—no serious head injury, just a nasty bump that would heal. The couple arrived home and did indeed curl up on the couch together with a plate of Christmas cookies and some of that spiked eggnog that gave everyone such a warm tingling feeling. This year, it was going to be a romantic holiday for two. If Bruce didn't fall asleep watching the movie like he usually did.

True to form, by the time his favorite scene in *A Christmas Story* came on, where Ralphie's friend Flick does the triple dog dare and sticks his tongue on a frozen flagpole with disastrous results, Bruce, who was stretched out on the couch, his head resting on Hayley's lap, began snoring softly. She reached down and kissed the top of his forehead and took a sip of her eggnog.

There was no other place she would rather be than right here this Christmas.

Island Food & Spirits
by
Hayley Powell

What a wild ride it's been in Bar Harbor this holiday season. First, poor Esther Willey's tragic demise at the annual church Christmas Bazaar, and then, to everyone's shock and horror, the involvement and subsequent arrest of Tawny Beauchemin for her wicked role in poor Esther's death. It's all anyone in town has been talking about! Word around town is that after Tawny's arraignment, her husband, Scooter Beauchemin, immediately put their stunning seaside mansion up for sale and skipped town while his wife awaits her trial. No one has heard from him or seen hide nor hair of him since. And then there was the drama we all endured when Scooter failed to use my best friend Liddy as his real estate agent. She's still raging on about that unforgivable slight.

But still, in true small-town fashion, the resilient residents of Bar Harbor have managed to put all the bad behind them and focus on the good with Christmas Day just around the corner.

My own plan for Christmas is to make my family's traditional Peppermint Bark, a recipe that has been passed down through the generations from my great-grandmother to my grandmother to my mother and to me, and I have recently passed it along to my own daughter, Gemma. So while Bruce enjoys his favorite Christmas eggnog cocktail in the living room watching another one of his favorite holiday comedies, *Elf*, on TV, I will retreat to the kitchen to whip up a few baking sheets of this sweet chocolate treat and await Randy's arrival. Randy seems to have a sixth sense whenever I make my Peppermint Bark, and always just happens to drop by unannounced right when they're ready to serve.

Randy is a chocolate fiend. He has been ever since he was a little kid. I remember one Christmas when I was twelve and Randy was ten. Our mother recruited us to help her make Peppermint Bark that she would box up and deliver to her closest friends to enjoy. We were ordered to break the bark into pieces after it hardened and put them in gift boxes. Well, like Lucy and Ethel working in the chocolate factory, Randy and I ate more than we put in the boxes. When our mother inspected our work and found the boxes nearly empty and the Peppermint Bark almost gone, she was none too pleased. She warned us not to eat another piece! I did not have to be told twice, fearing she might ground me and I would miss Mona's family's raucous New Year's Eve party, but Randy was so addicted to the Peppermint Bark he could not help himself. So finally, when our mother noticed his chocolate-smeared face yet again, he was ordered to go to his room until the morning when we would set out to deliver the boxes! There was some begging and crocodile tears. At one point he looked to me, the big sister, hoping for some support, but I couldn't resist popping a piece of bark in my mouth right in front of him when our mother's back was to us, which frustrated him even more. I know it was mean, but what can I say, I was twelve and could be a brat sometimes. Finally, Randy gave up, sighed and did as he was told, storming up the stairs and slamming his bedroom door behind him.

The following morning, I was up early and ready to head out to make our deliveries when our mother came into the kitchen with a worried expression on her face. She told me that Randy wasn't feeling well and had been up sick since the early hours of the morning.

I knew this must be serious, because Randy did not want to miss delivering the boxes. Usually we were gifted treats in return, and on the rare occasion we had a box of our peppermint bark left over, it was a win-win in Randy's eyes, so I feared this affliction might actually be serious.

Mom checked on Randy again, who was still pale but finally sleeping. She decided that she would call her close friend Celeste, Liddy's mom, to come over and stay with Randy so we could deliver our boxes. Celeste agreed and was there within ten minutes. So off we went.

When we arrived home hours later, Celeste greeted us at the door with the unsettling news that Randy was still not feeling well. She had even tried offering him a piece of Peppermint Bark, thinking he would eagerly gobble it up, but he turned positively green. Celeste thought he might need to see a doctor. Before she could call the doctor's office, however, our phone started ringing off the hook. My mother was fielding calls from all the homes we had been to earlier in the day. Her initial bewildered look slowly gave way to red-faced fury. She slammed down the phone, and within seconds another call came through, but she didn't bother answering it. She just made a beeline for the stairs, marching up and yelling Randy's name at the top of her lungs!

Curious, Celeste and I followed her upstairs to Randy's room, just in time to see a frantic Randy trying to crawl under his bed to hide and Mom lunging forward and grabbing his ankles, pulling a struggling Randy out from underneath the bed. She sat him down on the mattress and opened her mouth, ready to let loose with a monumental tirade, but before she had the chance, Randy burst into tears, wailing, "I'm so sorry, Mom!"

It did not take long for all the pieces of the puzzle to fall into place. Randy had snuck downstairs in the middle of the night and eaten five boxes of chocolate and was now sick with a tummy ache. This explained the five curious phone calls asking our mother why she had delivered empty boxes.

I knew this was my time to slip out of the room. Randy was going to be getting a really long lecture and I definitely did not want to be there for that, since I had already endured more than a few directed at me in my relatively short twelve years on this earth.

In the end, all turned out well. Our mother calmed down and made more Peppermint Bark for those that had been stiffed, and of course Randy was forbidden to eat any, but I'm sure he didn't mind because it took a few days for his stomach to feel better. Still, that unfortunate episode did little to squelch his love for the stuff, and the following Christmas he was right there stuffing pieces in his mouth again at every opportunity. Except this time, our mother took extra measures to protect her candy by installing a lock on one of our kitchen cupboards and hiding the key.

Randy's Favorite Peppermint Bark

Ingredients:
12 ounces semisweet chocolate, chopped
½ teaspoon peppermint extract
12 ounces white chocolate, chopped
10 candy canes, crushed

Line your baking sheet with parchment paper.

Fill the bottom of a large pot with 3 to 4 inches of water.

Bring the water to a simmer. Place a large heatproof bowl over the pot. Add your semisweet chocolate, stirring occasionally until melted.

Stir in the extract. Pour into your prepared baking sheet. Spread out the chocolate into an even layer. Refrigerate until set, about 30 minutes.

Over the same pot, place another bowl filled with the white chocolate. Stir until melted. Pour over the set chocolate, spreading evenly.

Sprinkle your crushed candy canes over the top. Place the sheet back into the refrigerator until fully set.

When set, remove the sheet and break apart the chocolate with your hands or with a rolling pin, depending on bark thickness.

Store in an airtight container at room temperature.

Great for gift giving!

I know that we should be making homemade eggnog, but sometimes we all just need an easy shortcut, so in this recipe I like to use store-bought eggnog. However, feel free to use your own homemade recipe, because in the end it always turns out delicious either way!

Bruce's Christmas Eggnog Cocktail

Ingredients:
1 ounce Amaretto
1 ounce vodka
2 ounces store-bought or homemade eggnog
Pinch cinnamon
Pinch nutmeg
Caramel sauce to rim the glass (I use the squeeze bottle of Ghirardelli caramel sauce)

Rim your cocktail glass with caramel sauce.

Add the eggnog, Amaretto, vodka, cinnamon, and nutmeg to a shaker filled with ice. Shake the mixture.

Strain into the cocktail glass. If necessary, add a little more cinnamon to taste.

Enjoy and Merry Christmas!

TWO CHRISTMAS MITTENS

Lynn Cahoon

Chapter One

The Lodge Culinary Department holiday party was the one event that Frank Hines allowed to be catered by an outside company. Unfortunately, a newer catering company out of Sun Valley had been given the contract instead of Mia's Morsels. Mia sighed as she watched the trays being passed around the large, dimly lit ballroom. She adjusted the black slinky halter dress she'd let Christina talk her into wearing tonight. Mia had to admit, it made her curly hairdo work, especially with the jeweled hair combs she'd slipped into the updo. A matching necklace and black heels finished the outfit. Now all she had to do was hang out with her coworkers for the next two hours and try to have fun and not judge the food Frank had contracted.

As the Lodge's new catering director, Mia had been part of the decorating team that had planned the festive decorations that went up right after Halloween every year. Now, a month and a half later, the Santa and friends décor would need refreshing after this weekend before the Christmas parties started in earnest. She'd suggested three different décor setups. One for a more general holiday theme for the Thanksgiving groups, one for Christmas parties, and then a refresh between that and the New Year events. But Frank had vetoed her suggestion for the large ballroom. Just like he'd vetoed Mia's Morsels as the caterer for this event. It was beginning to be a habit.

Christina Adams stood next to her and took a stuffed mushroom from the server. Christina was Mia's roommate and worked with her at Mia's Morsels when she wasn't finishing classes at the college in Twin. Christina shone as bright as her personality in a silver dress with a large tulle skirt. With her blond hair down and pulled away from her face with a small tiara, the girl looked like a princess tonight. Christina had plenty of appropriate party clothes, since she'd never worn anything twice when she was under her mother's roof. She sniffed at the mushroom. "We would have rocked the food at this party. Probably for less than what this place charged."

"I know, but Frank was concerned about my connection with Mia's Morsels. He thought it might look like I had the inside track." Mia shook her head at the server holding out the mushroom tray.

"Our proposal had better food and a lower per-person cost. So instead of choosing us, he hires the catering company where his girlfriend works." Abigail Majors also waved away the tray. Abigail was currently managing Mia's catering business while Mia worked for the Lodge. The arrangement had been the only way to keep Mia's Morsels going after Frank had torpedoed their catering for the Lodge. "That seems fair. Not."

Mia smiled at Abigail, who not only worked for her but was also Mia's boyfriend's mother. Sometimes in a small town the connections got a little close. Especially when you added in the fact that in Magic Springs, Idaho, members of the local coven outnumbered the number of normal people in town. Even tonight at the Lodge's Christmas party, Mia recognized many of the coven members. Most had tried already to bring Mia and her grandmother back into the fold to rejoin the coven. Mia blamed her work schedule, but that excuse wouldn't work forever. She needed to make a decision. And soon.

Abigail wore a burgundy pantsuit that shone in the twinkling lights. She pulled her phone out of one of the front pockets and sighed. "It's Thomas. He's checking up on us. The boys are supposed to be scouting new tour sites for his company, and yet he has time to call just when the party gets good. He's afraid I'm going to fall for one of these business suits and leave him."

Mia just laughed. "I don't think so. He probably just wants to see how beautiful you look tonight. Let's make sure we get a picture of all four of us in front of the tree. If we can pull Grans away from that guy she's been talking to all night."

Abigail stepped away to take the call out in the hallway.

Mia scanned the room. Everyone seemed to be having a good time, but very few of the trays were being emptied. She'd been right about the food. It was sub-par. Next time she'd insist that Mia's Morsels be given a fighting chance. Maybe have a tasting contest before the contract was awarded. No one in their right mind would choose this garbage.

Christina pointed to a man near the doorway. He was talking with a woman in a red dress that sparkled even in the dim light. "That's one of my professors, Geoffrey Brewer. He knows your boss from when they went to school together. He says Frank's a jerk."

"He's in the Culinary Department?" Mia hadn't met any of Christina's professors because the school was in Twin Falls, a town about two hours away.

"Hospitality, actually. I guess he used to manage a bunch of hotels before he took on the teaching job."

Christina waved at the man, and when he recognized her, she waved him over. "I guess he's coming over to meet you. He's super nice."

"Okay, just make sure he knows I didn't cook this food." Mia grinned and then turned to meet Christina's professor.

"Well, at least the company is entertaining tonight." Geoffrey waved away a catering staff member who was now trying to get them to take a cocktail wiener on a stick. "Frank always was about going with the cheapest bid. Although, I've heard that most of the Lodge's events serve top-notch food."

"That's because Mia is usually in charge." Christina took Mia's shoulders in her hands. "Professor, I'd like you to meet my boss and friend, Mia Malone. She owns Mia's Morsels and is the Lodge's catering director."

Mia held out a hand. "And just to clarify, the Lodge didn't cater our own event this year. And neither did Mia's Morsels. A mistake I hope to not repeat next year."

"Well, not expecting staff to work during a staff party is at least a good notion on Frank's part." Geoffrey shook her hand. "I've heard great things about Mia's Morsels. Why did you take on the unfortunate position of working for Frank?"

"You know how small businesses are at the beginning." Mia tried to skirt the issue and not bad-mouth her boss. Geoffrey was doing it enough for both of them. "Christina talks a lot about you and the program. I'm afraid she's going to graduate in June and be swept up by a much higher paying job as soon as they know she's available."

Geoffrey hugged Christina and spilled a bit of his wine on her skirt. "She's the best student we have. She should bring in amazing job offers."

As he wandered off to refill his glass, Christina dabbed at her skirt. "Good thing he drinks white wine. I think the dry cleaners should be able to get this out. I've never seen him tipsy before."

"I would hope not. I hope he got a room nearby tonight and won't be driving back to Twin." Mia watched as he went over to the open bar. The bartender who worked for the Lodge shook his head and offered the professor a cup of coffee. At least he wouldn't be getting any more alcohol at the party.

"Oh, Professor Brewer has a house in Sun Valley. His wife works at some Hollywood film studio. Everyone says he works just to keep busy." Christina dropped her voice a little. "Mom keeps harping at me to invite him to the Boise house to meet Dad. She's looked up their investments, I guess."

"Well, if they have a house in Sun Valley, then your dad is probably dying to get him and his wife as clients." Christina's dad was a lawyer, and her mom was always on the lookout for new, wealthy clients. Unfortunately for the Adamses, both of their children had gone into the hospitality field, with Isaac, their oldest, working as a culinary director for the most prestigious hotel in the Boise area. And now, Christina worked for Mia. A job her mom would say was beneath her. But people had to eat, right? Mia's gaze caught her grandmother moving their way from across the room. "Here comes Grans."

"I'll grab us a couple more drinks. White wine again?" When Mia nodded, Christina hurried away toward the bartender.

Mia watched as Christina's professor moved away from the bar and headed out the door. Apparently being cut off had made it the end of the party for him. Mia threw a blessing at him and got back a vision from the Goddess showing her that he had a car and driver sitting out in the parking lot waiting for him.

"You can't worry about every drunk driver," her grandmother said as she followed Mia's gaze to watch Geoffrey stumble out of the room.

"Maybe not, but if he hadn't had a driver, I would have asked one of the staff to drive him home. We don't need that on our roads. Especially on snowy nights like this." The snow had just begun to fall when they'd come into the Lodge an hour before. "I'll use my power for good, as long as they let me."

"Okay, Glenda, I just wanted to tell you that Robert is taking me to Sun Valley for a late dinner. He'd assumed, since you catered the last Lodge staff party, the food would be edible, not this crap." Grans shook her head at the trays being passed.

A waiter frowned at them as he tried to push a tray of undercooked egg rolls.

"I wasn't in charge of making that decision." Mia waved Abigail over. "Before you leave, let's get a picture of the four of us at the tree."

Abigail hurried over, and then Christina met them at the tree. They took several pictures, including one of just Mia and Grans. Grans was in a little black dress with black heels. She still looked younger than her actual years—a magic spell gone wrong—but at least she looked closer to her age than Mia. Abigail showed them the last picture. "You two look like sisters."

Mia grinned as Grans shook her head. She handed the phone back to Abigail. "Not now, but we did."

"And I liked it that way." Grans gave her a kiss on her cheek. "We should have taken a picture of the two of us when we did look like sisters. I'll call you tomorrow."

Mia watched as her grandmother rejoined Robert, who stood by the door with her coat on his arm. She'd met him once before when they'd stopped by the school. Mia liked him. He seemed to fit in well with her grandmother's life. And, since he was involved in the local coven as well, nothing had to be hidden from his view. Hiding her witch life wasn't something her grandmother did well. Especially since she tended to make her potions in her bathtub.

Abigail tucked her phone back in her pocket. "I haven't seen Robert this happy since his wife passed several years ago. I mean, since before she passed. They were a cute couple, and it was obvious that they were still in love. I hope Mary Alice and Robert find the same joy."

"Mia's Morsels may be catering a wedding soon," Christina teased, and then pointed toward Mia. "Oh, my goodness. You should see your face. You look scared."

"I'm not sure who I'm scared for, Robert or Grans?" Mia nodded to a table. "Let's sit for a bit, then as soon as eight hits, let's get out of here. I've got lasagna ready to warm up in the oven, and if you want to stay over, Abigail, I've got a few bottles of wine in the house."

"Sounds like a real party." Abigail sat down and slipped off her shoes. "My feet are killing me. We used to do the party scene probably twice a month when we ran the grocery store. Now it's rare for me to get dressed up unless I'm catering. Then I'm in sensible shoes."

Mia giggled at the older woman's gripes. She liked spending time with Trent's mom. His dad, he still was an unknown, but his mom was fun.

"Since the boys are all gone, we should have a sleepover. I'll make brownies and we can watch rom-coms until we fall asleep." Christina sipped at the wine she'd gotten from the bartender. She kept looking at the door, distracted.

"Are you waiting for someone?" Mia asked.

Christina turned back and shook her head. "No, I'm just a little worried about Professor Brewer. I know Sun Valley isn't that far, but his place is up in the mountains and the roads aren't the best."

"He had a driver," Abigail told her.

Mia turned to her. She'd been told that by the Goddess, but sometimes the messages weren't totally clear. "How do you know?"

"Kate insists on it when she's out of town. Geoff has an issue with alcohol. It's been a problem for a while." Abigail saw the shocked look on Christina's face. "Oh, I'm sorry. He's your professor, isn't he? Just because someone has a drinking problem doesn't mean they're not a good person. He's just troubled."

"How do you know his wife?" Mia figured the answer was obvious, but she asked it anyway.

"She's a member of the coven. He's not. Not a magical bone in his body, so to speak, but Kate's quite adept at magic. It's probably why she's so good at her job. She makes magic in the movies for mortals."

About an hour later, Mia had made her final rounds at the party to say good night to her employees. She met Abigail and Christina at the ballroom door. "I'm ready to go whenever you are."

Abigail dangled her keys. "The designated driver is at your service. I've already told Thomas that we're having a girls' night at your house. He says to expect a delivery from the grocery store when we get there."

"What is he sending?" Mia asked as they got their coats from the coat check and bundled up. Now that they were heading home, she pulled a beanie over her head, tugging it down over the updo. She pulled on her warm gloves.

"I'm not sure, but you two can stay inside while I get

the SUV warmed up." Abigail pulled on her hat and winter gloves too. "I'd hate to see you fall in those shoes."

For the first time that night, Mia envied Abigail's pants. The fabric wouldn't be the warmest, but it was thicker than the tights she wore under her dress. "We're not that far and the Lodge keeps the sidewalks clear. We'll come with you."

"Definitely," Christina said, but her tone didn't sound as certain.

"Okay then, stay close." Abigail walked through the sliding doors and into the night. The snow was still falling, but it hadn't worked its way into a strong storm or blizzard, yet. The flakes looked lovely, wafting down in front of them to land on the still-black asphalt.

Mia just hoped the surface wasn't hiding black ice. They went around to the back, where employees were directed to park, and she watched as Abigail remote started the vehicle. She'd still have to clear the windows, but the inside might start warming up as soon as they climbed inside. "I call shotgun."

"That's not fair. I would have if my teeth weren't chattering so much," Christina said as they moved as a group toward the first row of cars. Abigail's car was in the second row, so they didn't have far to go. Christina paused and reached down, picking up something.

Mia paused as she turned to look at Christina's find. The item was a mitten knitted in a bright Christmas red. A picture of a snowflake was in the middle of the mitten.

"Look, someone dropped a mitten." Christina held it out for Abigail to see.

Abigail turned, and a small scream popped out of her mouth. "Don't pick up that . . ."

Christina froze, holding the item in front of her. "It's just a mitten."

"It's not just a mitten." Abigail stepped toward her and groaned. "You've already made contact."

"What do you mean?" Now Mia was worried about Trent's mom. It was just a mitten. "We should get in the car. I'll take the mitten to the front desk for lost and found."

"No. Don't you touch it too." Abigail dug in her tote and pulled out a plastic bag. "Here, put it in this. The mitten has powers."

"Oh, it's magic? Am I going to be a witch then?" Christina followed Abigail's direction and looked up at her hopefully. "Is it a Christmas wish mitten?"

Abigail cautiously sealed the bag and put it in her tote. Then she carefully stepped toward the car. "We need to get out of here."

"Okay." Mia shrugged and shook her head at Christina, indicating they should follow Abigail, only to be stopped again when Abigail pulled out her phone.

"Stay back."

"What are you doing?" Mia asked, looking around. "Is there ice on the road?"

Instead of answering, Abigail spoke into the phone. "I need to report a dead body. Please send Mark Baldwin to the Lodge. We'll be inside the lobby waiting for him."

Chapter Two

Mia pulled Abigail to the side after informing security that there was an issue in the parking lot and that the police had been called. They sat on a bench, trying to warm up. Mia could hear Christina's teeth chattering. So much for a fun evening out. The large Christmas tree sparkled by the lobby fireplace. "So who was out there? Who's dead?"

Abigail glanced over at Christina, then whispered to Mia, "Geoff Brewer."

"Professor Brewer?" Christina had heard. "He's dead?"

"It looked that way. He might have slipped on the way to his car and hit his head." Abigail threw out ideas on ways he might have died. "He was just lying there, blood seeping from his head."

Mia shivered. It wasn't because she wasn't cold, she was. But from Abigail's tone, Mia didn't think Professor Brewer had died accidentally. She leaned back, then remembered the mitten. "Abigail, why didn't you want Christina to pick up that mitten?"

Abigail glanced around the lobby. For the moment, no one was nearby or watching them. She took the bag holding the mitten out of her tote, keeping her gloves on as she stared at it. "There's a legend about a lost mitten. It's red with the snowflake design on it. It shows up only in December of each year. It's cursed. Whoever touches it will die within a week."

Christina gasped and pulled off her gloves. She studied her hands. "No rash, no lines going through my veins. Are you sure?"

"We need to get Christina back to the apartment and get your grandmother there. I don't want to involve the coven, not yet. They'd want to isolate her and probably wouldn't be able to solve this before, well . . ." Abigail met Mia's gaze. "Let's just get her home before there's an issue."

"I'll let Carl, the head of security here, know that Christina's sick and we need to take her home. Security can handle the body and the questions. Mark can come to the school if he wants to talk to us." Mia pulled Christina to her feet. "You take her to the car, and I'll meet you at the valet area."

Mia headed over to Carl on the other side of the lobby by the door. He had already moved his men out to the parking lot to protect the scene. He was on the phone when Mia arrived at the concierge desk. He looked up at her and shook his head. "Bad night. Frank's not going to be happy when I finally get ahold of him."

"You haven't talked to him yet? Isn't he supposed to be at this party?" Mia scanned the lobby. Most of the staff were still in the ballroom at the party, but she saw the questions on people's faces as they came into the Lodge after parking.

Carl made a face. "He called in late. Apparently, he and the girlfriend aren't getting along, so he didn't want to be here when she was here. He's not a strong people person anyway. And this isn't the first time he's been unavailable at night. He's not like the previous manager. I couldn't get

Corrina to go home. He doesn't seem to want to be here at all."

Not my issue, Mia thought. She saw Abigail's car pull up. "Hey, Christina isn't feeling well. We're taking her home and I don't think I'll be able to come back. Can you let Mark know to call me on my cell if he needs to talk to me? I'll be up for a while."

Carl glanced out at the SUV, which was now in front of the door. They could see Christina in the passenger seat looking sick. The curse must be starting to affect her. "She looks like she's going to hurl. Too many of those appetizers, I bet. Someone brought me a plate and they were horrible. Why didn't you cater the event?"

"Wasn't my choice. I've got to go. Thanks for passing on my message." Mia tapped the desk and turned to leave.

"Seriously? Frank said you didn't want to cater," Carl called after her.

Mia turned back and couldn't stop the words. "My catering company put in a bid. I wanted this. Frank chose the other company."

"I think he's trying to distance himself from the food now. There are going to be complaints. I'll make sure people know you were burned on this." He nodded to the door. "Go take care of that kid. I'll handle things here."

Mia tried to tamp down her anger. Frank Hines was a weasel. He didn't let her have the event, and now that his girlfriend had messed it up, it was Mia's fault. He wasn't a nice person, and he was a worse boss. All she needed was a few months, maybe a few years, to build up her emergency fund. But right now, she needed to focus on what was wrong with Christina.

She climbed in the back seat and nodded to Abigail. "Sorry, I got distracted by a Frank warning."

"Your boss is a tool." She held up a finger as the call she

was making connected. "Mary Alice, this is Abigail. We have an emergency. Can you meet us at the school?"

The sigh her grandmother let out could probably be heard in the lobby through the closed doors. "Fine. I'll have Robert drop me off. We were just finishing dinner anyway."

"Thanks, Grans," Mia called out, but she saw on the display that her grandmother had already hung up. "She sounds happy."

"She's always happy. Not." Christina grumbled from the front seat. "Why is it so bright for nighttime?"

Abigail and Mia shared a look as they exited the dark parking lot.

"Just close your eyes and we'll be home soon," Mia suggested as she stared out the window watching Mark's truck pull into the parking lot. He wasn't going to be happy that they'd left, but Christina was her major worry right now. She sent a prayer up to the Goddess, but they must be too far away from Gloria, her witch doll that hung in her kitchen. Gloria was her familiar, and a lot of times Mia just got back a giggle when she sent up her wishes and dreams. Not hearing anything was disconcerting.

Mia's phone rang. It was Trent. They had a few blocks to the school, so she answered. "Hey."

"Hey, yourself. What's wrong with Christina? Levi's going crazy over here trying to reach her. He's got a bad feeling."

Well, that wasn't surprising. The Majors boys felt emotions strongly, especially from people they cared about. She glanced at Abigail, but she was focused on the road. "Your mom thinks she got in the middle of an ancient curse."

"Like Egypt ancient?" Trent sounded confused.

"Tell him it's the mittens curse. Both boys know what

danger that one can cause." Abigail turned the vehicle onto the road that led to Mia's school.

"Did you hear that? It's the mittens curse."

Trent swore under his breath. "That's not good. Why didn't you warn her?"

"Because I didn't know about how dangerous a pair of Christmas mittens could be," Mia spat back. "No one warned me."

"Sorry, I just assumed. Anyway, maybe Levi and I should head back."

Mia pushed down the fear. "No, stay there. I'll call you in the morning if we need your help. You don't get a lot of time with your dad. I'd hate for you to call it short."

"Christina's important, to both of us," Trent countered.

Abigail was pulling the car into the school parking lot.

"I know she is, and I'll keep you in the loop, but I've got to go. We're at the school." Mia hung up before he could say anything else and tucked the phone into her coat. She pulled out her keys and hurried out of the car and to the front door. She unlocked it and turned on all the inside lights. Mr. Darcy sat on the middle of the stairs, watching her. "Stay there. Christina's been cursed. I need to go get her, and I don't want to worry about you wandering out. It's too cold for you to be outside."

Her cat nodded, and she assumed he must have understood what she'd said. Or at least Dorian Alexander, the ghost or soul of Grans's ex-boyfriend, understood. He'd been sharing a body with Mr. Darcy since his untimely death.

Mia hurried back outside to find Christina out of the car and Abigail helping her to the door. "We need to use the freight elevator rather than the stairs. I don't think she could make it up all three flights."

"Taking her upstairs will make it more difficult to get

her out again if we have to drive her to the hospital," Abigail countered.

"Will a hospital help her?" Mia paused and turned toward the van. "Maybe we should . . ."

Abigail shook her head. "No, dear, a hospital will only keep her alive. It's a last resort. We need to break the curse. Now."

A newer model Hummer pulled into the driveway. Robert pulled the car close to the door, then stepped out and opened the passenger side door for Grans. They kissed lightly, then she came toward the open front door and met the rest of the women.

"Why is she still out here? Let's get her upstairs to the apartment now. She needs to expend as little energy as possible to keep the spell from exploding." Grans pulled the door shut and locked it. "Ruined a perfectly promising night."

"I'm sorry," Mia said as they moved toward the elevator. "I didn't warn her because I didn't know."

"Most of these warnings come as part of the fairy tale discussion when witch children are very little. I should have insisted that if your mother wasn't going to take the family mantle, she turn you over to me so I could have trained you from childhood. We really must return to daily sessions to get you caught up. I may not be around for much longer." Grans paused at the stairs. "I'll meet you at the top. Put her in her room, and I'll start the potion in your kitchen."

Once they got Christina in her room, they took off the party dress and dressed her in Snoopy pj's. Then Mia went to the kitchen. "What can I help with?"

"I'll need to run to my house in the morning, but for right now I need you to go into the library and get the book on fairy tales. It's red and oversized. I saw it the last time I did research in your library." Grans looked up from the large soup pot she was using to make a potion. "I'm not sure if this first spell will work, but it will slow down the process so we can find the counter potion."

"She's going to be okay, right?" Christina was more of a sister to Mia than simply a friend and coworker. She would have been her sister-in-law if Mia had made the mistake of marrying her brother, Isaac. Instead, they'd become best friends and sisters of the heart. Which Mia thought was even better.

Grabbing the library key, Mia headed out of the apartment and crossed the hall to open the room that shared a wall with her apartment kitchen. The library had been there when the school was active and the books had stayed, even though the school had been shut down. The library looked like she'd stepped back in time. And it housed a few ghosts that haunted the room. Because of their presence, it wasn't a friendly place to sit and read, not yet. But Mia had high hopes for the room if she could ever free it of the ghosts.

She turned on all the lights and moved into the library after unlocking the door. She tried to put the key into a pocket, then realized she was still in the black dress she'd borrowed from Christina earlier that night. So instead, she tucked the key into her bra.

If this library were set up like any other, the book should be in the nonfiction fable section. Or something like that. She'd had a library science class, but that had been a while ago. She moved to the left wall and started scanning the book titles to find one that was close. She could have gone to the old-fashioned card catalog and looked it up, but she wanted to spend as little time in here as possible tonight. No random conversations with the resident ghosts if she could help it.

She saw the red book before she could read the spine. She started to reach for it but held back. The book was glowing. She poked it with one finger, and when it didn't burn or send her screaming, she gingerly picked it up. The book must have known they needed it. She hurried out of the library, closing and locking the door. When she reached the door to the apartment, she let out a long breath. The library shouldn't freak her out that bad, but it still did.

Mia hurried into the kitchen and set the book on the table where Abigail now sat, talking to her grandmother. She hung up the key and then grabbed a beer out of the fridge. She held it out to Abigail, who shook her head, and then to Grans, who took it. Mia got herself another one. "What do we know so far?"

Grans opened the red cover and found the story she was looking for in the table of contents. "From what I can see, Christina has been affected by the mitten." She pointed a finger at the bag with the single mitten. "So let's hear the story first. Then we'll know more about how we can solve this problem."

"Should I have Levi come back with Trent so he can kiss her?" Mia asked after taking a swig of the beer.

"Are you crazy? If she's cursed and he kisses her, he'll fall under the curse as well." Grans shook her head. "I blame your mother for those cute fairy tales she read to you when you were a child. I told her it would be a problem, but no, she wanted fairy princesses and handsome princes to inhabit your imagination. You would have been much more prepared with a good copy of *Grimms' Fairy Tales*. At least those were honest."

"I get it. Sleeping Beauty doesn't exist, and Cinderella is just a girl waiting to get married." Mia hated it when her grandmother ruined her favorite childhood stories.

"Well, not quite, but it will hold you until we start training again. Which I've got on January's schedule. I know you're busy with the job, but I'd like to see you Monday afternoons for at least four hours. That will get us started, but you also need to set up lab time to practice. So figure another two hours at a minimum to start." Her grandmother turned a page. "No, that spell is for cursed food, specifically apples."

Mia eyed her grandmother. "Like Snow White?"

Grans let out an exasperated sigh. "If you must trivialize our work into Saturday morning cartoons for children, yes. Like Snow White."

Mia went and poured the beer down the drain. Then she made herself a cup of coffee. It was going to be a long night. When she got back, her grandmother read aloud the story of the Christmas Mittens.

It was terrifying.

A pungent odor pulled Mia out of a dead sleep. She looked around the living room, where she'd gone to sit down just for a minute after the last verbal sparring with her grandmother. Grans could be snippy when you interrupted a date night. Mia moved Mr. Darcy off her lap and stood and stretched. As she made her way into the kitchen, she tried to get her eyes to focus. "What's going on?"

"I've found something to slow the progression. We still need to find the other mitten and back off the spell, but this should make her comfortable while we do." Grans stepped away from the stove, where a pot bubbled. It looked like neon green goop.

"You're going to get her to drink that?" Mia tried not to gag as she thought about taking the potion.

"One of the many reasons you need to train. Of course not, we're going to fill her bathtub with it and submerge most of her body in the potion. Someone will need to keep an eye on her, so I'll move in for a few days while you and Abigail find the other mitten." Grans rolled her shoulders. "She'll be in a type of coma, but it's just the potion keeping her safe. No one's expecting Christina to be anywhere for the next few days, right?"

Mia groaned. "Her mother is expecting her at a party tonight. Christina said it was a big deal and she had to promise her mom she'd be there."

"Then you'll need to attend in her place." Grans yawned. "I sent Abigail out to get the rest of the ingredients to make enough potion. Since you're awake to stir the current batch, I'm going to take a short nap until Abigail gets back. Then you can go to bed. You're going to have to drive to Boise tonight."

"I can't go in place of Christina. Mother Adams hates me," Mia called after her grandmother.

"Dear, you won't be going as you. I'll do a glamour spell. You'll look like Christina. Now, stir that pot and don't let it burn. We don't have time to do another one." Grans disappeared out of the kitchen and into the hallway to her room.

"Sure, send me to the Adamses' house undercover. You know this is a really bad idea," Mia said, but there wasn't anyone there to hear her. Except Gloria, her kitchen witch. And as it was her nature, Gloria giggled.

Mia hated when she did that.

Chapter Three

By the time Abigail returned with supplies and they woke Grans, it was two-thirty. Mia thought about just staying up, but Grans was right. If she had to drive to Boise tonight and back after the party, she needed some sleep. Grans could make up a potion to keep her awake, but she'd have to have one for the drive there and the drive back. And if it wore off before the party was over, she'd be sleeping on one of Mother Adams's fancy couches. Not a good look for Christina.

Christina and her mother were just starting to have a solid relationship. Mia didn't want to do anything to set that on the wrong path. She climbed into bed after taking off the party dress and placing it on a chair in her room. Mia closed her eyes and immediately fell asleep.

When she awoke later that morning, she heard voices out in the hallway. She got up and peeked out to see Abigail and Grans with empty buckets outside Christina's room. "Is everything okay?"

"Good, you're awake. You can help us move Christina. Just get on some old clothes. This potion can stain. We changed Christina into a white nightgown, so she should be good." Grans handed Abigail the empty bucket.

"She's going to have to throw that nightgown away

after this," Abigail said as she took the buckets back into the kitchen. "I'll be right back to help you move her."

Mia hoped it wasn't the new one that Christina had just bought, but she knew, as she got dressed, it more than likely was. She'd just have to explain that it was necessary to save her life. That should be sufficient, right?

Mr. Darcy meowed as Mia pulled on her jeans.

"Yeah, I think she's going to be mad too." She stared at the cat. "I just hope I don't make things worse when I go to her party."

Mr. Darcy shook his head like he couldn't believe all the stupid decisions the humans were making, and left her bedroom.

Mia finished getting ready and pulled her hair back into a clip.

Grans's eyes narrowed when Mia came into Christina's room. "Isn't that the sweater I got you last Christmas?"

Mia froze, looking down. She hated this sweater. Every time she tried to wear it and intentionally ruin it, the polyester blend just washed the possible stain away. Not meeting her grandmother's gaze, she hurried into the room and said, "This old thing? I don't think so. I've had it for years."

Abigail pointed to Christina's arms. "You grab the top of her. I'll get her feet. Mary Alice, you make sure we don't hit something on the way to the bathroom."

"Dorian, keep Mr. Darcy out of Christina's room for a bit. You know that cat loves her to death." Grans spoke to her ex-boyfriend, who took charge of Mr. Darcy and ran out of the room.

"Sometimes that's a little freaky," Mia admitted as she got into position. She met Abigail's gaze. "One, two, three . . ."

They lifted Christina and carried her into the bathroom.

Grans had already braided Christina's long blond hair and wrapped the braid around her head, attaching it with hair clips. Abigail dropped Christina's feet into the tub filled with green goop, and Mia gently lowered her friend's upper half into the potion. Grans pointed to Christina's shoulders. "Push those down. And put a pillow under her head. She's going to have a creaky neck once we get her out of there."

"Is this going to go down the drain, or will we have to bucket it out and dump it somewhere?" Mia pushed Christina's shoulders into the mess and then made sure her arms were under the surface.

"I guess we'll have to see. I don't think this should cause a problem." Grans didn't meet her gaze. "But that's a worry for another day. You two need to go find out what happened to that professor and see if the other mitten was with him. Christina might have just been in the wrong place when she picked up its mate."

"If Mark has it in evidence, I just say, hey, that's mine and have him give it to me?" Mia shook her head. "That's not going to happen. Anyway, why was Geoffrey out there to begin with? He had a driver. Do you think he forgot and went looking for his car?"

"In his state, you never know. I hope Mark doesn't have the mitten. I could see him thinking it's not important. Especially if it wasn't directly at the crime scene. The winds kicked up last night about the same time as the murder. Maybe it went under a car." Abigail leaned on the vanity, watching Christina. "I think her breath is less labored."

"Good, then it's working." Gran made shooing motions with her hands. "Go into the kitchen if you want to talk. Christina needs to save her energy for surviving, not listening to you guys."

Mia laid her palm on the top of Christina's head. "We're going to save you. Don't worry. Just stay alive."

Then Mia went to the kitchen, grabbing a tissue and wiping tears off her face. "The way I see it, we need to go talk to Mark Baldwin and Carl at the hotel. And I'd like to know where Frank was last night. He was supposed to be at the party. Maybe I should call him as a concerned Lodge employee."

Abigail looked at the clock. "You might want to wait until eight at least. You might wake him."

"And that's my problem, why?" Mia opened the fridge, hoping her humor didn't go undetected. Just to be safe, she added, "You're right. Let's make our game plan while I make us some omelets so we're not investigating on an empty stomach."

"And food might soak up some of the coffee I've been drinking this morning." Abigail smiled and pulled out a notepad. "One, we know the mittens were used to kill Professor Brewer."

"The mittens were used?" Mia paused chopping the peppers for the omelets. "How can a mitten kill someone?"

"I'm not exactly sure of the magic behind the mittens. Some say the curse has been around for years. Maybe back to the beginning of Magic Springs. Basically, if someone wants to use the mittens, they put them onto the victim's person. I suspect, for the unfortunate Mr. Brewer, the mittens were stuffed into the pockets of his outer coat. I bet he reached in and found the mitten we found and pulled it out. Then the other mitten did its work. He probably threw the mitten he found on the ground and walked away. You saw how far he got." Abigail stirred some hazelnut syrup into her coffee. "The mittens work fast."

"So by separating them, by taking one out of the coat and not the other one, it set off whatever spell killed Christina's professor. Then Christina picked up the mitten that was left behind and it started to kill her?" Mia focused on chopping mushrooms to put into the omelet. Maybe that's why she loved cooking so much. It didn't rely on magic to work or for her to be successful. When you believe in the existence of magic, then add in the number of witches in Magic Springs, and poof—you have random magic floating around town, just waiting to be ignited. Or if it wasn't random, a targeted spell sent to kill one person attacked someone else, who just happened to be in the crossfire. Which led to why her best friend was currently in a bathtub filled with a green protection spell.

Her life was never boring.

"Yes. That must have been what happened." Abigail met Mia's gaze. "So our first step is to find out who killed the professor. Then if we find the second mitten, we can put them together and that should stop Christina's symptoms. According to the story, the mittens have to be together so we can tell them that their work has been done. Otherwise, they'll continue to fight. And Christina will be in harm's way."

"You know how dumb that sounds." Mia dumped some of the chopped vegetables into the pan to cook.

"All the fairy tales we read to our children are based on a story told from parent to child over the years. Why do you believe in true love or the idea of a soul mate? Because a story we tell ourselves makes us believe it's true. Kids raised in magic don't question this process at all. We know that fairy tales might not be the exact truth, but they're based on a story that was always true."

Mia sighed. "Which is why Grans told me that Mom should have read me more fairy tales to keep my feet in both worlds."

"Exactly. First up, we need to find out who killed the

professor. Then we can convince the mittens that they've done their job. Otherwise, Christina won't be coming out of that coma, as each mitten will believe it has been set on a path for its owner." Abigail tapped her pen on the notepad. "Did Christina say anything about Geoffrey that might be helpful? Did he have enemies?"

"Working at a small college in a small Idaho town?" Mia stirred the onion and pepper mix, which made the kitchen smell amazing. Now, that kind of magic was the best. The aroma of food being cooked made houses feel like homes.

"Dear, we live in Magic Springs, which makes Twin Falls look like a booming metropolis. Besides, since he lived here and his wife is a coven member with magical history in her family, I'm not sure you can limit the possibility of enemies just around his job at the school."

Mia broke two eggs into a bowl and beat them with a bit of water. "Aren't you always supposed to look at the spouse in these kinds of murders? How was his relationship with his wife?"

Abigail wrote down the idea and Kate Brewer's name. "That's something else we need to discover."

Mia poured the eggs into the pan, making sure the mix of vegetables was covered. Something else was bothering her about last night. She shook her head. It didn't mean it was connected.

"I see you arguing with yourself over there. What else are you thinking? Did Christina have a fight with someone? Maybe Bethanie? Could the mittens have really been aimed at Christina?"

"I don't think so. Bethanie and Christina aren't really friends anymore. They had a falling out. Besides, why kill the professor if they really wanted Christina?" Mia was actually glad their friendship had ended. Bethanie was bad news. She let the eggs set in the pan as she thought about what she knew about the local witch. "Besides, Bethanie's out of town. She went back east to go to school after her dad was put in prison. She didn't want any reminders of him."

"That's sad." Abigail got up and took out two plates. "So we think the intended victim was Geoffrey Brewer, right?"

"I can't see it being Christina." After adding ham and cheese, Mia flipped the omelet in half and let it set for a few seconds to melt the cheese. Just a little longer. Mia worried about her friend. Grans said she'd be fine, but Mia had seen the worry in her eyes. If they didn't match up the mittens and take the curse off Christina soon, well, it wouldn't be good. She slipped the omelet onto a plate, then started a second one for Grans. She'd eat last. The most Mia could do in this moment was make sure people were fed. At least until the world woke up and they could go investigating and find whoever had hexed her friend.

She'd finished half of her omelet when the alarm went off and she saw Mark Baldwin's truck drive into her parking lot. She put the plate on the counter and hurried down to meet him at the door. The bad thing about living in a converted schoolhouse was that her apartment was located on the top floor, so she went up and down a lot of stairs during the day. The good thing about living in the schoolhouse was that on some days the trips up and down counted as her cardio workout.

She met Mark at the door. "Hey, what did you find out?"

"Not much. Sorry you had to find Professor Brewer. Do you have time to give me a statement? I need one from you, your sidekick, and Abigail Majors. I heard the three of you found him?" Mark had pulled out his notebook and was looking at his notes from a different interview.

"Actually, it was Abigail and me. Christina wasn't feeling well, so we'd left her at the edge of the canopy and went to get Abigail's SUV. I didn't feel right letting her walk out in the snow by herself." Mia knew that the security video would show all three of them leaving the area, but the bench just on the edge of the valet canopy wasn't covered by a camera. Mostly because employees liked to smoke there. She didn't need Mark pushing to talk to Christina. Especially since she was indisposed at the moment.

"Oh, I'm sorry she's under the weather. Was it a little too much champagne?" He was scribbling in his notebook.

Mia shrugged. "I'm not sure what got her, but she's still sleeping this morning. Maybe a bug?"

"Don't say that. Sarah's already got me changing clothes out on the back deck so she doesn't get any germs from the outside. She's determined to give birth to a happy and healthy baby."

"I'm sure he or she will be fine." Mia smiled at the soon-to-be mother's protections. "And you're right, Christina's not used to drinking so much. That could have been it. Who would want to kill Professor Brewer?"

Mark took off his hat, ran a hand over his thinning hair, and then put the hat back on. "Now, that is the question of the day. Is Abigail upstairs? Do you want to do this down here or in your apartment?"

"Let's do it down here. I'll go call Abigail and have her come downstairs and make us some coffee. Black, right?"

He took his hat off again and stomped the snow off his boots. "That sounds great. Should I set up over at that table?"

"That will work. I'll start coffee in my office." Mia hurried into her office and called Abigail on her cell. When she answered, she lowered her voice, hoping Mark wouldn't hear her. "Hey, can you come down? He wants to ask us some questions. I said we left Christina on the smokers' bench so she doesn't have to be interviewed."

"Smart idea. I'll be right down." Abigail hung up, and Mia finished making coffee. She heard Abigail talking to Mark as she poured him a cup. She hurried out to the living room. The several trees they'd put up for the holiday season were blinking sparkling lights. They hadn't finished the full Christmas treatment, but Trent was eager to Deck the Halls as soon as he came back into town. If it had been up to Mia, she would have left it as it was with just the trees.

Mark took a sip from the cup. "That hit the spot. Can one of you go to a different room so I can ask you questions without the other hearing? It's standard protocol."

"Of course. Abigail, do you want to go first? I need to check some supplies for the party we're catering next week anyway." Mia was glad she'd already warned Abigail about the lie she'd told on Christina's whereabouts. "I'll be in the kitchen."

"Sure. That way I can go back upstairs afterward and check on Christina. I've been so worried about her, I stayed over last night just in case Mia needed help." Abigail met Mia's gaze. Another touch point on why she was even here.

One lie always led to another. Mia just hoped the Goddess would forgive them the untruths since it was the only way to keep from talking about the cursed mittens. If she came out and told Mark that Christina was under a Sleeping Beauty spell and that Christmas mittens were trying to kill her, the Magic Springs chief of police might just take her to the station to be transported to a local mental hospital to get her thoughts right.

She unlocked the kitchen and stepped into a lushly furnished den. A woman Mia didn't recognize sat at the desk and smiled at her. Mia turned to see the kitchen door disappear and a wood door appear in its place. "What just happened?"

"Sorry for the transportation, but we're aware that Mark Baldwin is at your school, chatting with Abigail. We don't have long, so I'll get you acclimated fast. I'm Sabrina Newport. I'm head of the National Office of Regrettable Events. We're investigating the Geoffrey Brewer incident. And of course your assistant's current situation. You have the one mitten?"

"Yes, but how did I get here?" Mia felt woozy. "Are you investigating the professor's murder?"

"Yes and no. Typically, we try to stay out of witch-to-witch arguments. But since both Geoffrey and Miss Adams are human, I'm afraid we must investigate. Especially since magical items were used recklessly in the actions." Sabrina stood and walked around her desk. "I'll be arriving this evening. Hopefully we can get this all settled and the coven at Magic Springs back under cover before Monday. Otherwise, we might need to disband your coven."

"Not my coven. I'm not a member." Mia glanced around the room, which was starting to waver at the edges. "So you can help us heal Christina?"

Sabrina shrugged. "Possibly. Our primary concern, however, is to gather the mittens and take them out of circulation. If the human lives, well, that's just a bonus, right?"

"Actually, no, it's not just a bonus." Abigail now stood at the door, and Mia could see into the school's living room. The sun shone in that room behind Abigail. "We're saving Miss Adams's life. And if your investigation gets in our way, we'll fight you until she's safe. I hope you understand my meaning, Sabrina."

"Oh, I understand, Abigail." The woman appeared to shoot darts through her look at Abigail. "We just need to ask Mia some questions. If you handle this, we'll stay out of the way."

"We'll handle it. And sorry, Mia's needed here in our world. You'll have to interview her when you arrive here in person. Or if you do. When was the last time you left Italy, Sabrina? One hundred, two hundred years ago? We have airplanes now." Abigail took Mia's arm and pushed her toward the door. "I'll be right in after Sabrina and I talk. Mark's waiting for you."

As Mia moved through the doorway and back into the school, she felt a pull of energy pop between the two worlds. Blinking her eyes, she saw Mark watching her. Apparently, she didn't look like she'd materialized from another world, at least not to Mark. So that was good.

Chapter Four

That afternoon, Mia stood in her room, staring at herself in the mirror. Or more accurately, staring at Christina's reflection in the mirror. She looked exactly like her friend. She checked Christina's phone. She read off the most recent text and told Abigail and Grans the information. "Mother Adams bought Christina a new dress for the event. All I have to do is get there by six so I have time to change."

"That girl needs a new dress as much as Muffy needs a new dog toy." Grans spun Mia around to fluff her hair. "Just remember, you need to be back on the road to here by ten because your glamour is going to disappear at ten-thirty, more or less."

Mia stared at her grandmother. "And what do you mean by more or less?"

"That's why you need to be in the car and driving back here by ten. That should give you the wiggle room." Grans turned to Abigail. "Do you think she should leave earlier?"

"No, I think it will last until ten. Or even later. Just don't dawdle. You don't want to change in front of people. Christina's a size smaller than you are. You might not fit in the dress anymore." Abigail met Gran's gaze. "Shall we play some cards while we wait? Or watch a movie? I haven't seen *Practical Magic* for a while."

"You just like the midnight margarita scene." Grans smiled and reached down to pick up Muffy. Abigail had brought the little dog back with her when she'd gone to get supplies. "You better go. That woman probably has an ulterior motive for Christina being there tonight. Just be careful and don't get her stuck in some contract or dating some lawyer in Boise. I don't think Christina would appreciate that."

"Are you sure Sabrina and her gang won't be here before I'm back?" Mia glanced over to the bathroom where Christina was still sleeping in the tub of goop.

Abigail took her by the arms. "Trust us. We won't let anything happen to her. She's part of our family now too. You might not know it, but your grandmother and I are quite formidable in our magical skills. If the National Office gets here before you get home, they won't get even close to Christina. I've already talked to the coven, and they're taking our side in this as well. Christina won't be used as a pawn."

Mia swallowed hard. "Then I better go have fun at this party. Thank you."

"Christina isn't the only one that's part of the family now, Mia." Abigail kissed her on both cheeks. "Drive safe."

"And don't kick Isaac in the nether regions. I would, of course, but for some reason, Christina seems to like her brother." Grans gave Mia a hug as well. "Go get this over with."

Mia pulled on one of her own coats. She needed to be warm and covered, just in case the glamour didn't last as long as Grans had calculated.

Mr. Darcy sat at the door to Christina's bathroom and

watched them. Mia reached down and gave his head a rub. "You're in charge. Watch out for Christina."

And with that, the cat meowed and went into the bathroom. Mia glanced after him and saw he'd made a bed out of Christina's bathmat. Mr. Darcy was on the job.

Mia grabbed Christina's purse and took out the keys to her new Land Rover. She used the remote to start the engine and took a breath. "You two be good while I'm gone."

"Yes, mother," Grans replied.

For some reason, that didn't make Mia feel any more confident.

She drove the Land Rover out of town, waving at people as they waved at her. Christina must have made a lot of friends in Magic Springs, because Mia didn't know most of these people. She turned the music up as she turned onto the freeway. She had two hours and she wanted to think about who might have killed Professor Brewer. She'd gone back to the Lodge with Abigail this morning and talked to the few people who'd been there last night. But so far, according to rumors, the only one who seemed to have a motive was his wife, since he tended to have affairs. Frank's name had come up because there had been a rumor that Geoffrey was supposed to have gotten Mia's job.

Although if it was about her job, wouldn't she or Frank be the unlucky victim?

The music stopped as Christina's phone rang. Trent was calling. She told the car to answer. "How did you find me?"

"I talked to Mom and she told me your crazy plan. You're going to pretend to be Christina? You don't even know which fork to use at these fancy parties." Trent sounded grumpy.

"One, it's not a crazy plan. I couldn't tell Mother Adams

that Christina had been hit with a random mitten curse. And she couldn't not show up. They are just beginning to talk to each other." Mia pointed out all the good reasons that she should do this. "And I'll have you know, I attended my share of these dinners so I do know what fork to use."

"Okay, I'll give you the fork thing. But attending puts you in the position of not saying anything stupid to Mrs. Adams. What if Isaac says something about you? Can you keep your cool then?"

"I hope so. My plan is to dodge and weave. I'll talk to everyone I can and just avoid Isaac and his mother. Then no one will get hurt or upset." Mia sighed, glancing at Christina's face in the rearview mirror. "It might not be a great plan, but it's all I have. I don't want to mess up Christina's relationship with her mom. Speaking of parents, how's the trip going?"

"Trying to change the subject?" Trent laughed. "I don't blame you. The trip is fine. It's been nice to do things with Dad and Levi, but I think all of us really just want to be home. Dad said something about maybe coming home a day or so early."

"Well, just don't come back before we save Christina. I need your mother at the school, and I'm not sure we could explain this to someone else." Mia flipped on the turn signal and passed an older sedan going five miles under the speed limit. "While I'm playing Christina, your mom's going to call around and see if she can pick up any gossip about Brewer."

"Like if he was sleeping with his students?"

"Why would you say that?" Mia felt the frown on her face even though she couldn't see it.

"I hear rumors at the store too. Last month, a couple of his wife's friends were getting ready for a girls' night at

Kate's house and I heard them talking about poor Kate and her wandering husband. I can't believe how people talk about others in a public place. I was right there stocking wine when they were talking about a person who's supposed to be their friend and about her marriage falling apart."

"People love to talk. Especially about other people." Mia glanced at the clock on her display. "I think I timed this perfect. I shouldn't have too much time before the party starts, so I don't have to make small talk with Mother Adams."

"Just don't deck Isaac or his new girlfriend. I'm pretty sure that might blow your cover. Just think WWCD, over and over."

Mia had to think for a second, and then she laughed. "Okay, so it's all about What Would Christina Do tonight."

"And put in a good word for Levi. He thinks her mom doesn't like him," Trent added.

"He's standing next to you, isn't he?" Mia laughed. "Well, the problem is that Levi's not wrong. He's not a professional, he skis too much, and he isn't independently wealthy. I think if he fixed that last one, Mother Adams would be more open to him dating her daughter."

"I'll tell him to get right on that wealthy thing. Maybe he can invent something that everyone needs, file a patent, and then live off the royalties for the next hundred years." Trent paused. "See, I've got him thinking."

"I think he might be reconsidering his life with Christina, not how to become wealthy." She turned off the freeway at the Broadway exit. "I'm into Boise traffic. I'll call you on the way home. If you're too busy to talk, I'll understand."

"I'll be waiting to hear what the Boise upper crust is

thinking about life." He paused. "Be careful. Sometimes these glamours can drop at the worst times. If you feel woozy, get out of there."

"Warning taken." She took a deep breath. "Thanks for the support with this. I don't want to mess with Christina's life any more than I'm already doing by having her work for me."

When she hung up, she admired the Christmas lights the city had installed on the power poles lining the streets. The town was beautiful, even this section that housed the university. The stadium was lit up in blue and orange lights, a nod to the team's colors and the blue Smurf Turf on the football field. Boise was an unusual city, but most of the people were fun and easy to get along with. Except maybe the older Mr. and Mrs. Adams and their cheating son, Isaac. She drove through the collection of government buildings and then turned on Harrison Boulevard and toward the Adams house.

"How bad could one party be?" she asked aloud as she pulled her car into the driveway where a valet stood, ready to take her keys. She grabbed her tote and headed inside the house.

Mother Adams was in the living room and saw her come in. "Christina, there you are. I was worried there had been a crash on the freeway and you were going to be stuck in traffic. I told you to come earlier. We need to talk about something."

Mia paused at the bottom of the stairs, thankful that Mrs. Adams had given her a valid excuse. "Sorry, I was delayed by traffic. Is the dress in my old room? I'll run upstairs and change and come right back down. I'm sure you don't want your guests to see me like this."

Mother Adams gave Mia the look over. "You're right. Go change in your old room. I set up a guest room in there, but you have clothes and such in the closet. Tani refilled it after you moved all your stuff out."

Which you told Christina to do. But instead of reminding Christina's mother of that fact, Mia just smiled and headed upstairs. Tani must be one of the servants that worked for the Adamses. Since Christina might know her, Mia just ignored the mention. "Be back down in a jiffy."

When she reached Christina's old room, she locked the door and sank onto the bed. "Oh, Christina, I hope I do you proud tonight. If you could sit on my shoulder, that would be helpful."

In the distance, she heard laughter. Apparently, Gloria was having fun with Mia's predicament. At least someone was. Mia got dressed and then glanced in the mirror. Christina's face beamed out at her. "This is the stupidest thing I've done. You better appreciate this, missy."

Christina smiled at her. Or Mia smiled at herself. The lines were blurring a bit.

Mia took a deep breath and opened the door. She could hear people milling around downstairs. The party had started, and her countdown to leave and go home had started as well. She stepped out into the hallway and closed the bedroom door.

"Christina!" A woman grabbed her and pulled Mia into a hug. "I'm so glad you're here tonight. With everything that's going on I haven't had time to ask you, and I know it's a big ask, especially since you're friends with Mia."

Mia stepped out of the hug and stared at the woman. This had to be Isaac's new girlfriend. The woman he'd been sleeping with while they were still together. Jessica was the other woman. Mia had met her once, but she'd been so angry seeing the woman in Mia's robe, she hadn't actually looked at her. Jessica and Christina were friends, or at least friendly. Mia pasted on a smile, hoping it didn't look as fake as it felt. "Jessica, how are you? You look lovely."

"I would hope so since your brother's going to ask me to marry him tonight. Well, technically, he already did, but this is for the party." Jessica bounced in her tulle princess dress. She even had a tiara in her hair. The perfect soon-to-be daughter-in-law for Mother Adams. "I talked to your mom, and she said you'd probably say yes, but would you be my maid of honor?"

"Oh, well, of course I will." Mia hugged the other woman again. Christina was going to kill her. But she needed to bury the hatchet with her brother about the way he broke it off with Mia. And this seemed right. "I'm so happy for the two of you."

"Awesome. I was so worried. I told Isaac that you might not accept my offer. He, well, he recommended that I ask one of my friends. But we're going to be sisters forever. And that's more important, right?"

"Right." Mia glanced toward the balcony that looked over at the foyer. "Oh, people are already here. We should be mingling before dinner."

"You're right as usual. I can't believe how much I have to learn about proper etiquette." She tried to link her arm with Mia's. "Let's go."

Mia pulled back. "Actually, I just realized I forgot something. You go ahead."

"I can wait."

Mia shook her head. "Please don't. Go have fun. This is your night."

Jessica grinned and bounced toward the stairs. "You're right, of course. I guess I'm going to be saying that a lot."

Mia turned to her door, and as she opened it, a voice from the hall stopped her.

"You can't hide here forever, you know. Mom will find

you." Isaac stepped out from a corner and toward Mia. "You look amazing, little sister."

"Thanks, Isaac," Mia croaked out. "You look great yourself."

He brushed imaginary lint off the black suit. Then he looked in the direction Jessica had left the hallway. "All in a day's work. Jessica's very excited about tonight. I just needed a few minutes to step away from the sugar overload that is my future wife."

Mia smiled. Now that sounded like her Isaac. The man whom she'd fallen in love with so many years ago. He had a wicked sense of humor and didn't care what his family wanted him to do. He'd been hidden for years. "You better get used to the sweetness."

He sighed. "I will. Just give me a few seconds. Anyway, I wanted to ask you how Mia's doing? Does she like Magic Springs? How's the catering business going?"

"Mia?"

"Yeah, your boss? My ex-fiancée? I bet she's still steamed at me. But it was her own fault. She couldn't bend to Mom's wishes. And you know how persistent Mom can be." He turned his head away from Mia.

"Mia's fine. She's got a full life without you, so don't worry about it." Mia wanted to say so much more, but she also needed to pretend to be Christina. She moved toward the stairway. "Are we ready to go down?"

Isaac blocked her. "In a minute. I hear she's dating someone. He runs the grocery store. What's up with that? She's so much better than that."

Mia leaned against the doorframe. He wasn't letting this go. "Isaac, stop. It's over between you and Mia. You're announcing your engagement tonight."

He dropped his head as he stepped back, studying his

shoes. "I know. It's just, well, I miss her. She was amazing and I couldn't see it."

Mia wanted to give him a hug. Tell him she was fine. But she wasn't Mia tonight. She was Christina. And Christina wouldn't fall for this from her brother. So instead, she popped him in the arm with her fist. "Your loss, big brother. You messed up the best thing you ever had. So, I'm dying for a drink. What about you?"

As they made their way down the stairs, Mia took a big breath. Her first test was done, and she'd passed. Or at least made it through without blowing her cover. Now she just had to make it through three, maybe four more hours of torture. Christina was going to owe her big for this one. If I don't blow up Christina's life, Mia thought.

Chapter Five

As dinner progressed, the handsome man sitting next to Mia smiled. "Mrs. Adams thought we might have something in common since I have a cabin outside of Magic Springs."

"Oh, really?" Mia froze, her fork almost to the plate where what looked like a piece of fish on a small bed of mixed greens sat, waiting for her. So far, the food had been good, but served in tiny portions. Mia used to cater dinners like this, and she always was concerned that the diners hadn't been served enough calories to keep them alive. Of course, they did have their wine with dinner and then drinks afterward. Calories were calories. She turned to meet his gaze. "Where is your cabin?"

"Near where the coven holds their summer equinox celebration. But I haven't seen you at a coven meeting yet, Mia." He'd dropped his voice for the last word. He smiled as he saw her react. "I take it you didn't expect anyone from our *club* to attend tonight's gala?"

"Look, it's important for Mrs. Adams to think her daughter is here, so she is. Christina is a little tied up right now." Mia glanced around, hoping no one was listening. "I'd appreciate your cooperation."

"Of course. We'll talk more about this at the next meeting. January fifteenth at eight p.m. Can you join us?" The humor flickered in his eyes. "I'm Edward Phillips, by the way."

"Nice to meet you, Edward. Mia Malone, but you already knew that." She shook his hand and met his gaze. A tingle surged through her. She pushed back at the magic. "I'd rather you not check out my power. The glamour needs all my attention. So you're blackmailing me?"

"Sorry. Force of habit. I like to know who I'm dealing with." He held his hands up in a gesture of surrender. "A harsh word, but the intent is correct. I heard there was a problem with the Christmas mittens this year, but I didn't realize that Miss Adams was involved."

"She got caught up. Sabrina's group is on their way to handle the issue." Mia set her fork down. She glanced around at the table, but no one seemed to be watching them. She really didn't like the way this discussion was going. "I didn't realize the full coven was aware of this. Do you know anything about reversing the spell?"

"Hold on a minute." Edward wiped his mouth with his napkin and held out his hand. "Do you mind stepping into the living room with me? Too many ears in this room."

Mia paused for a second, hoping that this wasn't a trap. But she couldn't feel any negative vibes, so she nodded and stood.

Mother Adams frowned at her from her spot at the front of the table. "Christina, dinner isn't over."

"I know, but we'll be right back." She smiled and dropped her head. "Excuse us a minute. We've got to check on something."

As they walked out of the dining room, Isaac grinned at her and made a thumbs-up sign. Mia sighed. She leaned into Edward. "Please don't expect Christina to follow up on this fake interest. She's dating . . ."

"Levi Majors, I know. I told her mother that as well, but sometimes a little money can change a heart." He paused in the middle of the hallway where they were out of sight of the guests in the dining room. "Look, the mittens are powerful. And until you can find the other one, I'm afraid Miss Adams is in danger. The mitten thinks it's fulfilling a mission. Even though Mr. Brewer is already dead."

"Yeah, I know that." Mia pressed her lips together. "And rumors on why Geoffrey was killed?"

"The rumors going around in the coven are all focused on his inability to be faithful." Edward leaned on what was probably a really expensive side table.

Mia sighed. "So his wife killed him?"

Now Edward looked wary. "I don't think so. Kate is solid. She's served as coven leader before as well as on the board. She runs her own company. Besides, she has her own dalliances. I'm not sure she can get jealous. She stays, or stayed, married to Geoffrey because she liked having a home base. Someone to share her life with. She wasn't into monogamy."

"Okay, so now I have only one suspect—my boss." Mia blew out a breath. "We better get back to dinner before Christina's mom comes out to find us. She runs a tight ship, even with her parties."

Edward put a hand up to stop her from moving. "And I'll see you on the fifteenth?"

She nodded. "If you keep my secret, yes."

Mother Adams met her gaze as they came back into the dining room. Mia's plate was gone, and now there was a small bowl of noodles with several colorful chopped peppers on the top. Apparently, a new course waited for no one. She slipped into her chair and took a bite of the noodles. The dish was good. But before she left town to drive back to Magic Springs tonight, she was stopping and getting fast food. A big juicy burger would fill the empty hole in her stomach from not eating since breakfast.

After dinner, Isaac and Jessica did their dog and pony show, everyone clapped, and champagne was passed out on trays as quickly as possible. After the toast, she turned to Edward. "Thank you for the lovely dinner conversation. I'm heading back to Magic Springs tonight. Do you need a ride?"

"I'm staying in town for the holiday. Thanks for the offer though. It was nice to meet you." He leaned down and brushed his lips against hers. Then he leaned into her to whisper, "Tell Trent *and* Levi it was all an act. I'd hate to have both brothers mad at me for just one kiss."

"It was nice to meet you, Edward. And thanks for the information. If you hear anything else that might be useful, call me. We're running out of time." Mia saw Christina's face in the mirror over the fireplace watching her and Edward. "I don't want to lose her."

"She's very lovely." Edward squeezed her hand. "Thanks for making this setup less awkward."

"Well, since I'm not who you were set up to meet, I think that eases the awkwardness." Mia said good night and headed toward the stairs so she could go upstairs to change. She needed to get home and find that other mitten. Mother Adams blocked her way as she approached the stairwell. "Good evening, Mother. I've got to run. I've got a lab tomorrow."

"On a Sunday?" Mother Adams's eyes narrowed as she focused on her daughter.

Mia nodded. "It's a makeup. The professor was sick last week, so we have this lab on Sunday. Sorry, it was last minute or I would have loved to stay. Edward was very nice."

"He's from a good family and he's looking for a wife to start a family with." She spoke under her breath. "You should stay and become better acquainted."

"Mom, you know I'm dating Levi." Mia hoped Christina had made this clear or there was going to be a lot of points Christina had to clean up. "Edward is lovely, but I'm in a relationship."

"You may not be in a relationship for long. You go through men like candy. Edward is very eligible," Mother Adams repeated.

The one thing about Mother Adams was she was determined. And stubborn. But Mia was as well. She leaned over and gave her a kiss on the cheek. "I appreciate you trying to look out for me. We've come a long way, right? But right now I need to get back to Magic Springs and get some sleep before this test tomorrow."

Mother Adams's eyes narrowed. "I thought you said it was a lab, not a test."

"Oh, that's what I meant. A test. See, I'm so tired I'm mixing up words." Mia started up the stairs.

"Christina?" Mother Adams stopped Mia on the second step.

Mia turned around and tried to smile. "Yes?"

"Please be careful driving back. You have a lot to live for." Mother Adams smiled at the image of her only daughter, then turned and engaged a guest in a conversation that seemed to be about the woman's dress.

Once in her room, Mia leaned against the doorway after she locked it. Tonight hadn't gone exactly as she'd planned, but she'd learned one thing. Kate Brewer hadn't killed her husband because he was sleeping around. So why had he been killed? Maybe one of the women he'd been sleeping with had done the deed because he wouldn't leave his wife.

Maybes. Those were all she seemed to have right now. But she needed to get changed and out of here.

With the dress back in the bag, she hurried down the servant stairway and out to where the valets were all hanging out. She handed one the ticket she'd been given when she'd come to the Adamses' house. "I need my car."

"Not a problem. I'll have it out front in a few minutes. You can wait here or out front." He glanced at the box that held the keys and took out the set she'd handed him a few hours before. Mia made her way to the front door, avoiding the party at every turn. Then she sank onto a bench near the driveway to wait.

"A penny for your thoughts." Isaac sat down next to her.

"I'm not sure they're worth even that." Mia smiled at him. "I've got a makeup test tomorrow. I need to get back or I would have hung out longer. Congratulations on finding the one."

He leaned back and sighed. "Sis, that's the problem. I think I met 'the one' years ago and let her go because of Mom."

"Isaac, Mia's happy now." It felt weird talking about herself in the third person.

He nodded his head. "And I'm happy for her. I just don't want to sit and watch you make the same mistake. If you love this EMT guy, stand your ground. I'll support you."

Christina's Land Rover pulled up and the valet left it running, the door open. Mia stood up and gave Isaac a hug. "I'm so glad you're finding your way in the world. You're really a nice guy when you don't let your mother influence you."

He kissed her on the cheek, squeezing her arms. "You mean our mother, right? Mia used to say the same thing to me."

Mia froze. Was her glamour slipping, or was it just her words that were not framed right? "Yeah, our mom. Seriously, I need to get home. I'm beat. I'll be jamming out to Heart all the way home."

"You're taking on Mia's musical tastes as well." He walked her to the car and waited while she climbed inside. "You're really growing up, sis. I'm proud of you."

Mia smiled as she put on her seat belt. "Thanks, Isaac."

He shut the door, but he stood there, a frown on his face. He moved to reopen it as he appeared to have made a decision, but before he could, Mia pulled the car out to Harrison Boulevard. She needed to get away from Isaac before he realized who he was actually talking to. And from the look on his face, that realization was close. In her rearview mirror, she saw Jessica come out and put her arm around him, dragging him back to the party.

It was too bad that Christina hadn't heard the nice things her mom and Isaac had said about her. But Mia would make sure she told her friend. Just as soon as they could safely wake her up from her induced beauty sleep. That wording sounded so much better than a coma.

She found a hamburger place and ordered a meal with large fries and a large Coke. The caffeine in that should keep her awake for the two-hour drive home. She scarfed down the hamburger in the parking lot, then set the French fries in the cup holder next to the soda. She was ready for her road trip.

Her phone rang just after she got on the freeway. She'd plugged it into Christina's sound system in the Land Rover. It was Trent. "Great timing. I'm heading home."

"I know. I've been tracking you since you reached the Adamses' house," he admitted. "You seriously needed to get food after having dinner?"

"You should have seen what Mother Adams served. I

can't believe anyone can survive on food like that." Mia grabbed a couple of fries while they were still hot.

"That's why they're always so slim. They don't eat. Now me, I like a good fourteen-ounce steak and baked potato when I go out. Not a sliver of fish and a half cup of noodles."

Mia wondered just how detailed Trent's tracking spell had been. "I'm thinking you've been watching me. Doesn't the lodge you're staying in have cable?"

"Watching you is more entertaining. So you're going to attend a coven meeting?"

She grabbed more fries. Trent was frustrating. "You need to stop watching me. It's creepy."

"I don't do it normally. I was just concerned about you pretending to be Christina. I wasn't sure you could hold up the glamour. I wanted to give you an out by calling you if it started to slip."

"Sure, all the stalker boyfriends say that." She turned up the heat. The roads were clear since they hadn't had any snow for a few days, but the temperature was bitter cold and dropping as the night got settled over the valley. From Boise to the road that took her up the mountain, the terrain was desert. Not something people thought of when they imagined Idaho. But that was why the potatoes grew so well. The arid climate. And the canal system of irrigation farmers had implemented years ago. "Have you heard from your mom? The guy Mother Adams set me up with doesn't think Kate Brewer had anything to do with her husband's death."

"I relayed that information. Or actually, Levi did. Edward was very forthcoming about the murder and the Brewers' marriage, don't you think?"

Mia nodded. She'd been thinking the same thing. "He offered up the information quickly. I know the coven wants Grans and me to join, but Edward seemed ready to make a quick exchange. And yet he seemed surprised to hear about the upcoming visit from Sabrina and the National Office of Regrettable Events."

"Mom said he's part of the membership committee, so it could be they've been watching you and trying to gain an edge. Otherwise, well, she's doing a deep dive into him and seeing what his relationship was to Geoffrey and Kate."

"Good. At least we got more information tonight. It wasn't a total waste of my time. Has Abigail said anything about Christina? Is she okay?" Mia could see Christina in the bathtub covered with goop, and it made her shiver. Or something did. She looked in the rearview mirror and her own eyes looked back at her. The glamour was wearing off. She still had Christina's blond hair, but her own face looked back at her. At least if she got pulled over, she'd have a correct driver's license.

"Don't worry. Mom says she's fine. Your grandmother is watching her. Just get home safe. You've had a long day." He paused for a minute. "Do you want to talk about Isaac?"

Mia laughed. "I guess you got more than you expected when you listened in, didn't you?"

Trent took in a breath. "He's missing you."

"I never expected him to say any of that. Either to me or Christina. Maybe he's just getting cold feet. You know the grass is always greener. Jessica is nice. Not too bright, from what I've seen. She *is* dating Isaac. But maybe that's what Isaac needed." Mia thought about her ex-fiancé.

"Remember *you* dated Isaac. In fact, you were planning on marrying him," Trent reminded her with a chuckle.

"I've never said I was smart. Especially when it comes to men," Mia shot back, a smile on her face.

"Ouch, that hurt." He laughed, and then the conversation stalled. Finally, he said, "I know you're worried about Christina. We'll figure this out. Should I come home early?"

Mia sighed as she focused on the road. "Not yet. I don't think we're at the point of throwing everything we have at her to try to save her, but it may come to that."

"Have you thought about the Sleeping Beauty cure?"

Mia shook her head. "Grans says that's a fairy tale. I already asked about bringing back Levi."

"Your grandmother isn't correct. It's worked before, but it is a long shot. I'm not sure the power of love is enough to break the hold the mitten has on her. Our best bet is to reunite the mittens."

"That's your mother's take too. I'll go to the Lodge tomorrow. I need to chat with Frank and see why he wasn't at the party. I'm wondering about his connections to Geoffrey. A lot of the hotel staff seemed convinced that Geoffrey was going to have my job." Mia nodded, thinking about her less-than-friendly boss. "And we all know Frank loves to talk."

"Well, I'll leave that interview to you. I'd rather not chat with Frank Hines. I'd have to say a few things that might get you fired." Trent murmured something she couldn't hear. "Sorry, Levi just came in. Dad wants to head down to the bar and talk."

"Sounds fun." Mia knew that the older Majors was trying to bond with his sons. Thomas had been busy with work for years, and when he retired, he'd focused on building up this hunting and fishing guide business. Now with Abigail working, he needed to fill some empty hours so he'd turned to his sons. She just hoped the family bonding time wasn't too late. "I'll talk with you tomorrow. Stop tracking me."

"I will as soon as you pull into the school's parking lot,"

he promised. "I want to know if you fall asleep at the wheel."

"Lovely thought." Mia took another handful of fries. "Anyway, I'm turning on a podcast about food and heading home. Have a good night."

As she drove east toward home, she thought about the man she'd met at Mother Adams's party. Had it been a coincidence that she'd found someone for Christina who lived in Magic Springs? Or had the coven just found another inlet into Mia's life that they thought might push her into joining the coven?

She turned off worrying and focused on the podcast that was highlighting appetizers for parties. Now this was a subject that could keep her awake as she drove. And, bonus, there was a second podcast loaded on January comfort food that would take her all the way to her doorstep.

Chapter Six

Sunday morning, Mia checked on Christina before she made coffee. The girl looked like she was sleeping, but a worry line creased between her eyes.

"She's been dreaming," Grans said from behind Mia. She came around and moved Christina's arm back into the green goop. "And from what I've seen, they're not pleasant dreams. It's a side effect from being under so long. All her negative thoughts are cramming in since there's no conscious self to control them. I'm afraid if we keep her under too long, we might not get back the same Christina."

Mia couldn't bear the thought of not having her friend back. "What if we played music? Or turned on a movie?"

Abigail had joined them. "I think it's time for some romance and Christmas movies. Help me move her television in here. She'll get a dose of happy while she sleeps."

"If this ever happens to me, don't subject me to that. Turn on some music and I'll be fine," Grans grumbled as she cleaned a spot on the counter. "I don't need to be thinking there's some prince out there to save me."

Abigail squealed as she set the television down on the counter. "You're so smart, Mary Alice."

"What did I say now?" Grans looked at Mia like she might know.

"If we can't find the mitten, infusing her with happily-ever-after movies might give more power to the Sleeping Beauty cure," Abigail explained as she plugged the television in. She turned it on and found the correct channel. "Operation Saved by Love has begun."

"We need to keep all men out of this bathroom," Grans warned as she met Abigail and Mia's gaze. "She'll imprint on whoever comes into the room."

"Don't tell Mother Adams that. She'll send Edward to save her." Mia squeezed her friend's hand.

"I'll make a sign for the door. Do not enter. Sewer leakage. That should scare anyone away." Abigail giggled.

"Just don't let Mark Baldwin in here. Sarah would kill Christina if she went after him," Mia added.

"If you two don't stop, she's going to imprint on someone without the guy being present. No talking about men near her. At all." Grans pushed the other two women out of the bathroom. "Now go make us some breakfast. I'm starving. And since I was up most of the night, I'm going to take a nap while you two go hunting for clues today."

Mia paused in the hallway. "Will she be okay while you nap?"

"Oh, yes, the danger is in the first twenty-four hours. Now that we're past that, she'll be safe in the goop. It's learned what she needs." Grans went to the fridge and took out a soda. "I need some quick sugar to keep myself awake while you cook. Then I'm crashing. Don't wake me unless it's completely unavoidable."

After breakfast, and after Mia and Abigail had checked on Christina one more time, they left the apartment. Mr. Darcy and Dorian were on watch in the living room, and Mia heard the television go on after she'd locked the door.

"What are they watching?" Abigail asked as they went down the stairs.

"I'm thinking it's a version of *A Christmas Carol*. They've found all kinds of remakes I didn't know existed. Dorian sure loves that story." Mia smiled as she went outside. "If you would have told me a year ago that my cat would be watching television with a witch soul that shared his body, I would have run away from you screaming. Now, we discuss their likes and dislikes as if it's the most normal thing in the world."

Abigail unlocked her SUV, which had been warming up in the parking lot. "Not the world, maybe. But this is Magic Springs. I take it we're going to the Lodge first?"

"Yes, and then to the Brewers' house. And maybe coven headquarters. Will anyone be there? At least in the library?" Mia climbed into the front seat and sighed. Abigail had also turned on the heated seats. She'd used them last night when she drove Christina's Land Rover. Her old van barely had seat belts. She really needed a new car.

"I didn't think you used the coven library." Abigail drove out of the school parking lot.

Mia shrugged. "I tried not to use it. But this seems to be an emergency. And, since I already agreed to attend a meeting, I might as well use that promise to my advantage. I can always say no later."

"You might rethink that when you see their library. It's glorious. Many witches have joined the coven just for the advantage of studying in the library. It's said to have volumes from before the colonies were settled." Abigail turned to look at her. "Being a coven member isn't always a bad thing."

"I know. But I like my independence. And then there's the Trent thing. We both know that the coven wouldn't like my dating him, and it might even uncover his secret. I don't want to be the one that outs him." She studied Abigail. "I suspect that's one of the reasons you and Thomas haven't been active in coven activities lately."

Abigail nodded. "The less said about that issue, the better. But you're right. It would be an issue. I've heard unofficial talk about you hopefully marrying into one of the more powerful families who are in one of the eastern covens. They believe that type of union might strengthen all covens. Kind of a super witch from your offspring."

"Now, see, that's why I don't join groups. I'm not just committing my time and effort, but now they want to bring my unborn kids into the discussion. And what if I don't love this witch from the arranged marriage they want to set up? Or I don't want to have kids? No one asks the woman what she wants to do." Mia shook her head, trying to tamp down her anger. "This library better be worth all the hassle. I'm not even a member and I'm upset at the coven leadership for something that they haven't done to me yet."

"I know you love Trent. But when you get involved in world affairs, sometimes they can skew your decisions." Abigail parked the car in the Lodge lot. She turned off the engine and turned toward Mia. "I suspect they're going to appeal to your love of humanity. There has been a lot of talk lately about our kind dying out. Fewer witches have been joining covens all over the world. They think it's because there are fewer witches. I believe, like you, the others are choosing not to be a part of an antiquated system that isn't in their best interest."

"Well, that's a heavy conversation for a morning ride. So why don't we shelve that problem and go find a killer so I can save my best friend's life." Mia squeezed Abigail's arm. "After that, we'll grab some tea and talk about saving the witching world."

"I love how you think. You go talk to your boss and I'm going to chat with the front desk staff. They always know everything that's going on in a hotel." Abigail climbed out of the SUV and met Mia on the sidewalk.

When they got inside, Mia went one way, Abigail the other. Mia saw her lean on the front desk and start to chat with a young man who was working on the computer. If anyone could charm information out of someone, it was Abigail. Mia went down a staff hallway and knocked on Frank's door.

"Come in," his gruff voice answered.

Mia walked into the stuffy room filled with notebooks. The prior Lodge manager had been in the middle of a history project on the Lodge's many guests. Frank had been here almost one year and still hadn't decided what to do with all the notebooks. He nodded to the one chair that wasn't filled with binders. "Mia, I'm glad you stopped by. I wanted an unbiased report on the catering for the staff party. I've heard some complaints."

"The food was awful," Mia said flatly as she sat down. "You should have either let the kitchen do it or hired my old company. I would have given you a discount."

"Okay, I get it. I'm sure your evaluation is a little self-serving, but it matches all the complaint calls and notes I've gotten over the past two days." He held up a pile of comment cards. "And then that guy dies after attending the party. I'm just hoping the coroner's cause of death isn't food poisoning. That would be embarrassing. Of course, since we didn't cook the food, the catering company would be on the hook, not us."

"Well, that *is* a bright side of the whole death thing." Mia leaned back in her chair. Frank was a tool. "I didn't see you at the party."

"No, I stayed away. I didn't want to run into Rebecca.

We kind of broke up at the beginning of the month. She asked about exchanging gifts and I told her that me giving her company the staff party contract was her gift. I guess she was expecting more." He threw the comment cards in the wastebasket. "At least I don't have to make that mistake again. I have the Lodge's reputation to uphold."

"Yes, that's important." Mia saw this wasn't going anywhere. Frank hadn't been at the party because he was hiding from his ex-girlfriend. Nothing there. She started to stand but thought of one more question Frank might have the answer to. "Hey, do you know why Professor Brewer was even at the event? Was he related to someone who worked here?"

Frank leaned forward, and Mia didn't like his smile. It was the kind that evil villains wore when they were divulging a secret in a movie. "He wasn't related to anyone. He was sleeping with one of the cooks on day shift. Tasha Alberts. She's the blonde."

Like that would make her stand out. Most of the kitchen staff wore head coverings. At least when Mia saw them. But then she remembered the bombshell from the party that had been talking to the professor before he came over to greet Christina. She'd been in a red dress and looked like one of the Lodge's guests, not a staff member. "Oh, her?"

"Yeah, I heard she went all out for the party. Marilyn Monroe red dress and all." Frank leaned back in his chair. "I might have to fire her so I can ask her out on a date. Especially now that Geoffrey's out of the way."

"That's a little self-centered. You need to be careful. People will start thinking you killed Geoffrey if you start dating her too soon." Mia hoped by pointing this out, Frank wouldn't go and fire the grieving girlfriend. But he had given her some more information she hadn't had yesterday. And it matched what Edward had told her—the Brewers had an open marriage. "Hey, was Professor Brewer up for the catering director position when I got it?"

Frank picked up a stack of papers and straightened the stack. He looked a little pale. "He was one of the candidates, yes."

"So why did you pick me?" Mia leaned forward, wondering if he'd be honest.

Frank shrugged. "Geoffrey came with baggage. I would have had to listen to his stupid stories about his big house and wealthy wife. I had enough of that crap from him when we were in college. It's hard to be a scholarship kid at an Ivy League school."

"Okay, then." Mia thought it was mostly the truth. She also knew that Geoffrey would probably have demanded a higher salary, even though Mia had more experience. "I'll see you later this week."

As she went to find Abigail, she wondered which explanation would be more unbelievable to the town's conservative police chief—the fact that the couple had ties to the witching part of the community or that they weren't monogamous. Knowing the strength with which Mark loved his wife, Sarah, Mia thought the open marriage might be more unbelievable for him.

But it was a motive that he could understand and prove in a human court of law. Mia walked by the kitchen and wondered if Tasha Alberts was working. She went into the kitchen, and it was nearly deserted.

"You missed the madhouse this place was an hour ago." James came out of his office and greeted her with a quick hug. "You really should come to the Sunday buffet team breakfast. You'd love hearing the staff talk about the week and its share of weirdness. Did you know there was a couple staying here that only ate raw food? Including fish. Of course, that didn't stop them from drinking their weight in wine. Sometimes people are strange."

"Everyone has their own path." Mia glanced around the empty kitchen. "I was hoping to talk to Tasha Alberts."

"Well, that's going to be a problem. She emailed me her resignation this morning. No reason, just an address in Boise to send her final check. I'd heard she was involved with the guy who was killed in the parking lot. Maybe she was just too upset to continue working here." James held up the printout he had brought out of his office. "I was just heading over to drop this into payroll's box."

"Can I look at her address?" Mia got out her phone to take a picture. Thinking quickly, she added, "I'd like to send her a sympathy card."

"Of course. You're part of the team now, aren't you. Sending her a card is a good idea. I'll have the kitchen staff sign one as well. Unless you think it should be all on one?" James handed over the paper.

"Oh, I think several cards would be nice." Mia felt bad about lying to him, but now she'd have to go and actually get a sympathy card to mail. "It must have been a huge shock."

"I hate passing on gossip." James paused and then laughed. "Okay, that's not true, I love talking gossip. Anyway, one of my sous chefs told me that Tasha was trying to talk that guy into leaving his wife and running off with her. She was deeply in love. At least, that's the rumor. And now with her leaving—"

"The story is proving to be true." Mia finished his story. She pointed to the phone number. "I can reach her there, if I wanted to call and tell her how sorry I was?"

He peered at the number. Then he pulled out his phone. "That's not the one I have. I'll write it here on the page and you can take another picture. Payroll might need it as well." He wrote the number down, then handed back the page.

"Thanks, James. I need to go. Christina isn't feeling well." She snapped a picture, then checked it before she left just to make sure she could read it.

"I heard she was under the weather. I hope she didn't get food poisoning. That caterer Frank hired was the worst. I can't believe she's even in the business." James opened the door to the hallway. "I'll see you tomorrow for the staff meeting?"

"I'm looking forward to it." She went through the doorway and paused.

"And you're a bad liar." James gave her air kisses and headed away from the lobby.

She watched him for a minute, then headed out to find Abigail. James was good people. He'd come to the job from Arizona, but he loved the four seasons and he'd stayed. Mia hoped that working for Frank wouldn't run him off. A strong kitchen manager chef like James had his choice of jobs any time he wanted a different one. She couldn't imagine working for the Lodge without James around. He was her rock here.

Abigail was sitting in the lobby, chatting with a woman Mia didn't recognize. Abigail stood as soon as she noticed Mia coming toward them. Mia watched as she said a quick goodbye, and Abigail hurried over to meet Mia. "Ready to go then?"

"Sure. So who was that?" She nodded to the woman who was now heading toward the elevators. She wasn't on staff. At least not anyone whom she knew.

"Oh, just an old friend. I hadn't seen her in ages. We went to school together and she's home visiting family. It's the holidays. You never know who you'll run into." Abigail started out to her SUV, starting it as she talked about the rumors from the front desk. It matched what James had told her about Tasha being hopelessly in love with the cad, Geoffrey. Abigail leaned out the window to chat as she dropped Mia off at the house. She needed to run home to water her plants and to grab some clean clothes. "I'll pick you up at one. I made us an appointment with Mrs. Brewer at one-thirty. She told her secretary to be expecting my call. I'm not sure how they knew."

"I'm thinking Edward." Mia thought a lot about the man who'd come to meet her in Boise. He'd had to know she was standing in for Christina if he was tied into the coven. She assumed everyone here knew about Christina's run-in with the Christmas mittens. She told Abigail that she'd be downstairs waiting when she returned, and then closed the door. She was already halfway upstairs when she realized Abigail hadn't told her the name of the woman she'd gone to school with.

Had that been an oversight? Or was Abigail hiding something from her?

She went into the apartment and decided to do some laundry while she waited. She wasn't hungry, since they'd just eaten. Instead she found herself sitting at the table, her laptop open. She started searching for information on Geoffrey and Kate.

And she found the mother lode.

The local paper had devoted the entire front page to the death and the couple's life. She was still reading when she saw Abigail pull back into the parking lot. She checked her watch. It was time to go chat with the source—Kate Brewer.

Chapter Seven

The "small" second home the Brewers kept in Sun Valley was the size of the school but a lot nicer. Mia estimated that it must be over five thousand square feet as they parked in front of the house, which looked a lot like a Swiss ski chalet. Abigail leaned up to get the full effect of the glass-covered front.

"I'd hate to have to wash those windows." Abigail took her arm as they made their way to the oversized front door. "Of course, Thomas hires out washing our windows, so I guess that's no different."

"Thomas spoils you." Mia took in the dark wood and stone building. The windows lightened it, but the effect was dazzling, especially in the sunlight. "Just think, if I hadn't jumped at saving the school, I could have owned a miniature version of this. Okay, maybe not this, but a small cottage on a mountain somewhere. Probably across the mountain ridge from Magic Springs."

"You love the school, I can tell." Abigail reached out and pushed the doorbell. "And when you decide to settle down, you can rent out that apartment for a nice chunk of your mortgage."

"Or I might just stay an old maid and keep the apartment," Mia teased.

Abigail shrugged. "I'm not sure my son's going to let that happen."

The door latch buzzed, and the door unlocked. The door cracked open a tiny bit. They heard a woman's voice on the intercom. "Come down the hall to your left. I'm in the sunroom."

"Okay, thank you." Mia felt weird trying to explain why they were there, but she wasn't being listened to. The monitor showed a red light on the top. She turned to Abigail. "Let's go find the woman behind the curtain."

"Nice twist on a *Wizard of Oz* theme." Abigail took in a breath. "This isn't intimidating at all. We can do this."

"She's a grieving widow, not a supervillain," Mia reminded herself as they wandered through the house, finally landing in the small room that had three walls of windows. Topiary lined the outside windows that looked out on the mountain range. "Beautiful day outside," she said to the woman who sat on the bench, watching them approach.

"I haven't noticed." The woman stood. Mia took in her first glimpse of Kate Brewer. Her platinum blond hair was pulled back into a clip. She had on a black shift dress and black tights and shoes. Her face was devoid of makeup, and the only piece of jewelry she wore was a large diamond set in a platinum ring on her left hand. "I'm sorry for not greeting you. I don't seem to have much energy."

"We're sorry to bother you at such a sad time." Abigail stepped closer. "I'm Abigail Majors, and this is Mia Malone."

"The coven told me you two would be looking into Geoffrey's death. You don't think this has anything to do with magic, do you?" Her eyes were gray, but they weren't as sedate as her outfit. Instead, they were bright and watchful.

"We don't know. My friend, she picked up a mitten. We need to find its mate. You didn't find anything like that in your husband's effects, did you?"

"The Christmas mittens? They were in play that night?" Kate covered her mouth with her hand. "I know about them, of course. Everyone does. But I've never known anyone to have been killed with the mittens."

Mia took out her phone and showed Kate a picture of the mitten. "Have you seen one of these? We really need to find one to save my friend."

Kate took the phone and barely glanced at it. She shook her head. "Sorry, I haven't seen it. The local police haven't turned over Geoffrey's personal items yet. The issue of the murder is holding everything up. I don't even know when I'll be able to plan a funeral."

"I'm sorry." Mia glanced at Abigail, who gently shook her head. Mia decided to ignore her friend's nonverbal advice. "Can we ask you a few questions?"

"If you think it might help, please. I loved my husband. I didn't want him dead. No matter what you might hear." Fire burned in those gray eyes, and Mia wondered if Kate had known about the affair. It didn't seem to be as open of a marriage as people had gossiped about.

"You weren't at the party on Friday," Mia started.

Kate held up a hand. "Look, I want to be up front with you. I knew about the affair. I didn't approve or appreciate it, but Geoffrey told me he was shutting it down. In fact, he told me he was going to do it Friday night. He wanted to talk to her in a public place. I guess she could get very physical and had distracted him several times when he'd tried to end the relationship."

Mia pressed her lips together. If a man wanted to end a relationship, he couldn't be tempted back into keeping it going. If he was determined. But she wasn't going to talk bad about a dead man. "Geoffrey went to the party to end the affair."

"Yes. He texted me about seven saying it was over. I got on a plane and came here to meet him for the week. I told him that until that situation was handled, I was staying in California. I arrived about two that morning, and the police met my plane at the airport to tell me about Geoffrey." She looked around the room. "I've been here since then. I can't seem to make plans to go back to California. I suppose I'll sell the house now. I just don't know."

"I've heard that you shouldn't make any decisions, or big decisions about your life, for a year after something like this happens. You need to give yourself time to heal. Then you can make a decision that you won't regret later." Mia glanced at Abigail, who shook her head again. Then Mia took a business card out of her purse. "I guess we're out of here then. If you hear anything about the mitten, would you call me?"

"Of course. I really hope you find it in time. Your friend, she's human, correct?" Kate stood as the other two women did.

"She is. I almost married her brother. We're really close." Mia smiled at a memory of Christina in high school when Mia had helped her pick out school clothes. Mother Adams hadn't liked any of the outfits and had taken Christina to New York the next weekend to shop again. "Thank you again for talking to us. I'm sorry for your loss."

"I think I'm staying here for a while," Kate said, sitting back down. "Can you show yourselves out?"

"Of course. Please take care of yourself." Abigail brushed her hand against Kate's shoulder.

As they walked away, Mia could hear Kate's gentle sobs behind them. When they got into the car, she turned to look at Abigail. "Well, that wasn't what I expected. She's truly grieving."

Abigail nodded. "I guess that doesn't prevent her having something to do with her husband's death, but I don't see it. She loved him."

"Or she's the best actress I know." Mia leaned against the seat. "The problem is, we aren't any closer to finding the mitten and curing Christina."

"Then let's go back to the scene of the crime. Maybe we can find something there that Baldwin's men overlooked. It's at least doing something. I can't just sit there while Christina's in that goop in the next room."

"Sounds like a plan." Mia needed time to think about what she'd learned. There was something that she'd heard that didn't ring true. Was it Kate's pronounced love for her husband? Or something else?

All she knew was she had a whopper of a headache.

When they got to the Lodge, Abigail parked out at the edge of the parking lot. A pile of snow was stacked next to where she parked. She pointed to the snow that a snowplow had dumped after scraping the parking lot. "If it's in there we won't find it until spring when everything melts."

"That's too late." Mia climbed out of the SUV and glared at the pile of snow.

Abigail pulled on her gloves. "Let's walk around it, just in case. If you see something red or silver, let me know. I'm going to do a locator spell, just to try. I'm not sure it will work, but what do we have to lose?"

Mia watched as Abigail waved her hands in a specific pattern and then repeated the sequence. Then she spoke words that Mia would have sworn were made up. Then that process was repeated. Mia couldn't see any change, but her knowledge of spell casting was limited. "I can't tell. Any results?"

Abigail sighed and shook her head. "The good news is that the mitten isn't in the snowbank. If it was, I would have had some kind of reaction. I got nothing."

"Okay, so that's good news?" Mia was confused.

Abigail nodded and put her hands in her pockets. "It is."

Mia nodded. "So we don't have to be digging in the snow or wait until spring."

"Exactly. Now we have to scan the parking lot, but don't think that magic is going to give you the exact location. We'll need to do our own footwork. It makes the journey more rewarding when you put some elbow grease in the mix."

"Okay, so now I feel so much better. As long as I work hard, we'll find the killer?" Mia pulled on her own gloves. This was going to be cold work. They'd be frozen stiff by the time they were done.

"The Goddess rewards hard work," Abigail said cheerfully.

Mia tried to keep an open mind, but sometimes Trent's mom got a little on her nerves. Especially since she'd been running Mia's company for the last few months. "That's what I hear."

Abigail paused, staring at her. "You don't believe that hard work is the answer?"

"Maybe." Mia started scanning a section of the parking lot. "I just think we make our own destiny."

"I'm not saying anything different. You're just hearing a difference." Abigail pointed to a small section of parking behind a power grid. "I'll head over there to check out that area."

"I'll take the left side and walk up and down the length of the lot." She held up her phone. "Call me if you need me."

"Will do." Abigail went over to the middle line and started slowly walking. Mia could feel that she had her magic pushed up to be sensitive to the mittens.

Mia headed over to the left side and plotted out her walking grid. She'd start in the farthest row. She might have to go wading into the snow later, but for now they'd start with the paved and scraped lot. This way, her feet wouldn't be too frozen before they called it quits.

Mia curled her fingers around the cup of soup that Grans had given her when they'd arrived back at the school. The search of the parking lot had come up empty. Nothing. Not a piece of frozen paper pointing a finger at a possible killer. No smoking gun. And worst of all, no mitten to match up with the one that was in Mia's bedroom safe.

They put off going to coven headquarters. Time for Christina was running out. Mia needed to find that second mitten.

Grans had made them all soup and sandwiches to stave off the cold when they came back to the school. Mia watched as her grandmother sipped the tomato bisque. She looked as tired as Mia felt. The spell keeping Christina alive must be affecting Grans's energy level.

"Robert came by today," Grans said as she set the soup cup down.

Mia froze. They'd been working on increasing Christina's acceptance of a Sleeping Beauty cure. The only man that needed to be here was Levi. Her one true love. At least that's what Mia hoped was true. Sometimes love took a while to find. Look at her. "But . . ."

Grans held up her hand before Mia could go on. "Don't worry, I talked to him downstairs on the front steps. Anyway, he said the coven is working on a counter curse for

Christina as well. It's unusual, but several members have reached out supporting our request for help."

"Several members?" Abigail narrowed her eyes as she set down her soup cup. "I sent in a request, but who else?"

"Robert said he did this morning, but he was told they were already working on it." Grans nodded at Abigail's surprise. "Yes, I thought it was weird as well. Robert did too, so he asked who else had contacted the coven. They said it was confidential, but the woman told him that we had Kate to thank for moving this up the ladder so quickly. I guess Robert has some pull with the receptionist who takes the requests."

"Why would Kate worry about Christina?" Mia picked up her sandwich. "Did she request that the coven help after our meeting this afternoon?"

"Robert was there this morning," Grans repeated.

"Huh. So the woman who told us she had been sitting in her house watching paint dry since she found out about the death of her husband had actually been alert enough to put out a call for help for Christina? Someone she'd never met. That's odd." Mia looked at the other two women. "Don't you think?"

Grans yawned. "We can't take Kate off the suspect list yet. She has a lot of money, and the coven responds to money. I'm surprised Sabrina hasn't arrived yet."

"Mary Alice, why don't you finish your dinner and head to bed. I'll stay up with Christina for a while." Abigail met Mia's gaze. "You know the National Office isn't as time sensitive as we usually need."

"Christina's fine. I just checked on her. We should be able to leave her alone for a few hours while we all sleep." Grans finished off her sandwich.

"Okay, this is an odd question, but if it's a National Office, why is Sabrina in Italy?" Mia finished her soup.

"Sabrina lives in Italy. The National headquarters is in Salem. They have a very small physical office. Most of the staff work from home." Abigail waved away the question as if Mia should have known the answer.

"Most witches do a field trip to headquarters while they're in high school." Grans put her cup in the sink. "Another reason why I should have raised you. Abigail. You don't have to stay up and watch Christina."

"I know, but I've got to call Thomas anyway, and that man loves to chatter." Abigail smiled as she finished her soup. "Mia, you can crash as well. I think you need sleep to clear your head. Don't you have work tomorrow?"

"Actually, no. Except for our staff meeting, I'm off until Wednesday. I worked last weekend and the start of this week on parties. We have a catering event Wednesday night, but it's planned out." Mia rolled her shoulders. "Can I help with the delivery this week since you're down a person?"

Abigail nodded. "That would be helpful. We've got a full delivery slate including several extra orders of treats for the holidays. We'll be baking cookies all day."

"Then it's a plan. I'll be your Christina for the next two days. Grans, you need to work up a batch of Sleeping Beauty cure, just in case we don't find the mitten. And Abigail, please don't tell Thomas how much you're working. He doesn't like you doing this in the first place, and I can't replace you."

Abigail waved her hand. "Don't you worry about my Mr. Majors. He's getting used to having a Sugar Mama. I'm putting all my wages into our retirement fund right now while the stocks are down."

"When are the guys coming back?" Mia asked.

"Wednesday, unless we need them earlier." Abigail pulled out her phone and checked something. "Their flight gets in midday, so they should be here by two at the latest."

Grans nodded. "If we don't find the mitten by then, we'll try the Sleeping Beauty cure. But I can't guarantee its results. The coven is working on a tracking spell for the mitten. Between the two groups, we should be able to bring Christina back to us by midweek."

"That would be amazing." Mia wanted it sooner than midweek, but she didn't want to rush Grans. Magic took time, especially if you wanted it done right.

"Well, I know it's only nine, but I'm beat. I'm going to bed." Grans clicked her fingers and Muffy, her dog, came running. "If you need me, just knock on my door. She's stable, but you never know."

Mia watched Grans slowly move out of the kitchen and toward the hallway. This week had taken a lot out of her. She looked older than she had in a long time. Mia rubbed her face, thinking about Geoffrey. She looked at Abigail. "Kate wasn't in town when her husband was killed. But sometime after that, she heard about Christina and asked the coven to step in and help her. I don't understand why."

"If I were suspicious, I'd think that Kate was feeling guilty about getting a mortal involved in the death of her husband." Abigail clarified what Mia had been thinking.

"I'm wondering whether Edward and Kate know each other. It's odd for me to meet a coven member the day after Christina was hexed." Mia put her dishes into the sink. "I know Kate feels bad about the death of her husband, but she could have had him killed and still feel bad."

"You need to try to call that chef Geoffrey was dating and see if she knows anything. Her leaving so quickly seems a little suspicious," Abigail pointed out. "Do you think nine is too late to call?"

Mia found the picture with the numbers from James. "Not if I'm planning next week's catering staff roster and lie and say that I didn't know she quit."

"Okay then."

Mia dialed the first number, but it had been disconnected. She tried the second one. It rang four times before someone picked up. "Hello? Is this Tasha Alberts?"

A hesitant yes came over the line.

"Hi, Tasha, this is Mia Malone. I'm the catering director for the Lodge, and I was just checking on your schedule for next week. We're going to be swamped with parties." Mia hoped the woman wouldn't just hang up on her.

"I don't work at the Lodge anymore. I moved to Boise," Tasha explained slowly.

"Oh, my phone list must be old. I'm sorry to bother you then. By the way, I saw you at the party on Friday. Where did you get that dress? It was heavenly." Mia switched tactics to keep Tasha on the line.

"Wasn't that amazing? A friend who has Hollywood connections loaned it to me. She's in touch with all the major designers. I've never worn a designer dress before," Tasha gushed, talking about the dress for several minutes.

"That sounds amazing. I'm getting ready for my engagement party." Mia saw Abigail grin, and she shook her head. "Anyway, I'd love to have something designer for that. Any chance your friend could help a girl out? You know how much we make as chefs. Even with adding director on my title, I'm not sure I can afford a designer gown."

The line was quiet for a minute. Then Tasha must have

made a decision. "I get it. I wouldn't have been able to afford it without Kate's help. You can't tell her I told you though. She's trying to keep our friendship on the down-low. You know how people get when they think they can scam something off you. She gets a lot of people who just pretend to be her friend."

"Kate Brewer? She got you that dress?"

Tasha giggled. "Everyone thought I've been dating her husband, but actually I've just been watching him for Kate. He's a terrible flirt, though. If I were Kate, I'd divorce him in a heartbeat."

Chapter Eight

Mia watched Abigail's face as she relayed the conversation again. Or at least the pieces that Abigail hadn't heard.

"She really said Kate should divorce him?" Abigail got some cookies out of the cupboard and set them in the middle of the table. "Sorry, I'm making myself at home. I need something sweet after a meal."

"No worries." Mia took a cookie and broke it in half. "Kate and Tasha were friends, according to Tasha's story. She was just pretending to be dating Geoffrey. Or maybe she was his plus-one to events so Kate didn't have to worry about him being picked up by a lonely student. Or him being more than a flirt."

"Modern relationships confuse me. In my day, you got married, you stayed married, and then you grew old and died together. Now it seems like people change out partners after one fight. A marriage isn't tested until you've gone through several fights and come out the other side." She glanced at her ringing phone. "And speaking of, Thomas must have realized he hadn't heard from me in a while. He's a good guy but a little needy at times. I'll talk with you tomorrow. Don't stay up for Christina. I've got her."

Mia watched Abigail move toward the living room as

she answered her husband's call. She cleaned off the table and put the dishes in the dishwasher. She started it and rolled her shoulders. She was beat and still a little chilled from spending so much time out in the Lodge parking lot. Mia decided to take a long bath before trying to sleep.

As she sat in the steaming water, her phone rang. It was Trent. "Hey, you caught me in the bath. I hope you're not still watching me, creeper."

"No, I told you I'd turn it off as soon as you got home Saturday night, and I did. But maybe I should be there." He chuckled. "I could wash your back."

"I'm so tired I don't think I would notice. How's the trip?" Mia had the phone on speaker as she sank deeper into the warm bubbly water.

"It's fine. Dad's missing Mom. He talks about her all the time. I guess she suggested that we do this boys' trip a few months ago. He wanted to take her on a cruise." He paused as he turned down the television in his hotel room. "She seems to be trying to get him to have at least a little life without her."

"What about his hunting trips?" Mia closed her eyes. "He's gone all the time."

"He sees that as business. This is just about the three of us, and he's lost in how to have fun. So we've been trying to get him out and doing things. We found a zip line today. It was cool, but you could tell Levi's head was back there with Christina. He's a lot like Dad. He's always thinking about her."

"And you, on the other hand, you can live without me for an entire week." The Majors men were all pretty close to their significant others. She thought Trent hadn't noticed it before in his brother.

"Hey now, I could definitely go a full week and a half without talking to you." He sighed. "And yet, to prove your point, we talked yesterday. Does the fact it's been crazy there with Christina give me any slack points?"

"Some. Hey, I wanted to run something by you." She told him about Kate and Geoffrey and the third wheel, Tasha. "From what she told me, she doesn't know Geoffrey's dead. She just up and quit. I think Kate's setting her up for something."

"But you liked Kate. You said she seemed genuinely upset at Geoffrey's death. Besides, she was on a plane when her husband was killed. And if this Tasha doesn't know Geoffrey's dead, she couldn't be the killer," Trent reminded her.

Mia nodded. "That's why my head's going in circles. I still think Kate's involved, even though the facts say differently. Why set her husband up to look like a cheat? Especially when you aren't in town a lot because of your work? Christina said he was really nice. She liked taking classes from him."

Trent was quiet.

Mia thought she'd lost him. "Hey, are you still there?"

"Yeah, sorry, I was thinking about the fact that Christina knew Geoffrey. She knew he was a good man. Maybe she found the mitten because someone wanted her to find it."

"Someone wanted her to be unconscious?"

"Not quite, but," Trent continued, "with you all focused on saving Christina, you haven't had a lot of time to investigate or think about why Geoffrey was killed. I think you need to go back to the first crime. Who killed Geoffrey?"

"Without looking at it with the filter of how to save Christina." She paused, thinking about his suggestion. "Do you think it will make a difference?"

He paused again. "I can't promise, but it feels right.

Why was Geoffrey killed? If you find that out, you might find the mitten to save Christina. But you can't focus on her. You need to focus on Geoffrey."

When Mia woke up the next morning, Trent's words echoed in her head. Why was Geoffrey killed? She decided to visit Mark Baldwin first thing this morning before her staff meeting started. Maybe talking to Mark would give her more insight into Geoffrey's death. And if that happened, maybe it would help save Christina. She got up and made coffee.

Abigail was the first one to join her in the kitchen. "Good morning, sunshine. You look rested. I hope you actually got some sleep last night. I don't smell a breakfast casserole baking."

"I haven't cooked anything yet." Mia grinned and poured Abigail a cup of coffee. "You look ready to go."

"I had a great night. Your guest bedroom is perfect." Abigail sipped her coffee. "It's nice getting up and already having coffee available. I might just decide to move in with you."

"I think Thomas would freak out." She nodded to the paper in front of her. "I was talking to Trent last night, and he said we should be focusing on Geoffrey. Not Christina. He says it's clouding my filter and I can't see the answer."

"That sounds like my son. He's so good at getting directly to the heart of the matter. With or without his powers." She dropped her gaze.

"Abigail, you and I both know that Trent's attempt at transferring his powers to Levi didn't work. Or at least didn't work the way the coven thinks it did. Trent's strong, as is Levi. Their connection is scary sometimes."

Abigail set her cup down. "I'm just always afraid I'm

going to slip and say something to someone in the coven. If they found out, they'd take Trent and study him. I might never see him again."

"And yet they wonder why I'm not jumping at the chance to join their little club. If you don't match what they think you should be like, they want to figure out why." Mia thought about the promise she'd made Edward to attend a meeting. Then she pushed the idea away. "Look, we need to figure out this puzzle first. Then we can solve world peace."

Abigail nodded, picking up her cup and sipping her coffee. "Okay, so the rumor is that the Brewers had an open marriage. And that he was seeing this Tasha on the side when Kate wasn't in town."

"And Kate had her own indiscretions, but Geoffrey didn't care," Mia added. "So who would have hated Geoffrey so much to kill him? According to Edward, it wasn't Kate. She adored her husband. I wonder what Mark has found out about their relationship. Did they have a prenup that would have given Geoffrey more money than Kate wanted to part with if they divorced?"

"That's a good question. I can mine my coven contacts to see what the rumors are around the money part. You know everyone loves to chat about who gets money or who's losing money. Geoffrey taught at a small regional college. You know his paycheck wasn't even paying the utilities on that house we visited."

"Well, maybe the utilities but not the mortgage." Mia wrote down another question on her list.

"Either way, he had to be a drain. Maybe she got tired of letting him spend her money." Abigail glanced at her watch. "I'm going to go down and start baking cookies. What time can I expect you?"

"Ten-ish. The meeting might not go that long. I'm heading to talk to Mark right at eight. The good news is, unless he's sick, he'll be at his desk then. Sarah kicks him out of the house just in time to drive to the police station and open it on time. She's punctual."

"Controlling would be a better word." Abigail smiled at Mia's reaction. "Just kidding, not."

Grans came into the kitchen. She looked refreshed. A night's sleep must have recharged her batteries. "You have to be talking about Sarah Baldwin."

Mia poured her a cup of coffee. "How did you guess?"

"Sarah's the most controlling woman in Magic Springs. You'd never guess that she gave up her family's magic to her little sister."

"Wait, what?" Mia stared at her grandmother. "Sarah's from a magical family? How on earth does she hide that from Mark?"

"They just don't talk about the coven in front of him. Sarah chose a mortal life rather than being a witch. She loved Mark and didn't want anything to get in the way of that. Her family has legacy issues, and I'm sure they wanted her to marry someone with as much power. Her sister married a coven leader from back east." Grans opened the bag of cookies that Mia had left on the table. "It was a big scandal when Sarah turned down her power."

"Did Mom have that issue when she decided not to take the power?" Mia had just assumed it was normal for people to choose another life.

"There's a reason she doesn't come here for holidays. She got a lot of crap from the coven members for walking away when she did. She mostly stays out of Magic Springs so she doesn't have to deal with that." Grans broke a second cookie in half. "So what's on the plan today? We need to get Christina out of that goop before she starts to shrivel up."

"Well, I'm going to go talk to Mark this morning. Then I'm helping Abigail with cooking. Maybe if we do something else, we'll realize what we've missed." Mia glanced around the table. "Do we need to make breakfast first?"

"No, I can do cereal. I'll take Muffy out first, then I'll start getting the Sleeping Beauty spell set up. When is Levi coming home?" Grans finished her second cookie and nodded to Muffy, who was sitting by the apartment door, waiting.

"Wednesday unless we need them earlier. You tell me." Abigail brushed off the cookie crumbs from her hands.

"She should be good until Wednesday. Her phone is ringing off the hook. Her mother." Grans took the phone out of her jacket pocket. "You might want to call her back before Mark Baldwin shows up on a missing person call. Muffy, I'm coming."

Mia stood. "I can take Muffy out."

Grans waved her away. "I need to stretch my legs anyway. You just get ready to go see Mark. And call that woman. I can feel the frustration every time she calls. She thinks Christina's ignoring her."

"Well, I'll have to keep it short. Maybe Christina has a cold. That's it. She's been sick since she got up Sunday morning. She went and took the test and then just went to bed. Did anyone else at the party complain about being ill?" Mia nodded. That was the way to deal with Mother Adams. Until Christina could actually talk to her on Wednesday. If not before.

"Whatever you have to do. And keep that phone downstairs. We don't need more strong feelings around Christina right now. She's vulnerable to any over-the-top emotions, not just love." Grans opened the door and called Muffy to follow. The little dog wagged his way through the door and out of the apartment.

"Okay, so now I have to call Mother Adams and talk to Mark Baldwin. It's beginning to look like Christmas from my to-do list," Mia groused.

Abigail laughed and refilled her coffee cup. Then she headed to the apartment door. "Just don't forget to come down and help me cook. Otherwise I'll be down there until time to make deliveries tomorrow."

"At least we're having a strong delivery season. Even if we haven't done a single catering event this month."

"Oh, we have two scheduled for next weekend. A tea for the Reading Society and a party for the bowling league. The estimate you gave them from the Lodge was too high for their budget. So they called me." Abigail tapped a finger on her lips. "Maybe that's how you can help out Mia's Morsels while you're at the Lodge. Give them a really high quote for the parties, and then they'll come to us."

"Yeah, but that only works if they have a different place to host or we can host it here. Maybe that's what we should advertise. A night at the haunted school for your party." Mia shrugged. "It couldn't hurt around Halloween."

"True. We'll make it out of this mess. I promise. And don't you even think you're going to have to work this weekend. I've got it covered, as long as Christina comes back to us by then. If that doesn't happen, well, I'm not sure what we're going to do."

"Let's just think good thoughts," Mia said, and then she groaned. She was starting to sound like her grandmother. "I'm calling Mother Adams, wish me luck."

"I'll bathe you in golden light for that call." Abigail left the apartment, and Mr. Darcy followed her.

For a minute, Mia sat staring at the phone. What if they couldn't save Christina? Was it fair for her to not tell her mom and let her say her goodbyes now? Mia shook her head. She wasn't going there. Besides, as soon as Mother Adams found Christina in the bathtub of goop, she'd freak, call the EMTs, and probably ban anyone besides her immediate family from the hospital room. Then they'd never save her.

Being a witch was hard when you were trying to deal with the mortal world. Some things they just didn't understand. Like magical healing. She took a deep breath and called Christina's mom, trying to sound like Christina. When the call was answered, she dropped her voice to a growl. "Hi, Mom. I'm sorry I haven't called you back. I've been so sick."

"You still are from what I'm hearing. I was ready to come up and take you to lunch today to see what you thought of Edward. He's very nice, isn't he?"

Mia could hear the hope in Mother Adams's voice. "Yes, he's nice, but Mom, we talked about this. I'm dating Levi. And not just because he lives in Magic Springs. Edward and I don't have anything in common."

"That's not true. You know a lot of the same people. He's always down here going to parties we attend. You didn't give him a chance. He said you were nice, but the two of you didn't click. Did you even try?"

"Did I try to seduce him when I have a boyfriend?" Mia bit her tongue for a second, giving her the time to frame her next words. "No, Mom. I didn't try that. I like Edward. And if things with Levi don't work out, I'll call him. But please, don't hold your breath on this and don't set me up on another blind date. It's embarrassing for both me and the unlucky guy."

"Well, I suppose if you're truly not interested in bettering your life . . ."

Mia laughed. "Bettering my life through marriage? No. I'm not interested in that. I am getting a degree and planning on having an amazing career in the hospitality industry. Just like my brother. I'm so glad you taught both your kids the value of party planning. It really reinforced my career choices. I better go lie down. I'm feeling worn out and I have a raging headache. I'll call this weekend."

And before Mother Adams could respond, Mia hung up.

Mia looked over at Gloria, her kitchen witch familiar. "Goddess, please forgive me for that last crack about party planning. I'm sure Mother Adams didn't mean to train both her kids in the fun of putting on a party. Even though it has been her own life's work."

Gloria giggled, and Mia thought that the Goddess found the comparison amusing as well. Mia knew that Mother Adams wouldn't, and she would have to let her friend know what she'd done. Maybe Christina could blame it on being delusional from a fever.

At least Mia felt better.

Chapter Nine

Mia could tell the moment Mark Baldwin saw her through his open door. She had just walked into the small Magic Springs police station. His face always gave away his thoughts. At least to her. The lobby was decorated with a small tree and a pile of presents underneath. If Mia guessed right, she'd say that Sarah had probably filled the boxes with presents for all the officers. She waited while Mark stood and called out to the officer sitting at the desk by the door. "Let her come on back. I might as well get this over with."

Mia smiled at the officer and then pushed through the small half door that divided the two-chair waiting area from the rest of the bullpen. The door had a smiling elf hung on it. Hardened criminals would find themselves being booked in an over-the-top Christmas experience. But again, it was Magic Springs. Hardened criminals didn't usually hang out in town.

Mia set the box of cookies she'd packed that morning on Mark's desk as she came into the office and sat down. "Good morning, how's Sarah?"

"She's huge and grumpy about it. If the doctor hadn't told me we weren't, I'd suspect we were having twins." He peeked into the box and pulled out a cookie. "I'll run these home at lunch. If she finds out I've eaten them without her, I'll be in trouble. She's having sweet cravings this week."

"I could have Abigail add a dozen to her delivery run tomorrow if you want." Mia pulled out a notebook so she'd remember to mention it.

"That would be great. She sent me to Majors yesterday, but they were out of the cookies she wanted. Some sort of snowballs? Her mom made them, and now Sarah can't find the recipe. Her sister is in Europe on a trip with her husband and she doesn't remember the recipe."

"They go by a lot of names, but I probably can whip her up a batch. It might not be exactly her mom's recipe, but maybe it will curb the cravings until her sister can get it to her." Mia wrote down Mexican Wedding Cookies, the name she knew for snowball cookies.

"That would be great. Now I'm sure you didn't come over just to drop off cookies. You know I can't talk about the murder at the Lodge, right?" He opened the box again and took out a second cookie.

"I know, but I'm worried about it. Does his murder have anything to do with Christina's school? You know that Geoffrey taught there." Mia laid on the concern in her voice.

"From what I can tell, no. The school checked out. No angry students. No rival professors. He was well liked by all. From what I can tell, it's either random, or . . ." He stopped, and his face went red.

"Or?" Mia prodded.

"Or it was something or someone from his relationships with women outside his marital vows. I've heard some strange things about his marriage. But his wife, she was on a plane when he was killed. I know she didn't do it." He picked up a cookie and then set it down. "People just get themselves into a pickle sometimes."

"Yes, they do." Mia realized Mark didn't know anything more than what she did. She stood and buttoned her coat. Then she stopped, holding her gloves in front of her. "Oh, random question. When your guys cleared the scene, no one found a red mitten with a silver snowflake on it, did they? I was wearing them after the party and I came home with only one. My mom made them for me, so I'd hate to break up the set."

He pulled out a folder and opened it. Scanning a page, he shook his head. "No mitten. There were strands of fake fur on his coat, but his date said she was wearing a black fur stole over her party dress." He paused and tapped the paper. "Funny thing about his date. I guess they got in a fight at the party and he left without her. She used to work at the Lodge with you."

"He had a date? But he was married." Mia slipped on her gloves.

"He was married. And he had a date going into the party. But not one coming out. If she hadn't still been at the party dancing with some chef from the Lodge when Brewer was found dead, I would have suspected her. Unless of course the coroner rules this an accident. The parking lot was slick. Maybe he just fell and hit his head. But if not, I think I've still got several people to interview who Mr. Brewer was seeing while his wife was in California working. Long-distance romances just set themselves up for this nonsense." His cell phone started ringing. "Sorry, it's Sarah. I need to get this."

Mia said her goodbyes. Sarah Baldwin probably had a spell on her husband to warn her when a discussion with any single female went too long. The coven would deny it, since they thought once you gave up your power, it was all gone. But Mia knew this wasn't true. At least not for everyone. She sent a *Hi, Sarah*, message through the Goddess and laughed when she felt the surprise on the other end. Then the connection ended.

Mia thought about the mitten. Someone had to have taken both mittens from Geoffrey's body and then dropped one on the way back to the Lodge. She decided to go back to the Lodge and see whether she could watch the security tapes again. If she was right, someone must have followed Geoffrey out into the parking lot, waited for the mittens to do their work, and then either come back into the Lodge before Mia's group left or got in a car and drove away with one mitten.

She started up the van and called Abigail while she waited for the inside of the car to warm up again. "Hey, I've got to run to the Lodge real quick and then I'll be back to help. Can we add a batch of cookies to the prep list?"

"Sure, what kind?"

She told Abigail about Sarah's craving, and Abigail promised to get the cookies started. "Oh, did you see anyone coming into the Lodge while we were going out Friday night?"

Abigail paused for a moment.

Finally she spoke. "I can't remember. It's funny. It's as if there's a blank spot between when we got our coats and when Christina picked up the mitten. That's odd, isn't it?"

Mia said goodbye and thought about what she remembered. Abigail was right, there was a blank spot. Someone had adjusted their memories of that night. She drove to the Lodge and went straight to the security desk.

Carl was there, and he greeted her with a smile. "You came in for the staff meeting? I would have thought you'd try to stay away on your days off. Your boss is a bit of a slave driver. At least at home you can tell him you'll do it later."

Mia groaned as she looked at her watch. Carl was right. The staff meeting was in less than an hour. "Hoping to get back home before he sees me. Can you do me a favor? Cue up Friday night's tape just before they found Professor Brewer? I lost a mitten and I was hoping I didn't have it when I went outside."

He pulled out the lost and found and took out a blue pair. "This is all that's been turned in. Are these yours?"

"No, sorry, it's red with a silver snowflake. I have one at the house but not the mate." She rolled her eyes. "I guess I had one too many on Friday night. Thank goodness Abigail drove."

"A lot of people had one too many that night. We put up several of the kitchen staff in rooms. Management approved a boys' room and a girls' room, so I know several people slept on the floor." He went to his computer, then waved her around the desk. "Here's fifteen minutes before you reported the incident."

"Okay, there we are getting our coats." She leaned closer to watch them walk toward the door. Then they vanished. "Roll that back. What happened there?"

Carl frowned and ran the digital feed again. "It must have been a power glitch. That happens sometimes and the cameras turn off. See, there's a difference of a minute in the time clock. Sorry, I didn't see your mittens."

She watched as the three of them disappeared off the screen again. She hadn't seen anyone come in, but if the killer had come inside then, they'd wiped away the evidence. And probably by magic, since Carl stated the power glitches happened a lot. "Thanks, I'll go check the ballroom and the kitchen."

"Check the coatroom too. Sometimes Mandy isn't as

careful with coats and mittens as she should be." Carl tapped his watch. "Don't let time get away from you."

Since Carl was watching, she went inside the coatroom first. A black fur was the lone item in the room. She almost left without checking it, but then she remembered what Mark had told her about the black fur on Geoffrey's coat. She approached it carefully, keeping her gloves on as she checked to see if the fur had pockets. And it did. This had to have been part of Tasha's outfit. She carefully checked the pockets, and they were empty. Except for a lone red bit of yarn fuzz. She set the fuzz on a counter and used her senses to feel for any power. It was faint, but it was there. And it was crying for its place on the mittens. She grabbed a bag and put the fuzz inside.

Looking at her watch, she saw she had just enough time to get home and sign on to the meeting, if she didn't get caught at the Lodge by Frank.

She opened the door and glanced out. Frank was coming out of the elevators to head toward the kitchen area. Which would bring him right between the coatroom and the front doors. She groaned, then watched as Carl headed over to intercept Frank. He led him away toward the back office, giving her time to escape. She saw Carl turn his head and wink at her as she hurried through the lobby to the doors.

Outside, she rushed to her van. While she was waiting for it to warm up, she called Tasha.

A groggy Tasha answered the phone. "What time is it?"

"Oh, just about nine. Anyway, this is Mia Malone. We talked yesterday? I wondered if you realize your black stole is still at the Lodge. Do you want me to hold it until you pick it up?" Mia held her breath.

"Oh, Kate's grabbing that and the dress from my locker. I couldn't fit both of them in my locker, so I had to leave the stole at coat check. She should be there soon to pick it up. I hear she came into town late Friday night. She called me Saturday morning, well, afternoon, and asked where the dress was." She mumbled something to someone else in the room. "Anyway, she said she'd grab it or send Edward. Look, I've got to go."

And with that, she hung up.

So Kate knew Edward. Unless there were two Edwards in the coven, Mia was beginning to think her meeting at Mother Adams's party wasn't just a coincidence. She sat in the parking lot staring at the Lodge door. If she went to the staff locker room, Frank would see her and make her attend the staff meeting in person. And then he'd have something else for her to do. Abigail needed help with the cooking. Mia put the van in gear and headed home. She'd come back this evening and check Tasha's locker. She hoped that Kate wouldn't come to clean it out before Mia could get there. And if she did, Mia would go over to her house and demand the other mitten.

She didn't know what game Kate Brewer was playing, but she knew she was deeply involved in her husband's murder. Now she just needed to figure out how to prove it and save Christina at the same time.

As soon as she got off the conference call, Mia ran to the kitchen to wash her hands and put on an apron. Abigail handed Mia a recipe and she started getting ready to bake. Bowl, spoon, dry ingredients were all on her table. Mia went back to the fridge a third time to get an ingredient for this recipe. Last trip, she hadn't grabbed butter.

Abigail walked over and glanced at the mise en place Mia had set up for her first cookie recipe. She arranged the ingredients by order of use in the baking. "You're distracted. What's going on?"

"I have this feeling that something bad is going to happen." Mia set the butter on the table and told Abigail about talking to Tasha and finding the mitten lint in the coat closet. "I would have told you sooner, but I wanted to at least get one batch of cookies in before we chatted. I have a feeling that the dress is the key. But I can't go back there now. We've got hours of cooking to do for the delivery tomorrow."

"Why don't you run now, and I'll make these cookies. I've called in reinforcements. The guys are coming home. I had a feeling too. I told Thomas to get Levi and Trent on a plane today, no matter what, and he called a few minutes ago to let me know they were boarding. If we can't find the mitten, we'll use the Sleeping Beauty cure." Abigail glanced at her watch. "If we need help cooking, we'll bring Trent and Thomas in this evening. They can at least pack up the deliveries for us."

"I'll get these done and then go." Mia grabbed a bowl and dumped in the butter so she could use the stand mixer to cream it with the sugar. "I'm regretting telling Mark we'd do these snowballs."

The kitchen door opened, and Grans hurried into the room. "We've got a problem. Christina's crashing. The goop isn't holding her anymore. We need to get Levi home, now."

"Already ahead of you. Luckily, it's a direct flight to Boise. They'll be on the ground by noon, so here by two?" Abigail took a towel and wiped some green goop out of Grans's silver hair.

"I wish we had that mitten. That would stop all this." Grans swatted Abigail's hand away and took the towel.

"I'm leaving now." Mia knew now why she was having the bad feeling. She should have taken the time at the Lodge to check the locker room. She turned off the mixer and grabbed her tote. "I'll go check Tasha's locker, and if the mitten isn't there, I'm going back to Kate's house and making her tell me where it is."

"Okay, but call me if you're heading over to the Brewers'. I don't want you to go there alone," Abigail called after her.

Mia heard Grans ask Abigail what was going on. At least she'd be up to speed when Mia got back, hopefully with the missing mitten. As she walked through the parking lot, she realized she'd left the keys to the van in the kitchen. She'd pulled it close to the back door so it would be easier to load tomorrow. She dug out Christina's Land Rover keys from her tote. She hadn't put them back in Christina's everyday purse on Saturday night. She remote started the car, then unlocked it. She had to wait for the car to warm up, and while she did, she called James.

He picked up on the second ring. "Hey, can you believe the nerve of Frank today? He made it seem like we'd chosen the caterer for the party."

"I wanted to strangle him through the computer screen. I need your help with something. Tasha Alberts left a dress in her locker. Kate Brewer is supposed to be picking it up, or maybe someone for her. If she gets there before I do, can you stall her?" Mia turned on the windshield wipers to help deice the window. The back window was already clear.

"Oddly enough, she's already here. I was just called downstairs to take her to the locker. I'm just waiting for my supply audit program to finish running. How long will it be for you to get here?"

"Ten minutes. Maybe take her some coffee and tell her you have to find the extra locker key? She shouldn't have Tasha's, but she might. If she does, you'll have to figure another way to distract her." Mia decided she could see through the windows. "It's really important that she doesn't get into that locker before I do. If you have to, take her to the coatroom to get the stole first."

"You're going to explain this later, right?" James asked. He groaned. "I just got another message from the front desk. She's in a hurry."

"I'll be there in five minutes as long as I don't hit traffic." Mia hung up the call. She prayed to the Goddess to have clear and safe roads to the Lodge. And for the Magic Springs traffic police officers to be on the other side of town.

She didn't get an answer. Not even a giggle from Gloria, so Mia figured the Goddess was working on her request.

Four minutes later, she pulled into the parking lot and left the car in front of the front door of the Lodge. Hank, from valet, approached her as she ran to the door. "Sorry, I'll be right in and out."

"Miss Malone, it's regulation to have employees park in the back lot," Hank called after her, but she just held up her hand with the keys as she hurried into the lobby. Kate and James were just going into the coatroom. He hadn't been able to stall her for long. James saw Mia run by and nodded. He'd try to give her more time.

She dialed Mark's number as she ran through the lobby and to the back area that held the kitchen and the employee breakroom and locker room. She got his voice mail. "Hey, Mark, I think I know who killed Geoffrey Brewer. I'm down at the Lodge, and I think I might have a clue to prove it if you want to get down here now."

Mia hung up and pushed through the door to the locker room. Tasha had told her that she had locker 403. Mia walked toward it and felt the fuzz in her tote pull toward the band of lockers. The other mitten was there. She used an unlocking spell on the old locker. She could claim it hadn't been locked when she got here. Staff members were always complaining that their lockers either didn't lock or wouldn't open. "Reserare," she commanded, and then tried to open the locker. The door stuck, but she jiggled it open. The designer dress skirt's fabric piled out of the locker, and Mia grabbed the hanger and brought the dress out. The dress didn't have pockets. She shook it, no mitten fell.

Then she turned back to the locker. A tire iron was in the locker along with a plastic bag with a single red mitten. Her tote pulled toward the locker, the bit of fuzz stronger now, trying to match up with its mitten. Mia grabbed the plastic bag and then took a picture of the locker with the red-tinged tire iron. She texted it to Mark.

Her phone rang as she was putting the dress back into the locker.

"Where are you?" Mark asked.

"The employee locker room at the Lodge. Look, I can't stay here and Kate Brewer is in the lobby getting ready to come here and get the dress. She's probably going to pretend to 'find' the tire iron." She saw the security chief walk past in the hallway. "Hold on a second, Mark. Hey, Carl?"

She explained that the police were on their way and he needed to keep everyone out of the locker room. Carl got on his cell and called in reinforcements. Mia went back to her phone call. "Okay, Mark, Carl's going to keep everyone away until you get here. Call me if you need something. I've got to get back to cooking."

"Mia, how did you find this?" Mark asked.

She hung up the phone, hoping he'd think that she didn't hear the question. She needed to figure out a reason she had gone to Tasha's locker and it couldn't be that she wanted to borrow the dress.

She saw that a security guard was now standing by the coatroom, blocking Kate from leaving. James nodded at her, and she ran to the car. She'd have a lot of explaining to do, but she had to get this mitten to its match. She could feel Christina's distress now, even at this distance.

The car was where Mia left it, but Hank had closed the door she'd left wide open. She waved at him and then took off to the house. She saw Hank coming out to talk to her, but again, that would have to be an apology for later. She didn't have the time. She called home.

When she arrived, she parked the Land Rover near the door and ran into the school and up the stairs. Grans met her in the living room with the other mitten.

She opened the bag and let Grans dump the one bag into the other. Sparks flew.

Abigail came out of Christina's room. "Did you match them?"

"Yes. How is she?" Mia sealed the bag with the two mittens cuddled up next to each other.

Abigail sighed as she sank against the wall. "No change."

Chapter Ten

"Are you sure?" Mia dropped her tote and ran into Christina's bathroom. Her face was pale and her breathing raspy. The mittens match hadn't changed anything. Mia touched her face. "Hold on, Christina, we're going to figure this out."

She went back to the living room and picked up the bag with the killer mittens. They were quiet now. Cuddled up together. Two peas in a pod.

"Levi should be here in a couple of hours. Then we can try the Sleeping Beauty cure." Abigail glanced at her phone. "They just landed in Boise."

"Tell them to hurry." Grans met Mia's gaze. "I'm not sure how much longer she can hold on."

Mia stared at the mittens. It should have worked. The lore around the mittens was that one person had to die when they were used. One person. Geoffrey had been killed by his wife. Well, not exactly by his wife, but she'd planned it. Mia was certain of that fact. Now to figure out who had helped her. Mia's phone rang. "Hello?"

"What had you running out of here like your school was on fire?" Mark Baldwin asked.

"Sorry, Mark, Christina's not feeling well. We may have to take her to the hospital. She's got some kind of virus."

What's going on?" Mia pulled out her notebook and another bag came out with it. She really needed to clean out her purse. There was something she was forgetting. She could feel it. With everything going on with Christina, she'd thought it had been around that, but now she needed to remember what it was that was said. It was important and on the tip of her tongue. Before she could grab it, Mark asked her another question.

"Why do you think Kate Brewer killed her husband?" Mark sounded as if he'd just shut a door. "I hate to do this, but even Sarah thinks you know something that might be important."

"I think she set Tasha Alberts up to look like she was having an affair with Geoffrey. Then once that was set, she had someone in town attack him. According to Tasha, she was just hanging out with Geoffrey to help out Kate. She'd been asked to keep an eye on him since Kate thought he was cheating when she was out of town. Tasha was going to tell him she wasn't interested that night." Mia flipped the notebook to what she'd written down after talking to Tasha.

"She told you a lot," Mark commented.

Mia sighed. She'd been expecting the lecture. "I know, I'm not an investigator, but I was concerned that someone was killed at the Lodge. I needed to know that it was personal. I don't want my staff in the way of some serial killer."

"That even sounded sincere." Mark laughed, but Mia could hear the fatigue in his tone. "Did you find out anything else?"

"There's a gap in the security tape just as the murder occurred. But I'm sure you've already seen that." She stared at the notes she'd made after talking to Tasha. There was something in that conversation she was missing.

"My tech guys just found it. You think someone jammed the signal to keep from being seen coming or going from the Lodge?" Mark paused. "You would have thought that someone would have seen a guy or gal with a bloody tire iron walk through the lobby."

"Unless they hid it in something." Mia knew that's why her memory was off. And why the video had been altered. Someone magical had killed Geoffrey for Kate Brewer and had walked through the Lodge to put the tire iron into Tasha's locker. A memory from Saturday night and Mother Adams's party came to her mind. Edward walking away from the door. Swinging an umbrella, even though there wasn't rain that night. Tasha had mentioned someone else picking up the dress. She stared at the notes she'd written down. She'd written down his name. Edward.

He hadn't been at Mother Adams's party to meet Christina or even Mia. He'd been there to see what she'd remembered, if anything. And maybe put a little more of a hex on her to keep her from remembering.

"Mark, I heard someone saying that Kate was seeing a guy from Magic Springs. An Edward Phillips. Maybe he helped her kill her husband." Mia pushed a little with the information, hoping that the magical boost wouldn't backfire. Mark was a good guy and an excellent investigator. If there was a trail between Kate and Edward, he'd find it. She could count on that.

"Funny thing, I've already been looking at Mr. Phillips. He was at the Lodge that night according to credit card receipts at the bar, but no one remembers seeing him. I wonder if he was watching for Geoffrey to leave so that his wife would have an iron-clad alibi. And, yes, I've heard the rumors about the two of them being together." He paused a moment. "I've got some interviews to set up. And some warrants to get, but thank you, Mia, you've been helpful. Sarah told me to tell you that you should come over for coffee one morning. She says you two need to talk. Well, she'll be drinking tea. She's been off caffeine for the pregnancy."

"I'll call her." Mia saw Grans leave the room, heading toward Christina's room. "I've got to go."

Mia hung up and went to tuck the notebook back into her tote. But the bag was blocking the opening. She took it out and realized she still had the mitten fuzz she'd found in the fur stole. Maybe this was what the mittens needed. She opened both bags and then dumped the fuzz on the mittens. It melted into the knit weave immediately.

Abigail came back from the kitchen. "They're on the road. They didn't even wait for their luggage. Levi will be here soon."

Grans came back into the room, relief exuding from her body language. "Tell them to go back for their bags. Christina's coming out of it. Maybe the mittens just needed some time to talk."

Mia glanced at the now-empty bag. "Actually, they were still missing a little bit of their essence. She's better?"

Grans nodded. "I need help getting her out of the goop. Then we'll take her to your bathroom while I make the goop dissolve. I'd hate to ruin your pipes. Abigail, call your husband, and Mia, come help me get her out of the bathtub. The spell has been broken."

The six of them were downstairs cooking later that night. Mia put the last batch of cookies into the oven and looked around her busy kitchen. Abigail and Thomas were setting up delivery orders and putting the delivery sacks on the table so they could be filled tomorrow morning. Grans was rinsing the last of the dishes to go into the dishwasher. Levi had just given Christina another bottle of water. He hadn't left her side since they'd arrived from the airport.

Trent came over to Mia and put his arms around her waist. "I'm not sure I can look at another Christmas cookie again. On the other hand, it looks like deliveries will go out tomorrow as planned. Should we go to the Lodge for dinner tonight? I think we're all wiped and not up for cooking."

"Sounds good." Mia leaned into him. "Mark Baldwin called and told me that they arrested Edward and Kate for the murder. I guess they found letters in Edward's house between him and Kate planning Geoffrey's murder. They've been planning this for years."

"Now how did you meet Edward?" He leaned his head on her shoulder and pulled her closer. "Wait, he was the guy at Mother Adams's who was hitting on you. I should have recognized him."

"He wasn't hitting on me. We can talk about it over dinner. I need to update Christina on some Mother Adams issues too, before she takes a call from her." Mia glanced around the room again and then smiled up at Trent. The room smelled like Christmas cookies. The Christmas mittens had been picked up by one of the coven leaders to go into their vault. Sabrina had called and told her that the case with the National Office of Regrettable Events was closed. And Mark had found justice for Professor Brewer. With a little help from her and the Goddess.

It had been a busy week.

"We're going to the Lodge for dinner. Who wants to drive?" Mia announced to the group as they all finished their tasks. "And dinner's on me to thank everyone for your help today."

Grans set the towel down she'd just used to dry off the sink area. "Maybe next year we can do something a little less strenuous like snowshoeing on Magic Mountain for our Christmas get-together."

Christina stood and stretched. "I know I could use some exercise. I feel like I've slept for days."

As the group left the kitchen to put on coats and decide on who was driving, Mia went over to talk to Christina. "I'm really glad you're back with us. What was it like?"

"I could hear you talking to me." Christina gave her a hug. "But I had this really weird dream where you were having dinner with my mom. And this hunky guy from Magic Springs."

Mia let her words sink in. Maybe some of Christina had been around when she'd gone to Boise for the dinner. "Christina, we need to talk. Especially before you talk to your mother."

They were gathered in the school's living room. It was set up now as a waiting room for classes and maybe somewhere groups could meet for parties. The tree lights twinkled as Trent came up and stood next to Mia. "I think we should add a Santa Village by the stairwell."

Mia turned her head and watched him. "It already looks like Santa's workshop in here. And you want to do more?"

He gave her a hug. "What can I say, I love Christmas."

MURDEROUS MITTENS

Maddie Day

Chapter One

Quiet can be peaceful. At other times it's ominous, as if something bad—disaster, tragedy, even violence—looms.

I nursed my glass of pinot noir in the Colinas wine bar that December afternoon. It was quiet here in Vino y Vida, as it was in the whole town, and for the moment felt peaceful. The peace was a welcome contrast to the always-moving energy of the Los Angeles area where I lived and worked. I was the only patron sitting at the bar, although a smattering of wine tasters occupied tables. I wondered if the quiet would last through the holidays.

Still, traveling to Northern California from my home in Pasadena a week before Christmas to visit my twin sister might have been a mistake. Allie's real estate business was suddenly so crazy busy she'd suggested I head over to Vino y Vida in the historical complex and taste local vintages until she could join me.

The bartender, a striking older woman whose dark hair bore a proud streak of white, had introduced herself as Val but turned away to help other customers. I wished I'd brought a book. Or my tablet. Scrolling through my phone got old, fast. I took a sip and gazed around at the thick adobe walls adorned with framed antique wine posters and maps of the Alexander Valley. Glass doors led to a terrace overlooking the Russian River, but when I'd arrived, all the repurposed barrel tables out there had been occupied.

A tall, lanky woman who I guessed was near my own early-forties age lowered herself onto the next barstool. She gave me a quick smile, then focused on the blackboard where today's pourings were listed. She glanced back at me with light blue eyes.

"What are you having?" she asked.

"An Alexander Valley pinot noir, apparently made right down the road. It's quite nice. I'm Cece Barton, by the way."

The other woman's face brightened. "Cameron Flaherty. Cam." She extended her hand. "Nice to meet you, Cece. Do you live in town, or are you a tourist like I am?"

"My home is in the Los Angeles area, in Pasadena. But my sister Allie has lived here for a while, and I came north to be with her for Christmas."

"Wait. Allie Halstead, with the bed-and-breakfast in the big Victorian down the street?" She tucked a lock of red hair behind her ear.

"She's my older sister." I bobbed my head. "Older by a whopping four minutes. They named us Alicia and Cecelia, which lasted about an hour."

Cam's smile broadened. "I have a suite in the B&B. I checked in an hour ago."

"I'm staying there too. Let me guess. She recommended walking over to Vino y Vida."

"Exactly."

Val hurried over and spoke to Cam. "What can I get you to drink, ma'am?"

Cam gave the same little wince I used to react with. When the general populace decides you merit being addressed as ma'am rather than miss, it's a milestone, and not one those in Cam's—or my—age bracket generally celebrated.

"I'd like what she's having, please." Cam pointed at my glass.

"You got it. I'm Val Harper, and I manage this lovely establishment." She selected a stemmed glass with a fat bowl and filled it a little over half full.

Cam thanked her and lifted the glass, facing me. "Cheers."

I clinked her glass and took a sip. "What brings you to Colinas, Cam?"

She sipped the wine and set down her glass. "I own and run a certified organic farm in Massachusetts."

My eyes widened. "That's different."

"Yep. I'm trying to widen my practices, and I heard about a few innovative farms out here practicing permaculture and other forms of sustainability. My darling sainted husband said he'd keep our little girl for the week and told me to go."

"Good husband. How old is your daughter?"

"Ruthie is every day of her two years and eleven months." Cam shook her head, smiling. "She was an early talker, and she basically rambles and asks questions constantly. Pete's going to have his hands full." She pulled out her phone and showed me pictures of a sturdy little girl with red curls.

"She's adorable, but don't blink. Your Ruthie will be nineteen in a minute."

"I'm sure. Why, do you have a nineteen-year-old?" Cam asked.

"I do. She's in college." And that was all I intended to say about Zoe.

We chatted further about my job managing a nonprofit

in Pasadena and about Cam's detective husband, who worked for the state police.

"Policing must be dangerous work," I said. "I've never met a detective before."

"It can be. Sometimes what he does is super boring, though."

Val reappeared. "Did I hear one of you talking about permaculture?"

"I mentioned it," Cam said. "I'm interested in knowing more about the practice for my farm back in New England."

"I can't say I personally have an interest." Val sniffed. "But I'm the president of the Colinas Garden Club, which has been in existence for a hundred years. Thea Robinet, one of our members, insists on suggesting speakers about all these nutty . . . I mean, innovative new practices."

I stifled a laugh at her course correction from "nutty" to "innovative." Cam gave me the side-eye, and her mouth looked as if she was also suppressing a laugh. Soon enough, Val would find herself in the minority. Innovation was always the way of the future.

"Either of you ladies heading up to ski at Tahoe after Christmas?" Val asked.

"Not me." I shook my head. I'd never skied and didn't see the need to start now.

"I'm returning to Massachusetts before the holiday," Cam said. "Why, is the skiing good at Lake Tahoe? I've heard of the lake but not in the context of winter sports."

"It can be, and the view is spectacular." Val reached under the bar and laid several pairs of mittens on the surface. Two were black, and the fabric of one was in a blue-and-white snowflake pattern. All had a long cuff. "I make and sell these. They're stretchy, so one size fits all."

I picked up a pair and tried out the stretch. It expanded

easily but also went back to shape. The weather in Colinas was chillier than in Southern California. It hadn't gotten over sixty degrees today. I'd driven up yesterday and was already glad I'd packed my thickest fleece sweatshirt. Did I need mittens, too?

"I can always use a new pair of mittens," Cam said. "Our winters back home are cold. And these long hands would appreciate the stretch." She laid a hand flat on the bar. With unvarnished and closely trimmed nails, it wasn't beefy, but she did have extra-long fingers to match her height. "How much are they?"

"Thirty each, but I'll sell you two pair for fifty." Val folded her arms.

That seemed a little pricey for mittens. On the other hand, they were handmade.

"I'll think about it," Cam said. "Thanks for showing them to us."

"You interested?" Val asked me.

"Not right now, thank you," I said. "Why don't you have a display of them out on the counter? You might get more customers that way."

Val tossed her head. "The manager of this cluster of buildings frowns on me selling anything but wine in here. Ridiculous, but true. And unfortunately, he—Otto Harper—is my ex-husband."

Ouch. Having to work for an ex would be no fun.

"What else is in the complex?" Cam asked.

"Alexander Books and the Acorn art gallery down that way." Val gestured with her head. "The Colinas History Museum next door in the other direction. All four businesses are in antique adobes. Town owns the property, and a board of directors makes the big decisions." She made her way around the bar to help a customer.

I sipped my wine.

Cam covered a yawn. "Sorry. It's been a long day, and it's eight o'clock at home."

"No worries."

"Listen, I'm going to go visit a couple of farms in the area tomorrow. Would you like to come along?" Cam asked.

I cocked my head. Why not? "I'd love to, thanks. I came up here to hang out with Allie, but she's really busy with her business, and my twin nephews are in school. Who knew people wanted to rush to buy houses at the end of December?"

Chapter Two

Cam drove us back to Colinas at a bit after noon the next day after visiting the Permaculture Skills Center and farm in Sebastopol.

"Do you want to grab lunch together?" I asked.

"Sure. Where do you recommend?"

"Edie's Diner is great, and the owner is a friend of Allie's."

"Sounds perfect. Tell me where to go."

We were still ten minutes from town, but I pointed her in the right direction. "Cam, I'm curious," I said. "Do you make actual money as a farmer?"

She laughed. "Depends on what you mean by actual. I bring in money, but I also lay it out for seeds and equipment. I'm lucky to have a dedicated group of subscribers to my CSA. They love the farm share program, they're absolute fanatics for local eating, and they volunteer with weeding and helping me harvest. I don't have to hire any employees."

"They're lucky. I try to buy from the farmers' market near my house, but I can't always get there when they're open."

"I hear you. Anyway, I'm grateful to have a husband

with health insurance for the family. Compared with what I earned as a software engineer? No, I'm not making much actual money. But I'm happy and around my kiddo. I'm growing food for my family and for others, and I'm doing good things for the earth."

"The place we just toured is, too, right?" I asked. "I know zero about permaculture, despite my having been a home gardener for a long time."

"It's pretty cool stuff, with the water management techniques and permanent food plantings. Permaculture is really a big step beyond sustainability."

"Take the next turn," I said.

A few minutes later, Cam parked in front of the shiny silver diner. A big sign proclaimed, "God bless America and Edie's Diner, too."

Soon we were seated on red banquettes in a booth as retro-fifties as the rest of the place. Ed Ramirez, a big man of about sixty with barely any silver in his full head of dark hair, approached with menus and a broad smile.

"Cece, I heard you were back. I'm delighted. I'm Ed Ramirez," he said to Cam. "Welcome to Edie's Diner."

"Thank you, Ed. My name is Cam Flaherty. I'm visiting from Massachusetts."

"And she's staying at Allie's," I added.

"Then you're in good hands, Cam," Ed said. "Can I get you both coffee, or something else?"

"He has a liquor license," I explained to her. "I'd like an oatmeal stout, Ed."

"Perfect for a chilly day," he said. "You, Cam?"

"Why not? I'm on vacation. What do you have for IPAs?"

"We don't have draft, but I can get you a pint can of Bodega Head."

"Perfect," Cam said.

Ed said he'd give us a couple of minutes to decide on food. I read through the menu, but I'd already decided on a cheese-and-chili tamale with a side of black beans. Talk about comfort food in cold weather.

"Last night Val didn't seem to appreciate the garden club member trying to bring the organization into the current decade by including speakers on permaculture," Cam murmured.

"She didn't. Thea somebody, wasn't it?"

A woman seated near us at the counter swiveled on her red vinyl stool. "What was that?"

I blinked. "I'm sorry?"

"My name's Thea. As far as I know, I'm the only Thea in Colinas. And I'm vice president of the garden club."

"Thea Robinet?" Cam asked.

Thea nodded without smiling. Her face had the look of a hawk, with intense eyes and a curving nose. I thought she was probably closer to fifty than forty.

"Nice to meet you." Cam stood and held out her hand. "I'm Cam Flaherty."

Thea slid off her stool to shake hands. I blinked again. Cam had to be five foot ten. Thea, who wore tight black jeans and a Levi's jacket, was two inches taller than Cam. Her cropped spiked hair gave her still more height. At five foot eight, I didn't usually feel diminutive. I did right now.

"Would you like to join Cece and me, Thea?" Cam sat and scooted in on the bench.

"Please do. I'm Cece Barton." I smiled.

Thea seemed to assess us. "All right. Thank you." She grabbed her coffee and joined us, sitting next to Cam.

Ed returned with our drinks and asked for our orders. "Got it. Veggie tamale plate for Cece, California burger for Cam, hold the raw onion, and Colinas Benedict for Thea. Back in a flash, ladies."

Cam and I did a quick glass clink, and I took a sip of a thick, dark libation that went down perfectly.

"What's Colinas Benedict, Thea?" I asked.

"Like eggs Benedict, but with locally made thick-cut bacon instead of Canadian and the addition of avocado."

"It sounds great." Except for the bacon. I'm a vegetarian who eats fish, but I'd be willing to bet Ed would sub in smoked salmon for me instead of the pork product next time I was in.

"So, ladies, what did you hear about me?" Thea folded her hands on the table. She breathed through her mouth, as if her sinuses were stuffed up.

"Cece and I met in Vino y Vida yesterday," Cam began.

"I get it." Thea's mouth pulled into a line. "Val was bad-mouthing me again."

"Not exactly," I ventured. "But she didn't seem to support the direction you want to take the garden club."

"She needs to go, and soon." Thea drained her coffee. "Hey, Ed, can I get a Bloody Mary, please? And make it weak on the tomato juice."

"The club doesn't have room for both of you?" Cam asked.

"No. Val wants to keep us in the white-lady white-glove era. I want our local Hmong farmers to join, and the women who run Gaia Vineyards, and everyone in between."

The door clanged open, making the bell on it ring furiously. Allie stood casting her glance around. She spotted me and hurried down the aisle.

"Hey, Al." I smiled at her. "You're in time for lunch."

My twin slid in next to me. "I can't eat."

"Why not?" I took a second look at her. She wasn't projecting her usual nicely put-together real estate agent look right now. Her cap of well-cut (and touched-up) blond hair was windblown, and not in a stylish way. Her face was pale under ill-applied makeup. Her earrings didn't match, her Patagonia sweatshirt was zipped up to the neck—very not Allie—and her navy slacks had a smudge of chocolate on the knee. One might expect disarray from a mom of twin ten-year-old boys, but not from this particular mother, Alicia Halstead. "Allie, are the boys okay?"

"What? They're fine. They're at school. Hey, Thea, Cam."

Ed brought our plates and Thea's drink. "Get you anything, Allie?"

"If that's a Bloody Mary, I want what Thea's having."

He went behind the counter, but he kept an eye on Allie, and his ears attuned, too, I suspected.

"There's no way around this." Allie looked at Thea and at Cam. She rested her gaze on me. "Val Harper was murdered during the night."

Chapter Three

My breath rushed in. Cam, frowning, brought a hand to her mouth. Ed delivered Allie's drink.

"Terrible news," he said softly.

Thea narrowed her eyes at Allie. "How do you know?"

Allie stared at her. My twin and I didn't share ESP, exactly, but right now I was a hundred percent certain she was thinking, "What kind of a question is that?" I was thinking it, too. In my mind I also heard Thea say Val "needs to go, and soon."

"I heard it on the local action channel," Allie finally replied.

Whatever an action channel was. It didn't matter. Allie was nothing if not tuned in to what happened in Colinas.

She twisted to face me. "And because a Sonoma County sheriff's detective came to see me."

"What?" My voice rose. "Why?"

Ed cleared his throat. "Val, may her soul rest with God, and Allie had had quite a few disagreements in recent months. In public."

Thea nodded as if she were aware of the spats or fights or whatever they were.

"But they can't possibly think you killed the poor

woman." I reached for her hand under the table and squeezed it.

"Someone did, though." Allie took a big swig of the Bloody Mary. "You should have heard the questions the cop was asking me."

"Did you have to go to the police station?" I asked.

Allie shook her head. "He grilled me at home. I'm glad the kids were already at school and, as you know, Cece, Fuller is away for a few days. It was only me and the extremely persistent Detective Quan."

"I'm sure they just want to rule you out, Allie," Ed said.

"Do either of you know Rafael Torres?" Thea gazed at Allie and up at Ed.

Allie shook her head.

"I ran into him not too long ago," Ed said. "Back when I was home from college in the summers, I helped out with the summer recreation program. He was there every year. He's ten or twelve years younger than me, and he said he teaches at the high school now."

"So you know he's Val's younger brother," Thea said.

"Right," Ed said. "I'd actually forgotten, since Val changed her name when she married. I didn't know her at all back in the day."

Cam, who wasn't acquainted with anyone involved, seemed keenly interested in the conversation. I wondered whether it was the lurid factor of murder in this scenic little town she'd come to visit or something more.

"Well, the two siblings were estranged," Thea went on. "I'm not entirely sure why. The last time I saw him, he was expressing a lot of anger toward Val. Maybe he finally snapped."

"How do you know Rafael?" Cam asked.

"Doesn't matter." Thea forked in a big bite of her lunch.

Seemed like it might matter. "What was he angry about?" I asked.

"None of your business." She held her hand in front of her full mouth as she spoke.

"You all should eat before your food gets any colder," Ed said. "Allie, you sure I can't get you anything?"

"Positive, but thanks, Ed."

"She can share with me," I said. To my sister I added, "You should eat, Al. Your drink'll knock you on your butt if you don't."

Ed grabbed a silverware roll from the counter and laid it down in front of Allie. "I have to get back to work."

I slid my plate closer to Allie before taking a bite of warm, starchy, delicious tamale, stuffed with melted cheese and covered with a thick, dark sauce so full of flavor it sang. Cam cut her burger in half, exposing a fat slice of ripe tomato and slices of avocado.

After she'd eaten a couple of bites, Cam set down the half. "The thing is, I have a bit of experience solving homicides."

This morning was full of surprises. "You do?" I took a sip of stout.

"Yes. Several years ago, I found a murder victim on my farm, and it was a man I'd had to fire the day before. Then, a few months later, a customer was killed and one of my volunteers—a friend—was accused of the crime. There were a few more homicides, too. It's how I met my husband, actually."

"So you know how to track down a killer." Thea sounded skeptical.

"Not alone, but I was able to help the police a bit."

"Isn't investigating murder terrifying?" I asked.

Cam smiled. "I've been scared a few times. But it taught me a lot about myself, too."

"I don't know anything about how the cops work," I said.

"I'm sure it's different in certain respects in every locale," Cam said.

"True." Allie nodded. "For example, Colinas has its own police department, but it relies on the Sonoma County Sheriff's Department for things like murder investigations."

"Yep." Thea bobbed her head with a definitive move.

It sounded like she spoke from experience. Allie finally took a bite of my tamale. She made an appreciative noise and took another.

"Thea, I know Val was divorced," I began. "But did she have other family? Parents still alive, or children? Somebody must be mourning her." Even if Thea wasn't.

She gave a shrug. "I didn't know her well. You'd have to ask Otto or Rafael or someone else." She popped in the last bite of her meal, drained her drink, and stood. She dug a twenty-dollar bill out of her jacket pocket and laid it on the table. "Nice to meet you ladies. Good to see you, Allie. I have to shove off." She strode down the row and out the door, her heavy boots clunking.

"She got out of here in a hurry." Cam gazed at the door.

"Something's up with her," Allie said.

"How do you know her, Al?" I asked.

"I don't, really," my twin said. "I've seen her name in the local rag. She competes in triathlons and has won a couple. And occasionally she helps her girlfriend at the farmers' market. I always stop at Narini's stand on market day. We'll have to go Sunday, Cece. The Raj Orchards olive oil is to die for, and her cured olives are fabulous. You're here through Monday, right, Cam?"

"Yes, and I'd like to meet an olive farmer, even though it's too cold to grow them where I live. By girlfriend, do you mean Narini is Thea's friend or her romantic partner?"

"The latter, from what I've seen." Allie's phone gave off two abrupt buzzes. She slapped her forehead. "Rats. I'm late to meet a client for a showing." She slid out of the booth but downed the rest of her drink before she left.

"Al, take a minute in front of a mirror first, okay?" I smiled to soften my message. She was super discombobulated if she planned to meet a client looking like that. "And pop a breath mint in your mouth."

Chapter Four

After I paid the lunch bill, insisting to Cam the meal was my treat, she drove off to tour another farm. I slid on my swingy purple fleece coat with the big buttons and began the short trip back to Allie's, letting myself move at a slow stroll. This wasn't a power walk, and I'd already done my morning Pilates routine in my room in the big Victorian.

I'd visited Colinas at least once a year for the fifteen years since Allie moved here, but I'd rarely been alone in the town. Edie's was on Las Marias Road, which bisected the main drag of Manzanita Boulevard. I hung a right and moseyed down a block on a residential street parallel to Manzanita. I was headed away from Allie's, but I wanted more time to think. For me, slow walking helped make thinking happen.

How awful that Val's life had been cut short by an act of violence. It was a tragedy anyone ever was murdered. But this was here and now, and, according to Allie, the detective thought she might have done it.

How had Val been killed? Maybe she'd closed the wine bar late and someone wanted to steal the till, although so few people paid cash anymore, that seemed unlikely to be a motive. The murder could have been for a personal reason, the settling of an old hurt or debt. But was she shot? Strangled? Poisoned, coshed over the head, or pushed in front of a train? Had her throat been cut? When the detective considered if a particular person committed a crime, they probably also weighed whether that person was able to use that method. Not everybody would be tall or strong enough to strangle or hit their victim.

I shook my head. I had no way of knowing. Anyway, everybody said, "I could kill that guy" on occasion. Thea herself had expressed wanting Val gone. At the time I'd assumed she meant out of the leadership of the garden club. Maybe she did, or maybe she meant something worse. Had Thea found a way to murder Val Harper? Or the killer might have been the ex-husband. The estranged brother. A random stranger.

What I knew for certain was it was not Alicia Van Ness Halstead. No. Possible. Way.

While Cam might have had successes in the past at putting killers behind bars, and apparently with her farm, her marriage, and her ability to bear children, I myself had not racked up a string of successes in my life. These days it was a thing to identify by your pronouns—"She, her. They, them. He, him." I identified by "Fail, fail."

I hadn't finished college, instead dropping out to get married. I'd never had a defined career. Instead I'd worked retail, had a job with a landscaping firm, and managed a gift shop, until I settled into my current position administering a nonprofit organization in Pasadena. My marriage had been unhappy and had had a terrible ending.

Yes, I'd given birth to a beautiful, healthy, brilliant little girl, who was still all of those things except little. But after her father died ten years ago, I wasn't able to comfort Zoe in a way we could both get past her anger at Greg's loss. I knew her fury was grief expressed as anger, but the resentment remained. These days she spoke to me when I reached out, except it was almost always a reluctant conversation. At least she was close to my mom—Allie's and my mom—and Zoe now attended college where her Gran was a professor. They'd both be here for Christmas.

So, yeah, I'd failed at almost everything in my adult life. But . . . Allie being suspected of murder? I needed to get to the bottom of that ASAP, and I couldn't let fear of failure get in my way. I knew my twin hadn't done it, whatever *it* was. I hoped this farmer Cam Flaherty, *aka* amateur sleuth, might be able to help.

I turned onto Manzanita and paused in front of Exchange Bakery and Gourmet Provisions. Allie was busy, and her husband, Fuller, was out of town. The least I could do was cook dinner tonight for two sets of twins.

Chapter Five

My arms were laden with paper shopping bags full of pasta, olives, gourmet tomato sauce, a hunk of nutty Parmesan, a bottle of Chianti, six ripe peaches, and a quart of vanilla ice cream when I turned down the side walkway of Allie's house. I halted. A slight man in a dark blazer was knocking on the side door.

I unfroze my feet and strode toward him. "Can I help you?"

He turned toward me and flashed a badge at me. He put it away as quickly. This might be the detective who was questioning Allie earlier.

"Sheriff's Deputy Detective Quan, ma'am. I'm looking for a Ms. Cecelia Barton."

"Excuse me, Detective Quan. I didn't get a good look at your ID." I set my bags on the pavement.

"You're being careful. Good. My apologies." He extended it again and waited until I read it and nodded.

"Thank you. I'm Cecelia Barton. What can I do for you?"

"You are Alicia's sister, I gather. I'd like to have a short conversation with you, if it's convenient."

I bobbed my head. "I am, it is, and I have melting ice cream at my feet. Would you like to come inside?"

"Thank you." As I unlocked the door, he hoisted both

my bags and brought them in, setting them on the island of the spacious renovated kitchen.

"I appreciate that." I stowed the ice cream and left the rest. I faced him. "Have a seat." I gestured at the kitchen table near the wall of windows to the backyard. I needed to clear Allie's name. If I was nice to this guy, it all might happen faster and more easily. Up to now he'd been nothing but polite.

He pulled out a small tablet, or maybe it was a big phone. "I understand you're staying here during your visit, Ms. Barton."

"I am."

"Had you ever met Valencia Harper?"

Valencia? A name as beautiful as Allie's. "Yes, I met Val yesterday afternoon in Vino y Vida at about four or five o'clock. We chatted a little. I'd never seen her before and didn't see her again."

He tapped in a note. "Please walk me through your movements last evening."

"I came back here. I ate dinner with Allie and her sons. I went to bed."

"Where in the house is the room you're occupying?"

"It's actually directly above this one."

"With windows on the driveway," he said.

"Yes."

"Were you aware of your sister leaving the premises?"

"What? No, of course not. Where would she go?" As soon as I uttered those words, I wished I could take them back.

"Are you positive her car didn't leave the property?"

I thought back. "Well, no. I mean, I wear earplugs to sleep when I travel, and my curtains were closed. I should think I would hear her car, but . . ." I let my voice trail off. "But listen, Detective. My sister would never, ever leave her boys asleep without telling me she was going out and when she'd be back. More important, she does not have it in her to kill anyone. I'm serious. You can't possibly suspect her."

He neither defended nor denied. "What about this other guest, a Cameron Flaherty? I understand you've been spending time with her."

How did he know that?

"What do you know about her?" he asked.

"Not much. She's an organic farmer from Massachusetts. She has a husband—also a police detective, but with the state police out there—and a young daughter. Cam's here to look into newer farming techniques. She arrived only yesterday, and I met her for the first time at the wine bar. Why?"

"Merely gathering the facts, ma'am." He stood. "Have you spoken with your sister about her altercations with the deceased?"

"No, and I don't intend to. She didn't kill Val Harper, sir. And you can put that in your notes."

Chapter Six

I came downstairs at nine that night after reading my nephews to sleep in their bunkbeds. They were both fluent readers, but they loved listening to a chapter of Harry Potter before bed—and I loved being their audio narrator. I found Allie on the couch in the family room adjoining the kitchen, feet up on the coffee table, working her tablet. She patted the cushion next to her.

"I'll put this away. Come sit with me."

I sat.

"Or, better yet, let me get us each a glass." She jumped up and came back a moment later with two snifters of cognac.

"Korbel?" I asked.

"Always." She held her glass to clink with mine. She swirled and inhaled the fumes before sipping. "Thanks for doing dinner, Cece. It was a real treat, and the boys loved it."

"Even if Arthur did pick out the olives."

"Yes, but Franklin ate every one of them." She smiled. "You know what he whispered when he said good night to me?"

I shook my head.

"He said it would be super awesome if you lived in Colinas. I think so, too. What's keeping you in Pasadena, sis?"

I counted things off on my fingers. "House. Garden. Job. And the only home Zoe has ever known." Move up here? It had never occurred to me.

"I suppose. But new surroundings might be the change that girl needs to finally move beyond Greg's death." She elbowed me. "And you could be near family. Think about it, okay?"

"I will, if you tell me what on earth you argued with Val about."

Her face fell.

"I didn't get a chance to tell you," I went on. "Quan was here when I showed up with the groceries."

"He was?"

"Yes. His primary goal seemed to be to get me to admit I could not swear you didn't go out last night."

"Cece! I didn't go anywhere. I can't believe you wouldn't vouch for me." She moved away on the couch.

"Listen. I insisted under no circumstances would you have gone out without telling me where you were going and when you'd be back. Not with the boys asleep. But you know I wear earplugs when I sleep. And this is the law, Al. I couldn't lie to him and say I knew for certain you were here all night." I reached over for her hand. "I also made it quite clear you would never, ever kill anyone."

She let me take her hand, but she wouldn't make eye contact.

"Hey, come on," I murmured. "Don't be mad."

"I'm not mad, honest." She twisted to look at me. "I'm scared. What if this sheriff dude doesn't believe me? What if they make me go to jail?"

"That's not going to happen, Al. I'm going to help, and I think Cam will, too."

"Sheesh, I forgot all about her." Allie gave her head a shake. "Some innkeeper I am. I hope she has what she needs."

"She's in the new suite. I'm sure she's comfortable." Allie and Fuller had carried out extensive renovations a year or two ago, part of which included adding a downstairs B&B suite with a small sitting room, a mini-kitchen area, and a private entrance from the outside. I would move in there after Cam left. "She went off to another farm after lunch. She probably grabbed a bite of dinner out and let herself in. She must still have jet lag."

"You're right."

"Anyway, you heard what Cam said about solving a few homicides. She and I can put our heads together tomorrow. But—"

Allie cut in. "But first you need to know what my history with Val is. She and I both served on the CCC, the Colinas Community Coalition. Well, I still do. It's all about keeping downtown beautiful and bringing the local community together as well as the community of tourists. We've done things like put cornhole games and a life-sized chess set in the park and sponsor the scarecrow light post contest in October. On Saturday we're staging a pop-up holiday craft fair in the park."

"Doesn't a Chamber of Commerce usually run stuff like community boosting?" I asked.

"Yes, but the Chamber here has been kind of dysfunctional recently. Our group, made up of business owners and civic groups, has the blessing of the city council." She let out a sigh. "Except Val and I were co-chairs, and we clashed repeatedly about the vision for the group, the direction we wanted to take downtown."

"In what ways?"

"For one thing, she wanted to let chain stores into the

historic district. Cece, we fought hard a decade ago to keep them out of here. Nobody wants chains and box stores downtown. Plus, Val thought Manzanita Boulevard should be flashier, richer looking. It's not us."

"No. But you didn't start a fistfight or anything." I sipped my cognac. The warmth going down was a comfort but also a reminder to take it slowly.

"Not exactly. One time after a meeting she looked like she was about to shove me. I sidestepped, and she fell forward. She claimed I'd pushed her to the ground, but I hadn't."

"Yikes. Were there any witnesses?" I asked.

"No. It was only the two of us. But we'd argued plenty of times in front of others. I'm sure somebody squealed to Quan and that's why he's interested in talking with me. Grilling me was more what it was like, honestly." Allie tasted her drink. "It all came to a head recently. Val was seeking support to push me out of the leadership. I don't like that kind of tactic and was kind of rallying my own supporters. The whole thing was a mess. But nothing to commit murder over."

I cradled the bowl of my glass in both palms. A murder had been committed for a reason, though. How could I find out what—and who?

Chapter Seven

I was returning from seeing my nephews off on the school bus at eight the next morning when Cam, wearing a hoodie and tennies, emerged from around the side of Allie's house.

"Morning, Cece," she said. "Coming back from a walk?"

"Just to the end of the block. I put the darlings on the bus. They're ten, and Franklin insists he can walk himself down. He says he'll be safe. But Arthur is both accident prone and easily distracted. Allie feels safer if someone sees them both off."

Cam made a face. "I was determined to raise a free-range kiddo. But there's a lot to worry about these days. I shudder at the thought of my Ruthie walking to a bus alone, even though I know we'll get there. Plus, she's much more outgoing than I was as a child. She says hello to every single person she sees on the street. If they don't respond, she says it again. It's as if she's running for mayor. I feel like the potential for disaster lurks in all corners."

"Allie was friendly like that when we were young. Heck, she still is." I laughed. "Are you out for a bit of exercise?"

"Yes. Want to join me?"

"Sure. Let me give Allie a shout and grab a key if she's

going out." I ducked into the house and was back in two minutes.

Cam caught me up on the farmers she'd spoken with yesterday afternoon. "I have two more places to tour today. While we walk, do you want to toss around ideas about the murder?"

"That'd be super helpful. I've never had the slightest inclination toward wanting to solve a crime."

"I get it. But when a person you know and love is threatened—or your livelihood is—you kind of have no choice."

I nodded. "No choice is exactly how it feels." Cam had taken a right from the house, which meant we were headed away from downtown. "If we continue in this direction, pretty soon we'll lose the sidewalk. Let's go around the block and head back toward town. There's a nice trail around Halstead Park."

"Sounds good. Wait a sec. Halstead Park, as in Allie's last name?"

"The same. Her husband's family has been here for over a century. Fuller's double-great-grandfather was one of the first Black professionals to establish a business here, and he became a major philanthropist. Being generous runs in the family, and the town named the park after Fuller's grandpa."

"Awesome," Cam said. "So far I haven't seen too many people of color in the valley, and I haven't had a chance to meet your nephews yet."

"You will soon. Listen, last night Allie filled me in on the CCC, the Colinas Community Coalition." I told Cam what Allie had said about the group's mission and about the conflict between her and Val.

"Val sounds like a piece of work," Cam murmured.

"I know. And a complicated one. Yesterday Thea was

saying Val wanted to keep the garden club in the dark ages, sort of. But Allie portrayed her role in the CCC as wanting too much modernization, with chain stores and richer decor."

"Every coin has five sides, as my great-uncle Albert is fond of saying."

"I guess. I'd like to have a word with Val's brother if I can figure out how to approach him. Thea said they had a flare-up not long ago, didn't she?" I asked.

"More or less. And Ed mentioned Rafael teaches at the high school."

"Right," I said. "I can look up what time classes get out and find him there. I hope. Or . . . wait. It's the Friday before Christmas vacation. School might be closed, unless they go to school for a few days next week."

"Allie will know," Cam said.

"Better yet, I'll ask Franklin. He's always on top of the schedule. The kid is ten going on doctoral candidate. Let's cross Manzanita here. We can hit the park trail over there." I gestured at the corner of Halstead Park, which occupied an entire block. *Huh.* What was going on over there? Trucks were backed up to the curb, and people were busily erecting pop-up tents.

By the time we waited for traffic and crossed, one booth was already rigged out with garlands and red ribbons.

"I remember," I said. "It's the holiday fair. I'll have to take the boys off Allie's hands tomorrow and bring them over. I can help them pick out gifts for their parents." I could look for a few presents, too. I needed to find special gifts for Zoe, Mom, and Allie's whole family.

"You're the best auntie." Cam's smile was wistful. "I'm an only child. Pete has a niece and a nephew, but they were taciturn middle schoolers when we married. Now they're uncommunicative high school students."

"Maybe you can connect better with them once they're out on their own."

"I hope so." She gave a quiet smile. "But my best friend Ruth—who we named Ruthie after—is like an aunt to my girl. She spoils her and takes her on playdates and buys her the best play clothes, in addition to handing down stuff from her own kiddos."

"See? When we don't have blood family, we make our own."

"True. And I'm close to her girls, her twins. They even call me Auntie Cam."

We slowed our pace, watching the fair setup in progress. A man with thin sandy-colored hair was having trouble getting the legs of a folding table to cooperate.

"Let me help," I said. Between us we got the legs secured and the table flipped upright.

"Thanks, ma'am." About my height, he wasn't thickset but looked like he might work physically for a living, with strong, thick hands and a ruddy neck.

"You're welcome," I said.

"I don't know what's wrong with me today. All left feet and rubber hands." He rubbed his brow as if it hurt.

"I get like that at times," Cam said. "What are you going to sell in this booth, sir?"

"Nothing, except memberships to the Colinas Historical Society. We'll also give away information about the complex down t'other end of Manzanita." He gestured with his chin.

"Can you tell us more about the complex?" I asked. "I love local history." Or so I could pretend. "I'm Cece Barton, by the way, and this is my friend Cam Flaherty. We're tourists." I extended my hand. I mostly was a tourist. Same with Cam.

"Otto Harper." He pumped my hand. "Born and raised up right here in the valley."

Bingo. Another person on the list I was hoping to speak with.

"Good to meet both you gals," he added.

"Likewise, Otto," Cam said.

"Now, the historical complex should be any tourist's first stop in Colinas," he began. "All the buildings are antique adobes. You first get the overview of the town, like, and its past at the history museum. Then you can buy a map or a book or whatnot at the bookstore, check out Acorn Fine Art's original souvenirs, and finish up with a glass of vino overlooking the river." He rubbed those beefy hands together after finishing what sounded like a tourist brochure spiel, minus the "like" and the "whatnot."

"I heard a woman in town died under unfortunate circumstances this week, a Val Harper." I mustered my most sympathetic face. "Was she your wife? If so, my deepest condolences."

He took a step back as if I'd slugged him. "Valencia was my ex-wife. It's horrible, what happened to her." His mouth pulled down at the corners.

"She served us a glass of wine on Wednesday, didn't she, Cece?" Cam asked. "I'm sorry for your loss, sir."

He eyed Cam and me. "How'd you two know about her murder, anyhow? Her name ain't been released yet."

"Somebody connected with town told me," Cam said.

"Yeah, there's always a blabbermouth in City Hall." He pressed his lips together.

"Have the police made any headway yet?" I asked.

"No, but I got a pretty good idea who done it. Yes, I surely do."

I'd opened my mouth to ask more questions when Cam spoke.

"Good luck with the fair tomorrow." She motioned for me to continue down the path with her.

After we were out of earshot, I said, "I was about to ask him if he knew how she died and who might have done it."

"I thought so. If I might offer a word of advice, you need to take it a little more slowly, Cece. You start grilling a guy like him and you run the risk of him getting suspicious. You'll never learn anything."

"Is this week one of Amateur Detecting 101?" I asked.

"Could be." She smiled.

"Thanks for the lesson. I mean it. This is a whole new world for me."

Chapter Eight

After our outing, Cam retreated to her suite to get ready for her day. I popped my head into the kitchen, where Allie sat at the kitchen table with her laptop and various papers spread around. I helped myself to a mug of coffee, dosed it with cream, and sat across from my sister.

"Good walk?" Allie asked, not looking up.

"Yes. We met Val's ex setting up for the holiday fair."

"Otto." Now Allie looked at me. "Learn anything?"

"Not much, except he seemed in shock she'd been murdered."

"That's no surprise. He can hardly say, 'Good riddance,' can he?"

"You haven't heard how she died, have you?" I asked.

"No, and Quan hasn't been back, either." She typed for a moment. "I'm sorry, sis, but I have to get this offer in ASAP, or the house'll get snapped up by another buyer."

"Good luck. I'm going to go upstairs and do a little research on my own laptop." I grabbed an apple out of the bowl and trudged up to my room with it and the mug.

Cam had suggested undertaking online digging if I had time, which was brilliant. I fired up the laptop and settled in at the desk overlooking the driveway.

The driveway. It still bugged me I hadn't been able to

verify Allie's presence in the house to Detective Quan for the night of the murder. Even if I'd been awake, my sister could have left the house quietly, since her bedroom was downstairs. She drove an all-electric car, which was silent. If she'd left the headlights off until she reached the street, I might not have noticed her departure. None of which she would have done, anyway.

I shook my head and mounted a search for Colinas Community Coalition. The members seemed to include most of the Manzanita Boulevard businesses, from the banks to Hoppy Hills brewpub to Edie's Diner to the hair salon, Shear Illusions. The Colinas Garden Club was a member, as was Allie's real estate agency and the local Lions Club, among other non-storefront businesses and organizations.

Maybe I could go up and down the street and talk to owners. Doing so seemed daunting. I couldn't walk up and ask them if they'd had issues with Val and had killed her. I'd have to think about another approach.

Letting out a breath, I turned to Otto Harper. What did he do when he wasn't managing the complex? The job couldn't take much time. It probably involved only collecting rent and reporting to the board. He'd looked strong and a little rough, as if he spent a lot of time outdoors.

It didn't take me long to find Harper Landscaping Services, owned by Otto Harper. He apparently designed residential gardens and patios but also mowed lawns and took away leaves. No wonder his hands were strong, although it made me wonder why he'd had trouble with the table earlier. Maybe Val's interest in gardening came from him? I couldn't find out where he lived. What if he'd designed a showcase garden in the house the couple had shared but she'd gotten the home in the settlement? Resentment might have fueled rage, leading to murder. And being house-rich but cash-poor could explain her pushing to sell her handmade mittens.

Allie probably knew where Val lived, except I didn't want to bother her during her urgent task.

I searched next for Val's brother, Rafael Torres. I easily found him on the high school website. He was older than I was but younger than Val, possibly by as much as ten years, unless this picture was dated. They resembled each other, with the same dark hair and the same white streak. But where her features were heavier, Rafael's looked lighter, leaner. He taught science and math at the school and coached the cross-country team.

He wouldn't last long with teenagers in a school setting if he had an anger issue. It was Thea who mentioned he'd been expressing a lot of anger about his sister. Directly afterward, Thea had clammed up about how she knew him and what in particular had made him angry. *Interesting.*

It was time to see if I could discover how Val was killed, with what, where, and at what time. Our parents had played Clue with Allie and me when we were young. Funny how a motive was never discussed in the game and all the crimes featured the same suspect pool. I wasn't going to be able to rely on one of the six old standbys, though I'd always chosen Professor Plum as my alter ego. Allie wanted to be Miss Scarlett, which was totally in character.

I searched for "Colinas homicide." *Odd.* There had been a few murders over the decades, but Val's wasn't top and center. It wasn't in the list at all.

I added "Valencia Torres Harper." Still zip. Perhaps the news wasn't public yet, but that seemed unlikely. I tried "Murder Colinas Historical Complex." That was the key. I leaned in and read.

> Longtime Colinas resident found dead outside the Vino y Vida wine bar by a passerby walking a dog early Thursday morning. Foul play is suspected. Authorities are withholding the identity of the victim pending notification of next of kin. Any witnesses to an altercation or suspicious movements in the vicinity on Wednesday night or in the early hours of Thursday morning are urged to contact the Sonoma County Sheriff at the following number.

It gave the number and continued for another paragraph.

> "Colinas residents should exercise all due caution, but we have every confidence in our Sonoma County law enforcement officers to swiftly apprehend the criminal," said Colinas mayor Malia Guttierez. "Our thoughts and prayers are with the victim's family."

I sat back. The fact that Rafael was Val's brother seemed common knowledge. Apparently the police hadn't been able to locate him, or maybe he wasn't ready to have the news made public yet. It could be that he was on leave from the high school. Or maybe Val had other kin the police wanted to inform, relatives from whom she wasn't estranged.

On second reading, I confirmed the article didn't specify how Val died.

I closed the computer. I always needed more steps in my day. It was time for me to get moving.

Chapter Nine

After I pulled open the door to Valley Savings and Loan, I stood there. The bank was housed in a century-old stone building that had originally been a general store. Tellers still worked behind plexiglass barriers to protect them from unmasked customers spewing virus particles. In their green shirts, they were busy taking deposits, cashing checks, and carrying out all the other business of a trusted local bank. A green-blazered bank officer in a glass-walled office bent over paperwork with two women.

I turned and made my way back out. I didn't know how to do this detective thing in person. I couldn't imagine confronting a teller and asking them if they knew who killed Val Harper. It wasn't the right question, but I had no idea what the right one would be.

A little farther down and across the boulevard sat Bowen's Apothecary, a classic family-run drugstore and pharmacy. I considered crossing over. Nope. Cam might know which words to use. Detective Quan surely would understand how to inquire, and people didn't have the option of refusing him. For me, it was one more chalk mark in the Fail column. I didn't enjoy the feeling, but I was used to it.

I made my way across the side street and found myself

back at Exchange Bakery and Gourmet Provisions. I might not know what questions to ask, but I sure knew how to sink my teeth into a chocolate-filled croissant. My cereal-and-banana breakfast with my nephews felt like a long time ago.

When I'd lived in Japan as a young mother with Greg and toddler Zoe, I had no job other than housewife and mom. I'd learned, to my surprise, Japanese bakeries excelled at French pastries. I ate plenty of delicious Japanese food, but there was one small coffee shop I would walk to with my daughter in her stroller. The owners fawned over my little blond *gaijin* girl, and we would hang out for an hour. I'd sip coffee, she'd have a chocolate milk, and we'd snack and look at books. If she fell asleep on the way there, I was rewarded with precious adult time to myself to read and think. And I always ordered a *pain au chocolat*.

The bakery counter here had a line. I poked around over on the provisions side to wait out the customers. In front of the area displaying gourmet oils and vinegars, a woman with a mass of curly dark hair cascading down her back pulled bottles out of a box and rearranged what already sat on the shelf to accommodate them.

I peeked over her shoulder. The company label on the olive oil bottles read Raj Orchards.

"I recently heard about this olive oil." I stepped to her side, then saw her T-shirt's insignia: Raj Orchards Fine Olive Products.

"It's the best." She smiled. "Hi. I'm Narini." She extended an elbow, which I bumped with mine.

"Cece." I gazed at the bottles. One kind was flavored with garlic. Another with habanero peppers. A third featured Mediterranean herbs such as basil, oregano, and rosemary. And one label claimed the oil was sand- and mineral-filtered and triple cold pressed by a farmer standing on her head. Not really, but the words described a complicated process I couldn't comprehend. I checked the prices and managed not to choke out loud at seventeen bucks for a slim bottle holding under thirteen ounces.

On the other hand, I was presented with the chance to quiz a person associated with Thea.

"My sister, Allie, says she often stops at your stand at the farmers' market on Sundays," I said.

"Allie's great. I haven't seen you around before."

"I'm up here for the holidays." I watched Narini's hands as she arranged the last bottles. Her brown forearms were muscular, and her clipped nails were stained around the edges, maybe from working with olives.

"You live in the city or in SoCal?" She faced me, a tiny jewel sparkling in the side of her slender nose.

"Pasadena." I picked up one of the garlic-infused bottles and pretended to study it. "I met a friend of yours yesterday. Thea Robinet?"

Narini tilted her head. "Thea's my friend."

"I heard she and Val Harper, may she rest in peace, had a lot of conflict having to do with the garden club."

"They disagreed about the club's direction going forward, yes." She narrowed her eyes at me. "Why do you ask?"

I swallowed. I didn't want to blow this. "I met another visitor to town who's really interested in permaculture and sustainability. She has a farm back east, and . . ." I ran out of words. I shrugged and tried to smile. "I guess I mean to say, I think Thea has a point."

"She does." Narini's cheeks turned pink. "She's a visionary, Cece. She knows what's going to help the environment and therefore all of us." She glanced down at her belly. "And our future."

I now saw a bulge I hadn't noticed before. Narini was pregnant. Maybe halfway along, with at least a few months to go before she gave birth, maybe more. Allie thought she and Thea were a couple. Married? Maybe. And about to be parents, likely thanks to a sperm donor.

What the olive grower wasn't was suspicious of me. But if she loved Thea and thought Val was threatening her and thereby their family's future, Narini could have used those strong arms and hands to remove the threat.

Chapter Ten

Despite striking out, information-wise, downtown, my plan all along had been to end up at the historical complex to see if I might learn anything from the location. I planned to try to talk to a few folks and maybe grab a glass of wine at Vino y Vida, too, if it was even open.

Zoe and I had toured the museum one of the first times we'd come to visit, but she'd been little, and it was so long ago I didn't remember much about it. I supposed Greg must have been with us at first, too. The wine bar and the shops were much newer, and I'd never shopped in them. When I'd visited Colinas more recently, it had been all about connecting the three cousins and hanging out with my twin and her husband. I hadn't done any touristing or wine bar hopping, either.

The Colinas History Museum looked normal from this end, except for a sign on the door reading, "Closed due to circumstances beyond our control. Open Saturday usual hours." Murder was the definition of being beyond one's control—except for the killer's. I wondered if Otto ran the museum and worked in it in addition to his tasks as the complex manager, or if someone else was in charge of the displays. Either way, I didn't blame whoever it was for closing up for the day.

As I rounded the building to the small cluster of businesses stretching along the Russian River, I slowed my step. Beyond the wine bar and to the left, overlooking the water, was a long rectangular bocce court filled with sand. I'd seen two couples playing on Wednesday but hadn't paid it much attention. Yellow police tape now stretched in a five-foot perimeter all the way around the court. Yellow cones with diagonal black stripes warned people away from approaching the area.

I took several more steps. A young woman in the khaki shirt and dark olive pants of the county sheriff's department moved toward me.

"No farther than the door of the wine bar, please, ma'am." Her hair was pulled back in a long braid hanging down her back. She kept one hand on her heavy service belt, and she held her other arm loose but ready at her side. I would have known she was a cop even without the uniform.

"Are the bookstore and the art gallery closed?" I asked.

"Yes, ma'am, for the time being."

"Too bad. I'd planned to Christmas shop in both places." I smiled and tried to step around her, to see what she'd do. She moved in the same direction.

"We expect they'll be allowed to reopen by tomorrow, if not sooner." The officer was an imperturbable Buddhist boulder blocking the way.

I lowered my voice to a low confidential tone. "So, what happened here?"

"You have a good day, ma'am." She stood her ground.

I pivoted toward the wine bar and barely refrained from saluting. I shook my head. This sleuthing business was giving me an irreverent attitude that wasn't a bit like me.

Chapter Eleven

The inside of Vino y Vida was empty except for a remarkable woman who stood behind the bar, except "stood" wasn't the right word. She moved her hips to a catchy song that sounded African playing loud on the speakers. Statuesque in height and build, she'd wound a gray braid around her head, a braid festooned with purple ribbon. A purple-and-green cotton tunic would be nearly knee-length on anyone else. On her it barely grazed her thighs. A dozen bangles adorned each wrist.

"Welcome," she called. "Come on in. We're open, except nobody knows it." She reached over and turned down the music.

"Thanks." I approached the bar and slid onto a stool. "What are you pouring today?"

"Anything and everything. What do you have a taste for?"

"Mmm. I haven't eaten lunch yet. Maybe light and bubbly?" The *pain au chocolat* didn't count as lunch, not in my book.

"I have a local *vinho verde*. It's light and, while not bubbly exactly, it's sparkly."

"I'd love to try it. I had a Portuguese friend when I lived in Japan, of all places, and he introduced me to *vinho verde.*" The name meant "green wine," which didn't sound appetizing, but it was delicious.

She set a full stemmed glass in front of me, then splashed more wine into a glass below the countertop. Up close I could see the lines in her tanned face. I thought she must be close to seventy years old, and I was delighted she wore what she wished and moved how it felt good to her—the heck with what anyone thought. I approved.

She lifted a straight-sided juice glass full of the pale wine and said, "*Saúde.*"

I returned the cheers and took a sip. "My name is Cece Barton."

"I'm Mooncat."

A unique name.

"And you can't tell the boss I'm having a nip of wine," she added before I could ask about her name.

"Who's the boss?" Here I went again, faking innocence. Too late now.

"I meant it literally, Cece." Her expression grew somber, and her eyes dragged at the corners. "You can't tell her, because she's dead."

I gave a slow nod. "Is she the woman who was murdered a couple of days ago?"

"She is. Valencia Harper. Did you ever hear a prettier first name?"

"It's beautiful," I said.

"How did you know Val was the victim?" Mooncat sniffed and swiped at a tear.

At least one person was grieving for Val.

"They haven't released her name yet," she added.

"I was in here for a glass Wednesday afternoon and met her. My sister read the news on a local action page."

"It's such a loss."

"I'm sorry, Mooncat. Were you good friends with her?"

"Not really. She and I weren't close, per se, but she was a fair boss, and anyway, nobody deserves to be murdered."

"True." I thought of the police tape a few yards away. "Was Val killed here in the complex?"

"Yes." She set her elbows on the bar and leaned toward me. "On the bocce court," she whispered.

"After she closed up here that night?"

"It must have been. What's worse, Cece, is they used one of her own handicrafts." Mooncat's eyes looked haunted. "She was cracked over the head with a bocce ball inside a handmade freakin' mitten and then left to die." She shuddered and pulled a pair of black mittens up from under the counter, as Val had done only two days earlier.

"How horrible," I said. The image of a person swinging one of those stretchy mittens holding a two-pound weight over their head and onto Val's skull was worth a shudder. "Poor Val."

"Can you believe it?"

"She tried to sell me her mittens. They're certainly stretchy enough to fit a bocce ball inside." And the long cuff would be easy to grip.

Mooncat gave a slow nod as she replaced the pair out of sight.

I made a flash decision. "Val had argued with my twin sister. The county sheriff's detective thinks Allie might have killed her, which is more ludicrous than snow falling on the Santa Monica pier. You worked for Val. Can you think of anyone who hated her, who might have needed her out of their lives?"

"You're asking if I know who Val's enemies were?"

"Yes." I might sit through a rehash of Rafael, Otto, or Thea. With any luck she'd know of a person I hadn't heard of yet.

"Other than her ex-husband, I assume?"

"I've heard about Otto. I actually met him this morning."

"She has a baby brother she adored, but he holds a grudge against her, or maybe it was the other way around. And I saw a spat between Val and her next-in-command at the garden club, Thea Robinet." Mooncat swiped at the counter. She straightened a couple of open wine bottles. She took a sip from her juice glass.

I waited.

"Also, an olive farmer in the valley has butted heads with Val more than once," she murmured. "I'm not clear on why. Narini was in here with Thea that time. She was irate and all up in Val's business."

"What's Narini's last name?" In Gourmet Provisions, Narini had been arranging Raj Orchards bottles, but maybe she had a different surname. I didn't know if it was her farm or her family's, or if she only worked there.

Mooncat folded her arms over her impressive bust. "What are you, some kind of detective? Why are you asking all these questions?"

Uh-oh. "As I said, it's because my twin sister is being looked at as a murderer. She's not. Just like I'm not a detective." I swallowed. "But if I can help find the real killer, everyone in town will feel safer. And Allie won't have to worry about going to jail and leaving her little boys without their mom."

Also, why was Mooncat reluctant to tell me about Narini and Val's fight?

Chapter Twelve

"What happened to the afternoon lull, Ed?" I asked from my perch on the last stool at Edie's counter. It was two-thirty, and I was completely, absolutely famished.

Every stool and every booth was full. Senior citizens and high school seniors alike jockeyed for space, with families and groups of young adults filling the rest of the space.

Ed swiped the counter and laid a fresh paper placemat and silverware roll in front of me. "What day is it, Cece?"

"Um, Friday?"

"Yes, Friday, the eighteenth of December, the last Friday before Christmas. Schools had a half day."

So much for my plan to hit the high school after I left here and find Rafael at the end of the school day. My window had come and gone. I shouldn't have gone to see him alone, anyway. What if he was a murderer?

"Nobody has their shopping finished," Ed continued. "People are traveling. And, guess what else?"

"What?"

"Hanukkah starts Sunday." He smoothed down his red Edie's polo shirt. "Which means more families and more shopping. For me, it's all good. But you can expect crowds everywhere through Christmas Eve."

"I guess I'll have to set my expectations. It is the holidays, after all." Holidays with an unsolved homicide casting a slate-colored cloud over everything. "For now, I'd like a salmon burger with the works except onions, and a side of sweet potato fries, please."

"A libation?"

"I don't think so, thanks. Water is fine."

He hurried off to put in my order and take more. An older woman waited on booths, and through the open window to the kitchen I saw a young man short-order cooking. They all helped one another in what looked like a well-practiced choreography.

I spied a text from Cam.

Where are you? What's happening?

I wrote right back.

Late lunch at Edie's. Join me?

BRT

Good, she'd be right over. I wanted to hash through with her what I'd learned since the morning, and the reactions I'd noted.

Before my burger arrived, I checked my email and national news, plus the one social media site where I spent any time. I thanked Ed and ate one-handed so I could scroll through local news channels. I got sidetracked, as one does, by a notice about the Phunniest Pun Contest right here in Colinas, followed by a story on the Healdsburg Prune Packers, the minor-league baseball team.

When I glanced up to see Cam standing next to me, I'd already finished my burger and half the fries. "When did you sneak in?"

"At about three-fifteen, right before you'd almost deprived me of your last fries." She smiled as she swooped in to grab a few from the pile remaining. "I mean, a minute ago. What were you absorbed in reading?"

"It's an article on a local baseball team. But I've always been a focused reader. I was reading with my fourth-grade class in the school library once, and my teacher had to shake my shoulder. The fire alarm was going off and the place had emptied. Why don't you . . ." I glanced around. "Oh." Every seat was still full.

"What, join you? Happy to, but impossible. It being Friday afternoon, I was considering a beer instead, since I ate lunch at a normal hour. What do you say we check out Hoppy Hills?"

"Sounds good. Finish the rest of those, if you want." Which was kind of a moot point, since only two fries remained on the plate. I laid a twenty on the counter, plenty for the lunch plus a good tip. I stood and looked around for Ed.

He was behind the far end of the lunch counter talking to a woman with salt-and-pepper hair who appeared to be rather impatiently waiting for a seat. A slender man stood just inside the door. I took another look. He was in his forties, possibly late forties. His dark hair bore a white stripe, an unusual look. Could he be Rafael Torres? I elbowed Cam and tried to point unobtrusively with my chin. "I think—"

"Rafael," Ed boomed. "Come in, come in. You are welcome." He hurried, beaming, toward the newcomer.

"Maybe we'll stay put another minute?" Cam murmured.

"We will."

A moment later, Ed led the woman as well as Rafael toward us. "Cece Barton, meet Rafael Torres. And this is Cam . . . I apologize, Cam, I can't remember your last name."

"Flaherty." She smiled at Rafael.

"But I'm afraid this nice lady has been waiting for

Cece's seat, Rafael," Ed said. "I'm sure another table or stool will open up soon."

"Good to meet you, Rafael," I said. "Cam and I were about to go for a beer at the brewpub around the corner. Would you like to join us there? You don't mind, Ed, do you?"

"Not a bit," Ed said, giving a knowing nod.

Rafael looked a bit bewildered. "Well, if you ladies are sure. It's been quite a week, and I appreciate the offer."

"We're sure," Cam said. "Come with us."

"Enjoy your lunch, ma'am," I said to the woman, who also appeared bewildered. "Talk to you soon, Ed."

I followed Cam and Rafael out, more than happy that Cam could lead the questioning, if questioning was what was going to transpire. I'd already proved less than competent in getting information out of people.

Chapter Thirteen

We found a vacant booth in the back corner of the Hoppy Hills pub where we might be able to hear each other. The lights on strings draped along the walls were hop-shaped, with pointed overlapping scales making them look like thin artichokes. A lamp on each table was shaped the same way. Christmas carols sung by various current and former artists played, and the buzz of conversation from Friday afternoon drinkers was loud. The place smelled of beer and fried food and companionship.

After Rafael sat on one side of the booth, Cam and I slid in across from him. A waitperson of indeterminate gender with purple hair and lots of piercings came by to take our orders.

"Start with drinks?" the server asked.

"Your hoppiest IPA for me," I said. Rafael added a sour for himself, and Cam went for a porter.

"You got it," the server said. "Anybody want food?"

"I'll take a look at the menu." Rafael took another glance at the waitperson. "Is that Pat?"

"Hey, Mr. Torres, how are ya?"

"I'm fine. How are things going for you?"

"I'm doing much better, thank you." He—or she—turned away.

"I had them in AP physics," he said. "Brilliant kid who went through a rough patch. Not sure why they're waiting tables, but it's none of my business."

He was fluent with the indeterminate pronouns, as a teacher who worked with teens should be. I'd grown up before the new acceptance of gender fluidity in the language, but Zoe had made clear how important it was for friends of hers. I had no objection.

"How long have you been a teacher, Rafael?" I asked. It was an innocent enough question not to get me in trouble. We were here to glean information from him, after all.

"I've been at Colinas High since I left the navy twenty years ago and moved back home. I joined the service for the benefits, but I stayed on and taught at a base high school for a couple of years."

Pat delivered our beers.

"I'd like the black bean burger, please," Rafael told the server, "with cole slaw instead of fries."

"Can you add an order of the deep-fried artichoke hearts for the table, too?" Cam asked.

Pat nodded and turned away.

After cheers all around and a first sip, Rafael set down his glass.

"Where are you ladies from, and why did you abduct me?" He sounded amused rather than suspicious.

I couldn't help snorting. "We're both visitors. I live in Pasadena."

"And I'm out from Massachusetts," Cam said.

The server brought the appetizer. "Enjoy. Your burger will be up in a couple of minutes, Mr. Torres."

"Thanks, Pat." To us Rafael made a rolling motion with his hand. "So you're out wine tasting and making off with high school teachers?"

I waited for Cam to explain. I'd blow it if I tried.

"I'm not wine tasting as much as visiting farms in the area. Trying to take home new ideas for my organic farm north of Boston. California is often the leader in innovations of all kinds, particularly in the environment and in farming." Cam took a swig of beer, then folded her hands. "To be honest about why we invited you to join us, Rafael, it has to do with your sister's homicide."

His easy, affable expression slid away. His eyes took on a steely look, and he straightened his spine as only a former military person can.

"Yes?"

"I'd like to offer my sympathies," I said.

"We're sorry for your loss," Cam added.

He blinked, as if considering how to respond. "Thank you. Valencia and I weren't close in recent years." He laid his palms flat on the table.

Was he thinking of leaving? That wasn't part of our hastily conceived plan.

"The thing is," Cam continued, "Cece's own sister is a person of interest in Val's homicide, and we're trying to find the real killer and clear Allie's name."

"What makes you think you can do that?" He sounded skeptical. "You're visitors. You don't even live here."

I dipped an artichoke heart in a creamy lemony sauce and savored it.

"I've been a consultant to the police back home on several murder cases," Cam said.

"I see." Rafael followed my example with an artichoke heart, but he didn't seem to be enjoying the flavors of the crispy nugget as much as I had. Or maybe he was really hungry. He swallowed. "You know, the Sonoma County sheriff's deputy has already been to grill me."

"He talked to me, too," I said. "But I know my sister didn't kill Val. Do you know Allie Halstead?"

He did a double take. "Allie Halstead? Yes, I've met her more than once. She's your sister?"

"My twin."

"We wondered if you had any ideas about who might have murdered Val," Cam said. "Did she have enemies? People who held grudges against her?"

He lifted his beer, but instead of drinking it he closed his eyes and leaned back against the wall. I exchanged a glance with Cam. She helped herself to an artichoke heart, and I had another.

Rafael opened his eyes, straightening his posture again and squaring his shoulders. "Valencia was a difficult and unhappy person, ladies. She rubbed almost everyone the wrong way. We were quite close as children, despite an eight-year age gap between us. It was only the two of us, and I looked up to her for everything."

He closed his mouth when his food arrived, delivered by a different employee.

"She changed when she married Otto," he went on. "I went off to the navy and college. When I came back, Val was even more different."

"Did she have children?" Cam asked.

"Are your parents still alive?" I asked at the same time. I mouthed "Sorry" to Cam.

"Our parents died in an accident while I was at sea. Valencia and Otto had one child, a son, but he died in Mojave in a military training exercise. It was a terrible tragedy. He wasn't even killed in combat. Such a waste."

"Very much," I murmured. It was. Nobody should have to endure such a string of heartbreaks. Parents, nephew, now sister. I glanced at his left hand. He didn't wear a wedding ring, but a band of pale skin made me think he'd divorced not too long ago.

"I'm afraid my joining the military made the kid think it was a good thing to do." He stared into his beer. "I felt responsible for his death."

"Do you have children, Rafael?" Cam asked.

He smiled, his expression brightening. "I do, a boy and a girl. Those two are the main joys of my life. They're in high school now, and by some miracle they still like to hang out with me."

"Do they live with you or their mom?" I asked.

He stared at me, his nostrils flaring. "How did you know I was divorced? What is it with you two? All this BS sympathy when what you're really doing is investigating me?" His voice was low and harsh as he half stood.

"No." I held out the back of my own left hand and rubbed where a wedding band would be, a ring I'd removed as soon as I could after Greg died. "I simply noticed the pale skin where your ring had been not too long ago. Please sit down and eat."

Cam shot me an approving glance.

He glanced from me to her and back. He sat. He bit into his burger.

"We would still like to know if you have any idea who Val's enemies might be," Cam spoke softly. "So we can try to track them down."

I supposed we'd be overambitious to expect him to also explain what made him stop speaking to his big sister. I couldn't imagine ever cutting ties with my twin. But Allie wasn't Valencia Torres Harper. Not even close.

Chapter Fourteen

Takeout pizza consumed and children asleep by nine o'clock that night, Allie, Cam, and I put our heads together. Or, rather, we lounged on the family room comfy furniture sipping a fine port Allie had been saving.

"Did Rafael ever say who, in his opinion, Val's enemies were?" Allie asked.

"All he could come up with was Otto," Cam said. "But even then he blamed Val for the animosity between them more than her ex."

I wrinkled my nose. "We failed to ask why they'd divorced, or when. Do you know, Allie?"

"Did he tell you about their boy dying?" Allie asked.

"Yes. Awful." The son might have been Zoe's age. Children dying before their parents of any cause wasn't the natural order of things. I shivered to think of anything bad happening to my girl, much less something fatal.

"I think their marriage couldn't endure the loss," Allie said. "Or at least Val's side of it."

"Burying a child is one of the hardest things a couple ever has to do." Cam shook her head, a sad look on her face. "It's the ultimate test of their love as well as their communication skills."

"I don't even want to think about losing one of mine," Allie murmured.

"I don't think Rafael caught on to us suspecting him, did he, Cece?" Cam asked.

"For a minute he thought we were investigating him, which we are, when I asked him about where his kids lived." I explained about the wedding band tan line to Allie. "But then he relaxed."

"I didn't really find him acting suspiciously," Cam said. "On the other hand, we didn't ask about his alibi for the night Val was killed, which the sheriff should have already done."

Allie noiselessly drummed her fingers on the arm of the stuffed easy chair she'd curled up in. "So, he thinks everything is Val's fault. She changed. She couldn't deal with her kid's death. She was at fault with her brother. Kind of classic, isn't it?"

Interesting. "You mean, if he killed her, it was her fault?" I asked.

Allie bobbed her head.

"Do you know Rafael?" Cam asked Allie. "He seemed to think he'd met you."

"I don't really know him, but as he said, we've met. Thing is, my son Arthur is a really good distance runner, for a kid who's ten. He's also fast. He's begged me to take him to the high school's cross-country meets when they run locally, and I have a few times. Artie tries to race the big kids at the end of the course to the finish line. Mr. Torres has been nothing but sweet and supportive to my kid. He said he'd save Arthur a place on the team when he gets to high school. Artie was over the moon, as you can imagine. I'd hate to think Rafael killed his own sister."

"Still, he could have a dark side none of us has seen." I savored another taste of the warm, rich port.

"Also, circling back to his thoughts about who might have murdered his sister, if he's been distant from Val, he might not know of her conflict with Thea Robinet," Cam mused.

"Let me tell you who I talked to earlier," I said.

Cam sat forward.

"I happened to be poking around in Gourmet Provisions toward the end of the morning. Narini Raj was stocking olive oil. Naturally I struck up a conversation."

"Naturally." A smile played at Cam's lips.

"As we do." Allie smiled full-tilt.

"One thing I noticed, other than the astronomical prices on the olive oil, was how strong her arms are."

"She probably lifts vats of olives and cases of oil." Cam pushed up the sleeve of her sweater. She had strong forearms, too.

"She also seemed completely supportive of Thea's views on the direction the garden club—and society—should be heading," I said. "And get this. She's pregnant."

"Sperm donor?" Allie asked.

"I didn't ask. But if defending her sweetheart means the world to her, she's certainly strong enough to . . . oh, wait." I had more I hadn't told either of them.

"What?" Allie and Cam spoke at the same time.

"I learned more. The murder happened in the bocce court at the historical complex. The art gallery and bookstore are blocked off for now because of the bocce court. I wanted to take a closer look, but a sheriff's deputy was quite clear I couldn't go any farther. So I stopped in to Vino y Vida."

"Good idea," Allie said. "Val ran the place, after all."

"And?" Cam asked.

"Mooncat, a woman who works at Vino y Vida, knew the method of death." I gazed from Allie to Cam.

"And?" Allie sounded impatient.

"Val was bonked on the bean by a bocce ball in one of her own mittens. I didn't have a chance to tell either of you."

Cam's eyes grew wide, but Allie snickered.

"Sorry." My twin tried and failed to gulp down the laughter bubbling up. "It's . . . the thought of the headline. 'Bean Bonking Bocce Ball Blasts Bartender' put me over the edge." She giggled. The hand she clapped over her mouth didn't do a thing.

I started to feel a twin laughing spree coming on, something Allie and I had a long history of, as many sisters do. But when Cam cleared her throat, I made myself get serious.

"Bonk and bean might have been an unwise choice of words," Cam said. "The fact remains, a woman is dead. And Allie hasn't been cleared from the Person of Interest list, not that I've heard. We have work to do, girls."

Chapter Fifteen

I made sure I had each nephew firmly by the hand at ten the next morning before we, plus Cam, crossed Manzanita.

"Ready, geysers?" I asked, with the affectionate term for "guys" I'd used since they were little.

We four waded into the holiday craft fair in Halstead Park. I'd tucked a couple of cloth shopping bags into my backpack, and the boys each had money of their own. Franklin's was in a wallet in his front pocket.

"Auntie Cee, you should never carry a wallet in a back pocket," Franklin instructed. "It can throw off your spinal alignment when you sit on it, plus it invites pickpockets."

Arthur, being a kid who had lost two wallets and three house keys in the last year, had his cash zipped into a side pocket of his cargo pants.

Franklin carried a phone in his other front pocket. Allie had given it to him but said it was for emergencies only, such as if he and his brother got separated from me. Looking relieved not to have her sons for the first half of the day, she'd driven off to run an open house.

"Do you boys know what you're looking for as gifts for your parents?" Cam asked them.

"Nah," Arthur said in a bright tone. "But I'll know it when I see it."

"Mother loves glass things the light can shine through, and Dad would like fun socks," Franklin said. "I know because he said so."

"Those sound like good choices." Cam nodded approvingly.

The fair offered the usual array of booths displaying Christmas ornaments and red-and-green sweaters, Santa-themed pottery, cookie cutters, and holly-shaped gifts. We also passed a woman in a headscarf selling quilted table runners and tote bags in Christmas colors as well as in jewel tones of magenta, gold, and turquoise. Another booth displayed dreidels, dreidel art, hand-carved menorahs, and other Hanukkah-related items. This was called the holiday fair rather than the Christmas fair on purpose, according to Allie.

The atmosphere was bright and cheery as more people flooded in, but it was in contrast to leaden skies forecasting rain later. A lot later, I hoped, despite the perennial drought around here. Rain would ruin the fair.

The boys paused at a booth with wooden puzzles and games. Arthur investigated small boxes requiring different pieces to be arranged a certain way to open the box, and Franklin picked up another complicated gizmo with metal rings and pegs. The man running the booth began explaining how the puzzle games worked.

"The boys are quite different from each other, aren't they?" Cam murmured.

"In all ways except the few minutes surrounding their births." Six-minutes-older Franklin, today in the forest-green down vest he loved, took after his brilliant father, Fuller, with dark curly hair, a quiet studious manner, and the tentativeness of a born introvert. Arthur, wearing his favorite yellow jacket, was blond like Allie, although his curls were a honey-colored shade, and his eyes were brown, not blue. He was athletic and always on the move, had mild ADHD, and was a cheery kid who wore his extrovert badge on his sleeve.

"When will Fuller be back?" Cam asked. "I hope I can meet him before I leave Monday."

"I think he's scheduled to return tomorrow. You'll miss my mom and Zoe, though. They won't be here until the twenty-third." Christmas was soon. We had to get Allie's name cleared before then, and preferably today.

"Auntie Cee, look, juggling balls!" Arthur pointed down the row.

"Fine," I said. "But don't go any farther than that booth. I'll be right there."

He skipped down the row, Franklin hurrying behind him.

At the game tent, I bought two of the complex puzzle games the man had been explaining. "They come with instructions, right?"

"Yes, ma'am. Wrap those for you?"

"No, thanks." I paid him, shrugged off my pack, and slipped the handled bag inside.

"I'll find you," Cam said. "I want to buy one of these preschool puzzles for Ruthie."

To my surprise, the juggler was Rafael Torres. His booth was full of brightly colored soft stuffed balls and cubes, plus sets of things that looked like bowling pins on steroids. Both boys faced one wall of the booth, concentrating as they each threw one ball in the air and tried to transfer another ball to the right hand and then catch the airborne ball with their left.

"Do you make these?" I asked Rafael.

Franklin turned to look at me and dropped both his

balls. He shook his head, picked them up, and returned them to a basket nearby.

"I can't do it," he muttered to me.

"It's okay, honey." I ruffled his hair. "You have lots of other things you're good at."

"Don't worry about it, Franklin. I couldn't juggle at your age, either," Rafael said. "And, yes, Cece, I sew the ball covers and stuff them."

"That's pretty cool." A man who sewed and admitted it. I approved. "Do you also perform riding a unicycle and juggling knives?"

He laughed. "Haven't quite mastered those skills yet." He gazed at Arthur, who now nearly had both balls in the air at one time. "Nice job, Artie. Do a few more rounds and let me know when you're ready for a third."

"I'd like to learn to use a sewing machine," Franklin said.

"Your mom doesn't sew?" Rafael asked.

I laughed. "You don't know Allie very well. Frankie, next time Mommy brings you guys to my house in Pasadena, I'll teach you, okay? What do you want to make?"

"I want to make a lap quilt for Gran. Every time she sits on the couch, she says she's cold."

"You're very thoughtful, young man," Rafael said. "Maybe your aunt here could bring you over to my house after Christmas, and I could teach you." He gave me a warm smile and raised his eyebrows in a questioning look.

Whoa. Hang on a second. First of all, I didn't know whether he was a murderer. Second, was he hitting on me? Well, we were single mature people, and he was both fit and reasonably good-looking. Stranger things had happened.

All the warm and fuzzy went *poof* when Detective Quan sauntered up.

"Morning, Ms. Barton. Might I have a word with you, Mr. Torres?"

Rafael gaped. He glanced quickly around. To see if there was an escape route? Or wondering if townspeople were looking, maybe.

"I'm running a booth, Detective, as you can see."

"I understand." Quan clearly wasn't going to take no for an answer. "It won't take long. Perhaps around the back?"

Rafael's shoulders drooped.

"I'll hang out here, tell people you'll be right back," I offered.

"Thanks." His voice was so low I almost couldn't hear it. He followed Quan around the corner of the tent. It had walls, making it impossible to watch them.

Arthur caught both balls and stopped tossing them. "Is Mr. Torres in trouble?"

"I don't think so," I told him. "But the detective wants to talk with him."

"I think he's in trouble," Franklin whispered, big-eyed.

In one fast move, Arthur lay on the ground at the back of the tent and lifted up the wall a couple of inches.

"Arthur." I used my best auntie stage whisper, shaking my head and motioning toward me.

He didn't budge. Franklin looked alarmed at this mutiny.

I headed toward him. "Artie, now!"

He jumped up, glanced at me with a pale, frightened face, and took off running.

Chapter Sixteen

Cam hurried up. "Where's Arthur off to?"
"I don't know. Can you watch Rafael's booth? Frankie, honey, please explain to Mrs. Flaherty."

Cam nodded, although she rolled her eyes at my choice of names.

I set off at a jog, weaving through the crowds. I wasn't hopeful I could catch a kid one fourth my age and four times as fast. But whatever Arthur heard had terrified him. I had to find our boy and hold him. Make sure he knew he was safe. Stay with him until he felt better.

My nephews hadn't been privy to any of our discussions and musings about Val's murder. They might have picked up gossip at school, but neither had mentioned anything about the homicide at dinners or before bed. Inquisitive Franklin hadn't asked questions. Impulsive Arthur hadn't blurted out shocking statements or fourth-grade hearsay.

My heart sank when I thought about what Arthur might have heard. Quan might have mentioned Allie in connection with the killing. Thinking his mom could go to jail would make any kid run for it. Run for home, maybe. Was home where I should be looking?

I scanned the crowds for a moving blur of yellow at about adult shoulder height.

"Cece Barton," a man's voice hailed me. "You looking for anyone?"

I put on the brakes and whipped my head to the right. Otto Harper stood behind his historical complex table, which was now draped in a purple tablecloth reaching the ground. He pointed dramatically—and repeatedly, without speaking—straight down at the table.

"Yes, I am, Otto. My nephew Arthur got separated from us, and I'm really worried about him. Age ten, yellow jacket?"

Otto nodded and pointed down again. "Can't help you, unless you want a historical society brochure."

I nodded in return, indicating I understood, and slid out of my pack. I gave the table a wide berth and set my pack on a chair at the back of the booth. I squatted at the back of the table, lifted the cloth, and crawled in next to poor Artie. He sat with his knees drawn up to his chin, his arms wrapped around his legs.

He looked up at me, eyes wide and drawn. "Auntie Cee, what if—?"

"What if nothing." I scooted next to him and wrapped him in my arms. "I'm here. You're safe. Mommy is fine. Franklin is with Cam. You're safe." I hugged him tight. I'd held him like this often when he was a baby and Allie was busy feeding Franklin. I'd held Arthur close when he was an accident-prone toddler and up to when he was in kindergarten. He hadn't needed or sought out his auntie's bear hugs for a while, but right now? He didn't shrink away from this one.

"You want to tell me about it?" I asked softly.

He shook his head, hard, casting his gaze up to the underside of the table.

Aah. Maybe Quan had mentioned Otto's name to Rafael, and Arthur didn't want the man who'd given him refuge to know. Smart kid. From outside our cave, I heard Cam's voice and Franklin's.

"Are you ready to go out? I will protect you and your brother from anything, darling." I peered at his face. "I promise."

"Okay," he whispered.

I emerged first. Arthur followed.

"Thank you, Mr. Harper," he murmured.

Otto held out his hand to Arthur and shook the boy's smaller one. "Always good to know when to retreat and regroup. I will say, you're lucky to have this lady in the family."

"I know." Arthur took my hand and squeezed. He held on to it.

I was blessed to be able to be special auntie to these kids. Allie had played the role with Zoe when she was young, and she still did.

Franklin rushed up and threw his arms around his brother. He held on tight without speaking. Cam stood back. "Glad he's safe," she mouthed to me above their heads.

I nodded my fervent agreement.

"Kardiskar trinklo," Arthur said as he pulled apart.

"Trinklo kardiskar." Franklin smiled.

Otto cocked his head and wrinkled his brow with skepticism. Cam scrunched up her face as if bewildered.

"It's a twin thing" was all I could tell them. As different as they were, my only nephews had made up code words and secret language games since they were preverbal, almost. Allie and I had, as well. I expected that the daughters of Cam's friend Ruth had, too. It was part of being a tiny speck who'd grown into a person lying body-to-body for nine months with a sibling on the same path.

Fraternal twins, as we were, made up secret codes all the time. I couldn't imagine what identical twins came up with. Maybe they had mind melds and didn't need to bother with verbalized secret games.

"Here comes trouble." Otto gazed in the direction of Rafael's stand.

We all turned our heads to see Quan striding straight for us. I grabbed Arthur's hand again and covered it with both of mine. "You're good," I whispered. Franklin took his other hand.

"Trinklo kardiskar," the darker twin murmured.

"Kardiskar trinklo," was a faint response, but a response it was.

But Quan wasn't looking for the Halstead boys, or for Cam or me.

"Mr. Harper, may I have a word, please?" the detective said to Otto.

"We'll be moving along," I said. "Thank you, Otto."

"Would you mind waiting, Ms. Barton?" Quan asked me.

Great. I glanced at Cam.

"Why don't the three of us keep shopping, kids?" Cam asked. "I think I saw a candy cane shop up ahead."

Arthur perked up. "Let's go."

"How will Auntie Cee ever find us?" Franklin asked, brow furrowed. "Look at all these people."

"Cam will text me, honey." I patted my phone-carrying pocket with one hand and laid my other hand on his shoulder.

"All right," he said.

"Thank you, Cam. I'll see you geysers in a minute." My nephews were in good hands with the tall farmer.

When I turned back to the detective, he and Otto stood in the back of the booth. Otto had crossed his arms over his chest, and his feet were planted apart in a defiant stance. Quan, ever calm, questioned him. I thought I heard Rafael's name.

What did Quan want to talk with me about? I could catch him up on what I'd learned but, if they were doing their job, the sheriff's department should already know all of it. Val and Otto's history. Rafael's estrangement from her. Thea's conflict with Val, and her relationship with Narini. Plus everybody's alibi—or lack thereof—for Wednesday night.

Otto stormed out, brushing past me without pausing to apologize, and stomped down the row. Quan stepped toward me.

"He doesn't look happy, Detective."

"He's not. I'm not in the business of making people happy, Ms. Barton, until I make an arrest and a killer is convicted, which at least satisfies the victim's family." Hardly taking a breath, he said, "I haven't been able to reach your sister this morning. I need to speak with her."

I blinked. "I hope you're not about to arrest Allie, sir."

"Would you know where I can find her?" His expression was unreadable.

"She's hosting an open house for a property. I'm sure if you leave her a message, she'll return your call when she's free."

"When would that be?" he pressed.

"I don't know." Which wasn't strictly true, but all she'd said was she'd be back this afternoon. I could stonewall as well as he could. I gazed down the row. "Is Otto on your list?"

"My list?"

"Come on. Your list of people who might have murdered Val."

"Thank you for your time. If you see Alicia, please have her contact me." He turned and left.

Just as well. It was past time for me to put homicide out of my head and let dreams of sugar plums take over.

Chapter Seventeen

I found Cam and the boys and greeted them. "Everything's fine," I added.

One side of the booth featured exactly the kind of glass gifts Franklin had been after. Hand-blown balls streaked with blue or pink dangled from ribbons on a rack. Small stained-glass birds sat on a fence. Translucent ornaments hung from a wire tree. He carefully examined each one without touching. Arthur was a different story.

"Hands in your pockets, Artie," I reminded the twin as he began to reach for an ornament. Nobody could break a fragile item faster than he could, and Allie had long given him a concrete—and safe—action to do with his hands.

He obeyed, to my relief.

On the other side of the booth sat Mooncat with an array of mittens on a table in front of her. I took a second look. These were Val's mittens. I shuddered.

"Hey, Cece." Mooncat looked a little abashed. "She left a box of these under the bar. I had bought the fabric for her wholesale through a friend of mine, and she still owed me for it. I figured it wouldn't hurt to unload them here and recoup my costs."

Selling the murdered woman's crafts this soon after her death seemed a little macabre to me, but Val was beyond caring. I personally would be creeped out to wear a pair of these mittens knowing one of their kind had been used to kill their maker. "Why not?" I shrugged.

Cam stepped up next to me.

"Cam, this is Mooncat," I said. "She works at Vino y Vida. Mooncat, Cam Flaherty. She's staying at my sister's bed-and-breakfast."

They exchanged greetings. Cam went back to perusing the glass art.

Arthur joined me, examining each pair of mittens. "What do you think, Auntie Cee? Dad is always saying how cold his hands are. And Mommy would love these pink ones."

Just . . . no. "Maybe not, Artie. I happen to already know they'll both have new mittens under the tree on Christmas morning." I winked at him. And set myself a mental reminder to quickly find two pair of non-murderous mittens, stat. "Sorry," I said to Mooncat, except I wasn't.

Franklin bought a small glass ornament for his mother, one featuring a Western bluebird. He paid a price I was pretty sure the vendor had discounted for him. We continued on our way.

I tried to put on a good front, but I wasn't feeling much in the holiday spirit. I wished I knew what Quan wanted from Allie. And what he'd quizzed Otto about to make him storm away mad, not to mention what the detective had said to Rafael that resulted in worrying Arthur as it had. Maybe my nephew thought the running coach he looked up to was in trouble with the sheriff's detective or, worse, had killed Val. At least Artie had bounced back nicely. I'd try to get him to open up later, at home, when it was quiet and he'd had time to process his experience. Or Allie could.

"Where're the candy canes?" Arthur asked Cam, bouncing on his heels.

"You're in deep doo-doo now, my friend," I murmured to her. The last thing he needed was a blast of sugar.

"I don't know," she said to the boy. "Maybe the next row over?"

We strolled to the end and looped back up the next row. Franklin stopped halfway along to buy socks with Einstein's picture woven in. Cam purchased a pair of Sherlock Holmes socks for her detective husband, and I bought identical pairs featuring Marie Curie's image for my science-inclined daughter and mother.

"Still nothing, Arthur?" I asked.

"Nope. I'll know it when I see it. Just not mittens."

I spied a tall woman with a much shorter one strolling hand in hand. I peered at them. Yes, it was Thea and Narini. They paused at a jewelry vendor.

Arthur stopped to look at a booth full of items featuring dogs and cats. They were embroidered onto pillows, woven into scarves, printed on floor mats, you name it. There were also collars and tiny pet jackets and fun handmade toys for actual animals to play with.

Allie and I had had a cat for only a short time before she was consumed by sneezing, an allergy she'd passed down to Franklin but not to Arthur.

"I'm going to get a present here for Mom and Dad," he said. "They want to have a cat and a dog, but they can't because the Frang will sneeze his head off."

Which really meant Arthur wanted a pet, badly. Allie had confided they were considering adopting a hypoallergenic dog when the boys got a little older.

"Arturo wants somebody else to beat up on besides me." Franklin grinned and elbowed his brother.

"I'm going down there to talk with Thea and Narini for a sec," I said.

"I'll watch these guys," Cam said. "Hey, boys. The dog

on this pillow looks exactly like Dasha, Pete's Siberian Husky mix."

"You have a dog at home?" Arthur asked, excited.

I wandered toward the tall and the short. Narini's puffy jacket hid her pregnant belly, mostly. She fingered silver earrings on a display tree. Thea, today in tennies and what looked like a high-end wicking shirt and calf-length running pants, examined an array of bracelets slung on a dowel hanging sideways.

"Hey, ladies." I nodded to the proprietor. "Nice jewelry."

Narini twisted her head. "Hi. Cece, wasn't it?"

"Yes."

Thea gave me a look I couldn't interpret. "Where's your private-eye friend?"

"She's down the row a bit, with my sister's kids. She's a farmer, you know, not a PI."

Thea scoffed, "As if. Shouldn't you two leave the detecting to the sheriff, who actually knows what he's doing?"

Thea took a step nearer, looming over me. I felt threatened, even though we stood amid hundreds of other shoppers and vendors.

"Of course we're leaving things to the able Detective Quan." I mustered a smile I didn't feel. "It's too bad he hasn't made an arrest for the homicide yet, though."

"It'll be too bad when he busts your twin sister for the crime." She turned back to the bracelets.

Narini raised a dark eyebrow, the tiny silver ring threaded through it glinting in the light, but didn't say anything.

I wanted to object, to defend innocent Allie. I turned away, instead.

Chapter Eighteen

I felt shaken by Thea's looming presence and her accusation about Allie, and all this noise and holiday cheer was suddenly too much to bear. I spied trees at the far end of the row. This was a park, after all. When I glanced down the row, Cam and kids seemed to still be busy at the dog-and-cat booth.

I cut through between two booths to the park proper. I leaned against the gnarled trunk of an ancient live oak and took a moment to text Cam.

Taking a second to calm down after veiled threat from Thea. In park near trees but outside fair area. Text me when you're on the move. I owe you.

Hearing male voices not far away, I took a peek around the broad trunk. Otto and Rafael faced each other a few trees away, also outside of the fair area. Rafael's hands were in the pockets of his athletic pants, but his stance was defensive. A red-faced Otto gestured with one hand.

I ducked back behind the tree and listened with all my might. Isolating their voices from the buzz of the holiday shoppers wasn't easy. It was also one of my superpowers. I'd been a minor voyeur from way back, inventing stories about people I saw in public. And if I could catch a snippet of a stranger's conversation, even better.

Closing my eyes, I listened to these two who'd known Val intimately.

"You can't pin it on me, you know," Otto said. "Val and I were divorced. I had no call to kill her, and you'd best stop going around and saying so."

"Who's talking?" Rafael asked, his voice rising with indignation. "You're the one telling people I might have killed Valencia. My sister. My own flesh and blood! What kind of depraved mind would accuse me of murder?"

"I never did."

I could imagine Otto was shaking his head, his face growing ever redder.

"Jimmy Quan implied as much," Rafael countered.

"He can go stuff it where the sun don't shine." Otto's voice took on a sly tone. "I mean, I know you've been angry with her, but hey, you're the one who cut ties, not her. And it hurt her, a lot, man."

"Must be nice living in a fantasy world, Harper. She never once reached out to me."

A gust of chilly breeze blew by. To my horror, I felt a big sneeze coming on. Sneezing had been my reaction to a cold wind since I was a child. I buried my face in the crook of my arm and also brought my other hand over my nose to try to muffle the sound. One sneeze. Two. Three. Never more, never less.

I sniffed before I relaxed my arm. The guys had stopped talking. They must have heard me. I swore silently. I was royally—

"Cece?" Otto appeared in front of me.

I jumped a little. I might have squeaked.

"What are you doing here?" Otto glared.

Rafael materialized at Otto's side. "I know exactly what she was doing—eavesdropping on our conversation. You can pretend at being friendly all you want, Ms. Barton. But you're nothing but a snoop, and not a very good one." He clenched his hands into fists.

My heart went into overdrive. My own hands turned clammy and cold. "I was taking a break from all the noise." I heard the quaver in my voice. "Having a kind of standing meditation."

"What did you hear us say?" Otto took a step closer, his eyes narrowing.

"Nothing, honestly. You were . . ." *Uh-oh.* I caught myself in time from letting on I'd seen them, and where. "I mean, I heard men talking, but I didn't know it was you. I certainly couldn't hear the words."

"She's lying." Rafael extended his left arm and set his hand on the rough bark of the tree trunk next to my head. He leaned toward me. Otto blocked my escape on the other side.

I wanted to scream. Or pass out. Neither would help me. I thought furiously.

"Listen, I have to go meet my family. If you gentlemen will excuse me?" In one move, I ducked away from Rafael and slid past Otto. As I rushed away, I saw the best sight I'd seen this year. This decade.

Artie and Franklin raced toward me. "Auntie Cee, look!"

Cam followed at a long-legged lope. I hurried toward them and away from two angry men. I swallowed and knelt to greet the two boys I loved most in the world.

"What do you have?" I asked.

"Cheesy popcorn." Franklin held up a bulging paper bag. The front of his dark vest was dusted with a yellow powder.

"And candy canes!" Arthur's face was already tinged

with pink. He showed me a candy cane almost an inch in diameter. The end of the hook was already sucked down to a point.

"Good job," I said. "Did you thank Mrs. Flaherty for hanging out with you?"

Arthur, his candy cane back in his mouth, nodded.

"Yes, but she told us to call her Cam," Franklin said. "Besides, don't you know the title Mrs. is archaic, Auntie Cee? Its only purpose was to define a woman by her married status, and that's silly. Now we have Ms., which is much better."

"You're right. Thank you for the history and language lesson." I pushed up to standing. "Did Cam teach you that?"

"No, Gran did, a long time ago when I was nine."

His earnest face about did me in.

"Do you have more shopping to do?" Cam asked me. In an aside, she whispered, "Are you okay?"

"No to shopping, yes to okay. Tell you later." I took in a deep breath and let it out. "Shall we hit the road, geysers?"

Arthur began to skip away. He froze and whirled. "But what about visiting Santa?"

"Daddy's going to take us after he gets home," Franklin said. "Don't you remember? He told us before he left."

"Maybe." Arthur resumed his skipping, high on sugar.

Franklin opened the popcorn bag and offered it to me. "Want some?"

"Not right now, thanks."

He munched as he hurried to catch up with his twin, the twin I was really glad hadn't glimpsed his idol, Coach— and juggler—Torres looming over me wearing an angry expression. Or Artie's sort-of rescuer from an hour ago, the then-kindly Otto, recently transformed into a furious and suspicious threat.

"What went down out here, Cece?" Cam asked. "I thought you were, like, taking a breather. Next thing I know you're moving fast away from two angry dudes with close ties to Val."

"Yeah. It got a little scary there for a minute." I told her what they'd been saying and about my failed attempt to muffle three involuntary sneezes. "They closed in and accused me of eavesdropping and incompetently investigating." I gave a laugh, but it ended up a choked sob. "Both actually true."

"Hey, now. We're making progress. And the day is young yet. Take a deep breath in, and when you exhale, let out all the negativity and toxic feelings."

"You sound like a Californian." But I did as she advised. And it worked. For now.

Chapter Nineteen

By two-thirty, we'd all eaten sandwiches, and Allie was back. Having taken charge of her children again, the candy canes were safely locked away. The boys were upstairs in their room playing Minecraft. Cam had headed out to visit a farmer she'd read about.

"Did you sell the house?" I asked my twin over a cup of mint tea in the kitchen.

"We got four great offers. The market isn't as hot as it was, but this is a good property. It'll go for at least asking price, if not above." She took a drink of her own tea. "Did the youth behave themselves this morning? Thanks for hanging with them, by the way."

"I love doing it. They behaved, mostly."

"What did the younger one do this time?"

I told her about Arthur listening under the tent wall to Rafael and Quan.

"Whatever Artie heard seemed to terrify him, and he took off running. I found him safe under the historical complex information table. I crawled in there, too, and comforted him until he was ready to come out. I think he's fine, but I haven't tried to learn what he heard."

"Coach Torres and the detective? Yikes," Allie said.

"My only thought is that Quan mentioned you, and Artie

was scared you'd go to jail—or worse." I decided to keep what had happened at the fair with me and Otto and Rafael to myself for now.

"I'll get it out of him." She cast a glance at the stairs. "We have a sweet little routine we do when one of them—usually Arthur—has an experience that's hard to talk about."

"I knew you'd have ways," I said.

Allie drained her tea and sighed. "Cece, despite my flexible schedule, it's hard doing this working mom thing. I mean, look at this house. Do you happen to see folded laundry, clean floors, and Christmas decorations? Yeah, me neither. Fuller is traveling more these days with his consulting business. How in heck am I supposed to cope?"

I covered her hand with mine. "Have you considered a nanny?"

"I don't want anyone else raising my kids."

"I hear you. How about this? The boys are big enough to fold and put away all the laundry. And it's good for them to have chores. They can each clean a bathroom once a week, too."

She tilted her head, regarding me. "We always had our chore chart, didn't we? Maybe I fell into the trap of thinking I had to do it all, at least when Full is away."

"You don't have to." I drank down my tea.

"Getting back to Quan, was he going around questioning other people at the fair?"

"He totally was. In fact, he asked me where you were, and how to reach you. I said you were running an open house. I did not mention when you'd be free." I grinned. "You're welcome."

She slapped her forehead. "Right. I got a call and a text from him as the first prospective buyers came in. I forgot all about it."

"Might be good to get back to him when you get a chance."

"I will." As she picked up her phone, the kitchen door opened. "Baby!" Allie jumped up, the phone forgotten on the table.

Fuller, a wide smile splitting his handsome face, set down his suitcase and computer bag. "Hey, Cece."

"Welcome home, Fuller." I returned his smile. Allie's husband was a full-size version of Franklin, with slightly darker skin and curlier hair, plus glasses and a web of laugh lines.

He opened his arms wide, and Allie nearly leapt into them. They shared a long kiss and a longer embrace.

Allie ignored her now-ringing phone. "Do you want me to call the boys?" she asked him.

"I'll go find them in a minute. Right now a beer would be optimal, plus a quick catch-up with you and Cece."

"Coming right up." Allie couldn't stop smiling as she grabbed three beers from the fridge.

I stood to get glasses but accepted a hug from Fuller on the way.

"So you got an earlier flight?" Allie asked as she poured.

"I did. What I had to do on site was finished, and it's Christmastime. I wanted to be here." He squeezed her hand after she sat. "Cheers, ladies." He lifted his glass and we all followed suit.

"I took the kids to the holiday craft fair today," I said. "By the end, Arthur was worried we hadn't visited Santa. Franklin said you'd promised to take them after you got home."

"I did, and I will." He took a long drag of the beer. "*Aah*. Perfect. Now, wife, dearest, I might have a surprise in the trunk of my car. Want to see?"

"You bet." Allie stood.

"You, too, Cece," Fuller beckoned.

Outside, a long green pointy thing wrapped in white netting stuck out of the end of his car.

"Did you bring home a Christmas tree, you beautiful man?" Allie asked.

He nodded, beaming.

I slipped away, carrying my beer up to my room, leaving them to their joy at being together. My twin being happy meant the world to me. My own marriage had not been a happy one, but it was long over. I wasn't too old to find love again. Perhaps I would one day.

Right now my job remained clear. Find Val's killer and clear Allie's name. Period. Full stop.

Chapter Twenty

Cam and I strolled away from Yukiko, the Japanese restaurant in Colinas, at seven-thirty that night. After she'd returned from her outing, we'd agreed to grab a bite out and leave the Halsteads to hang out on their own. The kids were over the moon their father was home early and were super excited about setting up the tree. When we'd left, Fuller was busy bringing garlands and boxes of lights and ornaments in from the room over the garage.

I carried an umbrella, and Cam had brought one, too. The winter rainy season had finally begun. Both the clouds and the damp scent of the air made me think we'd need the protection before the evening was over. A shower had fallen a couple of hours ago but stopped, and I could almost hear the dry soil begging for more water.

"Want to grab a drink at Vino y Vida?" I asked. We'd avoided talking about murder over dinner, but I hoped to hash through what we knew and what we didn't.

"Sure."

The historical complex was only a couple of blocks farther down Manzanita. By now the police tape was gone, and the cones had been removed. No alert officer guarded the site to keep nosy visitors away. The bookstore and art gallery were lit up and open for holiday shopping.

Cam and I stood looking at the bocce court. It was mostly in darkness, lit only tangentially by light spilling out from the other establishments.

"I guess they don't expect night games," I said. "I haven't thought at all about the logistics of the homicide, the how of it."

"Right. The killer stole or bought a pair of Val's one-size-fit-all mittens."

"I wonder if she kept receipts."

"Good point," Cam said. "If she did, the police could trace which of the persons of interest bought a pair. Either way, they stuffed a bocce ball into one."

The image made me shudder. "So the balls must be left out here all the time." I wandered over to a rough-hewn cabinet on legs. It stood near the fence overlooking the river. I pulled open the door and peered in. Inside was a rack holding six of the heavy scored balls, with two slots empty. "Voilà."

"That part made it easy for them," Cam said. "They lured her out here after dark, after everything else was closed."

"It must have been a person she knew."

"I'd think so," Cam said. "Does that rule out Narini?"

"No. Mooncat said Narini had been in Val's face last week."

"Well, whoever it was held the mitten by the cuff, swung, and cracked Val on the head."

I shivered, imagining the action. The sound. Worst, the nerve of the attacker.

Cam gave me a sympathetic look. "Yes, it must have been brutal. And the person we're looking for has to be strong."

I stared at her. "But they all are. Otto is a landscaper. Rafael is tall, he's a runner, and who knows what else?

Thea competes in triathlons, which include swimming. She has strong arms. Narini's are the same."

"Good point."

"But then what?" I asked. "Did they drop the weapon and run? So much could have gone wrong with their plan." I folded my arms. "You know? I mean, there could be a security camera out here."

"Or shoppers might have walked by." The door to the bookstore opened and three women emerged, chatting about the books they'd bought as gifts. "Like them," Cam added.

"Speaking of which, let's check what time Alexander Books and the art gallery closed on Wednesday night."

"I like the way you think. I'll take the gallery, you ask at the bookstore."

We split up. The bookstore's hours were posted next to its door. The place seemed to close at six every night. Still, it was the holiday season. I pulled open the door and went in to be confronted by one of my favorite sights—rows and stacks and shelves full of books. I could do a little shopping while I was here. I'd helped the boys find gifts at the fair, but I hadn't bought any presents beyond socks myself, and books make the best gifts. Except this wasn't the time.

"Can I help you find anything?" A man whose glasses perched halfway down the bridge of his nose stood behind the counter. He smiled at me over the top of the readers.

I thought fast. I didn't want him to think I was asking about the murder. "Are you open every evening? I haven't finished my Christmas shopping yet."

"We are, ma'am, through next Thursday, Christmas Eve."

"Oh good. Wednesday is my easiest night to get out."

"I'm sorry if you tried us last week. I had a family emergency to deal with and had to close at five." He frowned. "It's too bad. I might have . . . well, never mind."

Maybe he didn't want to bring up Val's homicide and what he might have seen or been able to stop. I had no such compunctions.

"It's terrible about that poor woman's murder, isn't it?" I asked.

"Oh my, yes, and it happened right outside," he said. "I hope the sheriff solves it soon."

"I suppose they've been around asking for security cam footage?"

"We don't have a camera, more's the pity," he said. "Several of us have been asking the complex manager for one, but it hasn't happened yet."

The manager being Otto. Maybe he had a reason for failing to mount cameras.

"Too bad," I said.

He glanced around and lowered his voice. "Frankly, ma'am, it's been bad for business. The authorities made us stay closed Thursday all day and yesterday until midafternoon. Places like this make the bulk of our annual income from holiday spending. One day off can be a disaster."

"I hope it's resolved soon, and good luck with your sales. I have to go now, but I'll be back to shop."

"We appreciate the business. You have a good night, ma'am."

When I stepped outside, rain was falling. Cam stood under her umbrella next to the bocce court. I flipped my umbrella open and joined her.

"Acorn Fine Art was closed last Wednesday evening," she said.

"So was the bookstore." I gazed at the court and shivered again, from the cold as much as by the ghostly mental image of Val's demise. "How about that drink?"

Chapter Twenty-one

"Hey, ladies, come on in." Mooncat smiled from behind the Vino y Vida bar.

The place was warm, dry, and hopping, full of sippers and tasters. Nearly every seat was full, probably because the tables on the terrace were now being rained on. But it was also a Saturday night kicking off a holiday week.

Mooncat pointed to the only two empty stools at the bar. "Better grab these while you can."

"Thanks," Cam said.

We grabbed them. I furled my compact umbrella and let it languish on the floor at my feet. Cam leaned her noncollapsible loaner from Allie against the end of the bar.

"You two met this morning at the fair." I caught myself before I tried to introduce them twice in one day. "Did you sell out of mittens, Mooncat?"

"I did." She gestured at the blackboard on the wall behind the bar. "What can I get you to drink tonight?"

In addition to a cabernet sauvignon and a pinot grigio, the list included a Gewürztraminer, two dessert wines, and a port.

"Do you switch to sweeter offerings in the evening?" I asked Mooncat.

"We do." She kept her hands busy as she waited for us

to order, swiping the counter, putting glasses in a rack presumably headed for a dishwasher, and straightening a napkin holder. "People seem to prefer those after dinner."

"I'd like a glass of the Gewürztraminer, please," I said.

"For me the pinot grigio," Cam said. "I'm not into sweet wines at all."

Mooncat poured before bustling off to help others. As the lone employee in the wine bar tonight, she wore all the hats. It had to be stressful.

"Cheers." Cam held up her glass.

"Likewise." I sipped the cool, mildly sweet wine. "This is nice." Except I hadn't truly savored it. Talking through the action of the murder had cut into my heart. Each of those four people we'd named were entirely ordinary humans. They worked, they loved, they had interests and passions. Which of them had stepped over the line? Stuffing a heavy ball used for recreation into a piece of cold-weather hand protection couldn't have been a spur-of-the-moment crime. Hastily planned, maybe, when the killer realized they had Val alone past closing time and in the dark of night. But planned, nonetheless.

Our stools were at the end of the bar, with Cam's the last. On my left sat three men about my age. I hadn't seen any of them in association with the others in the case. I caught the eye of one.

"It's terrible about the poor woman's murder, isn't it?" I repeated the question I'd asked the bookstore dude.

"Totally, man," the guy said.

"Poor Val." The one next to me twisted and scooted his stool back to include Cam and me in their circle. "She was a great lady."

"You all knew her?" Cam leaned forward to ask.

"Sure. We're regulars in here," the first one said. "The rest of the bros in bowling league make fun of us for not joining them in a few brewskies after a game, but me and my buddies, we like wine better."

"Val was an awesome lady," my neighbor added.

"There must have been people around who didn't like her. Any ideas who it might have been?" I hoped I sounded casual.

"Nah, everybody loved her." He thought for a moment. "Well, obviously not everyone."

"Yeah, bro." The farther one spoke. "Like, she was murdered. But"—he addressed me—"we wouldn't know who did it."

"Did you ever see her gardens?" The fellow in the middle spoke up.

"No," I said.

"I work for her ex. Otto Harper made a totally stunning design on the property. It was drop-dead gorgeous." He grimaced.

One of his buddies elbowed him. "Nice choice of words, pal."

"Oh, man, sorry. The design still is gorgeous. Brilliant. Won an award and everything. But after the divorce? Val wouldn't let Harper onto the grounds, and it all went to you know where and gone."

"To Hades in a handbasket?" Cam asked.

"That pretty much describes it. Val really let it go, may she rest in peace." Otto's employee shook his head.

I was grateful he didn't precede his last remark by "I don't want to speak ill of the dead, but . . . ." which invariably led to the person speaking ill of the dead.

He went on. "She let weeds set seed, perennials went undivided, there was insect damage, you name it. It's a crime, and I don't mind saying so."

"What a shame," Cam said. "Don't you think Val being murdered is a worse crime?"

The guy reared back. "Well, obviously, but..." He seemed to run out of words and shut his mouth before he said anything even more stupid.

Out of the corner of my eye I saw the door open. I swiveled to face the entrance after I saw the newcomers were Thea and Narini. I held up a hand and waved. Mooncat was passing by the doorway carrying a tray full of empty glasses. She saw my gesture and spoke to Thea, gesturing toward me. Narini frowned and gave a quick head shake. Thea looked in our direction, at Narini, and back. She laid her hand on Narini's back, apparently persuading her to join us at the bar.

"Hey, guys," I said to the men. "Our friends are joining us, and one is pregnant. You'll pull the gentleman card, right?"

All three leapt off their stools.

"Thank you," I said.

"We were about to go, anyway." The landscaper drained the rest of his wine and set his glass on the bar.

"Have a good one, ladies." The man closest to me laid several twenties on the counter. "Enjoy your wine." He and his friends made their way out.

"How'd you clear these seats so fast, Cece?" Thea sat next to me. "Tell them we had cooties?" In contrast to this afternoon, she seemed relaxed and not a bit threatening.

Narini perched on the next stool over, albeit appearing reluctant.

"It's never a mistake to ask a man to be a gentleman," I said.

"You travel in rarified circles, Cece." Thea snorted. "Try asking on the New York subway and see what kind of results you get."

"They were here for bro time, not schmoozing with the ladies." Cam leaned over. "Hi, I'm Cam Flaherty." She extended a hand to Narini. "Visiting from Massachusetts."

"Good to meet you, Cam. Narini Raj."

"As in the Raj olive farm?" Cam's voice rose along with her eyebrows.

"The same," Narini said.

"I need to talk with you." Cam jumped up, grabbed her wine, and went around to sit on Narini's other side. "I'm a farmer, you see."

Mooncat slid behind the bar. "Let me get things cleaned up for you folks." She stashed the guys' wineglasses, pocketed the cash, and wiped off the bar in front of Thea and Narini. "Now, what can I get you?"

"Water for me, please," Narini said.

Mooncat gave a knowing look. "Good choice, Narini. Thea?"

"A glass of port. Thanks."

Yesterday—which felt like last week—Mooncat had evaded my question about why Narini had fought with Val. Maybe Narini would tell me herself, if I could figure out the right way to ask. And come to think of it, it was Thea who'd mentioned at Edie's about Rafael being angry with Val. With Cam having moved over to talk with Narini, I had Thea to myself.

"I've had that port," I said to Thea after Mooncat poured for her. "It's great, isn't it?"

She sipped. "Very smooth."

All of a sudden I was nervous about asking Thea questions. Cam was the experienced one, not me. And after Thea had loomed over me this afternoon, I was reluctant to wade into the weeds of asking what she knew without rousing her suspicions or ire. This detecting stuff wasn't easy and didn't feel safe. Given my high failure rate in life generally, I thought I'd shelve the whole thing. Or at least leave it to the detective.

Chapter Twenty-two

Sunday brought a lazy morning and a pancake breakfast prepared by Fuller, with the boys serving. Allie had invited Cam to join us for pancakes, but she said she would eat in her room and prepack for her early departure tomorrow morning. Allie always stocked the suite's kitchen with frozen sliced bagels, yogurt, jam, and a few pieces of fresh fruit, plus coffee and cream for guests to make their own breakfasts.

Bacon was also on the Halstead menu today, plus smoked salmon "bacon." I hadn't known salmon bacon was a thing, but it was chewy and salty and delicious, exactly like bacon should be.

"Auntie Cee, I'm thinking of becoming a pescatarian like you," Franklin piped up. "I love salmon bacon."

"It's good, isn't it?" I wasn't sure how a ten-year-old could resolve to stop eating meat. But if a kid existed who was able to rationalize the change in diet, it would be Franklin.

I'd already oohed-and-aahed over the light-bedecked tree, the array of nutcrackers on the garland-festooned mantel, and the new ornaments Fuller had brought back from his work trip to Washington, DC—a miniature model of the Capitol for Frankie and a tiny Nationals baseball bat for Artie.

Allie leaned toward me as we washed dishes alone in the kitchen. "I got Artie to open up about what he heard," she whispered.

"You did?"

"You were right. Quan pressed Rafael about my disagreements with Val."

"What would her estranged brother know about you arguing with her?" I asked.

"I heard the two of them were communicating again recently, like in the last weeks before she died."

"I can't believe you simply 'heard' that. You've been holding out on me, Al."

"I have not. It was last night while you were out." She rinsed the last plate and handed it to me to put in the dishwasher. "Rafael called and wanted to apologize for upsetting Arthur."

"Seriously? You'd given him your number?"

"No." She fixed a Look on me. "Listen, Cecelia Bedelia. I'm only the top-selling real estate agent in the Alexander Valley. If people can't figure out how to reach me on my cell, they don't deserve to be part of adult society."

"I'll grant you that. But it sounds like Rafael didn't upset Arthur, the detective did."

"Hmm. It was probably a bit of both. Rafael apparently told Quan he didn't know if I'd killed Val or not, but he—Rafael—certainly hadn't. That was what sent my boy running."

"And before then, Arthur hadn't known that anybody had been killed."

"He had not," Allie agreed. "Neither kid had."

I stopped moving. "I feel bad Artie didn't come right back to me, that he felt he had to escape."

Allie put her arm around my shoulders. "It wasn't anything about you, sis, honestly. Along with his attention deficit, my boy is really impulsive. He needed to hide from everything for a bit, that's how scared he was. Including from you. You know he adores you."

"I do." I gave her a quick hug. "And he bounced back so fast. I could hardly believe how quickly he was smiling and skipping and looking for gifts for you and Fuller."

"Plus anticipating monster candy canes, apparently." She smiled.

"Yeah. Sorry."

"It's the holidays. We'll get through all the sugar and back to our routine in January."

"You will." I gently scrubbed Fuller's favorite cast-iron skillet, one that I knew never to use soap on and how to re-season after it was clean and dry. "Can we get back to what Rafael said about ending his estrangement with Val?"

"Val told him she thought downtown should develop according to her vision. She said mine was wrong and poorly conceived and would ruin all the businesses."

"Wow."

"And she said she'd let the CCC know her views, which she did."

"But simply because you two had different visions for the future of downtown Colinas doesn't mean you murdered her." I made sure to keep my voice soft.

"It doesn't."

"Did Rafael tell you why they'd been estranged?" I asked. "Which is fancy talk for one of them not speaking to the other."

"It is. He hinted at her being mentally ill, but nobody else has ever spoken about her being unwell. No, he didn't really say."

"Mommy!" Franklin burst into the room. "Come see. You too, Auntie Cee."

"What are we going to see?" I asked.

He grabbed my hand. "Come on. It's a surprise."

"I'll be right there, sweetheart," Allie said. "I need to start the dishwasher."

I let my nephew pull me along even as I pondered Rafael's history with his sister. And his sideways foisting blame onto Allie while her own son was listening. Rafael was going to have to answer to me for saying so, and then some.

Chapter Twenty-three

Cam and I set out for the Colinas farmers' market at eleven, twin boys again in tow. Allie and Fuller had both looked grateful for the gift of a couple of hours alone together. Franklin carried his own cloth market bag, but Arthur insisted on using a nylon drawstring backpack, saying he liked his hands free. He had a point.

"Did you get your stuff organized?" I asked Cam.

"Pretty much. I'm probably going to check a bag going back, depending on what I pick up at the market today. Narini totally sold me on her olive oil last night, and I might find a few other gifty items I'll want to carry home."

"Will you see your parents for Christmas?" I asked.

"Not this year. They're going to Daddy's last remaining aunt in New Jersey. But they're coming for Ruthie's birthday in January."

"A Capricorn daughter?"

"Every bit of one." Cam smiled. "She loves building things, and she's always sure her way is the right way. Who knows, maybe she'll be the next great architect."

"I'd like to talk with you later about something Allie said this morning," I murmured to her as we waited for a signal to turn green.

"Oh? I'll be all ears."

We arrived a few minutes later at the municipal parking lot. On Sundays it was transformed into a village of pop-up tents, eager shoppers, toe-tapping live music, and delicious food, prepared as well as recently harvested.

I slowed, feeling eyes on me. I scanned the perimeter of the market. *There.* A tall figure in black disappeared around the corner of a tent. Thea? Or maybe Rafael. A shiver ran through me.

"We're getting tamales at the end, right, Auntie Cee?" Arthur asked, eyes bright.

"Of course," I replied, glad to be brought back to the moment by a delightful child. "Isn't that the best part?"

"Ooh, love me a fresh tamale," Cam said.

"They're very good," Franklin said in all seriousness. "And you can get one without meat if you want, Auntie Cee."

"I know," I said. "Remember, I came with you last Christmas?"

"You were here last Christmas, but the last time we went to the market together was in July," he said. "Don't worry, the tamale truck is here every week."

I ruffled his hair and took his hand as we followed Cam and Arthur down the first row of stands. In contrast to the craft fair yesterday, today was all about food. No vendor was allowed who hadn't produced their edible product on their own property. The booth owner didn't have to sell fresh-picked produce, although many did. But cheese was required to be small-scale produced. The same with bread, olives, pistachios, pickles, and all the other yummy foods on offer. Here was no place for carved puzzles or hand-blown glass. I liked the organizers forefronting the "farmer" in farmers' market.

Franklin and I paused and bought five artichokes on

foot-long stems while Cam and Arthur sampled pistachios in all flavors next door.

"Ooh! Whew." Artie fanned his mouth. "Auntie Cee, I'm dying here."

"He sampled a jalapeno pistachio." Cam didn't look alarmed.

"He loves hot food," Franklin said with a world-weary look. "Even when it hurts his mouth. He says it clears his sinuses. But ask my brother what a sinus is, and he has no idea." He shook his head.

I smiled. "You need a milkshake, Artie, and they might not have them here. But look. A cheese sample might help." I pointed at a booth called Sam the Cheese Man.

"I like to sample everything." Arthur skipped across the row to the cheeses.

After the cheese, we proceeded to taste tangy dill pickles and an amazing sourdough, which I had to buy a boule of. A family dinner for tomorrow was shaping up—artichokes, sourdough bread, salad, and fish on the grill, which I could pick up in the morning at the fish market. I snagged a baguette, too.

Cam got into a lengthy discussion with the organic farmer where I bought a bag of greens. The boys and I wandered along until we reached Harper Greenscapes. I was surprised to see Otto here. How could shrubs and perennials be considered edible? He stood amid dozens of pots of what looked like shoots and twigs.

I greeted him. "I thought everything here had to be food."

He grinned. "These will be. I'm selling starts for peach, pear, and avocado trees. Those are boysenberry and raspberry seedlings. And more. I talked the market manager into it."

"They shouldn't have agreed." Rafael materialized next to me. "Hey, boys," he said to Arthur and Franklin.

Arthur glanced at him, his face scrunching up in either anger or fear, I couldn't tell. I grabbed his hand and pulled him behind me. I wanted to keep hold of him in case he decided to flee again. Franklin joined his brother, the two murmuring their code words.

"Rafael," I said. His black long-sleeved waffle shirt and matching fleece vest chilled me. It might well have been him who was watching me earlier.

Otto glared at him. "If you don't like it, you can take it up with the market manager."

"Maybe I will." The teacher turned and sauntered away.

No love lost there.

"Shall we move on, boys?" I asked.

Arthur nodded. He dropped my hand but kept hold of his brother's.

"I'll tell my mother you have fruit trees for sale, Mr. Harper," Franklin said. "She's been proposing we turn our front lawn into a garden. Grass isn't a good environmental choice."

"But we need it to play on," Arthur muttered to his twin.

"We'll keep it in the back."

"You do that, son." Otto tore his gaze away from the row Rafael had disappeared down and handed Franklin one of his brochures. "Give this to your mom. You can't beat growing food, and it can be decorative, too."

I thanked him. I would have loved to stay and ask about his conflict with Rafael. Find out what Otto knew about Val and Rafael's split and reconciliation. And more. But my auntie responsibilities were more important. I couldn't let these boys hear me talking about murder.

Chapter Twenty-four

A few tents away we came to Raj Olives. Narini was in the booth, currently selling a pint of mixed green and cured olives to a customer. Arthur had already speared a toothpick into a bread cube and dipped it in oil when Narini turned to us. Something passed over her expression when she saw me. It was only for a second, but I thought it was alarm or maybe nervousness.

"These are my nephews, Arthur and Franklin Halstead, Narini," I said. "Boys, this is Ms. Raj."

Franklin said something polite. Arthur's eyes lit up around his mouthful.

"This tastes just like olives!" he exclaimed.

Narini laughed. "Because it comes from pressing olives. It sounds like you've had olive oil that maybe didn't taste the same."

"Yes," Franklin said. "I looked it up. Many of the commercial brands are other oils falsely repackaged."

"Sad but true," Narini said. Today over leggings she wore a deep pink shirt that brought a glow to her skin, with a down vest layered over it.

Franklin picked up a bottle and examined it. "Your oil is quite expensive."

"It's because we pay a fair wage to our employees," she

said. "A lot of work goes into growing, harvesting, and processing the olives."

"And you take the pits out, right?" Arthur hovered his toothpick over another piece of bread.

"We remove them from certain olives, yes."

"You've already sampled, Artie," I chided. "Leave some for other customers."

Narini smiled. "He can have more than one."

Franklin selected a fresh toothpick and dipped bread into a dark green oil. He savored the bite. "Definitely tastes of olives."

Cam joined us and greeted Narini. At the same time, Thea strode up from the other direction. She slid behind the table and laid her arm over Narini's shoulders in what looked like a proprietary stance. Narini seemed to shrink from the touch. She moved a step away. Relationship issues, maybe?

What really got my attention was Thea's black motorcycle jacket. Rather than Rafael, maybe it was she who'd been surveilling us as we approached the market. I still didn't know why anyone would. I mean, I didn't think Cam and I had been obvious about poking around here and there into the homicide. We'd done it only in the interest of making sure Allie didn't go to jail for a crime she didn't commit. Still, the thought of the actual murderer being on to us was uncomfortable in the extreme.

"I'm here to buy," Cam said. "Even though we can't grow olives on my farm, a small-scale-production olive oil is too special not to take a bottle home."

"It's like totally delicious, Cam," Arthur told her. "You should sample it."

He swiped at his mouth with the sleeve of his yellow jacket, smearing it with oil. Because . . . ten-year-old. I knew Allie wouldn't be upset. She was a way-too-relaxed mom to let a new stain upset her.

A mew sounded at my feet. I glanced down to see a black cat with white paws weaving around my ankles.

"Auntie Cee, look." Franklin squatted and scooped the cat into his arms. He petted her head. She purred.

"What a sweetheart." I stroked the cat's back. "Yours?" I asked Narini.

"Never seen her before."

Franklin sneezed. "Rats. Arturo, can you take her?"

"Sure." Arthur accepted the cat with slow, gentle moves. "Hey, Ms. Mittens," he murmured into her fur.

Her paws did look like mittens, and she wasn't wearing a collar, which didn't mean much. Most cats figure out how to get out of a collar in about fifty-three seconds, flat.

While the kids were busy with the cat and Cam was buying several of the slim bottles of oil, I also dipped and tasted. Oh, good heavens. I was going to have to purchase a bottle, too, and I'd get one for Allie while I was at it. If Narini took credit cards.

I glanced up to see Thea staring at me with stony eyes and a set to her mouth I didn't like. I countered with a friendly smile I didn't feel. She didn't return it and looked away.

After we finished our olive oil transactions, Arthur gave me a pleading look.

"We can keep Ms. Mittens, can't we?" he asked in his sweetest, highest voice.

"Please, Auntie Cee?" Franklin added.

"It's not my decision, boys," I said. "Look, she's well fed. She must belong to someone here."

"I've never seen anyone taking care of her." Thea arched an eyebrow. "She's usually around the market begging."

Interesting. Narini said she'd never seen the cat.

"See?" Arthur asked. "Nobody owns her."

As if cats were ever owned by anyone. My tabby Martin back home was testimony to feline independence. "But Frankie, you're allergic," I said. "You can't be sneezing all the time at home."

"We could keep her in the garage," Franklin said.

"Yeah, set up a little cubby for her in a big box with an old blanket and her food and stuff." Arthur still hadn't put her down, and she showed no inclination to want to be released.

"Even if she is a stray, the decision is up to your mom and dad." I hoisted my ever-heavier bag on my shoulder. "Come on. Aren't you hungry for tamales? Put her down, honey, and you both say goodbye to her. We can ask your parents after we get home."

With an adult-worthy sigh of reluctance, Arthur set Mittens on the ground and gave her one last stroke.

Franklin sneezed again. "Bye, Ms. Mittens."

I thanked Narini and turned to go, ushering my nephews ahead of me. Cam strolled with us. What lingered in my ears was the sound of an argument beginning in hushed voices behind me.

We stood in a line ten-deep at the tamale truck, with our new black-and-white friend keeping us company.

Rafael strode up. "Can I have a quick word, Cece?"

"Um, all right." I glanced at Cam. "Can you watch them for a second?"

"Sure," Cam said. "I'll treat everybody."

"Thank you."

Arthur shot Rafael a scowl.

"You're going to stay right here and hold my place, Artie, right?" I asked.

He nodded, then picked up Mittens and held her tight like a shield.

I stepped out of line and moved a couple of yards away to where Rafael stood.

"Yes?" I asked.

"I saw you talking with Thea Robinet and thought you might want to know a little thing about her."

Huh. I hadn't seen him watching. "Okay. What?"

"She and my sister had history predating their tiffs in the garden club. Valencia used to sell real estate. Thea accused her of cheating her."

"And what happened?"

"Val wouldn't cheat anyone. Thea lost."

"How did you know about it?" I pressed. "I thought you'd stopped speaking to Val years ago."

"I had, but the whole town knew."

"And why are you telling me this?"

"Seriously? Everybody also knows that you and your farmer friend are going around trying to be investigators."

I shook my head. "We're not, actually." I spied Cam and the boys nearing Tia Tamale's window. "I have to get back. Catch you later." I wasn't about to thank him for possibly lying to me. Except if what he said was true, Thea's resentment could have been smoldering for a long time. But had it boiled over into a murderous rage?

Chapter Twenty-five

"See how cozy Ms. Mittens is, Auntie Cee?" Franklin asked after he and Arthur nearly dragged me out to the garden shed at four o'clock.

The cat had followed us all the way home, with Arthur scooping her into his arms to cross streets. Allie and Fuller had agreed she could stay—not in the garage but in the shed in the backyard—on the condition that tomorrow they'd take Mittens to a vet and see if she had an ID chip in her.

I had to admit it was a very nice shed, and the boys had built her a veritable clubhouse.

"It's perfect, you guys," I now said. They'd found a big cardboard carton and set it on its side, adding a couple of old beach towels to the bottom. Next to the box sat a bowl of water and another of dry cat food, a donation from a feline-owning neighbor. It was never very cold here. A cat used to being outdoors could weather the temperature, and the shed door could be propped open enough for the cat to get in and out. I assumed she'd do her business under the shrubs. If they decided to keep her, Allie would kit her out with box and litter soon enough.

Cam and I left the boys baking Christmas cookies with Fuller twenty minutes later. Colinas was lighting a person-sized public menorah in the park to celebrate the first day of Hanukkah. The town had hung Christmas wreaths and candles from the lampposts. It seemed only fair to give the Jewish holiday equal time. A farmer Cam had met mentioned the ceremony to her, and I was always happy to experience new things, having never attended a Hanukkah anything yet in my life.

Sunset, when the event would start, was at 4:50. We walked briskly.

"It was awfully nice of Allie to include me in her invitation to family dinner tonight," Cam said.

"You've gotten to know everybody but Fuller since you've been here, and the boys love you," I said. "We'll have plenty of time to get back for supper. What time did she say?"

"Cocktails at six."

"Easy peasy."

With looming overcast skies, it seemed darker than usual at four-thirty. It was also chillier than it had yet been this trip, or maybe I was feeling the damp.

"I'm sorry I wasn't really able to help clear Allie's name before I left," Cam said.

"No worries. The detective must be close to locking up the murderer. At least I hope he is."

"He should be. One assumes he has access to cell phone records, search warrants, a team to check alibis, and more."

"I'll be sure to text you when they nail the guilty party for the crime." We had exchanged cell numbers a few days earlier.

"I'd appreciate it," Cam said.

We crossed Manzanita and headed into the center of Halstead Park.

"It's supposed to be in the gazebo," Cam said.

Sure enough, a small crowd was gathered around the circular roofed structure. Ed was across the way with his husband, who owned the art gallery. I didn't see anyone associated with Val's death, not even Detective Quan. Which was fine with me.

We'd arrived in time. A city councilperson tested the microphone and made a little speech about how Colinas strived to be welcoming to all. He introduced the rabbi from the Ahavas Achim synagogue, a woman in a blue sweater. She said a few things about the history of the holiday and the significance of lighting candles.

"I'll explain for those of you not of our faith," she began. "At home on the first night we light the middle candle and use it to light one more. I'll save you from the Hebrew names."

A few people laughed.

"Each night we add one more until the eighth night, when the menorah is full of light. But here we have the miracle of all the candles being lit at once." She gave a nod to a man standing near the wall of the gazebo.

The menorah sprang into being, the soft light of six-foot-tall candles filling the sky. The rabbi began singing what I assumed was a prayer. A number of people in the gathering chanted along. When the rabbi was finished, she thanked everyone for coming and wished us a peaceful and joyous week.

"What a lovely ceremony," I said. "The lit menorah is pretty, isn't it?"

"Very," Cam said. "Hey, there's the farmer who told me about this. I'm going to go say hi to her."

"And I'm going to see if I can get some elevation and take a picture of the lights in the dark. Yesterday I saw a rock formation over there." I gestured to my right.

"Meet you back here." She pointed herself at the farmer.

I headed off to where I'd seen a big boulder. The buzz of conversation faded behind me. I cast a glance back. If I could get a little more height, it would be a stunning photo.

On the other hand, it was dark away from the lights. I stumbled on an uneven patch of ground but caught myself. I paused to switch on my phone's flashlight. The light was dimmer than I expected. I hoped my battery wasn't running out of juice. All I really needed was enough power to take the picture. This was an older model phone and didn't hold a charge as well as it used to. Maybe I'd give myself an upgrade as a Christmas gift.

In front of me loomed the boulder. I headed around to the back, where the granite sloped more and would be easier to climb up. I slid the phone into my coat pocket and climbed. As I reached the top, I groaned. It didn't have a flat-enough surface to stand on, at least not while also keeping my balance in the dark. The last thing I wanted was to teeter and fall, cracking my head on the way down.

Instead, I lay belly-down on the rock, propping my elbows on the top. *There.* I aimed, framed, and got a perfect shot. I took three more for good measure.

Now I had to get myself down. Rather than try to find footholds in the dark, I decided to descend seater-rumpus. That is, on my rear end. But the turning was awkward. I was halfway over when I heard a noise. I froze. Someone was breathing. Through their mouth. *Thea.* She was the only person I'd met up here who breathed like that. And she was close. Too, too close.

Chapter Twenty-six

My heart raced. Could I scramble back to the top? What if she came after me and pushed me off the rock?

An iron grip clasped my ankle. *No!* I kicked out. Thea swore and let go, enabling me to complete my turn onto my rear. A tall dark-clad figure in the night below, she grabbed my foot again. I tried to kick loose. This time she held on.

"What are you doing, Thea?" I swallowed down my shaky voice, or attempted to. "Take your hand off my foot and let me get down."

"You'll get down," she snarled. She tugged, hard.

I began to slide. I bent my other knee, digging my heel into a crevice in the rock, but I couldn't find any handholds with my hands damp with nerves. I tightened my Pilates-strong core and kept my head up off the boulder. I was too far away from the gazebo to yell for help, and if I fumbled for my phone or the other weapon in my pocket, I knew I'd slip off the boulder and drop the device.

"Why are you doing this?" I heard the desperation in my voice and hated it. I thought furiously. I'd be better off on the ground. I might be able to escape. Except, she was much taller than me. And those triathlete's arms—

She yanked. I slid and thudded onto the ground on my back, my ankle still in her grasp. But I hadn't cracked my head on the boulder.

"You and your farmer have been asking way too many questions." Thea loomed over me, her voice low and threaening, still holding my ankle in her left hand. Something pendulous swung from her other hand.

My insides turned to ice. It had to be the eighth bocce ball in the other mitten of the pair.

"Did you kill Val?" I asked.

"Val." She spat out a laugh. "She tried to ruin me years ago, and she was still trying. She didn't deserve to live. Just like you don't."

I swore to myself. I locked the knee of the leg she held and tightened my thigh. She tried to twist my ankle, but with only one hand, she didn't have the strength. She couldn't swing the heavy mitten and hit my head while still gripping my ankle. I bent my other knee and coiled my strength.

Thea dropped my foot. I pulled back my bent leg, fast, and slammed a flat foot into her knee as she took a step closer to my head. She cried out and crumpled. I rolled in the other direction and jumped to my feet, pulling out of my left pocket the pepper spray I always carried.

She still clutched the mitten but moaned, her other hand on her knee. "You hurt me."

"Let go of the mitten, Thea."

She didn't.

I didn't trust her an inch, but I didn't want to use the foul spray if I didn't have to. I stepped away and stashed it. Instead I turned on the phone's flash and snapped a picture of her. She pushed up on an elbow and let out a string of expletives. I'd rarely heard worse. She lashed out with her foot. She missed.

No way was I sticking around in case she was faking her injury. I dashed around the corner of the boulder and ran toward the still-lit menorah, a beacon of safety in the dark. Shapes flashing lights on the ground moved toward me.

"Cece? Is that you?" Ed called.

"Cece!" Cam added her voice.

"I'm right here." I hurried toward them. "Please call the police, now. Thea is behind that big rock—or was—with a bocce ball in a mitten and what I hope is a really damaged knee."

"She attacked you." Cam pulled out her phone and called.

"She did." I swallowed.

"Yes," Cam said into the phone. "Halstead Park in Colinas. Thea Robinet attacked Cece Barton. Cece is okay. She was able to get away, but Thea is still at large, possibly disabled with an injury to her knee." Cam explained about the bocce ball and the boulder.

"Tell them she's Val's murderer." My voice quavered. "Same weapon. Inform Quan."

Ed laid his hands on my shoulders and peered at my face. "Are you all right?"

I nodded. "Mostly. I think. I'll assess later."

He crooked an elbow. I threaded my arm through it and leaned on him.

"Thank you." My rubber legs also thanked him.

"Does she have another weapon, Cece?" Cam asked.

"I didn't see one." I glanced behind me. Had Thea faked how much I'd damaged her knee? Should I have used the pepper spray? She could be crawling—or running—away right now. She might be crouched, ready to swing at the next person who came around the boulder. My pulse, which had started to return to normal, sped up again.

Aah. I'd never been so glad to hear sirens wail into action. They grew nearer with every second. Nothing would make me happier than letting the authorities handle this from here on out.

My cell rang with Allie's ringtone. I had to answer.

"Cee, where are you guys?"

"Oh. We're late for dinner. Sorry."

She didn't speak for a second. "Hey, you. What's wrong?" My twin always knew. "Sirens are going off all over town."

"Something happened, but we're all safe."

Two SUVs roared through the park and stopped at the gazebo. Spotlights blazed on. Sheriff's deputies came at a jog. An ambulance pulled in. Detective Quan strode toward us.

"I have to go. I'm fine, Al."

"Love you," she was saying as I disconnected.

Chapter Twenty-seven

Cam and I didn't get to Allie's until eight o'clock. Allie and I exchanged a major bear hug, during which I whispered I'd fill her in after the boys went to bed.

"We saved your dinners," Franklin said.

"Mama said they caught the bad guy," Arthur added, eyes sparkling. "Did you get to see the sheriff, Auntie Cee?"

"I did," I said. "And everything's fine, except I'm super hungry."

At Allie's urging, Cam and I sat and were served bowls of steaming vegetarian chili with fat squares of cornbread.

"Wine?" my twin offered.

Mouth full, I nodded.

By eight-thirty we'd eaten our fill. Cam complimented the chefs on the tree- and star-shaped cookies we also sampled. Fuller took the boys upstairs for bed. Allie and Cam cleared the table while I collapsed on the couch in the family room. They joined me after a minute, Allie holding the wine bottle. Cam sat in the easy chair.

"Okay, girls, dish." Allie topped up our glasses and poured herself one before plopping down next to me.

I stared at the deep red in my glass. "After the menorah lighting, it looked so pretty in the dark I wanted to take a picture from a distance. I headed over to the big rock formation."

"I know the one you mean," Allie said.

"Thea must have been spying on me and followed me out there. I never saw her, but after I snapped the picture, she attacked me from the back side of the boulder. She got me on the ground, and Al, she had a heavy ball in a stretchy mitten."

"Like she killed Val with," Cam said.

Allie reached for my hand. "But you got clear of her, you brave thing."

"I had to, didn't I?" I patted my flat abs. "It's all in the core. Plus, she couldn't keep hold of my foot and also swing the bocce ball at my head." I shuddered.

"Cece gave her a good strong kick in the knee and got the heck out of there, always a smart self-defense tactic," Cam said. "The cops did the rest."

The doorbell rang. Allie gave me a questioning look as she stood.

"That's probably the detective," I said. "I told him I'd be here."

She came back with Jim Quan. He declined a drink and perched on the edge of a straight chair.

"You're all right, Ms. Barton?" he began.

"Yes, thank you."

"Well, as you know, we apprehended Thea Robinet."

Cam and I had watched as a handcuffed Thea was wheeled to the ambulance on a stretcher, swearing all the way.

"You did quite the number on her knee," he continued.

"I had to stop her. I couldn't let her escape. I had pepper spray in my coat pocket, but I didn't use it."

Both Allie and Cam looked surprised.

I lifted a shoulder. "After a series of muggings in Pasadena a few years ago, a friend and I took a self-defense class. We learned how to use the spray, and I usually have a container in my coat and in my purse. But it's nasty stuff. Do you think I should have sprayed her?" I asked Quan.

"I think you disabled her and got away, exactly what we recommend. She's currently under arrest for aggravated assault with a deadly weapon."

"Do you have enough evidence to arrest Thea for Val Harper's murder?" Cam asked him.

"We believe so. In the victim's phone records we discovered text messages between her and Ms. Robinet. Thea had arranged a meeting between the two on the night of Val's death, a meeting to take place after the wine bar closed. Thea claimed she wanted to buy mittens for her large-handed brother and also discuss Garden Club business."

"And she lured Val onto the bocce court," I murmured.

"Yes." He nodded. "The ball she used for the murder matches the set in the historical complex."

"Which was missing two balls of the eight last evening, I noticed," I said.

"Exactly. We also have a witness who thinks she saw Thea leaving the historical complex that night at eleven o'clock."

"But why?" Allie asked. "What motive did she have for killing Val?"

"Long-simmering resentments of several kinds," Quan said.

"Do you know about the real estate deal?" I asked him.

His eyebrows went up. "We had a long conversation with Mr. Torres this afternoon," Quan said. "We're also aware of the garden club conflicts. In addition, the deceased was apparently a bit of a homophobe and had insulted Thea about her relationship with Ms. Raj."

"I hope Narini didn't have anything to do with the murder." Poor Narini, who would now be raising a child on her own.

"We have no evidence to suggest she did." Quan set his palms on his knees. "Do you ladies have any other questions for me?"

"I can't think of any," Cam said.

Allie shook her head.

He stood. "Ms. Barton and Ms. Flaherty, I know the two of you were doing a bit of your own investigation, and I understand why." He inclined his head toward Allie. "However, we always strongly recommend leaving the police work to trained professionals."

"Yes, sir," I said. "You can be sure I don't have the slightest inclination to ever get involved again in the future."

"Good. You all have a nice holiday."

I thanked him. Allie showed him out. Cam high-fived me.

"I'm glad to learn how much he was doing in the background," she said.

"It's his job." I sipped my wine. It definitely wasn't my job. Things were quiet again, in a peaceful way, not an ominous one. But I never wanted to see a mitten again, murderous or otherwise.

Author's Note

I'm delighted to introduce you in this novella to Cece Barton, the protagonist of my new Cece Barton Mysteries series, which begins with *Murder Uncorked*.

Despite being a decades-long resident of Massachusetts, I'm originally a fourth-generation Californian. When my editor asked me to write a new series set on the West Coast, I was excited to say yes.

When the offer of a novella came along, it was he who suggested I bring Cam Flaherty, the organic farmer from my Local Foods Mysteries, into the story. (The series was originally published under the name Edith Maxwell and has now been reissued as authored by Maddie Day.) I've enjoyed revisiting my favorite fictional organic farmer several years (in her life) after the events in *Mulch Ado About Murder*, the last Local Foods mystery. If you haven't yet had a chance to read those books, I hope you take a look.

I'd already planned for *Murder Uncorked* to take place in early October in fictional Colinas. Because Kensington planned to release this Christmas novella before the first series novel, "Murderous Mittens" became a perfect way to hand readers Cece's origin story, as it were. I could present her first foray into solving a murder, Allie's invitation for her to move north, and how the position of Vino y Vida manager happened to become available.

My uncle, Richard Reinhardt, and my late aunt, Joan Maxwell Reinhardt, built a second home in the hills of Geyserville in the Alexander Valley over fifty years ago, which I have visited since I was a college student. Jo and Dick's home in that fertile wine-growing region north of

San Francisco was the inspiration for this series' setting. I'm so grateful to Uncle Dick and my cousins for letting me use the house as a home base when I went out west last fall on a research trip to refresh my memory of the region's atmosphere and environment. Don't be surprised if an older gentleman named Richard makes an appearance in *Murder Uncorked* and the books that will follow.

I'm always grateful for my enthusiastic readers and fans. I hope you love Cece and gang as much as you do my Country Store and Cozy Capers Book Group Mysteries.